BEYOND BINARY

"Seventeen stories of genderqueer and sexually fluid people living, laughing, lusting and lying their way through the world. Seventeen points of light burning like beacons above the plain of "normal." Seventeen tales written mostly in the twenty-first century about the future, the past that never was, and alternate universes that might never be (or always have been). Seventeen authors working on the bow wave of their own writing, riding a surge of inspiration.

"These writers—the vast majority identify as female, a thrill all of its own—play with many versions of queer. The stories range from a 35-page novelette that begins at the raw edge of loneliness and ends in exuberant human connection, to a 6-page blink of quantum weirdness encompassing all possibilities. The stories teem with gay, trans, lesbian, bi, polyamorous, asexual, unspecified, and imaginary people-- as well as aliens, angels, and androids. But each ends with some oh-so-human satisfaction, resolution, or glad understanding. *Beyond Binary* is peopled by those who are brave, who say Yes--and not only survive but thrive.

"Some of these pieces are truly strange. Some are delicious romps. But in the end this is the rarest of anthologies: the sum is greater than its parts. Read it. Read it all."

— NICOLA GRIFFITH, winner of the Nebula Award,
the James Tiptree, Jr. Award, the World Fantasy Award
and six Lambda Literary Awards

"...chock full of strong stories that challenge your perceptions of gender identity and sexuality, but also turn your notions of reality itself upside down. Editor Brit Mandelo has done a great job of assembling some of the most provocative writers working in SF today."

— CHARLIE JANE ANDERS, io9.com

10110100101000110012101101001 01
00011001310110100101000110014 10
11010010100011001510110100101 00
01100161011010010100011001710 11
01001010001100181011010010100 01
10019101101001010001100121011 01
00101000110013101101001010001 10
01410110100101000110015101101 00
10100011001610110100101000110 01
71011010010100011001810110100 10
10001100191011010010100011001 21
01101001010001100131011010010 10
00110014101101001010001100151 01
10100101000110016101101001010 00
11001710110100101000110018101 10
10010100011001910110100101000 11
00121011010010100011001310110 10
01010001100141011010010100011 00
15101101001010001100161011010 01
01000110017101101001010001100 18
10110100101000110019101101001 01

BEYOND BINARY

011001510110100101000110016101 1
010010100011001710110100101000 1

Genderqueer and Sexually
Fluid Speculative Fiction

edited by brit mandelo

BEYOND BINARY

LETHE PRESS — MAPLE SHADE, NJ

Published in 2012 by Lethe Press, Inc.
118 Heritage Avenue • Maple Shade, NJ 08052-3018
www.lethepressbooks.com • lethepress@aol.com
ISBN: 1-59021-005-0
ISBN-13: 978-1-59021-005-5

These stories are works of fiction. Names, characters, places, and incidents are products of the authors' imaginations or are used fictitiously.

Set in Warnock and Helvetica Neue.
Cover and interior design: Alex Jeffers.
Cover image: © Sean Gladwell—Fotolia.com.

LIBRARY OF CONGRESS CATALOGING-IN-PUBLICATION DATA

Beyond binary : genderqueer and sexually fluid speculative fiction / edited by Brit Mandelo.
　　p. cm.
ISBN 978-1-59021-005-5 (pbk. : alk. paper)
1. Science fiction, American. 2. Gender identity--Fiction. 3. Fantasy fiction, American. I. Mandelo, Brit.
PS648.S3B53 2012
813'.08762083538--dc23

2012003633

TABLE OF CONTENTS

INTRODUCTION

Brit Mandelo

There are many ways to break, transcend, challenge, subvert, and fuck with strict binary ideas about gender, sexuality, and identity. Speculative writers like James Tiptree Jr./Alice Sheldon and Samuel Delany have done it for decades; in 1969, Ursula K. Le Guin's *The Left Hand of Darkness* posited a world in which people are agendered for the majority of their lives, and the novel won both the Hugo and the Nebula. We still have the Tiptree Award, devoted to fiction that plays with and challenges ideas about gender, and it's been going strong for two decades. After all, speculative fiction is the literature of questions, of challenges and imagination—and what better for us to question than the ways in which gender and sexuality have been rigidly defined, partitioned off, put in little boxes?

The thing is, stories about genderqueer and sexually fluid identities are still hard to find, even in a field active with speculation on gender and sexuality. They tend to pop up here and there, scattered throughout magazines and collections, and in queer publications that get less attention from the SF readership. This book is an effort to collect and present some of the best of those stories in one place.

I have a personal investment in the creation of this book, also—as a queer person whose gender expression is fluid, and whose sexual identity is moreso, I have longed for books that speak to and for people like

101101001010001001010101101001

me. Non-binary identities and expressions are often marginalized; our voices are silenced, our identities are effaced, and our stories go untold. That has begun to change with the publication of more and more genderqueer, bisexual, pansexual, and otherwise non-binary narratives, and I am overjoyed to be able to contribute. Putting together *Beyond Binary* has been a moving experience, and I hope that the end result can do as much for readers as it did for me.

BRIT MANDELO

The people in these stories do not accept the proscribed gendering of their bodies, and their bodies may not conform to normative, restrictive expectations. They refuse to choose "one or the other" in their gender, sexuality or relationships. They redefine what the terms "man" and "woman" can mean, how "he" and "she" may be used. And— most importantly—they embrace their own selves, their own definitions, and their own needs, physical and emotional. On our world or off of it, in our past or our future, or somewhere else entirely, these are stories in which the queer and the speculative unite to explore the ways in which we can go beyond binary.

In choosing these stories, I had two major concerns. First, I wanted to put together a tapestry of positive narratives that challenged all-too-common destructive tropes about queer and trans* people. There are no tragic "big reveal" stories here; no one is shocked by anyone else, and in the stories that feature physical discoveries, the lovers in question are always pleased and open to the wholeness of their partner's self. Second, I wanted to represent a broad range of gender and sexual identities, not only those exploring a spectrum but also those who occupy spaces outside of it. To that end, there are stories in which the protagonist is never once gendered by other characters or the author, stories with asexual protagonists, and stories in which sex is defined and enjoyed a little differently than mainstream expectations. There are a variety of relationship-structures, too; no limiting things to couples, here.

Finally, the thing that strikes me most about *Beyond Binary* is that I could do two or three or ten books of genderqueer and sexually fluid stories without ever representing everyone, and every way in which we can live, be, and love. In these pages you will encounter all manner of people who have made a flexible grid out of a binary, an incorporated whole out of a dualism, or refused the mess of labels entirely, and yet: there are so many more stories to be told. In particular, I feel the lack of alternative pronouns and the lack of intersex folks as tellers and protagonists of their own stories; and so here I acknowledge that there is ground not covered, and there are stories not told. This is not an encyclopedia—it is an attempt to contain even a fraction of the possibilities.

∞

In *Beyond Binary*, I hope that the reader will find freedom, acceptance, humor, love, and a wide variety of voices. I hope that the ways in which institutions, language, and clinical definitions have restricted identity will be exploded. I hope that normative ideas about bodies will be re-imagined. I hope that definitions of gender and sexuality will be broadened in a thousand ways. But, mostly, I hope that you—the person who makes these stories real as you read them—have a great time with these writers and their handsome, weird, wonderful tales.

Enjoy.

Brit Mandelo
Dec. 16, 2011

INTRODUCTION

101101001010003001010101101001

SEA OF CORTEZ

Sandra McDonald

The war is the best thing that ever happened to most of the guys on your ship—a wild storm of global upheaval that flung them out of the flat dull prairies or gritty coal mines of Appalachia and dropped them right here. Stranded on a floating oasis of two thousand men in the South Pacific, a goodly amount of them shirtless at any given time. Certainly the war's the best thing that ever happened to you. If it weren't for the Japs, you'd be freezing your toes off back in Iowa City, working in your dad's shoe store. Instead you're lying on this wool blanket on this steel deck, and Robbie Coleman's head is pillowed on your bare stomach. The sky is canary blue and cloudless, the sun smiling directly above the gun turrets.

"What are you thinking about?" Robbie asks, his voice low and lazy.

You're thinking that Paradise is the dozens of men paired up around you, smoking or dozing or reading dog-eared magazines. Most are bare chested, some are stripped down to shorts, and some are casually buck-naked. Acres of skin, tight and tattooed and smooth and hairy. The blue-green sea glitters to the horizon in all directions with no trace of land. One day the war will end and all this will vanish like a mirage. All the handsome men will return to where they came from. You will measure old ladies' feet and lace up winter boots on little kids trying to kick you. You'll live at home, the bachelor son. Once in awhile you'll go out of town for a secret tryst, but your parents will never meet your lovers and you will die alone, lonely, unfulfilled, longing for the pretty boys of war.

"I'm not thinking about anything," you say.

Robbie arches his arm and pinches your thigh. Not hard enough to sting. "Liar, pants on fire."

He's told you before that you think too much. Which is silly, since he's the educated one. Three months of college in his home town of San Diego before he decided to drop out and enlist. He's read every book on the ship at least twice, and that includes two plays by Shakespeare. You hated every minute of high school and never met a book you didn't want to bury under stale gym socks at the bottom of your locker.

It's not that you think too much, it's that you can peer through time. You look at the ship and can see it in the Philadelphia shipyards, a frame accumulating pipes and wires and bulkheads, a vast investment of labor and material. You also see it rusting away on the bottom of the ocean, a habitat for fish and plants and ghosts. The beginning and the end of most things is yours if you concentrate hard enough. Two ends of a pole, like the ones track athletes use for vaulting. You see Robbie, who like you is nineteen years old, and simultaneously picture him also as a baby sucking on his mother's teat and a bald husk of a man in a hospital bed. He's surrounded by his kids and grandkids. He dies peacefully, quietly.

But right now he's alive and questioning so you murmur, "I'm thinking about the movie tonight."

"I'm on watch," he says. "Besides, we've seen it."

Everyone has seen it. A soldier goes to a cantina looking for love and eventually Carmen Miranda sashays around with pineapples and bananas on her head. It's the strangest musical you've ever seen. You knew already Robbie would find a reason not to go. On the last movie night you sat in the back, holding hands, little kisses of soft lips and raspy stubble, with the ship's officers just a few rows ahead, not noticing or pretending not to notice. Hands sliding beneath waistbands. Tongues between soft lips, hands grasping heat and hardness. Nothing the two of you haven't done before.

Later, though, you saw him clutching a photo of his girlfriend Nancy as reverently as a Catholic holds a rosary. Nancy, who is eighteen and honey-haired, her penmanship round and blue on perfumed paper. Nancy with her pert nose and bright eyes and a smile so wide you could fall right in and drown in sweetness.

She's cute and all, but if you were a woman—and here's an area you definitely do not think about very often, a boarded up hurricane cellar of cobwebs, rat droppings, and rusty nails that lead to tetanus—if you'd been born a girl, you wouldn't be sitting around in California writing love notes to your sailor boyfriend. You'd be working in a steel plant or shipyard, doing your part for the war. On weekends you would wear blouses the color of freshly churned butter, and ride a bicycle so that air flutters up under your skirt, and sleep in short cotton nightgowns with lace on the cuffs and neckline. You would keep your hope chest stocked and organized until the man of your dreams proposed with a gold ring and a long-stemmed red rose.

In the photograph that Robbie treasures most, he and Nancy are sitting are on a beach blanket, laughing, his left arm casual around her shoulder, her head tilted toward him. Nancy's bathing suit has wide white straps and cones that make her breasts point out like cannons. He says they were visiting the Sea of Cortez. You think that's in Europe somewhere. Wasn't Cortez an explorer, like Columbus? If you ask, you'll sound like a dumb hick. You do know that Robbie thinks a lot about what Nancy would say about him kissing you, what his momma would think, what the chaplain would admonish over the rims of his square black glasses.

What exists between you is nothing unexpected on a floating prison of men who sleep, shit, and work together twenty four hours a day for months without relief.

Or so you tell yourself.

It's not love. It can't be love. Robbie can only love women.

∞

Here's what happens: a boatswain's mate named Williams has a fight with his buddy Lee, who is a cook, apparently because Lee has been spending time with two radiomen, Easton and DeRosa. Everyone calls them Fruit Salad or The Two Fruits, but not when officers can hear. A tolerant captain will look the other way but the fleet admiral has eyes everywhere and he won't hesitate to discharge a man for being homosexual. You've heard of sailors sent to psychiatric evaluation or imprisoned in the brig. They get kicked out with what looks like an honorable rating but is coded on blue paper, so that the Veterans Administration will deny benefits. Anyway, Williams and Lee broke up over Lee's too-obvious affinity with Fruit Salad. Williams isn't homosexual, or so he says. He's got a wife and two kids to prove it. But he needs a pal to blow off steam with, and he decides that pal should be you.

He's big in the shoulders, with anchor tattoos on both biceps and a thick corded neck. Narrow waist and dark, slick hair. Dangerous look to him. He's the kind of man who might throw you overboard if you crossed him, or at least teach you a lesson in a filthy alley. You like that he's fierce. He asks around and finds out that you don't like books, so the first gift he gets you is an almost-new issue of a Hollywood tabloid.

"I'm done reading it," he says, brushing your fingers as he hands it over.

The next gift is a little flask of whiskey that tastes vile but gives you a warm glow on an otherwise bad day of combat drills and foul weather.

The third gift is a backrub late one night in the ammunition room, you standing upright against the bulkhead with your right cheek pressed against the cool metal and your arms splayed as if you are under arrest. His large, callused hands dig into the tight muscles of your shoulders, blossoms of pain-relief-pleasure. In the secret hurricane cellar of your brain, you imagine yourself wearing a blue silk dress, sheer silk hosiery, a lace bra, black high-heeled pumps. You're a lady reporter come to do a Life magazine article about the war and he's lured you down here, is moving his hands down your hips, is thumbing his way into your secret passage. If you were wearing pearls, he'd pull them cool and firm against your throat, or slip them one by one inside you like exquisite gifts.

"Baby," he breathes. "Baby pie."

Which is maybe the dumbest endearment you've ever heard but you take it, you will take anything you can get. You know that people see what's happening. People always see. Robbie is a boatswain's mate like Williams and there's no way he can be oblivious. You want him to object, get mad, claim you, but he writes daily letters to Nancy and reads his Bible so much that the binding cracks open. You share cigarettes and go to the mess together and he slings his arm across your shoulders in the same familiar way, but if he's bothered about Williams, he's keeping it completely to himself.

Meanwhile there's a war to fight. You man the 16-inch guns. You fire at Manila, Panay, Leyte, Cebu. Places you never heard of back when you were failing geography in tenth grade. The roar of the weapons leaves your head ringing and makes your hands shake. The Japs dive out of the sky in suicide attacks. The anti-aircraft guns shoot and shoot and shoot, ships sink on the horizon, you can't sleep, you can't eat, and Williams is the one who pulls you into tiny spaces, gets you to your knees, tugs on your ears, stuffs your mouth. There's no sweet kissing. This is not like cuddling on the deck under the blazing sun. He teaches you how to take him, his tattoos moving like snakes in the dim light, and he leaves you sore and addicted and craving more.

"Tell me what you want," he orders in the dark, but you can't even tell yourself the truth, how can you tell him? You want lace underwear that rides against your thighs, and a garter belt snug around your waist, and a bra to fill with breasts you'll never have. You want cherry red lipstick and tiny bottles of perfume to spritz on your neck. You can see Williams home after the war, calling his wife "Baby pie" as he nails her into a new white mattress in a four-poster bed. She will look like Robbie's girlfriend Nancy. She will swell with a new baby, a satisfied gleam in her eyes. You will eat your mother's meatloaf and listen to the radio with your father and go to bed with a pistol under your pillow, dreaming of the day you can shoot yourself in the head.

You lie and tell Williams that you want more whiskey. Any warm glow is a good one.

∞

For three days, your ship is part of a task force attacking Japanese airfields. A dozen cruisers, battleships, carriers and destroyers assail Luzon. Their pilots dive out of the sky, trying to smash your decks and turrets. You can't even count how much metal is screeching across the sky. Your sense of the future starts to fail. Maybe the war will never end. It will simply stretch on forever, reeking of gunpowder and deafening with its monstrous noise, the sea tossing you up and down in with angry swells.

There's a reason they don't let women out here, you think. To witness destruction is to take it in, like inhaling poison, and once inside you it can never be expelled. Your strictly imaginary womb aches for the babies who will never be born because their fathers have been wiped away from the planet by steel and fire. But eventually this battle does end, and you crawl into Robbie's rack because you're too tired to climb into your own. He finds you there a half hour later, roughly shakes your shoulder.

"It's not big enough for two," he says, even though men are double-racked all around you. Some are weeping with relief and being comforted, with small words and soft gestures, by their buddies. They have seen too much.

"Let me sleep," you plead.

Annoyed, he hauls you out. You land on your knees on the deck.

"Sleep alone," he says.

You go find Williams. He's upright, exhausted, his face dark with stubble, a cigarette burning unnoticed in his hand. He's talking to one of The Two Fruits. When he sees you, his face gets all tight. You think he doesn't want to be seen with you. But then he pushes you into his rack and crawls in right after you, an impossibly tight fit, his body crushing yours. You want to be crushed. You want to be held immobile and safe, a woman safe in the arms of her man.

"Close your eyes, baby-pie," he says roughly.

The next morning, the seas are so rough that cooking is limited on the mess deck. You don't mind, because just looking at food exacerbates your growing seasickness. As you sip bad coffee you hear the latest ship's scandal. One of the officers found pornography and women's underwear in the boatswains' locker and there's going to be hell to pay. It's not regular pornography but "perverted" stuff—men posed in women's lingerie, men with fake breasts, men in long slinky dresses. Your face burns because you want to see it.

"The captain threw it all overboard," you hear Robbie say. "Rotten filth."

That afternoon a typhoon blasts through the task force, an unannounced guest at an already terrible party. Planes slide off carriers or smash into bulkheads. Three destroyers capsize and sink to the bottom of the Pacific. Your ship rolls so dangerously to starboard and port and starboard and port that men scream for fear you're about to go right down alongside the destroyers. This is what terror really is: knowing in your heart that you will drown entombed in metal, seawater rushing in to flood and trap and smother you. It will hurt. You will scream, but that will just let more water invade you. You will convulse and choke and scrabble for help that never comes. Then your body will hang suspended in dark cold water forever, a grave from which no one is ever rescued.

∞

Eight hundred men die in the storm, every death frantic and painful.

You live. You're safe, you don't drown, you emerge onto the deck to a gray windy sky with the typhoon extinguished. The captain orders a shipwide muster and head count. Three sailors are missing and presumed to have washed overboard in the confusion of the night. The youngest is BM3 Robert Allen Soward, of San Diego, California.

You don't believe it—not when your chief tells you, not when the captain confirms it, not when everyone in your corner of berthing slaps your shoulder and tells you they're sorry. The sea is too big, the waves too choppy, the ship is almost out of fuel. There is no chance of recovery.

"But I've seen him," you tell them. "He dies as an old man, surrounded by his kids. I can see it right now. He's in a bed, and they're surrounding him."

∞

Eventually the ship's doctor gives you some little white pills, makes you sleep twelve hours in the infirmary, and sends you back to work.

Grief is a sword. It splits your spinal cord from head to toe, making you unsteady on your feet. You walk into bulkheads and trip over hatches. Grief is also a knife. It slices through your brain and makes you forget he's dead. You think you see him in the mess, in the showers, on deck when the sun breaks through. It's a finely honed razor that leaves a million tiny cuts on your hands and face. They sting when you touch his locker or turn your face into the pillow you stole from his rack.

When did your vision fail? What can you trust, if not the inner sight that points you to the inevitable future?

You decide that he's still out there in the water, swimming his way back to Nancy and sunny California. He will be rescued by a passing a ship, swaddled in blankets, reunited with his one true love. He will die old and beloved, not cold and abandoned to the ocean.

This fantasy helps in only the smallest possible way.

SEA OF CORTEZ

10110100101000110010101101001

It's the beginning of 1945. The Japanese are not yet exhausted enough or horrified enough to surrender. You still have Williams, but he still has a wife and he has secrets, too. He gets packages in the mail but opens them in private. He barters tobacco and chewing gum and candy but won't show you all of the bounty he earns in return. Every morning when you wake you see your bleak, gray future unfolding in Iowa City. You think, sometimes, that it would be easier to drop off the side of the ship and sink into darkness, let the whales and sharks and fish finish you off. Cortez explored the sea and so will you, your every cell scattered by tide and swell.

But then the ship puts in for repairs at Ulithi, an atoll with crystal clear lagoons and gorgeous long beaches and sunsets like blood oranges. There are beer parties and midnight movies and a lot of men sneaking off into the jungle for some private R & R. Williams takes you to a cove where the ocean washes in and out just a few feet away. He spreads a blanket on the sand and crawls all over you and takes you apart inch by inch. You participate as required, thinking of Robbie adrift on currents and calling for your help. His hands and voice grow rougher.

"I don't know what you want," he says.

You don't know, either.

More ships pull into port. The Seabees finish up a big a rec center on Mogmog Island and there's a rumor that Bob Hope will be flying in next month with a USO army of singers and dancers. In the meantime, the Morale Committee is organizing a musical revue. Every ship will provide volunteers to do skits and numbers. The Two Fruits are first to sign up. They ask you to perform as well.

"Why me?" you ask.

DeRosa says, "Gets your mind off things."

"I can't sing."

Easton says, "It's a chorus. You can just mouth the words and let the stronger singers carry it."

You ask Williams if you should do it, but he has no opinion on the matter. Maybe he's losing interest in you. You saw him talking to his old buddy Lee the other day, Lee with the thick blond hair and bright blue eyes. You're disposable. Maybe you deserve to be disposed of. You tell Easton and DeRosa that you'll volunteer but when you get to practice you realize they left out the crucial detail that the entire show is in drag—grass skirts, coconut shell breasts, wigs, makeup.

"Absolutely not," you say, and try to flee.

The Two Fruits grab your arms and turn you back. "It's just for fun. No one cares."

The other chorus members from your ship are a laundryman, a barber, a corpsman, a chaplain's assistant, a radarman and three yeomen. They know how to put on makeup. They argue about the costumes. Too late you realize that every single one is homosexual and you're probably going to be branded as one, too, but what does it matter? The world is ending in fire and Robbie is floating in the Pacific and Williams wants to put his hand down someone else's pants. This might be the only time in your life that you will get to dance on stage for hundreds of drunk and cheering men. You certainly won't get cheered back in Iowa City.

"I want the blond wig," you tell them. "I want pink lipstick and a seashell necklace."

The night of the revue brings high winds that rock the Chinese lanterns strung outside. The lagoon is full of ships riding the high tide. Somewhere out there, the admiral and his captains are eating dinner in a wardroom full of brandy and cigars. In the auditorium, rowdy sailors drink beer and hooch, cheering for each act. The "Andrews Sisters" are three Seabees with pretty good voices. "Marlene Dietrich" has to retreat from an ardent fan who storms the stage. You're in the chorus for "Carmen Miranda" but she's late for her entrance. You and the others swing your four-foot-long wooden bananas and do the best you can, given that you're a little drunk and a lot worried that Williams will see you from the audience and walk away in disgust.

Robbie would have walked away. You know that.

But for these few glorious minutes you can forget Robbie. You can pretend you are the woman denied to you by biology. You are radiant and alluring and the men are cheering. They shine desire on you, they lust after your lithe legs and firm breasts, they are on their feet clapping—

Then you realize they're clapping for Carmen, who arrives like a Hollywood movie star. She's glorious. Six feet tall, black skirt, black top, bare midriff, bananas and oranges on her head, singing about how happy and gay she feels. She hasn't been to rehearsal all week long so you don't know who she really is. All you know is that you feel inadequate and small. Reduced to a sham, a weak imitation, while she struts and sings, and what kind of imposter are you?

Then she turns, and you see the anchor tattoos on her forearms.

The roar of the crowd becomes a sea of blood draining out of your head. Your vision dims to shadows. You make the fastest exit in the history of South Pacific musical theatre and a stage hand puts you on a chair before you faint entirely.

Ten minutes later, Williams exits to thunderous applause. He kicks off his shoes and tutti-frutti hat and stands before you as if waiting for you to strike him. You pull him outside, down a path, away from every prying eye. The full moon slips out from behind a cloud and bathes you both in white light.

"You're insane," you tell him.

"I'm crazy," he agrees.

This time you're the one who drives him backward, you're the one who pins him against a tree trunk. He wriggles against you gladly. You suck on his lips and neck and leave your lipstick on his bare skin.

"Carmen got appendicitis," he mutters. "I owed Lee a favor."

Which is a good story if you believe it. In the moonlight of a tropical island, you're not too worried about the details. You're kissing him and he's pushing you to the ground and your costumes are coming off, your grass skirt a bed to lie down on.

This is wartime, this is the best and worst thing that has ever happened to you, these are his hands on your hips, this is the body you must live in, and in the morning you realize you can't see the future anymore. Your gift is gone, if it ever was a gift at all.

All you see before you is shimmering blue, the unexplored Sea of Cortez.

∞

EYE OF THE STORM

Kelley Eskridge

I am a child of war. It's a poor way to start. My village was always ready to defend, or to placate, or to burn again. Eventually the fighting stopped, and left dozens of native graves and foreign babies. We war bastards banded together by instinct; most of us had the straw hair and flat faces of westerners, and we were easy marks. Native kids would find one or two of us alone and build their adrenaline with shouts of *Your father killed my father* until someone took the first step in with a raised arm or a stick. These encounters always ended in blood and cries—until the year I was fifteen, when a gang of village young played the daily round of kill-the-bastard and finally got it right: when Ad Homrun's older brother pulled her from under a pile of screaming boys and girls, and Ad's neck was broken and her right eye had burst. The others vanished like corn spirits and left us alone in a circle of trampled grass, Ad lying in Tom's arms, me trying to hold her head up at the right angle so that she would breathe again. It was my first grief.

It was no wonder our kind were always disappearing in the night. "You'll go too," my mother said for the first time when I was only seven. She would often make pronouncements as she cooked. I learned her opinions on everything from marjoram ("Dry it in bundles of six sticks and keep it away from dogs") to marriage ("Some cows feel safest in the butcher's barn") while she kneaded bread or stripped slugs off fresh-picked greens.

It shocked me to hear her talk about my leaving as if it were already done. Ad was still alive in her family's cottage a quarter mile from ours, and I believed that my world was settled; not perfect, but understandable, everything fast in its place. I peered from my corner by the fire while my mother pounded corn into meal, jabbing the pestle in my direction like a finger to make her point. "You'll go," she repeated. "Off to soldier, no doubt. Born to it, that's why. No one can escape what they're born to."

"I won't," I said.

"You'll go and be glad to."

"I won't! I want to stay with you."

"Hmph," she replied, but at supper she gave me an extra corncake with a dab of honey. Food was love as well as livelihood for her. She never punished me for being got upon her while her man screamed himself dead in the next room; but she never touched me or anyone else unless she had to. I grew up with food instead of kisses. I ate pastries and hot bread and sausage pies like a little goat, and used them as fuel to help me run faster than my tormentors.

One of the childhood games Ad and I played was to wrap up in sheepskin and swan up and down the grass between her cottage and the lane, pretending to be princes in disguise. We were both tall, after all, and looked noble in our woolly cloaks. What more did one need? To be the first child of a king, Tom Homrun said, and our king already had one. There could only be one prince, only one heir. The rest were just nobles, and there were more of them than anyone bothered to count. *What's the good of being a royal if you're as common as ticks on a dog?* my mother would say, with a cackle for her own wit. But I had heard too many stories about the prince. My aunt's third husband went to court for a meeting of royal regional accountants and told us in his letters that the prince was fair and strong and already had the air of a leader. *And puts me in mind of your Mars,* he wrote my mother; *something about the eyes.* My mother paused after she'd read that part aloud, and looked at me with a still face. It thrilled me to be likened to the prince, and Ad was rigid with envy until Tom carved her a special stick to use as a scepter in our games, with a promise that he would never make me one no matter how hard I pleaded. I could not care about her stick, about her silence and hurt feelings, even though she was my only friend. My head was full of daydreams of walking through the streets of Lemon City, of being seen by the prince's retainers and taken up into the citadel, marveled over, embraced, offered…what? My imagination failed me there, so I would start from the beginning and see it all again. I began giving the pigs orders, and delivering speeches of state to the group of alder trees near Nor Tellit's farm.

They were different speeches after Ad died. At first they were simply incoherent weepings delivered from a throat so thick with snot that I barely recognized my own voice. It sounded adult and terrible, and filled me with a furious energy that I didn't know how to use; until one afternoon when I had run dry of tears and instead picked up a fist-sized stone. I beat the alders until the rock was speckled with my blood. I washed my swollen hand in the village well and hoped that my rage would poison them all. Then I found Tom Homrun and asked him to teach me how to fight.

From the first I was like a pig at a slop pile, gulping down whatever he put in front of me, always rooting single-mindedly for more. He taught me to use my hands and elbows and knees, to judge distance, and to watch someone's body rather than their eyes. It was hard at first to trust him and his teaching: I'd always thought of him as a native, as a danger, in spite of his fondness for his yellow-haired bastard sister. And it hadn't occurred to me that he would have to touch me. Apart from Ad, I'd only touched my mother by accident, and the village kids in desperate defense: but this was new and electric. The first feel of his muscle against mine was so shocking that the hair on my arms and legs stood up. I was desperately uneasy to think that I might be moved by Tom after what I'd begun to feel for his sister, as if it were some kind of betrayal of Ad. But I was fascinated by the strength and the power of his body, the way it turned when he wished, held its balance, reached out and so easily made me vulnerable.

I was just sixteen when we began, and the sky was always grey with the start or end of snow. I learned to move when I was too cold, too sore, too tired. I learned to keep going. All the things I wanted—Ad, my mother, a life of endless hard blue days in the fields, and just one true friend with dark hair and a father still alive—all those precious things became buried under a crust of long outlander muscles. I began to imagine myself an arrow laid against the string, ready to fly. I looked at the village kids with my arrow's eyes, and they stayed out of my way.

By the summer I knew enough not to knock myself silly. I was tired of the same exercises and hungry now for more than just revenge: I wanted to be a warrior. "Show me how to use a sword," I begged Tom constantly, sometimes parrying an invisible adversary with a long stick.

"No," he said for the hundredth time.

"Why not?"

"There's no point until you get your full growth. You're tall as me now, but you might make another inch or two before you're done."

"You didn't make me wait to learn how to fight."

"Swords are different. They change your balance. You've got to make the sword part of yourself, it's not enough just to pick it up and wave it around. It's true that you've learned well," he added. "But you haven't learned everything."

"Then teach me everything."

"Leave it alone, Mars."

I had no idea I was going to do it: I had never given him anything but the obedience due a teacher. But I was so frustrated with behaving. "You teach me, damn you," I said, and swung the stick as hard as I could at his ribs.

He softened against the blow and absorbed it. The stick was dry and thin, but still it must have hurt. It sounded loud, perhaps because we were both so silent.

I stammered, "Tom, truly, I was wrong to do it, I just...."

"You're stupid, Mars." His voice was very quiet. "You're not the strongest, you never will be, and no sword will change that. I'm heavier and faster than you, and there's thousands more like me out there." He waved at the world beyond the fields, and when I turned my head, he reached out and twisted the branch away as easily as taking a stick from a puppy. "All you have are your wits and your body, if you can ever learn to use them."

What had we been doing, all these months? "I can use my body."

A bruise I'd given him at the corner of his mouth stretched into a purple line. Then his smile changed into the stiff look that people wear when they are forcing themselves to a thing they'd rather not do; like the day he'd butchered Ad's favorite nanny goat while she cried into my shoulder. I did not like him looking at me as if I were that goat.

"You want to learn everything." He nodded. "Well, then you shall." And he came for me.

I managed to keep him off me for more than a minute, a long stretch of seconds that burned the strength from the muscles in my arms and legs. But he was right; he was too strong, too fast. First he got me down, and then he beat me, his face set, his hands like stones against my ribs and my face. His last blow was to my nose, and when he finally stood, he was spattered with me.

"This is everything, Mars. This is what I have to teach you. Become the weapon. Do it, and no one will touch you in a fight. Otherwise it's only a matter of time before someone sends you to the next world in pieces."

I was trying to spit instead of swallow; it made it harder to breathe, and every cough jarred my broken nose.

"I regret this," he said remotely. "But every time we meet from now on will be like this until you win or you quit. If you quit, I'll teach you nothing ever again. That's the lesson. I don't think you can do it, you know. I don't think you're ready. I wish you hadn't pushed so hard." He spoke as if he were talking to a stranger on the road.

He left me at the field's edge, under a creamy blue sky and the alders that were scarred with months of practice; all those pointless hours. After a long time I dragged myself up and limped home, turning my head away as I passed the Homrun cottage so I would not have to see whether Tom was watching. I let my mother bind my ribs, avoiding her questions and the silence that followed. Then I wrapped myself up in wool blankets and shivered all night, bruised and betrayed, frightened, and hopelessly alone.

∞

He beat me badly half a dozen times in the next year. Between our fights, I practiced and worked and invented a thousand different ways to keep distance between us, to protect my body from his. None of it made a speck of difference.

The day came when I knew I could never win. There was no grand omen, no unmistakable sign. I was milking our goat, and I suddenly understood that Tom was right. Someone would always be faster or stronger, and until I learned my place I would always be hurt and lonely. It was time to make peace and stop dreaming of Lemon City. I should be planning a fall garden, and tending Ad's grave. So there, it was decided; and I went on pulling methodically at the little goat's dry teats until she bleated impatiently and kicked at me to let her go. Then I sat on the milking stump and stared around me at the cottage, the tall birch that shaded it, the yard with the goat and the chickens, the half-tumbled stone wall that bounded our piece of the world. If someone had come by and said, "What are you looking at, Mars?", I would have said *Nothing. Nothing.*

Massive storm clouds began moving up over my shoulder from the west. The shadow of the birch across the south wall faded, and the chickens scuttled into their coop and tucked themselves up in a rattling of feathers. The wind turned fierce and cold; and then the rain hammered down. I hunched on the stump until it occurred to me that I was freezing, that I should see that the stock were safe and then get inside; and when I tried to stand the wind knocked me over like a badly-pitched fence post. I pulled myself up. Again the wind shoved me down. And again. This time I landed on one of my half-dozen un-healed bruises. It hurt; and it made me so angry that I forgot about my numb hands and my despair. I stood again. There was a loud snap behind me. It took a long second to turn against the wind: by that time, the branch that the storm had torn from the birch tree was already slicing toward me like a thrown spear.

I took a moment to understand what was happening, to imagine the wood knifing through me, to see my grave next to Ad's. Then the branch reached me, and I slid forward and to the right as if to welcome it; and as we touched I whirled off and away, staggered but kept my balance, and watched the branch splinter against the shed. The goat squealed from behind the wall; and I laughed from my still, safe place in the center of the storm.

∞

I had an idea now, and the only way to test it was by getting beaten again, and so I did: but not as badly. When he'd finally let me up, Tom said, as always, "Do you give in?"

"No."

He was supposed to turn and walk away. Instead, he kept hold of my tunic with his left hand and wiped his bleeding mouth with his right. He took his time. Then he said, "What was that first move?"

I shrugged.

"Who taught you that?"

I shrugged again, as much as I was able with one shoulder sprained.

"I expect I'll be ready for it, next time." He opened his hand and dropped me on my back in the dirt, and set off down the road toward the village. He favored his right leg just slightly: it was the first sign of pain he had ever shown. But that wasn't what made me feel so good, what made the blood jizzle around under my skin: it was the way I'd felt fighting him. I treated him just like the flying birch limb—allowed him close, so close that we became a single storm; and for just a moment I was our center and I spun him as easily as if I were a wind and he a bent branch.

The next time went better for me, and the time after that. It became a great dance, a wild game, to see how close I could get to him, how little I could twist away and remain out of reach, just beyond his balance point. He was heavier than me, differently muscled: it taught me to go beyond strength and look instead for the instant of instability, the moment when I could make him overreach himself. It was exhilarating to enter into his dangerous space and to turn his weapons against him; it was delicious to be most safe when I was closest to my enemy. I didn't notice my hurts anymore, except when parts of me stopped working. Then I would retreat to my corner by the cottage fire, sipping comfrey tea and reliving each moment, sucking whatever learning I could from the memory of each blow. My body and his became the whole of my world.

And the world was changing. I got those last two inches of growth and my body flung itself frantically into adulthood. I suppose it must have been happening all along underneath the sweat and the bruises and the grinding misery. But now that I was noticing it, it seemed to have come upon me all at once, and it was a different feeling from the days when Ad's smile could make me feel impossibly clever. This was the lust I'd seen at the dark edges of the village common after the harvest celebration, the thing of skin and wordless noise. No one had told me it would feel like turning into an arrow from the inside out and wanting nothing more than something to sink myself into. Sometimes it was so strong that I would have thrown myself on the next person I met, if only there had been anyone who wouldn't have thrown me right back. But there was no one. I could only burn and rage and stuff it all back into the whirlwind inside me: make myself a storm.

And so one day I finally won, and it was Tom who lay on one elbow, spitting blood. When the inside of his mouth had clotted, he said, "Well." Then we were both silent for a while.

"Well," he said later.

And: "You'll be fine now. You're a match for anyone, the way you fight. It's okay to let you go now. You'll be safe."

And then he began to cry. When I bent over him to see if he was hurt more badly than I thought, he gripped my arm and kissed me. He did not stop me when I pulled away, and he did not try to hide his tears. I didn't understand then what kind of love it is that kills itself to make the beloved safe: I only knew that my world had shaken itself apart and come back together in a way that did not include me anymore.

I told my mother that night that I would leave in a week. She did not speak, and all I could say over and over was "I have to go," as if it were an apology or a plea. Later as I sat miserably in front of the fire, she touched the back of my head so softly that I wasn't sure if I was meant to feel it. Her fingers on my hair told me that she grieved, and that her fear for me was like sour milk on the back of her tongue, and that in spite of it all she forgave me for becoming myself, for growing up into someone who could suddenly remind her of how she got me. I had traded scars and bruises with the village kids for years, but never before had I hurt someone I loved just by being myself; and in one day I had done it to the only two people left to me. And so I felt my world hitch and shake like a wet dog, and my choices fell over me like drops of dirty water: none of them clean.

∞

I set off early, just past dawn. Over breakfast, my mother said, "Here's a thing for you," and handed me a long bundle. When I unwrapped it, the lamplight flickered across the blade inside and my mother's sad and knowing eyes.

"Don't look at me," she said. "That Tom Homrun brought it around three days past and said I wasn't to give it to you until you were leaving."

There was no scabbard. I made a secure place for the sword in my belt, across my left hip.

"Feel like a proper soldier now, I expect," my mother said quietly.

K
E
L
L
E
Y

E
S
K
R
I
D
G
E

"I just feel all off balance," I told her, and she smiled a little.

"You'll be all right, then." She nodded, then sighed, stood, fussed with my slingbag. "I've put up some traveling food for you. And a flask of water as well, you never know when the next spring might be dry."

I tried to smile.

"Which way are you heading?"

"East. In-country."

She nodded again. "I thought you might head west."

"Mum!" I was shocked. "Those are our enemies."

"You've had more enemies here than ever came out of the west, child," she said. "I just wondered."

I took a breath. "I would never do anything to hurt you, Mum. You've been nothing but good to me." Another breath. "Tell Tom…give him my thanks." Opening the door, the damp, grey air in my face. "I love you, Mum." Kissing her dry cheek. "I love you." Three steps out now, her standing in the door, half in shadow, one hand to her face. "Goodbye, Mum." Four more steps, walking backwards now, still looking at her. "Goodbye." Turning away; walking away; leaving. Her voice catching up with me, "I've loved you, Mars. Godspeed." The bend in the road.

∞

I was alone on the road for a week. Every day brought me something new: a stand of unfamiliar trees, a stream of green water, a red-hooded bird that swooped from tree to tree above me for a hundred paces before it flashed away into the woods. I walked steadily. I didn't think about home or the future. I became more thin. I played with the sword. It wasn't balanced well for me, but I thought a good smith could remedy that, and meanwhile I learned not to overreach myself with the new weight at the end of my arm. Carrying it on my hip gave me a persistent pain in my lower back, until I found a rolling walk that brought the sword forward without swinging it into my leg at each step. Ad would have called it swagger, but she would have liked it. There was one moment, in a yellow afternoon just as the road lifted itself along the rim of a valley, when I could hear her laugh as if she were only a step behind me, and I missed her as fiercely as in the first month after her death. And I kept going.

On the eighth day I met people.

I heard them before I saw them; two speaking, maybe more silent in their group. I stopped short and found myself sweating, as if their sound was warm water bubbling through the top layer of my skin. I hadn't thought at all about what to do with other people. I had met fewer than a dozen strangers in my life.

"I think there's something in the wood," one of the voices said brightly.

"A wolf?" A hint of laughter.

"A bear."

"A giant."

"A creature with the body of an eagle and a pig's head and teeth as big as your hands."

I was beginning to feel ridiculous; it made me move again. I came out of the trees into an open place where my road met another running north and south. Just beyond the crossroads, three people sat with their backs against a low stone wall that bounded a meadow. I slowed my step. I had no idea how one behaved, and I'm sure it showed. The woman who called to me had the same glittery amusement in her voice that I'd heard as she'd described all the fabulous monsters I might be.

"Why, it's not a bear. Ho, traveler." She nodded. I felt awkward, and I wondered if my voice would work properly after so long in its own company; so I only returned her nod, hitched up my belt, and kept walking. As soon as it was clear that I meant to pass them by, she scrambled to her feet, scattering breadcrumbs and a piece of cheese from her lap into the grass. "Luck, don't," the man said, and grabbed but missed her. She darted toward me. I turned to face her, my hands out, waiting.

"Ah ha," she said, and stopped out of my reach. "Perhaps a bear cub after all. I don't mean to detain you against your will, traveler. We have Shortline cheese to share, and we'd welcome news of the world beyond this road."

She was relaxed, smiling, but she watched my body rather than my face, and her knees were slightly bent, ready to move her in whatever direction she needed to go. She looked strong and capable, but I could see a weakness in her stance, a slight cant to her hips. *I could probably take her*, I thought.

I put my hands down. "The place I've come from is so small, you'd miss it if you looked down to scratch. But I can trade flatcakes for a wedge of cheese and your news."

"Fair enough," she said.

She was Lucky, and the man was Ro. The other, silent woman was Braxis. We ate cheese and my mother's cake in the afternoon sun, and they told me about the North, and I gave them what I knew about the West. I was nervous, but gradually their laughter, their worldliness, won me over. They never asked a question that was too personal, and they gave exactly as much information about themselves as I did, so I never felt at a disadvantage.

"What is it you want from me?" I asked finally. I don't know exactly what made me say it. Maybe it was the combination of the warm gold sun and the warm gold cheese, the bread and the cider from Braxis' wineskin. Maybe it was hearing about the great cities to the north, Shirkasar and Low Grayling, and the massive port of Hunemoth, the way they made me see the marketplaces and the moonlight on the marbled plazas of the noble houses. Maybe it was the looks the three of them traded when I answered their questions.

Braxis raised an eyebrow in my direction. It was Ro who answered.

"Okay, so you know when something's going on under your nose. That's good. Can you fight?"

I tensed. "I've told you how I grew up. I can fight."

"We're going to Lemon City, to the auditions. We need a fourth."

"What auditions?"

"Hoo hoo," Lucky said with a grin.

"Three times a year they hold an audition for the city guard," Ro said. "They only accept quads, they think it's the most stable configuration for training and fighting."

"So," I said. I thought of Tom under the alders, of Lemon City as I'd imagined it with Ad.

"So you probably noticed there are only three of us."

"You came all this way from Grayling without a fourth?"

"No, of course not," Ro said patiently. "He left us two days ago. He found true love in some stupid little town with probably only one bloodline, but he didn't care. He's a romantic, much good may it do him in the ass-end of nowhere."

"And you'd take me just like that, not knowing me at all."

"What do we need to know?" Lucky said. "You breathe, you can stand up without falling over. You're on the road to Lemon City, aren't you? Do you want a job or not?"

"You mean for money?" She shook her head as if she couldn't credit my being so dumb. But I'd expected to have to find honest work, meaning something dirty and bone-tiring, before I could start looking for someone to train with. The idea of getting tired, dirty, and paid to train was so exciting I could hardly believe it was real.

Ro said, "We'll offer you a trial on the road. Travel with us to Lemon City, and we'll see if we want to take it any farther."

"Not without a fight," Braxis said. We all looked at her; Ro and Lucky seemed as surprised that she'd spoken as they did at what she'd said.

"I don't take anyone on without knowing if they can hold their own," she said reasonably. "Not even on trial. That's the whole point of a quad, isn't it? Four walls, stable house. We need strong walls."

"They train you, Brax," Ro responded. "All we have to do is get past the gate."

"No," I said slowly. "She's right. And so are you: I do want to go to Lemon City, but it's got to be properly done." They looked at me with a variety of expressions: Braxis impassive, Ro with his head tilted and a wrinkle in his forehead, Lucky grinning with her arms akimbo.

"I can't explain it. But I need this to be something I can be proud of. It needs to be earned."

"Gods, another romantic," Ro muttered.

We climbed over the wall into the field, and laid aside our swords. Lemon City was just behind that cloud, and I was a hot wind. It was such an amazing feeling that I almost forgot I'd never really fought anyone except Tom, that I didn't yet know if I could. Then Braxis' strong arms reached for me.

When we were done, and Brax had finished coughing up grass, she said, "Fine. On the way there, you can teach us how to do that."

∞

We began to learn each other. Braxis woke up surly. Lucky sang walking songs out of tune, and she knew a hundred of them. Ro was good at resolving differences between others, and peevish when he didn't get his own way. I wasn't sure what they were discovering about me. I'd never lived with anyone except my mother: it was one more thing I didn't know how to do. I watched everything and tried not to offend anyone.

We got into the routine of making camp early in the afternoon, to keep the last hours of light for practicing swords and stormfighting. It didn't take them long to work out that I barely knew one end of my sword from the other. I was ashamed, and halfway expected them to kick me back up the road. They surprised me. "I've never seen anyone fight like you do," Ro said matter-of-factly. "If we can trade learning between us, it makes us all stronger." Then he set about showing me the basics.

Two weeks later it was Lucky who came toward me with her sword. I looked at Ro. He smiled. "I've given you enough so that you can at least keep up with what she's got to show you. She's the best of us."

I expected the thrust-and-parry exercises that I'd worked on with Ro, but Lucky came to stand to one side of me, just out of blade range. She extended her sword. "Follow me," was all she said, and then she was off in a step, turn, strike, block that moved straight into a new combination. She was fast. I stayed with her as best I could, and actually matched her about one move in seven.

"Not horrible," she said. "Let's try it again." We worked it over and over until finally she reached out and pried the sword out of my grip. "Those will hurt tomorrow," she said of the blisters on my palms. "You should have told me." But I was determined to hold my own with these people, so I only shrugged. My hands felt raw for days after; but I was stubborn. And it helped that I could teach as well as learn. It did not matter so much that I was the youngling, the inexperienced one, when their bodies worked to imitate mine, when their muscles fluttered and strained to please me.

And I had a new secret: I was beginning to understand the price for all those months that I'd wrestled my body's feelings back into my fighting. I could scrub Lucky's back after a cold creek bath, see Brax's nipples crinkle when she shrugged off her shirt at night, lie with my head pillowed on Ro's thigh—and never feel a thing except a growing sense of wonder at what complex and contradictory people I had found on my road. But when we met in practice, everything changed. The slide of Brax's leather-covered breast against my arm during a takedown put a point of heat at the tip of every nerve from my shoulder to my groin. Ro's weight on me when he tested the possibilities of a technique was voluptuous in a way I'd never imagined in my awkward days with Ad. Lucky's rain-wet body twisting underneath me excited me so much it was almost beyond bearing: but I learned to bear it, to stuff the pleasure back inside myself so that it wound through me endlessly like a cloud boiling with the weight of unreleased rain. In my days with Tom I had learned to fight through cold and pain and misery: now I learned to persist through pleasure so keen that sometimes it left me seared and breathless and not sure how to make my arms and legs keep working. I told no one; but I woke in the morning anticipating those hours, and slept at night with their taste in my throat. I was always ready to practice.

"I sweat like a bull," Brax said ruefully one day when we were all rubbing ourselves down afterwards. "But you always smell so good." I smiled and pulled my tunic on quickly to hide the shudders that still trembled through me.

It was a few days later that Ro approached me after supper, squatting down beside me near the fire. We smiled at each other and spent a quiet time stripping the bark off sticks and feeding it to the flames. Eventually, he said, "Share my blanket tonight?"

I'd seen from the first night how it was between them, bedding two at a time but in a relationship of three. I had already guessed at their idea of what a quad should be. I wondered how sophisticated people handled this sort of thing.

"No, but thank you," I said finally. "It's not you, Ro, you're a fine person, and I'm pleased to be part of your quad. It's just—"

"No need to explain," he said, which only made me feel more awkward. But the next day he treated me not much differently. By the afternoon I had recovered my equilibrium, and I'd noticed their quiet conversations, so I was only a little surprised to find Lucky at my elbow after practice.

"Let's take a walk," she said cheerfully. "Fetch water, or something."

"Fine," I said, and went to gather everyone's waterskins. "No need to rush," Braxis said. Ro nodded agreeably.

"Fine," I said again, and off we went.

We found a stream and loaded up with water, and then sat on the bank. I lay back with my head on my arms while Lucky fiddled with flower stems. Then she leaned over me and kissed me. Her mouth was dry and sweet. But nothing moved in me. I sat up and set her back from me as gently as I could. She didn't look angry, only amused. "Would Braxis have been a better choice for water duty today?"

"No, it's not that."

"Don't you know what you like, then?"

"You know what?" I said, "Let's go back to the others so I only have to have this conversation once."

We all sat around, and they chewed on hand-sized chunks of bread while I talked.

"Anyone would be proud to have you as lovers, all of you." It was nice to see the way they glowed for each other then, with nothing more than smiles or a quick touch before turning their attention back to me. "It's not about you."

I stopped, long enough that Braxis raised an eyebrow. It was hard to say the next thing. "If you need that from your fourth, then I'll help you find someone else when we get to Lemon City, and no hard feelings."

We were all quiet for a while. Finally Braxis wiped the crumbs off her hands. "Oh, well," she said. "Of course we don't want another fourth, Mars, we'd rather have you even if we can't have you, if you take my meaning." Lucky hooted, and I went red in the face, which just made Lucky worse.

"No, truly," Braxis went on when Ro had finally put a hammerlock on Lucky. "We like you. We're starting to fight well together. We learn from each other. We trust ourselves. We can be a good quad. The other," she shrugged, and Lucky made a rude gesture, "well, it's nice, but it isn't everything, is it?"

It stayed with me, that remark, while I did my share of the night chores, and later as I lay on my back in the dark, listening to Ro's snores and the small, eager sounds that Braxis and Lucky made together under a restless sky of black scudding clouds. It was strange to think about sex with them so intent on it just a knife-throw away. *It's nice but it's not everything*, Brax had said: but for those moments it sounded like it was everything for the two of them.

I hoped they stayed willing to take me as I was. I didn't know if I could explain that what they did wrapped in their blankets was like being offered the lees of fine wine. I could tell they thought I was still grieving for Ad, or Tom: let them believe that, if it would obscure the truth of what I had become and what stirred me now. *Keep your mouth shut, Mars,* I told myself, and twisted onto my side away from them. *They'll never understand and you'd never be able to explain. They'll think you're insane or perverted or worse, and they'll send you packing back to your no-name village before you can say 'oh go ahead and fuck me if that's what it takes to let me stay with you.'*

I never was much good at cheering myself up: but in spite of it all I finally fell asleep, and I woke to a hug from Braxis and pine tea from Ro, to a sleepy pat on the shoulder from Lucky, and for the first time in oh-so-long I felt the hope of belonging.

∞

It took weeks to get to Lemon City, mostly because we were in no hurry. There was always so much to do each day, so much exploring and talking and the hands-on work of turning ourselves into a fighting partnership. And other kinds of work, as well. In spite of what they'd said, the three of them made a concerted effort to seduce me, and I did not know how to reassure them that they had already succeeded, that they had turned me into a banked coal with a constant fire in my belly. "Damn your cold heart, Mars," Lucky spat at me one day, "I hope someday someone you really want turns you down flat, and then see how you like it!"

"Luck, it's not like that!" I called after her as she stalked off down a side trail into the woods.

"Leave her," Ro advised. "She'll accept it. We all will." He and Brax exchanged a wry look, and I felt terrible. I must be cold, I thought, cold and selfish. It was such a small thing to ask, to make people I loved happy. But it wasn't just my body they wanted, it was me, and they would never reach me that way, and then we would all still be unsatisfied. And I was not willing to explain. So it was my fault, my flaw. My failure.

I was packing my bedroll when Lucky came back. "Oh, stop," she said impatiently. "You know what I'm like, Mars, don't take it so personally. Just stay away from me tonight and I'll be fine in the morning." And she was; and the next afternoon, when she took hold of me so unknowingly, I gave her myself. I gave to all of them, a dozen times each day.

"The hardest part about all this," Brax said one evening as we all stretched out near our fire, "is overcoming all the sword training."

"Whaddya mean?" Ro mumbled around a mouthful of cheese.

"Well, the sword makes your arm longer and gives it a killing edge, so that you still strike or punch, sort of, but it's with the blade. But the stormfighting, well, like Mars is always saying, the whole point is to become the center of the fight and bring your enemy in to you. So with the sword we keep people out far enough to slice them up, and with the storm art we bring them in close enough to kiss. It does my head in sometimes trying to figure out where I'm supposed to be when."

"You think it's hard for you?" I replied. "You're not the one with half a dozen cuts on every arm and leg trying to learn it the other way around. I always let Lucky get too close."

"So maybe there's a way to do both." Lucky reached out to swipe a piece of cheese from Ro's lap.

"What do you mean?" Ro asked again.

"Pig. Give me some of that. I mean that maybe there's a way to combine the moves. All the sword dances I do are based on wheels, being able to turn and move in any direction with your body and the sword like spokes on a wheel. It's not that different from being at the center of a wind, or whatever."

"Gods around us," I said. She'd put a picture in my mind so clear that for a moment I wasn't sure which was more real, the Lucky who smiled quizzically at me from across the fire, or the one who suddenly rolled over her own sword and came up slashing at her opponent's knee. "She's right. You could do both. Think about it! Just think about it!" They were all bright-eyed now, caught in the spiral of my excitement that drew them in as surely as one of the armlocks we'd worked on that afternoon. "Imagine being able to fight long or short, with an edge or a tip or just your bare hand. They'd never know what to expect, they couldn't predict what you'd do next!"

"Okay, maybe," Lucky said. "It might work with that whole series that's based off the step in and behind, but what about the face-to-face? A sword's always a handicap when you're in that close."

"That's because everyone always goes weapon to weapon." Lucky looked blank. "If you have a sword, what's the other person going to do? Get a bigger sword if they can. Try to beat your sword. But we don't need that. Our weapon is the way we fight. Go in and take their sword away. Go in and do things with a sword that no one thinks possible. In my head I just saw you roll with your own blade and come up edge-ready. Maybe staying low would give us more options for being in close."

"Come here," Lucky said, and scrambled up, and we worked it out again and again until the fire was almost dead and we trod on Brax in the dark. "Stop this idiocy and go to sleep!" she growled; but the next day we were all ready to reinvent sword fighting, and we ate our dinner that night bloody and bruised and grinning like children.

∞

We came into Lemon City on a cold wind, just ahead of a hard autumn rain that dropped from a fast front of muddy clouds. We crowded under cover of a blacksmith's shed inside the city gates with a dozen other travelers, three gate guards, and two bad-tempered horses, while manure and straw and someone's basket washed away down the waterlogged street. Everything was grey and stinking. I couldn't help laughing, remembering my fantasies about golden streets full of important people in silk with me in the center, being whisked toward greatness.

When the rain had passed we walked in towards the heart of the city. My boots leaked, and my feet got wet, and Ro stepped in goat shit and swore.

"So far, I feel right at home," I told Lucky, who cackled wildly and reminded me for one sharp moment of my mother, bent over in laughter with her hands twisted in her apron and flour dust rising all around her.

We found an inn that they'd heard of, and got the second-to-last room left. We were lucky; the last room was no better than a sty, and went an hour later for the same rate as ours. The city was packed tighter than a farm sausage, our landlord told us with a satisfied smile. He took some of Ro's money for a pitcher of cider and settled one hip up against the common room table to tell us where to find the guard house for the coming auditions. The next were in two days' time. "And lots of competition for this one, of course," he said cheerfully, with a glance around the crowded room that made him scurry to another table with his tray of cider.

"What's that mean, of course?" Lucky wondered when he'd gone away.

I shrugged. Brax drank the last of her cider. "I hate it when they say of course," she muttered, and belched.

The next day was sunny, and we went out exploring. I left my sword for the day with the blacksmith near the city gate, who promised to lengthen the grip. From there we wandered to the market, and they laughed at my wide-eyed amazement. And everywhere we saw four-somes, young or seasoned, trying not to show their stress by keeping their faces impassive, so of course you could spot them a mile off. We followed some of them to the guards training camp, and waited in line to give our names to someone whose only job that day seemed to be telling stiff-faced hopefuls where and when to turn up for the next morning's trials. Then we found a place to perch where Lucky and Brax could size everyone up until they found something to feel superior about: a weak eye, too much weight on one foot, someone's hands looped under their belt so they couldn't reach their weapon easily. Eventually the strain got to be too much, and we went back to the inn for an afternoon meal and practice on a small patch of ground near the stable. Working up a sweat seemed to calm them down; and touching them erased everything else for me.

That night, I laid an extra coin on the table when the landlord brought our platter of chicken and pitcher of beer, and said, "Tell us what's so special about these auditions."

He looked genuinely surprised. "Anybody could tell you that," he said, but he put the coin in his sleeve pocket. "The prince has turned out half the palace guard again, and Captain Gerlain's scrambling for replacements. Those who do well are sure to end up with palace duty, although why any of you'd want it is beyond me."

"Why's that?"

"Our prince is mad, that's why, and the king's too far gone up his own backside to notice."

Lucky put a hand to her knife. "You mind yourself, man," she said calmly, and Brax and I tried not to grin at each other. Lucky could be startlingly conservative.

"Oh, and no offense intended to the king," he said easily. "But well done, he needs loyal soldiers around him. Particularly now he's old and sick, and too well medicated, at least that's what they say. You just get yourself hired on up there and keep an eye on him for us." He poured Lucky another drink. I admired the skill with which he'd turned the conflict aside.

None of us could eat, thinking about the next day, and the beer tasted off. We sat at the table, not talking much. Eventually we moved out to the snug, where the landlord had a fire going. It was warmer there than the common room, but no more relaxing. I turned the coming day over and over in my head as if it were a puzzle I couldn't put down until I'd solved it. Lucky and Ro sat close together: their calves touched, then their thighs, then Ro's hand found its way onto Lucky's arm and she sighed, leaned into him, looking suddenly small and soft. When I looked away, Brax was there, next to me.

She cupped her hard hand around my jaw and cheek and left ear. "Don't turn me away, Mars," she said quietly. "It's no night to be alone."

"You're right," I replied. "But let's try something a little different." I felt wild and daring, even though I knew she wouldn't understand. I took her by the hand and led her out to our practice area by the stable. They kept a lantern out there for late arrivals; it gave us just enough light to see motion, but the fine work would have to be done by instinct: by feel.

"You want to practice?" she said.

My heart was thudding under my ribs. This was the closest I had ever come to telling anyone what it was like with me. It was so tempting to say *Take me down, Brax, challenge me, control me, equal me, best me, love me.* But I only smiled and stepped into the small circle of light. "Put your hands on me," I whispered, soft enough so that she would not hear, and centered myself.

∞

They were fair auditions, and hard, and we were brilliant. I could tell they had never seen anything like us. The method was to put two quads into the arena with wooden swords. I learned later that they looked for how we fought, but that was only part of it. "The fighting is the easiest thing to teach," Captain Gerlain told me once. "What I look for is basic coordination, understanding of the body and how it works. And how the quad works together."

It was an incredible day, a blur of things swirled together: crisp air that smelled of fried bread from the camp kitchen and the sweat of a hundred nervous humans; the sounds of leather on skin and huffing breath interleaved with the faint music of temple singers practicing three streets away; and the touch of a hundred different hands, the

KELLEY ESKRIDGE

textures of their skin, the energies that ran between us as we laid hold of one another.

After he saw our stormfighting, Gerlain started putting other quads against us, so that we fought more than anyone else. Most of the fighters didn't know what to make of us, and I began to see that Gerlain was using us as a touchstone to test the others. Those who tried to learn from us, who adapted as best they could, had the good news with us when Gerlain's sergeant read out the names at the end of the day; and Gerlain himself stopped Lucky and said curtly, "You and your quad'll be teaching the rest an hour a day, after regular training, starting tomorrow afternoon. Work out your program with Sergeant Manto. And don't get above yourselves. Manto will be watching, and so will I."

"Hoo hoo!" said Lucky. "Let's get drunk!" But I was already intoxicated by the day, dizzy with the feel of so many strangers' skin against mine. And I was a guard. I whispered it to Ad as we walked back to the inn through the streets that now seemed familiar and welcoming. *I made it,* I told her. *Lemon City.* I thought of Tom, and my mother: *I'm safe, I found a place for myself.* I saw Ad with her sheepskin and her special stick; I felt Tom's tears on my skin, and my mother's hand on my hair. Then Ro was standing in the door to the inn, looking for me, waiting: and I went in.

∞

It was the stormfighting that kept us out of a job for such a long time. Gerlain and Manto saw it as a tactical advantage and a way to teach warriors not to rely on their swords. Tom would have approved. But many of our fellow soldiers did not. Our frank admission that it was still raw, as dangerous to the fighter as to the target, and our matter-of-fact approach to teaching, were the only things that kept us from being permanent outsiders in the guard. Even so, we made fewer friends than we might have.

"Can't let you go yet," Manto would shrug each month, when new postings were announced. "Need you to teach the newbs."

"Let someone else teach," Ro was arguing again.

"Who? There's no one here who knows it the way you do."

"That's because you keep posting them on as soon as they've halfway learned anything."

"Shucks," Manto grinned, showing her teeth. "You noticed."

"Manto, try to see this from our point of view...."

"Oh gods," I whispered to Lucky, "There he goes, being reasonable again. Do something."

"Right," she whispered back, and then stepped between Ro and Manto, pointing a finger at Ro when he tried to protest. She said pleasantly, "We came here to be guards, not baby-minders. You want us to teach, fine, we'll teach other guards. Until then, I think we'll just go get a beer." She turned and started for the gate, hooking a thumb into Ro's belt to pull him along. Brax sighed and reached for her gear. I gave Manto a cheerful smile and a goodbye salute.

"All right, children," Manto said, pitching her voice to halt Lucky and Ro. "Report to Andavista tomorrow at the palace. Take all your toys, you'll draw quarters up there."

Even Lucky was momentarily speechless.

Manto grinned again. "The orders have been in for a couple of weeks. I just wanted to see how much more time I could get out of you." She slapped me on the arm so hard I almost fell over. "Welcome to the army."

"Where the hell have you people been?" Sergeant Andavista snarled at us the next morning. "Been waiting for you for two weeks." There seemed to be no good answer to that, so we didn't even try. "Your rooms are at the end of the southwest gallery. Unpack and report back here to me in ten minutes. Move!"

The rooms had individual beds, for which I was grateful. The double-wide bunks at the training camp had made us all more tense with one another as time went on, and I was tired of sleeping on the floor—particularly after a good day's work, when my body felt hollowed out by the thousand moments of desire roused and sated and born again, every time we grappled, when I only wanted to sleep close to one of my unknowing lovers and drink in the smell of our sweat on their skin.

Andavista handed us off to the watch commander, who gave us new gear with the palace insignia and a brain-numbing recital of guard schedules. Then she found a man just coming off watch and drafted him to show us around. The soldier looked bone-tired, but he nodded agreeably enough and tried to hide his yawns as he led us up and down seemingly endless hallways. He pointed out the usual watch stations: main gate, trade entrances, public rooms, armory, the three floors of rooms where the bureaucrats lived and worked, and the fourteen floors of nobles' chambers, which he waved at dismissively. I remembered my mother saying *ticks on a dog.*

He brought us to a massive set of wooden doors strapped with iron. "Royal suite," he said economically. "Last stop on the tour. Can you find your own way back?"

We did, although it took the better part of an hour and made us all grumpy. "Not bad," the watch commander commented when we returned. "Last week's set had to be fetched out."

And so we settled. It wasn't much different from living in my village, except that I belonged. We learned soldiery and taught stormfighting and found time to practice by ourselves, to reinforce old ideas, to invent new ones. It was an easy routine to settle to, but I'd had my lessons too well from Tom to ever relax completely, and the rest of the quad had learned to trust my edge. And it helped in a turned-around way that news of us had spread up from the training ground, and there were soldiers we'd never met who resented us for being different, and were contemptuous of what they'd heard about stormfighting. Being the occasional target of pointed remarks or pointed elbows was new for Brax and Lucky and Ro; it kept them aware in a way that all my warnings never could. So on the day we found swords at our throats, we were ready.

They came for the king and prince during the midnight watch when we were stationed outside the royal wing. Ro thought he might have seen the king once, at the far end of the audience room, but these doors were the closest we had ever been to the people we were sworn to protect. And it was our first posting to this most private area of the palace. Perhaps that's why they chose our watch to try it. Or perhaps because they had dismissed the purposely slow practice drills of storm art as nothing more than fancy-fighting; it was a common enough belief among our detractors.

The first sign we had that anything was amiss was when two of the daywatch quads came up the hall. Brax stepped forward; it was her night to be in charge. "We're relieving you," their leader said. "Andavista wants you down at the gates."

"What's up?" Brax asked neutrally, but I could see the way her shoulders tensed.

The other shrugged. "Dunno. Some kind of commotion at the gates, security's being tightened inside. Andavista says jump, I reckon it's our job to ask which cliff he had in mind."

Brax stood silent for a moment, thinking. "Ro, go find Andavista or Saree and get it in person. No offense," she added to the two quads in front of her.

"None taken," their leader said; and then her sword was out and coming down on Brax. She struck hard and fast, but Brax was already under her arm and pushing her off center, taking only enough time to break the other woman's arm as she went down. The other seven moved in, Brax scrambled up with blood on her sword, and then they were on us.

I wasn't ready for the noise of it, the clattering of metal on metal, the yells, the way that everything reverberated in the closed space of the hallway. I could hear the bolts slamming into place in the doors behind us, and knew that at least someone was alerted: no one but Andavista or Gerlain would get inside now. Lucky was shouting but I couldn't tell what or who it was meant for. Then I saw Ro shaking his head even as he turned and cut another soldier's feet out from under him, and I understood. "Go on," I yelled. "Get help! We don't know how many more there might be!"

For a moment Ro looked terribly young. Then his face set, and he turned up the hall. It was bad strategy on the part of the assassins to arrive in a group, rather than splitting up and approaching from both directions; but they'd had to preserve the illusion of being ordered to the post. Two of them tried to head Ro off: he gutted one and kept going, and Brax stepped in front of the other. Three horrible moments later she made a rough, rattling sound and they both went down in a boneless tumble. Brax left a broad smear of blood on the wall behind her as she fell.

Lucky and I were side by side now, facing the four that were still standing. Out of the side of my right eye I could see Brax lying limp against the wall. Lucky was panting. There was a moment of silence in the hall; we all looked at each other, as if we'd suddenly found ourselves doing something unexpected and someone had stopped to ask, *what now?*

"Blow them down," I told Lucky, and we swirled into them like the lightning and the wind.

I'd never before fought for my life or another's. These people weren't Tom; I couldn't drop my sword and call *stop*. And these were our own we were facing, people we'd eaten with, insulted and argued with, and whose measure we had taken on the training field. Some of them were people I had taught, muscle to muscle, skin to skin. Now I reached for them in rage, and my touch was voracious. I went in close to one, up near his center, my arm fully extended under his and lifting up, taking his balance, thrusting my weight forward to put him down. It was sweet to feel him scrabbling under my hands, pulling at my tunic, trying to right himself, and then my sword was at his neck and I cut off his life in a ragged line. His trousers soiled with shit and he fell into a puddle at my feet. My body sang. I took the taste of his death between my teeth and stepped on his stomach to get to the woman behind him.

∞

I woke in our rooms. Ro was there, watching over me.

"How are you?"

"Don't touch me," I said.

He waited. "Brax and Lucky are going to be fine." I put a hand up to my head. "It was deep, to the bone, but it's not infected. They had to shave your head," he added, too late.

"Saree came around. Those two quads were hired to win a place in the guards and wait for the right moment. The one they took alive didn't last long enough to tell them who did the hiring. Poor bastard."

I felt empty and dirty, and I couldn't think of anything to say.

He swallowed, moved closer, but he was careful not to touch me. "Mars, I know it's the first time you've killed. It's hard, but we've all been through it. We can help you, if you'll let us."

"You don't understand," I said.

"I do, truly." He was so earnest. "I remember—"

I held up a hand. "Blessing on you, Ro, but it's not the killing, it's—I can't. I can't talk about it." I swung my legs off the other side of the bed, stood shakily, looked around for something to wear. My head hurt all the way down to my feet, but I wasn't as weak as I'd expected to be. Good. I found my tunic and overshirt, and a pair of dirty leggings.

"Where are you going?"

"I need to get out. I'll be fine," I added, seeing his face. "I won't leave the palace. I just want some time to think. I'm not looking for a ledge to jump off."

He managed a tight smile. I did not come close to him as I left.

I really did want to wander: to get lost. I had the wit to stay away from the public halls, and I did not want the company and the avid questions of other guards, so I steered toward the lower floors: the kitchens, the pantry, and the enclosed food gardens. I found a stair down from the scullery that led to a vast series of storerooms, smokerooms, wine cellars.

I thought about the killing.

The sword work wasn't so bad. The sensations of weapon contact were always more muted for me than hand-to-hand. But stormfighting was so much more intense: seducing my opponent into me, or thrusting myself into her space, or breathing in the smell of him while my hands turned him to my will. I'd got used to it being delicious, smooth, powerful, like gulping a mug of warm cream on a cold night. Until the hallway, until the man's throat spilled open under my sword, until I broke his partner open with my hands. With my hands—and the fizzing thrill through my body was overrun by something that felt like chunks of fire, like vomit in my veins. I hated it. It made me feel lonely in a way I'd never thought to feel again. So I sat down in the cellars of the palace and wept for something I'd lost, and then I wept some more for the greater loss to come.

My head hurt worse when I'd run dry of tears. I gathered myself up and went to find my quad.

∞

They were sitting quietly when I came into the room, not talking; Brax on one of the beds drowsing in the last of the sun through the west window, Lucky crowded in beside her with her bad leg propped on a pillow, Ro on the floor nearby leaning against the mattress so that his head was close to theirs.

"Ho, Mars," Lucky said gently.

They were so beautiful that for a handful of moments I could only look at them. When I opened my mouth I had no idea what might come out of it.

"I love you all so much," I said. I wasn't nervous anymore; it was time they knew me, and whatever happened next I would always have this picture of them, and the muscle-deep memory of all our times.

"Being with you three is like.... Gods, sometimes I imagine leaving home a day earlier or later. How easy it would have been to miss you on the road. What if I'd missed you? What would I be now?"

They were silent, watching me. I was the center of the world.

"That time on the road, when you asked me to...." I made a hapless sort of gesture, and Ro smiled. "You thought I was saying no, but what I was really saying was no, not like that." I swallowed. I wasn't sure how to say the next bit; and then Brax surprised me.

"The night before the guard trials, out behind the inn, when I thought we were practicing. We were really fucking, your way."

I felt like a lightning-struck tree, all soft pulp suddenly exposed to the world, ruptured and raw. And I did the thing more frightening than fighting Tom, or leaving home, or losing Ad. I whispered *yes*. Then I crossed my arms to hold myself in, and tried to find words to hold off the moment when they would send me away. "I didn't know until I met you on the road, and we began to practice, and every time we touched in this particular way I thought I would die from it. That's when I figured it out, you know. I was a virgin when I met you," and I couldn't help but smile, because it was so right. "For me, the touch of your palm on my wrist is the same as any act of love; it's my way of bringing our bodies together. It's no different from putting ourselves inside each other."

"Mars, it's—" Ro began.

"Don't you tell me it's okay!" I cut him off. "You're always the peacemaker, Ro, but you don't understand. You don't understand what I've done. Every time we've touched as fighters, all the teaching and the practice, it's all been sex for me, hours and hours of it with one of you or all of you, or other quads that we've taught. And you never knew. What's that but some kind of rape? It's bad enough with people I love, and then there's all those strangers. I've probably had more partners than all the whores in Ziren Square. And I can't help it, and gods know I can't stop because it's the most unbelievable...but what I did to all of you, that's unforgivable, but I was so afraid that you'd...well, I expect you can guess what I thought, and I'm sure you're thinking it now. No, wait," I said, to stop Brax from speaking. "Then there's this killing. You were right, Ro, I've never killed before, and it was horrible, it was disgusting because I still felt it even when I was pulling her arm out of its socket. And I didn't want to, I didn't want to, but I thought of what they'd done to Brax and then I was glad to hurt them and then there was this fierce, terrible wave.... Oh, gods, I'm sorry." I was panting now, clenching myself. "I'm sorry. But it's there, and I thought you should know." They were still silent; Brax and Lucky were holding hands so tightly that I could see their fingers going white, and Ro looked sad and patient. "I love you," I said, and then everything was beyond bearing, and I had to leave.

∞

I went back to the cellars because I didn't know where else to go. I did not belong anywhere now. I sat curled for hours next to one of the beer vats, numb and quiet, until I heard the chattering voices of cooking staff come to fetch a barrel for supper: I did not want to meet anyone, so I unkinked myself and went farther down the hallway until I found a small heavy door slightly ajar, old but with freshly oiled hinges that made no sound as I slid through.

I came into a vast, dim place, heavy with green and the smell of water. Not a garden: an enormous twilight conservatory in the guts of the oldest part of the palace. Even through my despair I could see the marvel of the place, feel its mystery. There were trees standing forty feet tall in porcelain tubs as big as our room upstairs. Light seeped through narrow windows above the treetops. There were wooden frames thick with ivy that bloomed in lightly perfumed purple and orange and blue. Everything felt old and unused, sliding toward ruin, with the particular heavy beauty of a rotting temple. The humid air, the taste of jasmine on my tongue, the stone walls that I could sense although I could not see them under so much green—everything collided inside me and mixed with my own madness to make me feel wild, curious, adrenalized as if I'd eaten too many of the dried granzi leaves that Brax liked to indulge in sometimes when we were off duty. The narrow path that twisted off between the potted trees was laid in the unmistakable patterns of desert tile. I followed the colors toward the sound of rain, and the sound turned into a fountain, a flat-bottomed circle lined with more bright tiles. Strings of water fell into it from a dozen ducts in the ceiling high overhead, onto the pool and the upraised face of the woman in it.

She was dancing. From the look of her, she'd been at it awhile: her hair was flung in sodden ropes against her dark skin, and the tips of her fingers were wrinkled, paler than the rest of her when she reached them up to grasp at the droplets in the air. She breathed in the hard, shallow gasps of someone who has taken her body almost as far as it can go. Her eyes were rolled up, showing white, and her mouth hung half-open. She whirled and kicked to a rhythm that pounded through her so strongly I could feel it as a backbeat to the juddering of my heart. Faster, faster she turned, and the water turned with her and flung itself back into the pool. I knew what I was seeing. It was more than a dance, it was a transportation, a transmigration, as if she could take the whole world into herself if she only reached a little higher, if she only turned once more. I knew how it must feel within her, burning, building, until her body shuddered one final time and she shouted, her head still back and her arms clawed up as if she would seize the ceiling and pull it down over her. Her eyes opened, bright blue against the brown. She saw me as she fell.

Bless her, I thought, *at least I'm not that alone.*

Her shout still echoed around the chamber, or at least I could still hear it in my head; but she was silent, lying on her side in the water, blue eyes watching me. I eased myself down onto one of the tiled benches bordering the walkway, to show her that I was not a threat or an idle gawper. There was a shawl bundled at the other end of the bench, and I was careful not to touch it. After a minute she rolled onto her back in the shallow pool and turned her blue gaze up to the high windows. Neither of us spoke. I was relaxed and completely attentive to everything she did: a breath drawn, a finger moved, a lick at a drop of water caught on her lip. When she finally pulled herself up to her knees, I was there with the shawl and an arm to help her raise herself the rest of the way. She draped the shawl around her shoulders but did not try to cover herself; she seemed unaware of being naked and wet with a stranger. I stood back when she stepped out of the pool.

She looked me up and down. She was medium tall, older by a few years, whip thin with oversized calf muscles and strong biceps. An old scar ran along one rib. The skin on her hands was rough. I pictured her in one of the kitchens, or perhaps tending the smokehouse where the sides of beef and boar had to be raised onto their high hooks.

"I hope you closed the door behind you," she said absently, in a dry and crackly voice.

"The door? Oh...yes, it's closed. No one will come in."

"You did."

"Yes. But no one else will come."

"They might."

"I won't let them."

She looked me up and down. "You're a guard," she said.

"Yes."

"So you'd kill anyone who tried to get in."

"I'd meet them at the door and send them on their way. If they tried to come in further, I'd stop them."

She drew a wrinkled finger across her throat.

"Not necessarily," I replied. "I might not have to kill them."

"Oh," she said. "I would. I wouldn't know how to stop them any other way. I don't know much about the middle ground."

She had begun to shake very slightly. "You're cold," I said, and pulled off my overshirt to offer her. She peered at it carefully before she put it on, dropping the shawl without a glance onto the wet floor.

"Most people don't talk to me," she said.

"I'll talk with you whenever you like," I said, thinking that I knew very well how people would treat her, particularly if she wandered up to the kitchens with one of the meat cleavers in her hand and tried to have this kind of conversation. Standing with her in the dim damp of the room felt like being in one of those in-between moments of an epic poem, where everyone takes a stanza or two to gather their breath before the next impossible task.

She appeared to be thinking, and I was in no hurry. Then she straightened the shirt around her and said, "Walk me back."

"Of course," I answered. I plucked her shawl out of the muck and fell in behind her with my hand on my sword, the way I'd been taught. She was so odd and formal, like a little chick covered in bristles: she wanted looking after. When we left the room, she watched to make sure that I closed the door firmly, then nodded as if satisfied and led me back up through the cellars. I was surprised when she bypassed the carvery and the scullery, and nervous when she took the stairs away from the kitchen, up toward the residential levels of the palace: I wasn't sure what to do if someone challenged us, and I did not want trouble with Andavista on top of the mess I'd already made with my quad. But she held her head high and kept going, and then we made a turn and almost ran into Saree talking something out with one of his seconds. *Oh icy hell,* I thought, and was absolutely astonished when Saree gave me an unreadable look and then bent his head. "Prince," he said, and she sailed by him like a great ship past a dinghy, trailing me behind. As I passed him, Saree pointed his finger at himself emphatically, and I nodded, and then followed the prince. We came to the great wooden doors of the royal suite, and the four guards there stiffened. They opened the doors clumsily, trying to see everything without appearing to look at us, and I knew the stories would start a minute after the watch changed when the four of them could get down to the commissary.

The hallway was a riot of rich colored tapestries, plants, paintings, a table stacked high with dusty books: and silent as a tomb. I wondered if the king was behind one of the many doors we passed. A servant came out of a room at the far end and hurried toward us with a muffled exclamation. The prince waved her off, and I handed her the shawl as she stepped back to let us pass. Then the prince stopped in front of one of the doors and turned to me. Her eyes were hard, like blue stained glass. I saluted and bowed.

"You saw me," she said, and her voice was like her eyes.

I imagined what it would be like to practice with my quad from now on, their knowing what it meant to me every time we touched, their distaste or their tolerance, my most private self on public display because I had not kept my secret. I understood how she might feel; and she deserved the truth.

"You were beautiful," I said. "You were like a storm."

She looked at me for a moment, then she took in a breath and blew it out again with the noise that children make when they pretend to be the wind. Her breath smelled like salt and oranges. The door shut between us.

"What happened?" Saree growled when I found him.

"The prince asked me to escort her back to her rooms," I said evenly.

"Where did you find her? Her servants have been looking for her for hours."

"In the hallway near the armory." It was the farthest place from the cellars that I could think of.

"Oh, really?" he rumbled. "She just happened to appear in the armory hallway soaking wet, and there you were?"

"Yessir," I answered. "Honestly, sir, I didn't even know who she was until we met you. I just didn't think that she should be—I mean—"

He relaxed. "I know what you mean, no need to say any more. But we'd like to know where she disappears to." I stayed quiet, and he lost interest in me. "Don't you have somewhere to be?" he said, and I saluted and got out of his sight as quickly as I could. My head was too stuffed full of tangled thoughts to make any sense of anything, and I didn't want to deal with Ro and Lucky and Brax until I felt clear. I took myself off into Lemon City for a long walk and did, in the end, get my wish: I got lost.

It was late when I came back to our rooms. The quad was there, and so was Andavista. They all wore the most peculiar expressions: Lucky was trying to send me seventeen different messages with eyes and body language, but all I got was the general impression that a lot had been going on while I'd been away. Then I looked beyond her, and saw the carrybags we'd brought with us all the way from the crossroads, packed now and waiting to be closed up.

"No, you idiot," Brax said. "Your things are in there too, we're being transferred. Don't look at me like that; everyone knows what you're thinking, we can always tell."

"Ummm," I said helplessly, and Ro grinned. Andavista stood up from where he'd been sitting, in our only chair. "Very touching. Sort it out later. You, I've just about run out of patience waiting for you, but I've got direct orders to fetch you all personally. I suppose I can be thankful you didn't decide to stay out all night. Particularly since this lot wouldn't say where you could be found." He squinted at me. "Well, at least you're not stupid enough to turn up drunk. Now, all of you, get your things and follow me."

He stomped out of the room and we scrambled to shoulder our gear and follow him. I shooed Lucky out of the way and picked up our biggest pack. "Get away from that, you can't carry it with your leg." She grimaced impatiently. "What's going on?" I whispered.

"You tell me," she whispered back. "All we got is some wild story at dinner about you and the prince, and then Andavista saying he's giving us a new home and everyone who's not on watch finding an excuse to wander by our rooms and goggle at us."

"Shut up and move," Andavista snarled without turning, so we did, Ro and I carrying everything between us while Brax braced Lucky with her good arm. Of course I knew where we must be going, but I could scarcely credit it: I'd only been nice, and certainly more free in my manner than what was due to her. But I was right: we went through the by-now-familiar wooden doors and into a room just beyond, where sleepy-eyed servants were busily beating the dust out of a rug and several coverlets, with a new fire in the hearth and a pitcher of mulled wine on a mostly-clean table. And my overshirt, carefully folded on the mantel.

Andavista said, "You've been assigned as the prince's personal guard. You're with her wherever she goes, all of you, which means more time on duty than before. She breakfasts at midmorning, you two—" looking at me and Ro, "—report to her then. If she forgets to let you out for meals, let me know. I expect a full report every day from one of you, personally to either me or Saree, no exceptions. You'll go back to teaching when you're all off the sick list, at least until you've got others good enough to take over. Where you find the time is your problem. And don't get above yourselves, I'll be watching. And don't let so much as a mouse near her," he added, in a different tone. Then he glared around the room and left. The servants scuttled out behind him.

My three pounced on me with questions before the door was closed. "Wait, wait," I said, trying to gather my wits while Ro poured us a cup of wine. Between hot swallows, I told them about meeting the prince, curiously content even though we all knew why I'd been downcellar in the first place, the unfinished business between us.

"Unbelievable," Lucky said. "How do you do it, Mars?"

Brax said, "I wouldn't go planting any gardens here, Luck. She's thrown out more guards than we have ancestors. She could change her mind anytime."

"I don't think so," I said. "She's never taken a personal guard before that I know of, just the shift watches outside the door. Can you imagine some of our mates in the barracks standing outside the conservatory doors while she.... She'd have been a laughingstock years ago."

"So why now?" Ro said.

"I understand her." They looked at me. "Maybe I'm mad, too, I don't know, but seeing her dance—you know what I think? I think she wants someone to share with. I told her she was beautiful, and she was. Maybe no one else ever has. But whatever you think of her, you mustn't—you mustn't hurt her."

"Oh, Mars," Lucky said sadly. "Of course we won't."

"I know, I'm sorry. It's just—"

"We know what it is," Ro said. "And we decided we didn't want to talk about it until you and Lucky and Brax are better. And that's the end of it," he said as I opened my mouth to speak. "Now, who gets the bed nearest the fire?"

∞

We and the prince began getting used to each other. She spent a lot of time watching us; it was a bit unnerving at first. She tested us in little ways. She led us on some incredible expeditions into the belly of the palace. She seemed more and more trusting of us; but she did not dance. She seemed to be waiting for something.

And so was I. Every arc of motion that returned to Brax's arm was one step closer to all my worst fears. By unspoken agreement, we did not practice, and the others stopped making love in front of me. There was a particular kind of tension between us that I could not define, but that made me miserable when I let myself think about what it all might mean, and what I had to lose. I wondered if the prince felt it and thought it was directed at her: it made me try even harder to be easy and gentle with her, who'd had so much less than I.

Ro and I came back to our rooms one night to find Lucky and Brax already toasting each other with a mug of beer from a barrel swiped on our last trip to the cellars. "Back on duty tomorrow," Lucky grinned around a mouthful of foam. "Hoo hoo!" She poured, and we all drank. I felt numb.

"Oh, sweet Mars," Ro said, "don't look like that. Don't you know we see right through you?" Then he took my cup away and opened his arms and folded me into himself, and Lucky and Brax were behind me, gathering me in, stripping off my clothes and theirs. "I don't know if I can—" I began to say, and Brax murmured, "Shut up, Mars." Then Ro shifted his weight and sent me backwards into Brax's waiting arms, and she pinned me down for a lightning second while she brushed her breast against my mouth, and then rolled us so that I was on top and Ro's arms came around me in a lock, and I hesitated and he whispered *Go on* and I turned the way we'd taught ourselves and felt his thigh slide across my back and heard his breath hitch, and mine hitched too.

And then it was Lucky with her leg across mine, strength to strength, my heart beating faster and faster, everything a blue-heat fire from my groin to the tips of my fingers. They traded me back and forth like that for some endless time, and each moment that they controlled me they would take some pleasure for themselves, a tongue in my mouth or a wristlock that placed my hand on some part of them that would make them moan; and I moaned too, and then answered their technique with one of my own and changed the dance. Then Brax reached for Ro, and Lucky and I continued while beyond us they brought each other to shouts; and then Lucky was gone to Brax and it was Ro with me, whispering *Best me if you can,* and then Brax with her strong arms; until finally the world stopped shuddering and we lay in a heap together in front of the fire. And later some of us cried, and were comforted.

∞

We are the prince's guard. When she sits in a tower window and sings endless songs to the seabirds, we are at the door. When she roams the hallways at night peering through keyholes, we are the shadows that fly at her shoulder. She dances for us now, and we protect her from prying eyes; and when she is ecstatic and spent, when she is lucid and can find some measure of peace, we take her back to her rooms and talk of the world, of the rainbow-painted roofs of Hunemoth and the way that cheese is made in Shortline. She is safer now; she has us to see her as she is, and love her.

And there is still time for ourselves, to teach, to learn, to gossip with other guards and steal currant buns from our favorite cook. Sometimes the prince sends us off to Lemon City for a day, to collect fallen feathers from the road or strings of desert beads from the market; to bring back descriptions of her beggars and smiths and shopkeepers; to gather travelers' stories from the inns. Sometimes we carry home a flagon of spicy Marhai wine, and when she sleeps, we drink and trade wild stories until the moon is down. Sometimes we sleep cuddled like puppies in our blankets. Sometimes we fight.

∞

FISHERMAN

Nalo Hopkinson

"You work as what; a fisherman?"

I nearly jump clean out my skin at the sound of she voice, tough like sugar cane when you done chew the fibres dry. "Fisherm...?" I stutter.

She sweet like cane too? Shame make me fling the thought 'way from me. Lord Jesus, is what make me come here any atall? I turn away from the window, from the pure wonder of watching through one big piece of clear glass at the hibiscus bush outside. Only Boysie house in the village have a glass window, and it have a crack running crossways through it. The rest of we have wooden jalousie shutters. I look back at she proud, round face with the plucked brows and the lipstick red on she plump lips. The words fall out from my mouth: "I...I stink of fish, don't it?"

A smile spread on she beautiful brown face, like when you draw your finger through molasses on a plate. "Sit down nuh, doux-doux, you in your nice clean press white shirt? I glad you dress up to come and see me."

"All right." I siddown right to the edge of the chair with my hands in my lap, not holding the chair arms. I frighten for leave even a sniff of fish on the expensive tapestry. Everything in this cathouse worth more than me. I frighten for touch anything, least of all the glory of the woman standing in front of me now, bubbies and hips pushing out of she dress, forcing the cloth to shape like the roundness of she. The women where I living all look like what them does do: market woman, shave ice seller, baby mother. But she look like a picture in a magazine. Is silk that she wearing? How I to know, I who only make for wear crocus bag shirt and daddy old dungarees?

She move little closer, till she nearly touching my knees. From outside in the parlour I hearing two-three of the boys and them laughing over shots of red rum and talking with some of the whores that ain't working for the moment. I hear Lennie voice, and Two-Tone, though I can't really make out what them saying. Them done already? I draw back little more on the fancy chair.

The woman frown at me as if to say, *who you is any atall?* The look on she face put me in mind of when you does pull up your line out of the water sometimes to find a ugly fish gasping on the end of it, and instead of a fin, it have a small hand with three boneless fingers where no hand supposed to grow. She say, "You have a fainty smell of the sea hanging round you, is all, like this sea-shell here."

She lean over and pick up a big conch shell from she windowsill. It clean and pink on the inside with pointy brown parts jooking out on the outside.

She wearing a perfume I can't even describe, my head too full up with confusion. Something like how Granny did smell that time when I was small and Daddy take me to visit she in town. Granny did smell all baby powder and coconut grater-cake. Something like the ladies-of-the-night flowers too, that does bloom in my garden.

I slide back little more again in the chair, but she only move closer. "Here," she say, putting the shell to my nose. "Smell."

I sniff. Is the smell I smell every living day Papa God bring, when I baking my behind out on the boat in the sun hot and callousing up my hands pulling in the net next to the rest of the fishermen and them. I ain't know what to say to she, so I make a noise like, "Mm...?"

"Don't that nice?" She laugh a little bit, siddown in my lap, all warm, covering both my legs, the solid, sure weight and the perfume of she.

My heart start to fire *budupbudup* in my chest.

She say, "Don't that just get all up inside your nose and make you think of the blue waves dancing, and the little red crabs running sideways and waving they big gundy claw at you, and that green green frilly seaweed that look like it would taste fresh like lettuce in your mouth? Don't that smell make your mind run on the sea?"

"It make my mind run on work," I tell she.

She smile little bit. She put the shell back. "Work done for tonight," she tell me. "Now is time to play." She smoky laugh come in cracked and full up of holes. She voice put me in mind of the big rusty bell down by the beach what we does ring when we pull in the catch to let the women and them know them could come and buy fish. Through them holes in the bell you could hear the sea waves crashing on the beach. Sometimes I does feel to ring the bell just for so, just to hear the tongue of the clapper shout "fish, fish!" in it bright, break-up voice, but I have more sense than to make the village women mad at me.

She chest brush my arm as she lean over. She start to undo my shirt buttons. *No, not the shirt.* I take she hands and hold them in my own, hold her soft hands in my two hard own that smell like dead fish and fish scale and fish entrails.

The madam smile and run a warm, soft finger over my lips. I woulda push she off me right then and run go home. In fact I make to do it, but she pick up she two feet from off the floor and is then I get to feel the full weight and solidness of she.

"You go throw me off onto the hard ground, then?" she say with a flirty smile in she voice.

One time, five fifty-pound sack of chicken feed tumble from Boysie truck and land on me; two hundred fifty pounds drop me *baps* to the ground. Boysie had was to come and pull me out. Is heavy same way so she feel in my lap, grounding me. This woman wasn't going no-where she ain't want to go.

"I...." I start to reply, and she lean she face in close to mine, frowning at me the whole while like if I is a grouper with a freak hand. She put she two lips on my own. I frighten I frighten I frighten so till my breath catch like fish bone in my throat. Warm and soft she mouth feel against mine, so soft. My mouth was little bit open. I ain't know if to close it, if to back back, if to laugh. I ain't know this thing that people does do, I never do it before. The sea bear Daddy away before he could tell me about it.

She breath come in between my lips. Papa God, why nobody ever tell me you could taste the spice and warmth of somebody breath and never want to draw your face away again? Something warm and wet touch inside my lips and pull away, like a wave on a beach. She tongue! Nasty! I jerk my head, but she have it holding between she two hands, soft hands with the strength of fishing net. I feel the slip slip slip of she tongue again. She must be know what she doing. I let myself taste, and I realise it ain't so nasty in truth, just hot and wet with the life of she. My own tongue reach out, trembling, and tip to twiny conch tip touch she own. She mouth water and mine mingle. It have a tear in the corner of one of my eyes, I feel it twinkling there. I hear a small sound start from the back of my throat. When she move she face away from me, I nearly beg she not to stop.

She grin at me. My breath only coming in little sips, I feeling feverish, and what happening down between my legs I ain't even want to think about. I strong. I could move my head away, even though she still holding it. But I don't want to be rude. I cast my eyes down instead and find myself staring at the two fat bubbies spilling out of she dress, round and full like the hops bread you does eat with shark, but brown, skin-dark brown.

I pull my eyes up into she face again.

"Listen to me now," she say, "I do that because I feel to. If you want to kiss the other women so you must ask permission first. Else them might box you two lick and scream for Jackobennie. You understand me?"

Jackobennie is the man who let me in the door of this cathouse, smirking at me like he know all my secrets. Jackobennie have a chest a bull would give he life to own and a right arm to make a leg of ham jealous. I don't want to cross Jackobennie atall atall.

"You understand me?" she ask again.

Daddy always used to say my mouth would get me in trouble. I open it to answer she yes, and what the rascal mouth say but, "No, I ain't understand. Why I could lick inside your mouth like that but not them own? I could pay."

She laugh that belly laugh till I think my thighs go break from the shaking. "Oh sweetness, I believe a treasure come in my door this day, a jewel beyond price."

"Don't laugh at me." If is one thing I can't brook, is nobody laughing at me. The fishermen did never want me to be one of them. I had was to show up at the boat every blessèd morning and listen to the nasty things them was saying about me. Had to work beside people who would spit just to look on me. Till them come to realise I could do the work too. I hear enough mockery, get enough mako make 'pon me to last all my days.

She look right in my eyes, right on through to my soul. She nod. "I would never laugh after you, my brave one, to waltz in here in your fisherman clothes."

Is only the fisherman she could see? "No, is not my work clothes I wearing. Is my good pair of pants and my nice brown shoes."

"And you even shine the shoes and all. And press a crease into the pants. I see that. I does notice when people dress up for me. And Jackobennie tell me you bring more than enough money. That nice, sweetness. I realise is your first time here. Is only the rules of my house I telling you; whatever you want to do, you must ask the girls and they first. And them have the right to refuse."

After I don't even know what to ask! Pastor would call it the sin of pride, to waltz in the place thinking my money could stand in place of good manners. "I sorry, Missis; I ain't know."

Surprise flare on she face. She draw back little bit to look at me good. "And like you really sorry, too. Yes, you is a treasure, all right. No need to be sorry, darling. You ain't do nothing wrong."

The ladies-of-the-night scent of she going all up inside my nostrils. The other men and they does laugh after me that I have a flower bush growing beside the pigeon peas and the tomatoes, so womanish, but I like to cut the flowers and put inside the house to brighten up the place with their softness and sweet smell. I have a blue glass bottle that I find wash up on the shore one day. The sand had scour it so it wasn't shining like glass no more. From the licking of the sea and the scrape of the sand, it had a texture under my fingertips like stone. I like that. I does put the flowers in it and put them on my table, the one what Daddy help me make.

"So, why you never come with the other fishermen? When you pull up to the dock all by yourself in that little dinghy, I get suspicious one time. I never see you before."

All the while she talking, and me mesmerized by she serious brown eyes, and too much to feel and think about at once, I never realise she did sliding she hand down inside my blouse, down until she fingers and thumb slide round one of my bubbies and feel the weight of it. Jesus Lord, she go call Jackobennie now! I make to jump up again, terror making me stronger, but this time she look at me with kindness. It make me weak. "Big strong woman," she whisper.

She know! All this time, she know? I couldn't move from that chair, even if Papa God heself was to come down to earth and command me. I just sitting there, weak and trembling, while she undo the shirt slow, one button at a time, drag it out of my pants, and lay my bubbies bare to the open air. The nipples crinkle up one time and I shame I shame. Nothing to do but sit there, exposed and trembling like conch when you drag it out of the shell to die.

I squinch my eyes closed tight, but feel a hot tear escape from under my eyelid and track down my face. So long nobody ain't see me cry. I feel to dead. I wait to hear the scorn from she dry-ashes voice.

"Sweetheart?" Gentle hands closing back my shirt, but not drawing away; resting warm on the fat shameful weight of my bubbies. "Mister Fisherman?"

Yes. Is that I is. A fisherman. I draw in the breath I been keeping out, a long, shuddery one. She hands rise and fall with my chest. I open my eyes, but I can't stand to look in she face. I away gaze out the window, past the clean pink shell to the blue wall of the sea far away. What make me leave my home this day any at all, eh?

"Look at me, nuh? What you name?"

I dash way the tear with the back of my hand, sniff back the snot. "K.C."

"Casey?"

"Letter K, letter C. For 'Kelly Carol:' K.C. I sorry I take up your time, Missis. You want me to go?" I chance a quick glance at her. She get that weighing and measuring look again. The warmth of she hands through my shirt feeling nice. Can't think 'bout that.

"Why you come here in the first place, K.C.?"

I tilt my head away from her, look down at my shoes, my nice shine shoes. Oh God, how to explain? "Is just I...look, I not make for this, I not a.... I did only want some company, the way the other men and they does talk about all the time. All blessèd week we pulling on the nets together, all of we. And some of the men does even treat me like one of them, you know? A fisherman, doing my job. Then Saturday nights after we go to market them does leave me and come here, even Lennie, and I hear next day how sweet allyou is, all of allyou in this cathouse. Every week it happen so and every Saturday night I stay home in my wattle and daub hut and watch at the kerosene lamp burning till is time to go to bed. Nobody but me. But I catch plenty fish and sell in the market today, I had enough money, and after them all come here I follow them in one of Lennie small boats. I just figure is time, my turn now…. But I will go away. I don't belong here." My heart feeling heavy in my chest. I sit and wait for she to banish me.

She laugh like a dolphin leaping. "K.C., you don't have to go nowhere. Look at me, nuh?"

The short distance I had was to drag my eyes from the window to she face was like I going to dead, like somebody dragging a sharp knife along the belly of a fish that twisting in your hands. My two eyes and she own make four, and I feel my belly bottom drop out same way so that fish guts would tumble like rope from it body.

She start to count off on she fingers: "You come in clean clothes; you bathe too, I could smell the carbolic soap on your skin; you not too drunk to have sense; you come prepared to pay; you have manners. Now tell me; why I would turn away such a ideal customer?"

"I…because I…."

"You ever fuck before?"

"No!" My face burning up for shame. I hear the word plenty time. I see dogs doing it in the road. I not sure what it have to do with me. But I want to find out.

She give me one mischievous grin. "Well doux-doux, is your lucky night tonight; you going to learn from the mistress of this house!"

Oh God.

Softly she say, "You go let me touch you, K.C.? Mister fisherman?"

My heart flapping in my chest like a mullet on a jetty. She must be can feel it jumping under she hands. I whisper, "Yes, please."

And next thing I know, my shirt get drag open all the way. She say, "Take it off, nuh? I want to see the muscles in your arms."

My arms? I busy feeling shamed, fraid for she to watch at my bubbies—nobody see them all these years—but is my arms she want to see? For the first time this night, I crack one little smile. I pull off the shirt, stand there holding it careful by the collar so it wouldn't get rampfle. She step in closer and squeeze my one arm, and when she look at me, the look make something in my crotch jump again. Is a look of somebody who want something. My smile freeze. I ain't know what to do with my face. My eyes start to drop to the floor again. But she put she hand under my chin. "Watch at me in my eyes, K.C.; like man does look at woman."

My blasted tongue run away with me again. "And what it have to look at? You seeing more of me than I seeing of you."

A grin that could swallow a house. "True. Help me fix that then, nuh?" And she present me with she back, one hand cock-up on she hip. "Undo my dress for me, please?"

She had comb she hair up onto her head with a sweep and a frill like wedding cake icing, only black. The purple silk of the gown come down low on she back so I could see all that brown skin, smelling like sweet flowers. The fancy dress-back fasten with one set of hook and eye and button and bow. I tall, nearly tall like Two-Tone, but this woman little bit taller than me, even. I reach up to the top of she dress-back. I manage to undo three button and a hook before a button just pop off in my hand. "Fuck man, I can't manage these fancy things; I ain't make for them. Missis, I done bust up your dress, I sorry."

She feel behind she, run one long brown finger over the place where the button tear from. Quicker than my eyes could follow, she undo the dress the rest of the way. I see she big round bamsie naked and smooth under there, but she step away and turn to face me before I could see enough. "Give me the button."

I hand it to she. She laugh little bit and drop it down between she bubbies. "Oh. Look what I gone and do. Come and find it for me, nuh?"

Is like somebody nail my two foot-them to the floor. I couldn't move. I feel like my head going to bust apart. I just watch at she. She step so close to me I could smell she breath warm on my lips. I want to taste that breath again. She whisper, "Find my button for me, K.C."

I don't know when my hands reach on she shoulders. Is like I watching a picture film of me sliding my hands down that soft skin to the opening of the dress, moving my hands in and taking she two tot-tots in each hand. They big and heavy, would be about three pound each on the scale. If I was to price this lady pound for pound, I could never afford she. I move my hand in to the warm, damp place in between she bubbies. The flower smell rising warm off she. My fingers only trembling, trembling, but I pick out the button. I give it back. She stand there, watching in my eyes. Is when I see she smile that I realise I put the fingers that reach the button in my mouth. She taste salt and smell sweet. She push the dress off one shoulder, then the next one. It land on she hips and catch there. Can't go no further past the swelling of she belly and bamsie without help. And me, I only watching at the full and swing and round of she bubbies and is like my tongue swell up and my whole body it hot it hot it hot like fire.

"You like me?" she say.

"I...I think so."

"Help me take off my dress the rest of the way?" She telling me I could touch she. My mother was the last somebody what make me touch their body, when I was helping Daddy look after she before she dead. Mummy was wasting away them times there. She skin was dry and crackly like the brown paper we does wrap the fish in. But this skin on this lady belly and hips put me in mind of that time Daddy take me to visit my granny in the town; how Granny put me on she knee and give me cocoa-tea to drink that she make by grating the cocoa and nutmeg into the hot water; how Granny did wearing a brown velvet dress and I never touch velvet, before neither since, and I just sit there so on Granny knee, running my thumb across a little piece of she sleeve over and over again, drinking hot cocoa-tea with plenty condensed milk. This woman skin under my hands put me in mind of that somehow, of velvet and hot cocoa with thick, sweet condensed milk and the delicious fat floating on top. As I pass my hands over this woman hips to draw down the dress the rest of the way, I feel to just stop there and do that all evening, to just touch she flesh over and over again like a piece of brown velvet.

Then she make a kind of little wiggle and the dress drop right down on the ground and is like I get transfix. My two eye-them get full up of beauty and if God did strike me dead right there I woulda die happy.

She only smiling, smiling. "Like you like what you see, eh Fisherman?"

"Yes, Ma'am."

She step out the dress and go over to the bed. She lie back on it and I mark how she bubbies roll to either side when she do so. Today I bring back two fat, round pumpkin from the market, rolling around in my basket. The soup from those pumpkins going to be nice. I taste the salt on my lips still from when I touch she bubbies and lick my fingers after.

She say, "Come over here, K.C."

I go and sit on the edge of the bed, not too close. And now I shame again, for it have a white crochet spread on the bed, and white pillow cases on the pillows and them, with some yellow and pink embroidery edging the pillowcases. I can't get my fisherman stink all over this lady nice bed!

"Take off your shoes and your pants, K.C."

So I do that, giving thanks that I could turn my back on she and not see she watching when I get naked.

"The underwears too."

I drag off my underpants, the one good ones with no stain. I fold them up small small and put them at the foot of the bed. I leave my hand on them. They still warm from my body. I feel to never leave that warmth.

"Come into bed with me."

So then I had was to turn around to climb on the bed. I feel so big and boobaloops and clumsy. I roll back the bedspread, careful and sit down on the sheet. I pull my knees up to my chest. I watch at she feet. Pretty feet. No callous though.

She rise up in the bed, sit facing me. She ease the crochet bedspread out from under she body and roll it all the way down to the end of the bed. What she go do now? I nearly perishing for fright. "Lie back, K.C."

So I do that, stiff like one piece of plank. She lean over me, she chest hanging nearly in my face. If she come down any lower, how I go breathe? She start passing she hands over my two shoulders, side to side. Big, warm hands. Big like mine. All these years, is this my skin been hungry for. I feel my whole body getting warm, melting into the soft bed. I close my eyes.

"Nice?" she ask.

"Mm-hmm."

She hands pass side to side, side to side, so hot and nice on my skin. And then the hands go under my bubbies, weighing. I jump and my eyes start open, but the look on she face ain't telling me nothing. I turn a piece of board again, just lying there. She run she thumbs over my nipples and I swear I feel it right down to my crotch. Is so I does do myself nights when the skin hunger get too bad, but Jesus God how it powerful when somebody else do it for you! My breath coming hard, making little sounds. Can't make she see, can't make she hear. I go to push she hands away.

"Is all right, K.C. Nothing for shame. Relax, nuh?"

"I doing it right?"

"When it feeling good, you doing it right."

I must be doing it plenty right, then. I put my head on the pillow again. She start to squeeze my bubbies, to pull and tug at them. I ain't know how much time past, I just get lost in what she hands doing. The little noises I making coming louder now. I wonder if Lennie could hear me, and Two-Tone, but I decide I ain't care.

The woman hands on my belly now, massaging the big swell of it. Between my legs my blood only beating, beating. I want…no, I ain't want that. How anybody could want that? But when she push my legs apart, when that big, warm hand cover my whole pum-pum and squeeze, I swear it try to leap into she hands. She push apart my legs little more, spread my pum-pum lips open. Oy-oy-oy I shame, but I couldn't stand to stop she. She press on that place, the place between my legs I find to rub so long ago. I forget how to breathe. "Look your little parson's nose there," she giggle. She take she hand away and I nearly beg she to put it back. She lick she fingers. She must be did watching my face, how it get disgust, for she say, "You never taste yourself?"

"Yes." My voice come out small.

"Well, then." She put the fingers back. Oh, God, the wetness she bring on she fingers just sliding and sliding on the button. And she rub and she rub and little more I thrashing round on the bed till she had was to lie over me with all she weight to make me keep still, make me stay open under she fingers and something coming from deep inside me it buzzing buzzing buzzing from way inside my body like I don't know what but it coming and I can't stop it, don't want to stop it and I barely hear myself and the noises I making and then it hit me like lightning and it ride me like a storm and I shout something, I ain't know what and inside my pum-pum squeezing so hard and nice. I only sweating and trembling when the something drop me back on the bed. "Fuck."

"Exactly." She laugh, move off me. "You have a mouth like a fisherman, too."

Sweat drenching me, salt drying on my skin. My belly feeling all fluttery inside. I couldn't look at she. One time long long ago, one night time in my bed, I touch myself long time like she just touch me and I get a feeling little bit like she just give me, but it frighten me. I thought I was deading. I thought is because is nastiness I was doing. I pull my hand away, and the feeling stop. And though I figure out afterwards that I wasn't go dead, though I do that thing between my legs plenty times since and it feel nice, I never manage after that to make the feeling come back so strong again. "What we go do now?" I ask she.

"How you know we ain't finish, K.C.?"

I peek over my bubbies and belly at she. She sitting in between my legs like if it ain't have nothing wrong with that. She two massive legs pinning my own big ones down, brown on brown. I see she cocoa pod pum-pum, spread open pink and glistening, going to brown at the edges. Lord, what a thing. "I ain't feel finish yet, I feel like it have more."

She give me that rapscallion smile. "Oh yes, it could have plenty more."

She start to stroke my button again, gentle. I glad for that, for it feeling tender. Nice, though. I ain't really get surprised when she push a finger inside my pum-pum. Then another one. I do that myself, plenty times. I thought is only me do that. Me and my nastiness. I start to relax back on she fine white bedspread again, but all of a sudden I sitting up and pulling she hands away. "No. Stop."

She stop one time. "You don't like it?"

"I.... I don't know." Then I bust out with, "I just feel.... I not a glove you does wear for you to go inside me like that."

She just stroke my thighs, with a look on she face like she thinking. "All right then. Let we try something else."

Just like that? "Is all right?"

"Yes, K.C. Everybody different. You must tell me what you like and don't like. Move over so I could lie down."

I make room for she. She lie down on she back with one knee bend. "Touch me like I touch you."

Lord, but this thing hard to do. The way the boys and them talk, I did think it would be easy; just pay the woman and she fix you up.

I do she like she do me. I massage she shoulders, I play with she bubbies. So strange. Like touching my own, almost.

"Pull them."

I ain't know what she mean. She put she nipples between my fingers.

"Pull."

I tug little bit.

"Harder."

So I 'buse up she breasts for she. It look like she good and like it, though. She breathing coming in heavy. It make me feel good. Powerful. I knead she belly, and she spread open she legs for me. The pum-pum smell rise from she, like I used to smelling it on myself. I know that smell like my life. I start to relax. I rub she little button, but that ain't seem to sweet she so much. She only screwing up she face and twitching little bit when I touch she. I stop. "I not doing it right."

"It ain't have no right nor wrong, my fisherman. Just stroke it from the top to the bottom, very gentle."

Oho. Treat she tot-tots hard on top, she pum-pum soft down below. I could do that. I make the touch light, so light. In two-twos she start to say, "Mm," and "Ah," quiet-quiet like the first soft breeze of morning. I look at she face. She head only rolling from side to side, she eyes shut tight. She nipples crinkle up and jooking out. I feel if to kiss them. I wonder if I could do that? She belly shuddering. I think she liking it.

Something wetting my hand, down there where I stroking she. I look down. She pum-pum getting wet and warm and sticky. The salt and sweat smell rising up from she stronger. Now what to do? I ain't know what to do.

Do me like I do you, that is what she tell me. Maybe she don't mind being a glove. So I slip one finger inside the pum-pum. She kinda give a little squeak. It hot in there, and slippery. It only squeezing and squeezing my finger, tight. "Like this, Missis?"

"Oh God like that. Go in and out for me, nuh? No, no; only partway out. Yes, yes, K.C. like that."

I get a rhythm going; in, out, in.

"More fingers, K.C."

I could do that.

"More."

Four fingers inside she, fulling she up. She squeezing tight like a handshake now, and only getting wetter. And every push I push, my hand going in farther. I get lost in the warm wet and sucking and the little moans she making. She spreading she knees wider, tilting up she hips to get my fingers deeper in.

"Oh God more."

More? Is only my thumb leave behind. I tuck it in close with the others and push that inside she too. She start to groan. I say, "I hurting you?" I start to pull my hand out.

"If you only take it out," she pant, "I swear I box you here tonight." She spread she two feet to either side of the bed, move she pum-pum up to meet me hand. "Push it, K.C. Push."

And is like a space opening up deep inside the poonani. Like it pulling. Like it hungry. I push a few little minutes more, with she groaning and rolling she head around. And next thing I know, is no lie, my whole hand pass through the tightest place inside she and slide into she poonani right up to the wrist! She groan, "Fuck me, K.C.!"

She hips bucking like anything. A strong woman this. I had was to brace myself, wrap one arm around she thigh and hold on tight. So close in there, I close my hand up into a fist. I pull back my hand partway, and push it in again. Pull back, push in. Pull back, push in. She start to bawl 'bout don't stop, fuck she, don't stop. I could do that. I hold on to she bucking body and I fuck she. Me, K.C. She only throwing sheself around steady on the bed. The way she head tossing, all she hair come loose from that pretty hairstyle. It twisting and knotting all over the two pillows. She belly shaking, she bubbies bouncing up and down, she thighs clamp onto me. And she bawling, bawling. This woman bawling like any baby here in this bed. I ride with she. I feel my own pum-pum getting warm, my button swelling and throbbing between my legs. I fuck she, I fuck she. She moan, she twist herself up. My shoulders burning from all the work I doing, but I just imagine I pulling in the net with the boys and them. Push your hand out, pull it back. Push it out, pull it back. Push, pull. I smelling pum-pum all 'round me and my sweat and she own.

All of a sudden, something deep inside she start to squeeze my hand fast-fast-fast like a pounding heart, so strong I frighten my hand going to sprain. She arch she back up right off the bed and she scream, "Oh GOD I love a mannish woman!" And more too besides, but them wasn't exactly words.

Hmm. Mannish woman. I like better to be she fisherman. Now is not the time to tell she that, though.

The pounding inside she stop. She give a little sigh and reach down and grab my wrist to hold it quiet. She flop back down on the bed with that mischevious grin on she face again.

Somebody knock on the door. I jump and freeze. If I come out too fast, I might hurt she.

"Mary Anne?" Everything all right?" Is a man voice.

She start to laugh. I could feel it right down in she belly. "Jackobennie, you too fast. I with a customer. Leave we some privacy."

A deep chuckle roll into the room. "Sorry, girl. I ain't mean to disturb allyou; I gone."

I could hear the heavy weight of he footsteps as he walk away. Jackobennie is a giant of a man. My whole body start to feel cold one time. "You is Jackobennie woman?"

She lie back and close she eyes, squeeze my hand that jam up inside she. She smile. "Jackobennie is my right-hand man. He and me know one other since God was a little boy in short pants. Jackobennie does make sure me and the rest of the girls stay safe. Sometimes customers does act stupid. Don't fret your head about Jackobennie, K.C. You is a well-behaved customer."

I smile.

"Move the heel of your hand up and down for me, nuh? Ai! Gentle!"

I could do that. A sucking sound come from inside she poonani as she flesh move away little bit from my hand.

"Good. Now come out, slow."

My shoulder muscles burn as I pull out. My hand come back to me wet and wrinkly. I raise the hand to my mouth. It smell like she, like me. I taste it. I know that taste.

"Here." Mary Anne hand me a towel from out the bedside table. I wipe my hands.

My bubbies tingling.

Mary Anne sit up, she belly resting on she thighs like a calabash. When she grin at me again, I feel all warm inside.

"So, fisherman," she say, "What you think of your first time?"

"Nice. Strange. But nice."

"Like you. You going to come back and see me sometimes?"

"You want me to come back?"

"It have plenty more I could show you, sweetness."

My pum-pum feeling like a big, warm smile. I just done fuck somebody. The grin that break out on my face must be did brighter than the sun.

For that grin, she say, she kiss me again.

After she and me done clean weselves up she count the money and tuck it into she bosom. She take my hand. Nobody do that since I was a small child. We step outside the room and walk down the hall to the parlour.

Bright lights. All the chatting stop one time. Everybody looking at we. Lennie skinning up he face like he smelling something rotten. Two-Tone, with the cards still in he hand, busting a grin from one side of he jaw to the next and shaking he head. "Lord, K.C.," he laugh. "Is what you was doing inside there with that woman?"

Mary Anne walk with me over to the bar. "Is what you think he was doing, Two-Tone? Bartender, give the man a beer there. House paying."

I hear the chair scrape and I turn round one time to face the storm. I did know it was coming. Everything I get in this life, I had was to fight for. Lennie throw down his cards and slam his hand on the table. The shot glasses jump. "'Man?' Don't make joke, woman! Is nastiness allyou was doing! Is against nature!"

I step between Lennie and Mary Anne, but she come out from behind me. She push out one broad hip and cotch up she hand on it. "Lennie," she say, loud so everyone in the bar was looking now. "Against nature? And the way you too love to push your totie up inside my behind—ain't that is against nature too?"

And one set of belly laugh cut loose in the place. Jackobennie, man mountain, thundering, slapping his hand on the bar. The little, light-skin bartender with he long fingers only giggling and snapping he white towel in the air. The rest of my crew holding their sides and shaking with laugh. Ramesh. Errol. Matchstick. Two of the whores jump up from their tables and start to wind each other down, back to belly. "Like this, Lennie? Eh?" the one in back shout, jooking she crotch in she mini-skirt crotch up against the behind of the one in front of she. Lennie face just shut down.

I barely have time to notice how the mini-skirt woman voice hard, how she shoulders broader than my own, when Lennie rush Mary Anne, reach for she neck. Jackobennie jump and hold he, but is my hand grab Lennie wrist. Lennie spit at me: "Bullah woman!"

He try to break my hold. I hang on. I could do that.

"Lennie man, calm down!" Jackobennie say, wrestling Lennie by he shoulders. But Lennie not paying him no mind. He only trying to box me, he eyes boring hate into me like them could jook inside my brain and strike me dead. Mary Anne not saying anything. I can't see she. She all right? I holding Lennie back with the arm I had inside she. It getting weary. But I hang on. Lennie know he could pull net twice as hard as me. But like he forget I could go longer.

"Lennie," Jackobennie rumble right beside Lennie ear. He put he hand on Lennie shoulder. Lennie try to shrug it away.

"Let me go, I say! Fucking bullah woman and she fucking whore! I going knock she head right off she shoulders!"

I just keep holding on. My hand trembling, but I don't let go. Mary Anne step in between me and Lennie, and I see Jackobennie fingers tighten on Lennie shoulder. "Lennie," Mary Anne say, hard and fast, "If you make any more comess in my house tonight, you never going set foot in here again."

Lennie look from me to she, he eyes bull-red in he angry face.

"No more of this sweet behind for you, Lennie. Who else you going find to let you do that thing with them?"

Lennie shake my hand off he wrist. It look like he cool down little bit, so I let he. He try to stare down Mary Anne. Jackobennie never move away from he the whole time; that big, heavy hand resting like a threat on Lennie shoulder. From behind the two of them I hear Two-Tone say, "The woman right you know, Lennie. You have to have some manners inside she establishment. And all these years K.C. been doing everything else we men does do, you think she ain't go do this too?"

"It not right!" Lennie spit, glaring at Mary Anne.

I barely hear what Jackobennie whisper to Lennie, grinning the whole while: "And what you pay me and Mary Anne to do to you that time? That wrong too?"

Lennie glance over he shoulder like is the devil heself latch on there. He go still. It get quiet in the place again. I see he shoulders sag. "All right," he mutter. "Let me go. I ain't go hurt nobody."

Jackobennie release him. Lennie dust heself off and sit back down to table. He growl to Two-Tone, "Let we finish we game and go home, yes."

I glance at the whore with the deep voice and the broad shoulders and the tiny, tiny skirt. She? smile and roll she eyes at me.

Mary Anne throw she arms round my waist. I smile at she. "Thanks."

"Only the best for the best customers."

I hug she back, this armful of woman. I think the perfume smell and woman smell of she going stay with me whole week.

But I know Lennie and me story ain't done yet. I have to stand up to he now, in the light, else I go be looking over my shoulder every time it get dark from now on. "Just now," I excuse myself to Mary Anne.

"All right, darling."

Lennie and Two-Tone look up when I reach to their table. I pull a chair, I turn it backwards. I throw my leg over it (poonani still feeling warm and nice under my clothes) and I sit down. "Lennie," I say. He ain't say nothing.

Mary Anne and Jackobennie come to the table with three beers. "On the house," Jackobennie tell we. "To thank everybody for being gentlemen." He look hard at Lennie as he and Mary Anne put down the beers. Two-Tone thank them, but Lennie just pick up his and start guzzling it down. Mary Anne wink at me as they walk away.

I take a sip from my beer. Cold and nice, just so I like it. I swallow two more times, think about what I going to say. "Lennie, you is a man, right?"

"Blasted right!" He slam the empty bottle down onto the table.

"Big, hard-back, long-pants-wearing man?"

"Yes." He look at me with suspicion.

"Work and sweat for your living? Try to treat everybody fair?"

"I never cheat you, K.C.!"

"Is true. You wish if I never try to work with allyou neither, but once you see I could pull my weight, you treat me like all the rest."

"So long as you know your place!" He scowl and shake the beer bottle at me. "But coming in here brazen like this!"

"You is a man, yes."

He look at me, confused. I see Two-Tone frowning too. I nod my head, sip some more beer. "Work hard in the hot sun, don't do nobody wrong. Have a right to fuck any way you want."

"But not you! You is a woman!"

To rass. Time to done with this. "Lennie, you is a man. And I? I is a fisherman."

And I swear all the glasses in the place ring like the fishing bell, the way Two-Tone start to make noise in the place. "Oh God, K.C., in all my born days, I never meet no-one like you!" He put down he cards and he hold he belly and he laugh.

"What, you taking the bullah woman side now?" Lennie sulk.

"Man, Lennie, hold some strain," Two-Tone say. "K.C. not judging you for what you like to do. I not judging you, and you know Mary Anne not judging you, for you bringing you good good dollars and give she. K.C. work hard beside you every day, she never ask no man to look after she. She have a right to play hard too."

Is not only me does work hard, neither. Mary Anne. All the whores. I realise is not only man have a right to fuck how he want. When a truth come to you simple like that, it does full you up and make you feel warm, make you want to tell everybody. I must ask Mary Anne sometime if she think I right. But for now I just smile and look down at my nice clean shine shoes. I drink some more beer and look Lennie right in he eye, friendly. He scowl at me, but I ain't look away. Is he look down finally.

He pick up he cards. "You playing or what?" he say to Two-Tone.

"Deal me in next hand," I say. God, he go do it?

Lennie glance sideways at me over he cards. Look down at the cards. Then quiet, "You have money after you done spending everything on Mary Anne?"

"Yes, man." I done being careful. "I have enough to whip both of al-lyou behind."

"Oh, yes?" Lennie say. "Well, don't get too attached to it. I bet you I leave this place tonight with you money and my own."

He throw down he cards. Two-Tone inspect them, make a face, drop he cards on the table, and pull out two bills and lay them down. Lennie pocket the bills. He pick up the whole deck of cards and hand them to me. "Deal. Fisherman."

I feel the grin lighting up my face as I take the cards from he. "I could do that."

∞

PIRATE SOLUTIONS

Katherine Sparrow

MARY READ 1692-1720

You could feel their heat. Not a metaphor, I don't mean that, I mean literally the room grew warmer when they were in it. They were both so powerful. Whenever Anne and Jack (they weren't named that then, but that's who they were) strolled into the room you got contact highs from their lust. People who would never make out would find excuses to go to the bathroom together and come back with monster hickies. Everyone always wanted to sit near them because of their heat, and because they always said the thing you wish you'd said but only thought to say a billion blinks later.

When I first joined the Freebooter tech collective Anne and Jack were happy to have another girl in the group, but otherwise they ignored me. I could stare and stare at them all day long, hiding behind my black-rimmed glasses. But then one day Anne looked at me, and then Jack looked too, and we all just sort of fell toward each other. Like gravity. Like magic. Like there was a God.

You know that feeling you have all the time that if you were just somewhere else things would be better, more perfect, cooler? I never felt that around them, not for a second. They were the exact center of where I wanted to be.

Everything started when we were celebrating one night. It was just the three of us since the other ten had gotten popped at an anti-war direct action. We had just gotten over the flu so we stayed home and programmed like fiends. We worked for like twenty hours straight, and then finally quit and just didn't want to think anymore.

We made a fancy dinner in the crumbly kitchen, and Jack found this ancient bottle of rum in an old wooden box in the back of a closet. We always found crazy stuff in our squat, like control top pantyhose with mice living inside or huge cracked jars of mentholatum. The rum was a score. It was corked and dusty. The insides looked dark and thick as molasses.

Jack opened it and took a swig without even smelling it. He kissed Anne. Anne kissed me with sugarcoated lips and a toffee-leather-burnt-cream taste. I'm not usually gonzo for liquor, but I wanted more. Jack popped in some beats from an old ska cassette that had a pounding drum-line. We passed the bottle around and around, and a new kind of drunk rose up in me. Like swallowing light bulbs and glowing from the inside. Like being full of helium and wanting to jump all over the place. I bounced up and down a hundred times a minute as the rum snaked down my throat.

"More?"

"Yeah."

By the bottom of the bottle Jack swayed from side to side like he was on a boat, Anne waved her arms around like she was in a knife fight, and I bounced up and down a thousand times a minute.

"There's something in the bottom," Anne said, looking down the bottle like a spyglass. "Something gray. Looks like a bone. Or a piece of wood."

"Drink the worm!" Jack yelled as he began to play air-drums.

Anne tipped the bottle toward the ceiling and drank it all. She stuck out her tongue, black with rum. Nestled in the middle of it lay something shriveled. She bit down on it, then kissed Jack. Jack kissed me and pushed his tongue into my mouth. Shards of dust and death coated my tongue and teeth.

We swallowed. We choked and gasped for air.

I felt the hempen halter tighten around my neck and squeeze the life from me. I felt the fever-death of childbirth. I raged against the shortness of life and damn the church and England! Damn the lords and ladies and everything but brine is swine! I screamed as I died and then rose up from the murky tangle of seaweed and bulb kelp. I breathed in fresh air and stared astonished at Jack and Anne. My Jack. My Anne. We saw who we truly were. The sweetest hope, then laughter and dancing and....

The next morning we downloaded nautical maps, made lists of what we needed to take, and argued over what kind of ship we wanted. When the rest of the collective came home from jail, we told them where we were going, pointing to the little wisp of an island that almost disappeared at high tide and curled around like a question mark in the aqua waters of the Caribbean sea.

"Isla d'Oro."

"It's not marked."

"It's not named."

"Yes, but that's her name," Jack whispered.

"What are a bunch of programmers going to be on an island?"

"You'll see."

We didn't expect the rest of the collective to come, but after we told them our plan, they were all in.

We packed up our servers, boxes, solar panels, and a zillion cables and monitors. We tied them on top of our school bus. We dumpstered hundreds of oak pallets, tore them apart for good wood, and loaded up the back of the bus. We threw away our cell phones, watches, and radios. We drove east and south toward Florida. The bus didn't break down. Cops didn't harass us. We only got lost a couple of time. Fate or her little sister Luck rode with us all the way to Pensacola Bay.

We found our sloop in Brown's Marina—some millionaire had been restoring an old ship before he hung himself off the boom after losing his fortune. We bought her cheap and renamed her 'Rackham's Revenge.' She wasn't much to look at—rotten jacob's ladder, softened-wood poop, mold all over the lower decks—but the fo'c's'le and abaft masts rose straight and proud. On the crow's nest you could see her lines and wooding were planked true, and she was wide enough to carry our crew and cargo. It took all thirteen of our collective a month of patching wood, weather proofing, and tying knots as big as fists before she was seaworthy. Just before we set sail, Anne and I swung out in harnesses toward the mermaid figurehead on the prow. We pried the old lady off and nailed on our new ambassador—a fey looking man with golden horns, bare chest, and blue knickers that did little to conceal his small, proud erection. Jack stared at him and blushed, which made the likeness all the more apparent.

We set sail with oakum and tarred hands, and cheered as the wind picked up and blew us southeast. We navigated via sextant and compass, and learned the details of sailing as we went. We earned our sea legs, one mistake at a time. The sun rose, the moon set, and rain fell as waves slapped against our gunwales in choppy water.

Every day was talk-like-a-pirate-day, at first as a joke, and then because we loved it. Everyone got new pirate names, except Anne, Jack, and I, who'd already found ours. On sunny days we talked about our mission all day long as we lay on the deck and embroidered handmade patches onto our coats. We unfurled rubbery solar panels over the deck as soon as Anne and Malfunction hacked together a satellite feed and got us online. We programmed lazily, exploring our options and data-modeling.

It took us three weeks to get there. Three weeks of water and feeling like all the land in all the world might have disappeared.

"All hands ho and turn her starboard!" Skurve shouted from the crow. We watched our island grow larger as a steady nor' eastern blew us in.

"Lower the iron lady and load up the jolly boat!" Anne yelled.

We left two men on board. The rest of us rowed to Isla d'Oro who sat like a mirage on the water, just like I'd seen when I drank the rum. My hand trailed through the water as I leaned over the fore-bow. Yellow fish with swirly tails and translucent jellyfish with visible organs swam below. I jumped into the water as soon as we neared shore and swam with dolphin-kicks and butterfly strokes. I flopped onto the sand and stared up at the bluest sky.

The others reached shore. We ran up to the palm trees on the hill. Breathing hard, we sprinted across the flat rocks that led to the hills of the northern point of the island.

"There!" Jack cried and ran faster.

"There! Beneath the red rock and white stone!" Anne yelled.

We dug with shovels and pickaxes. We sweated and sang and didn't lose hope even when we reached five feet down and there was nothing. Ten feet down and the ground started crumbling inward. Water rose up from below. Then we heard a thunk.

With ropes and pulleys we hauled up a rusted metal trunk. Anne twisted the handle just so, pressed three metal ingots inlaid into the top, and kicked at the lock. It popped open.

Treasure. Beautiful treasure for us and us alone! It had lain here all these centuries, untouched and perfect. I counted the glowing bottles of rum with an anxious lust. The collective looked to us for permission. Anne, Jack, and I nodded our heads. The boys uncorked the first bottle and drank. I watched with envy. When it was my turn, I drank the bone-rum as if it was the only liquid that could quench my thirst.

Jack collected the empty bottles, wrote short messages inside, and chucked them into the sea.

∞

Anne Bonny 1690-1723

History cuts the rope between then and now, telling us it was all so different we couldn't possibly understand. They take away our stories to make us weak and forget that we have always been fighting. With the rum came memory.

Imagine the moment of mutiny, when the captain has just gone apeshit one too many times, and maybe he's about to kill someone you like, maybe a kid he pressganged, and men spontaneously rise up and take the boat. Of the beautiful things in the world, that's one of them.

We're much luckier than the original pirates. We were able to stock up on vitamin C, potable water, and food supplies. Jack, Mary, and I insisted on it. The others didn't understand, not really, until they drank the rum and remembered the hard times: the scurvy, the rat plagues, and the dying a little every day because there was never enough sleep or water or food.

It is a strange thing to discover one's destiny, or to be press-ganged into it, as the case may be. Our old anarch friends needed us, and so we came to the island.

We're here to find pirate solutions for pirate problems, Jack liked to say, and that was as good a description as any. We tamed the red-hooded crows and used them to watch for incoming boats. We swam down to the trans-Caribbean cable and spliced into it to forge a wicked OC384 connection. We perfected our hardtack. We programmed bits and pieces of software, creating action and reaction as solid as our anchor chain. We cooked whatever we caught—even squid the size of tetra.

There was never enough time in the day to get it all done. I could code for twelve hours and only get a little closer to our goal. Like swimming against the current, our progress, despite our best efforts, was slow.

One day I sat near the fire and played with sand, running it through my fingers. I watched the water. My head was full of code and the fear that I'd never get it all right. A stray comma can ruin everything. Mary sat beside me. Her short hair had grown longer. It made her look girlier, but she still had her edge. She still wore that "I'm shy, but really I'm a predator" look that made me want to devour her. Jack stood talking to the twins—Cannonball and Cutlass—but kept glancing over at us with yearning eyes. I stared back until he blushed and looked away. I know what you're thinking Jack, I thought. He's as easy to read as an open dirty-picture book.

Dred sauntered across the beach and crouched over the treasure chest. His long rope-snake hair trailed down his back. He popped open a bottle of rum. The rest of the collective suddenly showed up. We all pretended not to be lusting after it—not obsessed with who would get the bone. We all lied. Syrop passed around a platter of small, charred fish.

Crunch, crunch, crunch. Waves lapped at the sand, each one a little closer than the last as the tide came in. It reminded me of recursive loops and the way things done repeatedly, a little different each time, change the world.

Red grabbed his guitar and plucked out a tune that thrummed like a discordant mash-up. He chewed the ends of his red beard as he played. I drank rum and passed it on. Madwell got the bone and chewed slowly with a faraway look to him. The rum distorts reality, but the bone twists your soul into a different shape entirely.

We opened up another bottle. Skurve made rolly cigarettes from pipe tobacco, and the air filled with the smell of smoke and salt water. Jack played his bongos and began singing. No words, just ululating sound. Malfunction harmonized and sang about water, ocean, and freedom to do the impossible. It wasn't good music, but it was our music.

Rum like the sea's milk filled my throat. I stood and swayed as the tempo picked up. All the code, all the hacking problems fell away as I slowly spun around the blazing red tongues of fire. I picked up speed and began to dervish like an unstoppable, destructive virus. Others rose and we became the rage of everyone murdered too young to have made a difference. We flung curses and hope up and out into the world. The song grew louder. We jumped into the air like gravity might fail, and then pounded our legs into the sand. Cannonball faced Skurve. Their sunburned faces glowed in the firelight. They matched their movements into large, competitive gestures and then fell onto each other and rolled away from the firelight, making loud, gasping animal noises.

Mary ran at the fire and jumped over it, playing with skin, cloth, and safety. She landed on the other side and flung her over-long sleeves into the flames. When they caught fire she swung them around in circles and turned and ran like a phoenix, shrieking with laughter, into the sea. I followed her, watching as the water extinguished the flames. Mary turned and stared at me with an inner fire. She laughed as I dove into the water and emerged beside her. Jack stumbled in behind us, pausing for a moment as he watched us tear our clothes off. Then the liquid embrace took all of us and rocked waves over our flailing, twisting forms. My lovers whispered to me with every touch that all this folly was my destiny.

I woke up the next morning dry-mouthed and fuzzy on the beach. Others lay naked and scattered like seaweed across the sand. A bird screamed overhead. One of our crows swooped down on ebony wings. "Crawk! Caw!" she yelled.

I shielded my eyes and stared at the horizon. A boat, tacked hard and moving fast, stirred the waters of the world's edge. She was the kind of ship that didn't exist in this day and age, just like our ship. She's coming here. She's coming home, I thought. Things are going to get really interesting, or I'll eat the bottle with the bone.

∞

JACK RACKHAM, 1691-1720

The ship, like an itch, like a void, rode toward us all morning. Look away! Touch wood and spit! Ask the kraken for a reprieve, but still she grew larger. She sailed three times or more the size of our Revenge. Black sails like the fear of night whipped through the air. Golden Chinese characters stood scrawled upon her starboard.

I wanted her. I wanted our crew to stand on her bow and let the wind run ragged. I wanted that ship like I'd never wanted anything in my life.

An arm snaked around my waist and pulled me backwards. Anne whispered in my ear, "It's an old ship. Like ours, Jack. Think for a moment, okay?"

I turned to her and winked gallantly.

"Have you been in the rum already?" Anne asked.

"Maybe."

"Lay off until we meet them, okay?"

I nodded. Her words reeled me in. Pirate thoughts were seductive, and once I started thinking with them, like a song or a rhythm, it was hard to think any other way. "Sure," I said. "Sorry."

Anne punched my arm with force enough to raise a welt. She wandered off toward Mary who stood watching the horizon with a lovely frown.

We waited until we knew she headed straight toward us, and was not perhaps some themed cruise ship or fishermen's boat. We rowed out to Rackham's Revenge. If this storm on the water wished for battle, it would be at sea or nowhere else. But perhaps they were friends, not foe.

I buttoned a calico coat over my striped undershirt as I took the helm. I swayed with the sea swells and inhaled the sweaty musk of sea wind.

"Raise the sails, aft and fore!" The words fell like paper from my mouth, like old words written by dead men.

We sailed like an arrow aimed at her portside. Another bout of ship lust rippled through me, but this time I tamped it down like tobacco in the pipe. I mellowed it to a slow burn.

"Tighten the sails!" I ordered.

The distance between us narrowed. A figure rose and stood broad legged on the ship-bow. A billowing red silk coat whipped around him. He pointed at me.

A mighty voice rose from the shrouded ship, using a powerful bullhorn.

"We come to join you," a voice said with a heavy accent, and then repeated the words in Chinese.

"They're here for our treasure!" I yelled. "Or maybe not," another me added. I raised my bottle, but then remembered I had promised not to drink.

Suddenly, the wind fell from our sails and we lay dead in the water.

"No!" I yelled. "Damn the skies!" But it was not the winds of fate who failed me, but our crew who lowered the sails and readied the jolly boat. I glared at the yellow-bellies, but before I could order them back, Anne looked at me with eyes to wither my turnips.

"Relax," she hissed. "Mellow out."

Only when I saw the red captain walk to his small boat did I run to our jolly and let myself be lowered to the water.

Anne, Mary, Dred, and I rowed to them. Bits of white foam hit my face. Their small boat measured twice the length of ours. If I couldn't take their entire ship, perhaps I could steal their jolly?

Stop, I told myself, but the inner pirate looked through my eyes with a stubborn lust.

Our crew threw ropes across the water, and we drew our boats together. The red captain stepped forward and straddled both boats. I stared at her t-shirt, sure I was mistaken, but no! The captain of this magnificent ship was a woman?

I sighed. So what? No big deal, I told myself. She bore a shaved head with a scar that wound around her skull.

"Captain Jack," I muttered and managed a half-bow.

"Captain Ching," she said and nodded her head.

"Captain Shmaptain," Anne said.

"Would you like some tea?" Captain Ching asked in careful English. I was prepared for fisticuffs or swordplay. But tea?

"Uh. Sure."

She took a glass flask from the folds of her coat and passed it to me. It was tar black and smelled like wood chips. As I swung it to my mouth, I heard the clink of something within. Then the liquid touched my lips and a demonic desire flushed through me. The tea was mixed with bone-rum!

"Oh," I said, unmanned by this strange change of circumstance. Anne grabbed the bottle and drank, then passed it to the others.

We sailed back to Isla d'Oro and followed the Chinese women as they ran to where they pried a boulder from a hill and found their own hidden cache of bone-rum.

They told us the story of how their collective, the Wōkòu, had found an old bottle on the beach with a message inside. A message I myself had written. A day later they discovered a bottle of rum in Ching's government apartment. When they drank it they left behind their work of creating autonomous cyberspaces inside the great firewall of China and sailed here, much as we had done. They all wore cropped hair and glasses of a style most geekishly becoming.

We stood around like shy dogfish wanting to play with each other. Then Madwell showed one girl the software he was working on. She pushed him aside, pointed at a line of code, and corrected it.

All awkwardness fell away like foam on the surf. We gathered around monitors and spoke the true language we had in common. It cleaved my heart to the tenderest cut to see such ease and solidarity.

The next day another ship appeared on the horizon. And another. Ships flowed toward us like migrating auks, bringing flocks of geeks from across over the world.

The Marauders, the Corsairs, the Buccaneers, the Infidels, the Pieras Noblas, and dozens more sailed in. Each had received my message. Each found their own cache of bone-rum upon the island, and brought with them necessary skills we needed for our mission.

The Germans were big bratwurst-bellied men who'd welded together shipping crates to make their ship. The French were thin cross-dressers who'd never held down jobs and brought huge rounds of stinky cheeses with them. The Cubans were fierce and rowed in on houseboats. The Indians brought a treasury of spices. All of them understood, without quarrel or bickering, why they were called to Isla d'Oro. The rum was nothing in comparison to the real treasure we would steal.

Every night the captains joined me in gathering up the empty rum bottles, stuffing notes inside, and throwing them out to sea. Our message was simple: Join us.

Ships kept coming. They lay moored and silhouetted against the setting sun. I stared at them as I sat with another man's sad memories lodged within me. There'd been battles fought and lost, sunken boats, and a life much too short and violent. I settled my gaze on the horizon and wondered if this present story would also end with keelhauls and hangings.

∞

SAM FLOWERS, PRESENT DAY

Falling like flying. Air like freedom. Splash. Hard water turned warm as it wrapped around me. I sank and then surprised myself by thrashing upward, desperate for life. My head broke through into air. I treaded water and watched the thousand-light cruise ship churn away from me. What a shocker—I even suck at suicide.

Ah hell. Oh shit. I should have stayed on that boat. I should have taken pills instead.

I floated in the salty water and stared up at the big fat stars. Why am I here? Why is it all so empty? Bull kelp rose like a submerged sea raft beneath me. It carried me along in a sea current like a magic carpet full of sand flies. The night passed and the sun rose and burned me.

My life played before me like a plotless French movie: no girlfriend, boring office job, stringy hair.

You meant nothing. You were worthless.

Is that you God? Because you sound kind of mean. You sound just like I expected.

I gulped down salt water and cried. I picked sea leeches off my balls and stared at them. Dolphins came by and poked me with their stubby heads. They made stupid dolphin sounds as they took bull kelp into their mouths and swam.

"I'm not one of those dolphin lovers," I told them.

They swam on with their secret dolphin schemes.

My head turned into a rotten watermelon. My arms swelled like kielbasas. My nipples were ripe cherries. "When do I get to die?"

Aah-awk? said the dolphins.

I drank sea martinis and chatted with all the girls I'd never kissed. They had big breasts like flesh marshmallows. They were covered in glittery fish scales. When did all the girls become mermaids? The mermaids became pirates who rose up around me. They wore sea-gray clothes and grayer skin. They glared at me with watery gray eyes.

"Captain Calico Jack," one said and tipped his barnacled hat toward me. "Awrk?" he added.

"Fuck off," I said.

"Anne Bonny," another said. She spat flotsam at me.

"Mary Read." This one pointed a pistol at me and fired salt water.

"Skurve."

"Madwell."

"Dred."

Thirteen in all, they spoke to me like they were real. I laughed at them and tried to drown.

∞

"Wake him up. He needs to drink water."

"You think he found a bottle?"

"No."

"We should throw him back in the water, maybe."

"Are you talking about me? I feel like shit, Heaven sucks." I spoke through a cottony mouth. Palm trees swayed above me.

"He speaks. Hello."

A woman my age stood over me and nudged me with her knee.

"Ugh. I'm still alive, aren't I?"

"Yep. I'm Anne. She's Mary." Another one stood beside her. They were tanned like popular girls who'd lain out all summer. They had legs and seemed happy. I disliked them.

"I jumped from a cruise ship. Dolphins took me here. I wish they hadn't. Wish I'd drowned."

"Fascinating," Mary said.

"Is he up?" A thin man came up and put his arms around both girls. I hated him instantly.

"Hi, I'm Jack."

"Fascinating," I said and sat up. A bottle lay near me. I grabbed it and drank.

"That's not—" Jack said.

Rum burned my throat.

I looked at them and saw gray-blue pirates. The image flickered away. "Freebooting lunatics," I muttered, then wondered what free-booting meant.

Anne brought me a water bottle and I drank, but wouldn't let them take the rum. I stumbled to my feet with a bottle in each hand and saw hundreds of computer geeks hunched over computers wrapped up clear plastic casings. Each geek was either too thin or fat, and had an obvious disregard toward basic hygiene. Cables lay bundled and interconnected across the sand. "Christ. I'm marooned with nerds? Thanks, God." I glared upward.

Mary, Anne, and Jack headed toward empty monitors and key-boards.

"Steady as she goes, mates," a man in a pink shirt yelled.

"Keep true! Tack hard! Apt get install Chaos! Then mutiny! Then freedom! Keep true!"

"Activate the mock-autonomous-network!"

"Activated!"

"Employ the water diversion! Launch vegan!"

People typed furiously. "You all suck brine," I said, angered by how vibrant they all seemed. I raised the bottle. I needed water, but it was the wrong hand and I took another swig of rum.

∞

I swayed and almost fell onto the wooden planks of a ship deck see-sawing back and forth.

What?

I looked around and saw a pirate ship with a billowing jolly roger whipping off the ship's mast overhead. Around me a salty crew scrambled to stay upright as the ship tilted toward a huge wave. Six men put all their weight behind a cannon and pushed it to the ship's edge. They kicked wooden wedges behind the wheels, and then ran to the next cannon. A captain held a spyglass and stood with one foot on a wooden box, staring forward. As he lowered it I saw it was Jack.

I ran to him. "I don't understand...."

He snarled and thrust the spyglass into his pocket. He grabbed the helm and spun the wheel hard to the right.

I looked across the water and saw ships flying St. George's Cross.

England? "We're fighting England?"

Jack raised his weathered rifle. He fired toward the ships. He turned and said, "A sea battle is a hard death, child. Make your peace. Ready yourself for the end!"

We swooped down into another stomach-wrenching wave. To our left I spied another ship. She flew a ragged red flag. To our right lay another. Maybe this is death. Maybe this is me dying. I hoped, and then hoped it wasn't.

With the next wave I fell down hard onto the ship's splintery deck.

∞

Except I didn't.

My knees hit hot sand.

"I'm hallucinating," I said. "I'm probably dying." No one even looked up from the computers. I stood and wandered among them as a sound like a thousand crabs scuttling over the sand ebbed and flowed as they typed away.

A woman yelled, "The autonomous network churns trouble up from the deep!"

"Does she slow? Does she bow under the weight?"

"She does, but slowly! We wait! We must wait to slip in the bold and slythy kraken, hold steady!"

"Yar, ye swashbuckling assholes," I said. The rum was making me talk funny. I tried to drink some water, but I got rum again by accident.

∞

Yelling rose all around me and I stood on the pirate ship again. A massive English galleon sailed toward us. We were a rowboat in comparison. We were mosquitoes. Other galleons followed the ships to our left and right as they sped away.

Black cannon nubs pushed out from the lower decks of the English ship. A cannon boom hit the air, followed quickly by two more. Our ship rocked backwards. Clouds of smoke billowed up from below. One man laid limp and screaming on deck with stumps where his legs should be. Another man caught fire and jumped overboard.

Jack scowled and raised his rifle. He shot once more toward the galleon.

Boom. Wood sprayed up from the decks below.

Boom. A cannonball lodged into our mast. A groaning wooden scream filled the air.

Boom. Three more men dead.

Our ship began to sink. Men staggered forward and lit one of our two cannons. A black mass zoomed toward the galleon. A hit! Then another!

Yet still we sank. Still the galleon fired upon us without mercy. I ran to Jack. "What can I do?"

∞

Nothing.

Because I stood on a beach, delusional and disoriented. "I'm dying!" I yelled. I raised the correct bottle this time and drank water.

A man swearing in Italian stormed toward the sea and threw his laptop into it. He yelled and cursed.

"Cloak the feed! Fire at will!" a woman said, her head looking up from her monitor for a moment, before hunching over again.

"She's slowing down! She's crippled!"

"Hold steady! Wait until she's three-quarters gone!"

More rum found its way to my lips. I would have sworn my hand never raised the bottle, even as the rum slid down my throat.

∞

A wave crested the edge of the pirate ship and hit me. It pushed me off the deck and into the ocean. Among the waves were dozens of men yelling and drowning.

Boom! A cannonball punched another hole into our ship.

Boom! Our mast tottered over.

The galleon turned and left us to our watery death. Someone clutched my arm. It was just a kid, barely even a teenager. A wave crashed into us. When I resurfaced he was gone. With the next wave I didn't come up but breathed salt water into my lungs. My chest convulsed, struggling to get air. There was none. I sank down into water that grew darker with every yard. I hit bottom and died. Finally, I thought as the last of me floated away. Finally, it's over.

∞

But no.

I fell forward onto the deck of a different pirate ship. A female captain stood along the ship's edge and watched sinking ships in the distance as we sped off, unseen. Tears ran down her face. We sailed around the edge of an island until we were out of sight, and she strode toward a huge trunk sitting on deck. She knelt and opened it. I walked forward and saw dozens of scrolls piled up inside. The ship circled the island. On the far side of it we turned into an inlet full of pirate ships. We sailed into the bay to the sound of yelling and clapping.

∞

I awoke to water streaming over my face. I opened my mouth and drank. When I'd had enough, I pushed the flask aside. Mary helped me upright. She smiled and I saw her pirate—like a glowing ember—lodged within her. Beside her stood Anne and Jack, tired but unscathed.

Behind them computers lay tangled on the beach. I heard the sound of music and celebration coming from behind the palm trees.

"What happened?" I asked.

"A battle."

"We shut down the internet for a couple of hours via a dummy network. Freaked everyone out," Mary grinned. "Hell of a diversion."

"Before it fell, we hacked into some Cayman accounts, diverted funds, and then destroyed all records and backups. That was the hardest part, but the Moroccans and Chinese cracked it. We stole some islands," Anne said.

"What?"

"Seventy-four uninhabited islands." Jack grinned. "That's what our old friends wanted. That's what we want too. A home. More ships will be coming to join us."

"It will take them awhile to figure out what we did. By then, we might even be ready for them," Mary said.

"I saw a sea battle."

Jack nodded. "Twas fearsome and bloody. Would you like a drink?" He held up an almost empty bottle of rum.

I wasn't thirsty any more, but I took the bottle and drank. A piece of bone slid into my mouth. I hesitated, and then bit into it. Rope squeezed my neck as the landed lords looked on and applauded. I cursed them all with my last breath. Then the noose loosened, and I was reborn.

∞

"A WILD AND A WICKED YOUTH"

Ellen Kushner

"He's dead, mother."

"Who's dead, Richard?"

His mother did not look up from rolling out her pastry. They lived in the country; things died. And her son did not seem particularly upset. But then, he seldom did. She was raising him not to be afraid of anything if she could help it.

"The man in the orchard."

Octavia St Vier carefully put down her rolling pin, wiped her hands on her apron, and tucked up her skirts. At the door she slipped into her wooden clogs, because it was spring and the ground was still muddy. The boy followed her out to the orchard, where a man lay still as the grave under an apple tree, his hands clutching tight at something on his chest.

"Oh, love, he's not dead."

"He smells dead," said her son.

Octavia chuckled. "He does that. He's dead drunk, is all, and old and probably sick. He's got good boots, but they're all worn out, see? He must have come a long way."

"What's he holding?" Before she could think to stop him, her son reached between the old man's hands to tug at the end of what he clutched in the folds of his messy cloak.

Like a corpse in a comedy, the old man sat suddenly bolt upright, still gripping one end of the long pointed object whose other end was in her son's hands. It was the end of a sword, sheathed in cracked leather. Octavia was not usually a screamer, but she screamed.

"Rarrrrrr," the old man growled furiously. It seemed to be all he could manage at the moment, but his meaning was clear.

"Richard," Octavia said, as carefully as if she were back at her girl-hood elocution lessons—though this was not the sort of sentence they had been designed for—"put the man's sword down."

She could tell her son didn't want to. His hand was closed around the pommel, encircled itself by a swirl of metal which no doubt had its own special name as well. It was a beautiful object; its function was clearly to keep anything outside from touching the hand within.

The old man growled again. He tugged on the sword, but he was so weak, and her son's grip held so fast, that it only separated scabbard from blade. Octavia saw hard steel emerge from the leather. "Rich-ard...." She used the Voice of Command that every mother knows. *"Now."*

Her son dropped the sword abruptly, and just as abruptly scrambled up the nearest tree. He broke off a branch, which was strictly forbid-den, and waved it at the sky.

The old man pulled the weapon back into his personal aura of funk, rags, hunger, and age. He coughed, hawked, spat, repeated that, and dragged himself up until his back was to the apple tree's trunk.

"Quick little nipper," he said. "'Sgonna break his neck."

Octavia shielded her eyes to look up at the boy in the tree. "Oh," she said, "he never falls. You get used to it. Would you like some water?"

∞

The old man didn't clean up particularly well, but he did clean up. When he was sober, he cut wood and carried water for their little cottage. He had very strong arms. He did stay sober long enough to spend all of one day and most of the next sanding every inch of his rust-pocked blade—there was quite a lot of it, it was nearly as tall as the boy's shoulder—and then oiling it, over and over. He wouldn't let anyone help. Richard did offer. But the old man said he made him nervous, always wriggling about like that, couldn't he keep still for one god-blasted moment, and get off that table, no not up into the rafters you're enough to give a man palpitations now get outta here if you can't keep still.

"It's my house," Richard said. "You're just charity."

"Am not neither. I'm a servant. That's what it's come to. Fetch and carry for madam your mother, but at least I've got my pride, and what does she want all those books for anyway? And where's your daddy?"

It wasn't like he hadn't heard that one before. "She left him behind," he said. "He couldn't keep up. She likes the books better. And me." Richard lifted a book off the shelf. He was supposed to ask permission first, but she wasn't around to ask. "There's pictures. Animals' insides. Inside-out. See?"

He found a particularly garish one. Last year he'd been scared to look too closely at it, but now that he was big it filled him with horrific delight. He thrust it suddenly up into the old man's face.

But the old man reacted a great deal more strongly than even a very horrible picture should have warranted. As soon as Richard shoved the book at him he jumped backwards, knocking over his chair, one arm thrown back, his other arm forward to strike the book from they boy's hand.

Quickly the boy pivoted, drawing his mother's book out of harm's way. He had no desire to have his ass handed to him on a platter, the official punishment for messing up books.

The old man fell back, panting. "You saw that coming," he wheezed. "You devil's whelp."

He lunged at him again. Richard protected the book.

The old man started chasing him around the room, taking swipes at him from different angles, high, low, sideways . . . It was scary, but also funny. There was no way the old man was going to touch him, after all. Richard could always see just what he was aiming for, just where his hand would fall—except, of course, that it never could.

Not a screamer, Octavia let out a yell when she walked into the room. *"What in the Seven Hells are you doing with my son?"*

The old man stopped cold. He drew himself up, carefully taking deep breaths of air so he could be steady enough to say clearly, "Madam, I am training him. In the art of the sword. It cannot have escaped your notice that he has an aptitude."

Octavia put down the dead starling that she was carrying. "I'm afraid it has," she said. "But do go on."

Richard practiced in the orchard with a stick. His best friend, Crispin, wanted to practice too, but Crispin's parents had impressed upon him that lords did not fight with steel. It wasn't noble; you hired others to do it for you, like washing dishes or ironing shirts or figuring accounts.

"But it's not steel," Richard explained; "it's wood. It's just a stick, Crispin; come on."

The old man had no interest in teaching Crispin, and anyway it might have gotten back to his father, so Richard just showed his friend everything he learned, and they practiced together. Privately, Richard thought Crispin wasn't very good, but he kept the thought to himself. Crispin had a temper. He was capable of taking umbrage for days at a time, which was dull, but could usually be resolved either in a fistfight or an elaborate ritual apology orchestrated by Crispin.

Richard didn't mind that. Crispin was inventive. It was never the same thing twice and it was never boring—and never all that hard, really. Richard was perfectly capable of crossing the brook on the dead log blindfolded, or of fetching the bird's nest down from under the topmost eave by Crispin's mother's window. He did get in trouble the time he climbed up the chimney, because chimneys are dirty and his mother had to waste her time washing all his clothes out. But Crispin gave him his best throwing stick to make up for it, so that worked out all right. And Crispin's other ideas were just as good as his vengeful ones. Crispin was the one who figured out how they could get the cakes meant for the visitors on Last Night and make it look like the cat had done it. And Crispin was the one who covered for him the time they borrowed his father's hunting spears to play Kings in the orchard, when they forgot to bring them back in time. They never told on each other, no matter what.

Crispin's father was all right, except for his prejudice against steel. He winked when the boys were caught stealing apples from his orchards, and even let Richard ride the horses that were out to pasture; if he could catch one, he could ride it, that was the deal (as long as it wasn't a brood mare) and Crispin with him.

Crispin's father was Lord Trevelyan, and had a seat on the Council of Lords, but he didn't like the City, and never went there if he could help it. Every Quarter Day, Trevelyan's steward brought Richard's mother the money her family sent from the city to keep her there. A certain amount of it went right back to town, to be spent on books of Natural History the next time Lady Trevelyan went there to shop. Lady Trevelyan was stylish and liked theatre. She went to the city every year. She did not buy the books herself, of course, and probably would have liked to forget all about them, but her husband had instructed that they be seen to, along with everything else the estate required from town.

What mattered was that the money came, and came regularly. Without it, his mother said, they would have to go live in a cave somewhere—and not a nice cave, either. "Why couldn't we just go live with your family?" Richard asked.

"Their house is too small."

"You said it had seventeen rooms."

"Seventeen rooms, and no air to breathe. And no place to cut up bats."

"Mother, when you find out how bats can fly, will you write a book?"

"Maybe. But I think it would be more interesting to learn about how frogs breathe, then, don't you?"

So she always counted the money carefully when it came in, and hid it in her special hiding place, a big book called *Toads and their Discontents*. There were some pictures of Toads, all right, but their Discontents had been hollowed out to make a stash for coins.

Shortly after the latest Quarter Day, the old swordsman disappeared. Octavia St Vier anxiously counted her stash, but all the coins were still there.

She gave some to him the next time he came and went, though. It had been a beautiful summer, a poet's summer of white roses and green-gold grain, and tinted apples swelling on the bough against a sky so blue it didn't seem quite real. Richard found that he remembered most of the old man's teaching from when he was little, and the old man was so pleased that he showed him more ways to make the pretend steel dance at the end of his arm—*Make it part of your arm, boyo!*—and to dance away from it, to out-guess the other blade and make your body less of a target.

Crispin got bored, and then annoyed. "All you ever want to do is play swords anymore!"

"It's good," Richard said, striking at an oak tree with a wooden lathe flexible enough to bear it.

"No, it's not. It's just the same thing, over and over."

"No, it's not." Richard imagined a slightly larger opponent, and shifted his wrist. "Come on, Crispin, I'll show you how to disarm someone in three moves."

"No!" Crispin kicked the oak. He was smart enough not to kick Richard when Richard was armed. "What are you stabbing that tree for?" he taunted. "Are you trying to kill it?"

"Nope." Richard kept drilling.

"You're trying to kill it because you're scared to climb it."

"No, I'm not."

"Prove it."

So he did.

"The black mare's in the field," Crispin told him when he'd hauled himself all the way up to the branch Richard was on, by dint of telling himself it didn't matter.

"The racer?"

"Yah."

"How long?"

"Dunno."

"Can we catch her?"

"We can try. Unless you'd rather play swords against trees. She's pretty fierce."

Richard threw an acorn at Crispin. Crispin ducked, and nearly fell out of the tree.

"Don't do that," he said stiffly, holding on for dear life. "Or I'll never let you near our horses again."

"Let's get down," Richard said. He eased himself down first, leaving Crispin to follow where he couldn't be seen. Crispin got mad if you criticized his climbing, or noticed he needed help. The rule was, he had to ask for it first, even if he took a long time. Otherwise he got mad.

Crispin arrived at the bottom all covered in bark. "Let's go swimming first," he said, so they did that. On the way home, they discovered Crispin's little sister unattended, so they borrowed her to make a pageant wagon of Queen Diane Going to War with the garden wheelbarrow and the one-horned goat, which didn't turn out as well as they'd hoped, although that wasn't their fault; if she'd only kept still and not shrieked so loud, nothing would have happened. Nonetheless, it got them both thrashed, and separated for a week. Richard didn't mind that much, as it gave him more time to practice. All that stretching really did help the ache of the beating go away faster, too.

The old man was going back to the city for the winter, where a body could get warm, he said, and the booze, while of lesser quality, was cheaper, if you knew where to go: "Riverside," he said, and Octavia said, "That's a place of last resort."

"No, lady," he gestured at the cottage; "*this* is."

But when she handed him the money, he said, "What's this for?"

"For teaching my son."

He took it, and went his way, just as the apples were ripening to fall. He came back the next year, and the next, and he stayed a little longer each time. He told them he had a niece in Covington, with four daughters ugly as homemade sin. He told them the Northern mountains were so cold your teeth froze and fell out if you didn't keep your mouth shut. And he told them the city was crazy about a new swordsman, De Maris, who'd perfected a spiraling triple thrust the eye could hardly follow.

"Could you fake it?" Richard asked, and the old man clouted him (and missed). They figured it out together.

Octavia gave him more money when he went. But maybe that was a mistake, because then he didn't come back. The old fellow might have just dropped dead, or been robbed, or he might have spent it all on a tearing binge. It hardly mattered. But she had meant him to buy a sword for Richard with it, and that mattered some.

So she went up to the Trevelyan manor, to see what could be done. Surely, she thought, they had plenty of swords there. Nobles owned swords, even if they didn't duel themselves. There were ritual swordsmen you hired for weddings, and, well, guards and things.

The manor servants knew her, although they didn't like her much. They were all country people, and she was a city girl with a bastard son and some very weird habits. Still, it wasn't their business to keep her from their lord if he wanted to see her. And so she made her best remembered courtesy to Lord Trevelyan, who was at a table in his muniments room doing something he didn't mind being interrupted at. Octavia St Vier was a very pretty woman, even in a sun-faded gown, her hair bundled up in a turban and smudges on both her elbows.

"You've been so kind," she said; "I won't take much of your time. It's about Richard."

"Oh, dear," said Lord Trevelyan good-humoredly. "Has he corrupted Crispin, or has Crispin corrupted him?" She looked at him inquiringly. "Boys do these things, you know," he went on. "It's nobody's fault; it's just a phase. I'm not concerned, and you shouldn't be, either."

"Crispin doesn't really like the sword," she said.

His tutor had taught him about metaphor, but he realized that wasn't what she meant. He also realized that this poor woman knew nothing about boys, and that he should, as his lady wife often told him, have kept his mouth shut.

"Ah, yes," he said. "The sword."

"Richard loves it, though."

"I hear that he shows promise."

"Really?" She said it a little frostily, as her own mother might have done. "Have people been talking about it?"

"Not at all," he hastened to assure her, although it was not true. People did notice Octavia St Vier's rather striking boy—and the drunken swordmaster talked in the village where he got his drink, pretty much nonstop. But he just said, "Crispin's not as subtle as he thinks he is."

"Oh." She smiled. She really was a very pretty woman. The St Viers might be a family of bankers, but they were bankers of good stock and excellent breeding. "Well, would you help me, then?"

"Yes," he said, "of course." It was her eyes; they were the most amazing color. Almost more violet than blue, fringed with heavy dark lashes....

"I'd like a sword, then. For my son. Do you have any old ones you don't need?"

"I can look," he said. He leaned around the table. "I'm so sorry. I don't mean to stare, but you've got a smudge on your elbow. Right there."

"Oh!" she said, when he touched her. His thumb was so large and warm, and, "Oh!" she said again, as she let herself be drawn to him. "I have to tell you, I haven't done this in a very long time."

"Ten years?" he said, and she said, "Fourteen."

"Ah, fourteen, of course. I'm sorry."

"It's all right. Yes, he's just turned thirteen. And may I have the sword?"

"You," he said gallantly, "may have anything you wish."

∞

Richard's mother brought him a sword. It was a gift, she said, from Lord Trevelyan—but he wasn't to thank him for it; she had already done so, and it would only embarrass him.

Richard did not ask permission to take the sword to show Crispin. It was his sword now, and he could do as he liked with it. He had already polished it with sand and oil, which it badly needed. Truth to tell, Lord Trevelyan had had a hard time laying his hands on a disposable dueling sword. There were battle swords in the old armory, each with a family story attached. There were dress swords for formal occasions, but he knew Octavia would not be content with one of those. Nor should she be. The boy deserved better. For the first time, Trevelyan considered the future of his unusual tenants. Perhaps he should pay to have the boy trained properly; send to the city for a serious swordmaster—or even have the boy sent there to learn. Richard St Vier was already devoted to Crispin. When Crispin came of age, he might have St Vier as his own personal swordsman, to guard him in the city when he took the family seat in the Council of Lords (a burden Trevelyan would be only too happy to have lifted from him) to fight Crispin's inevitable young man's battles over love and honor there, even to stand guard, wreathed in flowers, someday, at Crispin's wedding. Trevelyan smiled at the thought: a boon companion for his son, a lifelong friend who knew the ways of steel....

Crispin was tying fishing flies. It was his latest passion; one of their tenants was the local expert, and Crispin had taken to haunting his farmhouse with a mix of flattery, threats and bribes to get him to disclose his secrets one by one.

"Look!" Carefully, Richard brandished his blade, but low to the ground where it couldn't hurt anything. It was not as razor-sharp as a true duelist's would be, but it still had a point, and an edge.

Crispin nodded, but didn't look up. "Steady...." he said around the thread in his mouth, anchored to one finger against his hook. "Wait—" With a needle, he teased at the feather on the hook. "There!" He held up something between an insect and a dead leaf.

"Nice," Richard said.

"So. Let's see." Crispin gently balanced his fly on the table and looked up. "So you finally got a real one. Is it sharp?"

"Not very. Want to practice? I'll tip the point for you, don't worry."

"Not now. I want to fish. It's nearly dusk. The pike will be biting."

"I'll let you use the real sword." It cost Richard something, but he said it. "I'll use the wooden one."

"*No*, I tell you! I've been working all day on my Speckled King. It's now or never. I've got to try it!" Crispin picked up his rod, the fly on its hook reverently cupped in one palm.

"Oh, all right. I'll come with you, then."

Richard slung his heavy sword back in the makeshift hanger at his hip, and followed the lord's son out through the courtyard and down the drive and across the fields to where the river ran sluggish, choked with weeds. The afternoon was perfectly golden. He felt that it was meant for adventure, for challenge, for chasing the sun down wherever it went—not for standing very still and waiting for something small and stupid underwater to be fooled onto the dinner table by a feather and a piece of string. Nevertheless he joined his friend on the riverbank, and watched Crispin expertly cast the line.

It was true that the boys had already corrupted each other, in precisely the way that Crispin's father had meant. It was, for them, just another thing to do with their bodies, like climbing or swimming or running races—and with certain similarities there, as well; they experimented with speed and distance, and competed with each other. Fishing was serious, though. Richard prepared to wait. He wondered if it would distract Crispin, or the fish, if he practiced just a little, and decided not to chance it. Crispin fussed at the pole, and cast the line again.

Gnats hummed on the water. A dragonfly mated with another.

"Tomorrow," Richard began, and Crispin said, "*Shh!* I think I've got one." He raised the tip of his rod, and his line tightened. Richard watched Crispin's face—the fierce concentration as he pulled, released, tightened the line again, and gave a sudden jerk as his opponent lashed the surface of the water. It was a pike, a big one, with a sharp pointed snout, its jaws snapping with the hook. It struggled against the pull of the line, and Crispin struggled with it as it raised white water and then rose into the air—it looked almost as if the fish were trying to wrestle him into its own element, holding him at the end of the nearly-invisible line, coming toward him, going away, dancing on the wind. Finally it spun in, a writhing silver streak of a pike that landed on the grass beside him with a desperate thud, enormous and frantic for breath.

"Ha!" Crispin cried, viewing his prize as it gasped out its life—and "Ha!" Richard cried, as he plunged his blade fiercely into its side, where he figured the heart should be.

The fish lay still, then flopped once more and collapsed. Richard withdrew his blade, a little raggedly, and fish guts leaked out its silver sides.

"Why did you do that?" Crispin said quietly.

"It was dying anyway."

"You ruined it."

"It was a noble opponent," Richard said grandly. "I gave it a merciful death."

"You don't give a fish a merciful death." Crispin's voice was tight with rage. "It's not a deer or a hound or something. It's a *fish*."

"I *know* it's a fish, so what does it matter?"

"Look at it!" Crispin's fists were clenched. "It looks completely stupid now." The pike's fierce mouth, lined with teeth, gaped haplessly, the hook still in it, the feathers of the fly like something it had caught and didn't quite know what to do with.

"Well I'm sorry, then," said Richard. "But you can still eat it. It's still good."

"I don't *want* it!" Crispin shouted. "You've *ruined* it!"

"Well at least get your fly back out of it. It's a terrific fly. Really."

"No it's not. It was, but you ruined it. You like to ruin everything, don't you?"

Oh, no, Richard thought. He knew where this was going, and that there was pretty much no stopping it. It didn't even occur to him to walk away; that would only prolong things. He had to stay and see it out.

"Go away," Crispin said. "You're not my friend."

"Yes I am. I was your friend this morning. I'm your friend, still, now."

Crispin kicked the fish. A little goo ran out its mouth. Its eyes were open. It did look pretty stupid.

"You said you were sorry, but you didn't really mean it."

"Yes I did. I am. I'm sorry I ruined your fish. It's a great fish."

"Prove it, then."

Here it comes, thought Richard. He felt a little involuntary shiver. "How?"

He waited. Crispin was thinking.

The longer Crispin thought, the worse things were. It would be something awful. Would he have to eat the fish raw? He wondered if he could.

"Give me your sword," Crispin said.

"No!" That was too much.

"I'll give it back."

"Swear?"

"If you do as I say. *I* don't want it," Crispin said scornfully. "It's just a beat up piece of junk."

Richard put his hand on the pommel at his hip. "Swear anyway."

Crispin rolled his eyes, but he swore one of their oaths: "May the Seven Gods eat my liver live if I don't give it back to you. After you've apologized."

"All right, then." Richard drew his blade, and held it out.

"Not that way. You must kneel. Kneel to me, and offer it properly."

He knelt in front of Crispin in the grass, the sword balanced across his two hands. It was heavy this way.

"All right," his friend said.

"Is this enough?"

"For now." Crispin was smiling the unpleasant smile that meant he'd thought of something else. Richard wondered what it was. It was worth staying to find out. His arms ached, but not unbearably.

"Are you going to take it, Crispin, or not?"

"Give it to me."

Richard held it out a little further, and Crispin grasped the hilt. The weight leaving him was like a drink of water on a hot day.

"Now stand up."

He stood.

Solemnly, Crispin leveled the sword at his chest. Richard looked down at the tip of the blade against his shirt. This was hard. It took almost everything he had to hold himself in check, not to fight back.

Crispin nodded.

"You have passed the first test," Crispin intoned. He put the sword aside. Richard hoped it wouldn't get too wet on the grass. The sun was getting lower. But it wasn't dark yet.

"And now, the second. Are you ready?" Richard nodded. "Take off my boot."

He knelt by Crispin's leg and pulled his left boot off the way he'd seen the valet pull off Lord Trevelyan's after the hunt. Crispin steadied himself with a hand on Richard's shoulder, but that was all right; he had to: the whole thing wouldn't work if Crispin fell.

"Now my stocking."

Richard eased the wrinkled stocking off his foot. It smelt not disagreeably of leather, wool, and Crispin himself. "What should I do with it?"

"Put it somewhere you can find it again. This won't take long."

Crispin's bare foot was balanced on his thigh, just above his bent knee. Crispin was like an acrobat, poised for flight. Or if there had been a tree above them, he might have been about to hoist his friend up into its branches for the sweetest fruit. He could see all sorts of possibilities, but Richard knew from rich experience that nothing he could imagine was remotely like what Crispin would say. And, indeed, it was not.

"Now, put your tongue between my toes."

"*What?*"

Crispin said nothing, did nothing. The foot was there. Crispin was there. The words had been spoken. They were never taken back.

The foot was there. Richard bent his head to it.

Something in his body tingled. He didn't like it. It was just a stupid foot. It should have nothing to do with the way he was feeling.

He tasted essence of Crispin. Crispin's fingers were in his hair, holding tight. He moved on to the next toe. The feeling grew. He really hated it, and he really didn't. He didn't seem to have a choice, actually. He was feeling it whether he wanted to or not. It felt more dangerous than anything he'd ever done, and he didn't hate that, either. He ran his tongue along another toe, and felt Crispin shudder.

"All right," his friend said. "That's enough." But Richard didn't raise his head. "The offense— The offense is purified. The deed is pardoned." Those were the ritual words. Richard should have stopped, but he didn't.

"The deed is—"

Richard went for another toe.

Crispin let himself fall. His bare foot caught Richard on the side of the mouth, but Richard could tell he hadn't meant it to, and let himself fall, too. They rolled on the ground together, struggling against each other for some sort of relief in a fight they didn't know how to win. They pressed their bodies tight against each other, reaching for each other's skin through their clothes, and finally had the sense to tear them off and give each other the release they'd gotten in the past. It felt different this time, more frightening, more uncontrolled, more essential—and more complete, when they had both done, as though they had made an offering to the world they hadn't meant to.

"The offense is purified," Richard breathed into Crispin's ear.

"The deed is pardoned," Crispin whispered to the grass.

They got up and cleaned themselves off, and put their clothing back together, and went home.

The next day, Richard helped his mother clean the loft out. The day after that, Crispin took him riding on a real saddlehorse. They passed through a field with high hedges, but did not dismount to experiment with each other behind them. That particular experiment was over, now. They never spoke of it again.

∞

The old swordsman came back at the end of summer, and spent the winter with them. He didn't say much, and he didn't drink much, either. He was yellowish and hollow-eyed, skin slack on his face, hands trembling when he didn't watch them.

Richard showed him his new sword. The old man whistled low. "That's a real old relic, that is. A pride of ages past. Wonder where they dug that up?" He hefted it, made a few passes with surprising speed. "Wasn't junk once. Nice balance. Length's all wrong for you, boy—'smeant for a bigger man. Have to work extra hard now, wontcha?"

He wasn't fun to have around. Some days he never got out of the grubby tangle of blankets and cloaks he huddled in a little too close to the hearth and its ashes. On what must have been his good days, though, he'd heft his own blade, or the fireplace poker, whichever was nearest, and smack at Richard's leg or his sword, if either was within reach; he'd growl something in the back of his throat, and then simply go at him as if Richard were some kind of demon he needed to vanquish. Eventually he'd calm down, and start criticizing, or explaining. That was worth the wait. But it was hard.

"I've gotten bad," Richard complained, the fifth time of being smacked along his ribs with the flat of the man's blade. He was waking up bruised. "I've forgotten everything you taught me."

"No, you've not." The old man cackled. "You've grown, is what it is. Arms and legs in a whole new place each morning. Trying, ennit?"

"Very." Richard risked a pass, and was rewarded with a touch.

"Move the table," Octavia said absently, standing at it exploring a bat's insides. They had actually left it on the other side of the room some days ago, but she wasn't paying attention.

"Well, don't break anything, then." She might have meant a bowl, or her son's arm—or probably both.

Nothing got broken. Richard grew all that winter. He was getting hair in unaccustomed places. His voice was not reliable. It made him all the more eager to master the sword.

"You'll be a beauty," the man would taunt him, trying to break his concentration while they sparred. "Good thing you know how to use this thing, because you'll be fighting them off with it."

That was good. The last thing he wanted was people pestering him. This fall the goose girl had started following him around, never leaving him alone—and when he ignored her, she actually *threw* things at him, so he gave her a thrashing—a light one—but still, to his surprise, his mother had given *him* one when she heard, to see how he liked it. She said it was for his own good, but he knew that she was just good and angry. She told him he must never, ever lift his hand against a woman or a girl, not even if they were being very irritating. Not even if they struck him first. Because son, she said, soon you will be much stronger than they. You could hurt someone badly without even meaning to. So it won't be fair. And besides, soon you'll be in a position to, ah, to put them at risk— But we'll talk about that next year, shall we?

"What if her brother comes after me?" Village boys had bullied him a lot when he was small.

She gave him the same answer now that she'd given then to such good effect: "Oh, him you can try and kill, if you can."

∞

He didn't see much of Crispin that winter. The snows were unusually deep, and Crispin was at studies of his own. His father had sent to the city for a University man to teach Crispin mathematics and geometry and orthography and things. When he saw his friend, Crispin told Richard that this was unquestionably the worst year of his life so far. And he didn't see why he had to learn all this stuff when he was going to have secretaries and bailiffs to do the important writing and figuring for him—which earned him a clout from his father, who explained that if he didn't know how to do those things for himself, he'd be cheated blind and the whole estate go to wrack and ruin. And no, it wasn't a bit like not studying the sword. Some things were indeed best left to specialists; he wasn't expected to be able to shoe his own mare, either, was he? Next year he was to have Logic, and Rhetoric, and Dancing.

"Stand fast," he told Richard St Vier. "Don't let them teach you to read, whatever they say. Next time she remembers, just tell her you're too busy or something."

"I'll tell her it's bad for my eyesight."

"Whatever it takes. Trust me, it's the beginning of the end."

Crispin was considering running away if things got much worse. But not to the city; that's where all these horrors came from. Maybe he'd jump a boat upriver, if Richard would come with him.

Richard said he'd consider it.

And so they waited 'til spring.

The old man was better in the spring. He sat out in the sunshine on a bench next to the rain barrel against the wall, like a pea sprout waiting to unfurl in the sun. He dueled Richard up and down the yard, to the terror of the hens, who wouldn't lay for a week. Octavia complained about the chickens, and the old man got all huffy, and said he would go. She was sorry to hurt his feelings, but she was really just as glad to get her cottage back to herself.

They missed him the next year, though. Octavia felt bad, especially as she was pretty sure he must be dead. He couldn't last forever, and he hadn't looked good, even in spring. However, Richard had uncovered the exciting news that Lord Trevelyan's new valet from the city had studied the sword there, as well.

Richard had given up on Crispin as a dueling partner. Crispin said he had too much to study already, and when they had time to do things together, they had better be something fun. Neither of them had to say that Crispin wasn't any kind of match for Richard any more (except in drill, which even Richard couldn't consider fun).

In an agony of need, Richard plotted how to approach the new valet. Should he be casual, off-hand, and only plead if he had to? Or should he abandon all pretense, and simply beg for a lesson?

In the end, it was Lady Trevelyan who decided the matter. Crispin's mother was back from the city, a month early because of an outbreak of fever there, and bored out of her mind. It was her idea to stage a demonstration bout at the Harvest Feast.

By the time Octavia had heard about it, Richard had already gleefully said yes, and it was too late for her to make a fuss about any son of hers displaying himself like a mountebank for the entertainment of people who had nothing better to do than watch other people poking at each other with hypertrophied table knives. It was just as well, really; she had the awful feeling she might have ended up sounding exactly like her mother.

Still, it would have been nice if Hester Trevelyan could have troubled herself to make a courtesy call to explain to Octavia herself that the swords would be tipped, and there would be no First Blood in this duel, the way there was in the city. A mother's heart, after all. Or didn't Lady Trevelyan think she had one? Octavia had Richard's boots re-soled, and made sure he had a nice, clean shirt.

Late on the holiday, Octavia braided her hair on top of her head, fixed it with gold pins, and put on her Festival best—not the dress she'd run away in, which had gone to useful patches long ago, but the one she'd stashed to be married in whenever she and her dashing lover got 'round to it: a glittery and flimsy contraption a decade out of date which still fit her perfectly, and made her look like a storybook queen.

When she made her entrance on the Trevelyan grounds, everyone stared. The country folk standing behind the ribbons marking off the fight space sniggered, because they'd never seen anything like it; but Hester Trevelyan, who had worn something very similar at her own coming out ball, looked hard at Richard St Vier's mother. Then she scanned the crowd for Crispin, and called him to her.

"Your friend's mother," she said; "go fetch her—*politely*, Crispin—and tell her she must come and sit with us."

Octavia had been dreading this. She did not want to sit and attempt to make conversation with Hester Trevelyan in front of or with Hester

Trevelyan's husband. Still, one must be gracious. She followed Crispin and arranged herself decorously in a chair on the other side of Lady Trevelyan, and smiled and nodded at everything that was said to her, but that was about all.

Hester found the woman very strange, and not at all appealing, lacking, as she'd always suspected, any agreeable conversation. But she put herself out to be affable. It had clearly been awhile since Richard St Vier's mother had been in any sort of decent company, and perhaps she was worrying about her son. The woman's eyes kept straying across the yard to where the torches were waiting to be lit around the bonfire, and the Harvest tables all set up.

Usually, Hester explained, her dear friends the Perrys held the swordfight *after* the bonfires had been lit. They also brought dancers down from their Northern estates to perform the traditional horn dance beforehand—and that was thrilling to see. But because once the fires were started (and the Harvest drinking seriously begun, though she didn't actually say that) people got a little wild, they'd thought it best here to begin with the duel while it was still clear daylight. She hoped Mistress St Vier wasn't anxious. Master Thorne, the swordsman valet, was really as gentle as a lamb. She would see.

Octavia had seen Richard running around with Crispin, eating cakes and apples and throwing the cores across the yard at people. She was glad he wasn't nervous. His shirt couldn't be helped; it had been clean when he left the house.

Hester waved a strip of silk at the men with the horns—they were hunting horns, brought into service for a somewhat cracked but nonetheless thrilling fanfare. Richard and Master Thorne entered from opposite sides of the yard.

Master Thorne moved with a smooth elegance Octavia hadn't seen since she'd left the city. He was arrayed—there was no other word for it—arrayed in green satin, or something that shone like it, his breeches without a wrinkle, his shirt immaculate white. He set his jacket aside, and rolled up his sleeves as meticulously as a master chef decorating a cake. It was a treat to watch, the way they folded neatly into place. She stole a glance at Richard, who was both watching the man intently to see if he knew tricks, and fidgeting with impatience. That particular fidget was well known to her.

Crispin had begged to serve as Richard's aide, but Lady Trevelyan had put her foot down; it wouldn't be seemly for the son of the house, not even at Festival. So it was to a footman that Richard handed his sword while he took off his jacket. His mother watched him hesitate a moment before deciding to leave his sleeves as they were. Then he and Thorne advanced to the middle of the field, saluted each other, and began to circle.

It was only a half-circle, really. Richard lunged and struck, and Thorne fell back. People gasped, or clapped, or both.

"Whoops!" said Thorne. "I must have slipped. Shall we try again?"

"Please do!" Lady Trevelyan commanded. She had planned on her entertainment lasting longer than this.

The duelists saluted, and assumed guard. Richard struck Thorne in the chest again.

"Well done!" cried Thorne. He held up one hand for a pause, and then rolled up a fallen sleeve. "You're very quick, my friend. Shall we continue?"

He did not wait for an answer, just went on guard again, and immediately struck at Richard. Richard didn't even parry, he simply stepped out of the way—or so it seemed from the outside. Thorne thrust, and thrust again. Richard sidestepped, parried, parried again, but did not return his blows.

Octavia recognized the drill from her hen yard. Richard was running Thorne through his paces. He was reading Thorne's vocabulary of the sword, maybe even learning as he went, but it was nothing but a drill to him.

"Stop!" Lord Trevelyan stood up. The fighters turned to him. "Richard, are you going to fight, or just—just—"

"I'm sorry," Richard replied. He turned to his opponent. "Want me to go a little slower, sir?"

Master Thorne turned red. He glared at the boy, shook out his arms, and breathed deep. He passed one sleeve over his face—and then he laughed.

"Yes," he said; "go a little slower, will you? It's Harvest Feast, and the Champions fight for the honor of the house and the virtue of the land. Let's give the people what they came for, shall we?"

The duel was so slow that even Octavia could follow the moves; for the first time she understood what it was her son could do. It was a

A WILD AND A WICKED YOUTH

textbook lesson—but it thrilled the country folk, who'd never seen real swordplay before.

Richard wasn't quite grown up enough to let Thorne beat him. So when Thorne finally tired of showing Richard and the crowd just about everything he knew, he obligingly opened himself for St Vier's final blow.

"How long did you study?" Richard asked Thorne later.

"Oh, just long enough to put on a show. I figured I could get work as a house guard if valeting got thin. Lots of city men do that. It's always good to have a second skill to fall back on."

"So do you think I should learn how to valet?" Richard asked with distaste.

"You?" Thorne shook his head. "Not you."

∞

When Richard was sixteen, the old man came back.

Richard could smell the fumes of him from the cottage, before he entered and found him there, peeling potatoes for his mother at the big chestnut table as though he'd never been away.

"Look at this dagger," the old fellow wheezed. "Worn thin as one of the King's own Forest Leaves. Now I peel with it, do I?"

"Use the paring knife." Richard held it out to him.

The old man flinched. "Put that down on the table," he said. "It's bad luck passing a knife hand to hand. Cuts the friendship. Didn't you know that?"

It hadn't been that kind of flinch.

"Want to spar?" Richard asked.

"Spar? With you? Hell, no. I hurt, boy; everything hurts. Everything hurts, and I can hardly see. Spar with you?"

"Oh, come on." Richard felt himself jiggle with impatience. "I'll nail my feet to the turf. We'll just do standing. You can just check my wrist-work."

The old man wiped a rheumy red eye. "Told you, I can hardly see."

"You've been chopping onions. What's for supper?"

"Onions. Stew. How the hell should I know? I'm just the servant here. You're the man, St Vier. The man of the house, the man of the hour...."

"Cut it out." Well, he'd smelt it before he came in. There was the tell-tale jug, propped against the chimney piece.

Octavia came in with a fistful of thyme. "There you are, Richard. Look who's dropped in for dinner."

"I didn't come for your cooking, lady," the old man said. "I came for the feast."

"What feast?"

"Don't get out much, do you?" He hawked and spat into the fire. "The whole county's buzzing with it. Thought you'd know. There'll be a feast, after. And alms galore, I shouldn't wonder. And booze."

Octavia pressed her back to the door for support, knowing she'd need it. "What's happened?"

"Your man Trevleyan's on his way out. Thought you'd know."

No one had told them. It was close to autumn; everyone would be busy with the harvest or the hunt; they'd been staying out of the way. True, Lord Trevelyan had been ill for a bit in summer, but last they'd heard, it had passed.

Richard drew a long breath. "He isn't dead now. Maybe it will be all right."

"Maybe," his mother said. She started chopping thyme, thinking, Well, I've still got a long lease on the cottage.... Maybe Crispin will take Richard into his service.... I wonder if Thorne will stay on....

She handed the old man another onion. "Make yourself useful," she said.

But Richard took it from him. "You're going to slice your thumbs off." The old man's hands were shaking. Richard put the jug into them. "Just drink," Richard said; "I'll cut."

In the morning, very early, he was gone. They found his sword out by the gate, and a horn button in the hedge. Octavia followed her heart to the orchard, expecting to find him lying under the very tree where they had first discovered him passed out with a sword in his hands. But there was nothing there, only a few apples, rotting in the grass.

Three days later, Lord Trevelyan died. The valet, Master Thorne, came himself to the cottage to tell them.

"Should I go see Crispin?" Richard asked.

Thorne fingered the frayed rushes of a chair back. "Maybe. I don't know. He's doing his best, but it's hard on him. Any man grieves when his father passes; but Crispin is Lord Trevelyan now. He's not himself, really; none of them are. The lady's distracted. I didn't know it would be this bad. You never know 'til it happens, do you?" He sipped the infusion Octavia gave him.

"So should I go now?"

"You might do that." Master Thorne nodded slowly. He looked ten years older. "Yes, go ahead; I'll just sit here for awhile and drink this, if you don't mind."

∞

Richard walked softly through the halls of the Trevelyan manor. He'd known it all his life, but it felt different now. Not the lord's death, exactly—but the effect it had on everyone. The people that he passed were quiet; they barely acknowledged him. The sounds of the hall were all wrong: footsteps in them too fast or too slow, voices too gentle or too low. Richard felt lost. It was as if the shape of the hall had changed. He closed his eyes.

"What are you doing here?"

Lady Trevelyan stood before him, dressed in black, her long bright hair bound back behind her, falling like a girl's. Her eyes were red-rimmed, and her face had the same pulled look as Master Thorne's.

"I came to see if Crispin was all right." She just stared at him. "I'm Richard St Vier," he said. He wanted to fidget under her gaze. But something about the focus of her stare now kept him still and watchful.

"Yes," she said at last; "I know who you are. The swordsman. That peculiar woman's son."

She was grieving, he reminded himself. People were said to go mad with grief. Maybe this was it.

"I'm Crispin's friend," he said.

"Well, you mustn't see him now. He's very busy. You can't see him, really. It's not good. He's Lord Trevelyan now, you know."

He wanted to retort, "I do know." But she felt weirdly dangerous to him, like Crispin on one of his dares. So he just nodded.

"Come with me," she said suddenly. Without waiting for a reply, she turned and walked away. The swirling edge of her black skirt struck his ankle.

Richard followed her down the silent halls. People bowed and curtsied as she passed with him in her wake. She opened the door to a little room, and beckoned him in with her, and shut it behind them.

The walls of the round room were heavy with fabric, dresses hanging on peg after peg.

"My closet," she said. "Old gowns. I was going to sort through them, but now it doesn't matter, does it? I may as well dye them all black, and wear them to death."

"They're pretty," he said politely.

She fingered a green and gold dress. "I wore this one to the Halliday Ball. I was going to have it cut down for Melissa . . . Children grow up so fast, don't they?"

She looked up at him. She was a tiny woman. Crispin's bones hadn't come from her. "Would you like to see me in it?" she asked wistfully.

What kind of a question was that? He licked his lips. He really should go.

A swoosh of icy blue hissed across his skin. "Or do you think this one's better?"

The cold and cloudy thing was in his arms. It smelt metallic.

"That's silk brocade, Richard St Vier. Blush of Dawn, the color's called. It's to remind you of early morning, when you wake up with your lover." She brushed the fabric over his lips. "Thus. Do you like it?"

He looked over at the door. Silk was expensive; he couldn't just drop it on the floor. Maybe there was a hook it went back on—

She followed his gaze to the wall. "Do you like the pink silk better?" She held a new gown up against herself, the glowing pink cloud eclipsing the black of her dress. "This becomes me, don't you think?"

He nodded. His mouth was dry.

"Come closer," she said.

He knew the challenge when he heard it. He took a step toward her.

"Touch me," she said. He knew where he was, now: walking the fallen tree, stealing something and bringing it back....

"Where?"

"Wherever you like."

He put his hand on the side of her face. She turned her head and licked his palm, and he started as if he had been kicked. He hadn't expected that, to feel that again here, now, that dangerous thrill at the base of his spine. He shuddered with the pleasure he did not like.

"Hold me," she said. He put his arms around her. She smelt of lavender, and blown-out candle wicks.

"Be my friend," she whispered across his lips.

"I will," he whispered back.

Lady Trevelyan laughed low, and sighed. She knotted her fingers in his hair, and pulled his head down to her, biting his lips as she kissed him. He shivered, and pressed himself against her. She lifted her inky skirts, and pulled him closer, fingering his breeches. He didn't even know where his own hands were. He didn't know where anything was, except one thing. His heart was slamming with the danger of how much he wanted it. His eyes were closed, and he could hardly breathe. Every time she touched him he tried to think what a terrible thing this was, but it came out completely different: he had to stop thinking entirely, because thinking that it was dangerous just made him want it more. She was saying something, but he couldn't hear it. She was helping him, that was what mattered. She was helping him—and then suddenly it was over, and she was shouting:

"You idiot! Pink *peau de soie*—ruined!" She shoved him away. His sight came back. He reached for his breeches, fallen around his knees. "What do you think you're doing? Who do you think you are?" Her face and neck were flushed, eyes sharp and bright. "You're nobody. You're no one. What are you doing here? Who do you think you are?"

He did up his buttons, stumbled out into the hall.

The door was closed; he couldn't hear her now. He started walking back the way he'd come—or some way, anyway. It wasn't a part of the house he knew.

"Richard!"

Not Crispin. Not now.

"Richard!"

Not now.

"Richard, damn you—you *stand* when I call you!"

Richard stood. He had his back to Crispin; he couldn't look at him now. "What?" he asked. "What do you want?"

"What do I *want*? " Crispin demanded shrilly. "What the hell's wrong with you? What do you think I want?"

"Whatever it is, I don't have it."

"No, you don't, do you?" Crispin said bitterly. "God. I thought you were my friend."

"I guess I'm not, then. I guess I'm not your friend."

Crispin threw a punch at him.

And Richard returned it. He didn't hold back.

It wasn't a fair fight, not really. They'd never been even in this game.

It was, Richard reflected after, a good thing they'd neither of them had swords; but he still left Crispin, Lord Trevelyan, a wheezing mess crumpled on the floor.

Then he went home and told his mother what he'd done.

∞

She had known that it would come someday, but this was so much sooner than she'd hoped.

"You have to go, my love," she said. "Lord Trevelyan's dead. His lady won't protect you, and Crispin certainly won't."

Richard nodded. He wanted to say, "It's only Crispin," or "He'll get over it." But Crispin was Trevelyan now.

"Where should I go?" he said instead. He pictured the mountains, where bold men ran with the deer. He pictured another countryside, much like this; another cottage by a stream, or maybe a forest....

"To the city," his mother said. "It's the only place that you can lose yourself enough."

"The city?" He'd never been there. He didn't know anyone. The house with no air was there, and the place of last resort. But even as he thought it, he felt that curious thrill down his spine, and knew he wanted it, even though he shouldn't.

"The city," he said. "Yes."

"Don't be frightened," his mother said.

He said, "I'm not."

She pulled out the book on Toads, opening to the hollow where the money was. "Here," she said. "Start with this. You'll earn more when you get there."

He did not ask her, "How?" He thought he knew.

∞

10110100101000111001010110 1001

PROSPERINE WHEN IT SIZZLES

Tansy Rayner Roberts

My mistress is never more confident than when engaging in nefarious activities. "Duchesse Claudine Augustille Recherche Dubois," she announced to the factotum of the spice shop. "Accompanied by M. Pepin."

The factotum looked alarmed. "Madame, one is not supposed to use one's real name."

My mistress paused to consider the etiquette of this. "Would it help if I pretended to be M. Pepin, and he pretended to be La Duchesse?"

"Just write M. and Mme. Noir," I urged.

The factotum looked relieved. "Very good, Monsieur."

"Nonsense, Pepin," protested La Duchesse as I steered her through the shop. "How am I expected to remember a name like *Noir*? Pseudonyms require subtlety, panache...possibly something from classic literature?"

"I will try to conjure something more literary next time," I promised her.

Past the foul-smelling shelves and bins of the shop, we found ourselves within one of the more sinister dens of the city of Prosperine. At first it appeared to be nothing out of the ordinary — a selection of well-heeled ladies and gentlemen sat at tables in order to chat, to read from slender volumes, or to embroider while drinking dishes of coffee.

But the flashes of metallic grey, LED green, and holographic purple were hard to ignore. For every gentleman with a book, there were another three swapping data crystals. For every lady with embroidery on her knee, there were several with glowing nano-wands or flat screens.

Even setting foot in an establishment like this was illegal on New Ceres. For an aristocrat such as my mistress, there was a great deal to lose. Only one week earlier, the Count and Countess of Chevre had been arrested in Anglais for hosting a scientifiction salon in a speakeasy such as this one. They were currently awaiting trial for sacrilege and treason, and there was talk that the Lumoscenti were pressuring the Lady Governor to withdraw the Chevre family's rank and titles back three generations.

"Eyes open, Pepin," said my mistress as we walked among our fellow criminals. "And don't drink the coffee. It smells positively rancid."

I recognized the boy first, though I had only seen him at a distance on state occasions. Conrad Nathaniel DeVries had dyed his hair recently, but his black-splashed locks could not disguise the evident family resemblance, including a particularly pointed nose.

I nudged my mistress, and indicated the table where Conrad sat with a group of similarly raucous and badly dressed young gentlemen. They were playing some kind of offworld game with holographic battleships that shot glowing pellets across a flat glass gameboard, and had reached that stage of drunkenness where simply everything is hilarious.

My mistress moved into position behind Conrad before calling attention to herself by plucking at his sleeve. "Young sir," she murmured. "A word, if you please?"

He shook her off without looking. "Take your wares elsewhere, wench."

His friends laughed at that, but one of them caught the look in La Duchesse's eyes, and the laughter stilled in his throat.

"For your mother's sake, sir," my mistress said, with glass in her voice. "A moment of your time."

Conrad whirled at her, eyes bright with absinthe and rage. "Who are you to use my mother's name—" There he stopped, for he recognized the woman before him. "What are you doing here?"

La Duchesse smiled a winning smile. "Merely a duty visit, my sweet. I knew him in swaddling clothes," she confided to his friends, even as she drew the resisting lad into her perfumed bosom. As he struggled in her embrace, she whispered into his ear. She was too discreet for even I to hear the words, but I guessed something of what she had said to him.

Don't be an ass, Nate. The Lumoscenti are coming. This place is being raided tonight, and you know perfectly well that you can't be caught here.

Everything moved fast after that. Even as the young rascal made his apologies to withdraw, a low whistle sounded from the spice shop frontage.

"The Golden Priests!" someone cried. Many of the patrons simply slipped their contraband out of sight, but others upturned tables and scrambled for the back door.

"Not there," La Duchesse said in disgust as the brat made to bolt. "This way, Nate. Follow me."

"My name is Conrad," he spat at her in disgust. "You're not my mother."

"Saints be praised for that, at least," she said, and dragged him towards a wall thick with tapestries.

There were yelps and howls from outside. "Priests at the exit?" I said, not in the least surprised.

"La Policia, I expect," said my mistress. "This isn't an everyday raid." She pushed us both behind the tapestries. "Is there a door, Pepin?"

There was, though it was old and unused, with a firm lock upon it. "How did you know?"

"No time for questions!"

Within three months of employment in La Duchesse's household, I had found it necessary to learn the art of picking locks. A beauty such as this one, however, required time and finesse that I did not have. I drew a fountain pen from my inner pocket, thumbed it to draw a fine laser bead and sliced the lock neatly from the door.

Conrad gulped at the hissing sound of metal parting.

"That's right, lad," La Duchesse said grimly. "We're all criminals here."

Steps led down to a cellar. Conrad clattered down them, and I followed with La Duchesse after bolting the door from this side.

"There's a tunnel behind the barrels," she said, without looking to check. "It leads up and out to the alley near the bookshop."

"That's why you had Damon wait there with the phaeton," I said, admiringly. The bookshop was in another street entirely to both the spice shop's front and back entrances.

She rolled her eyes. "Really, Pepin, I am no amateur in these matters. Make haste, before they find the door behind the tapestry."

Conrad hesitated by the barrels. I motioned for him to start moving them, and after a moment, he did. Sure enough, there was a small hole in the wall — wide enough for a man to crawl through. Not a woman in current fashions, though. "You'll have to leave your skirts," I told La Duchesse.

"I'm not coming with you. What are you waiting for?' she barked at Conrad, and he dived into the tunnel as if his life depended on it. In a manner of speaking, of course, it did.

"Leaving you behind was not our plan," I protested.

"Of course it was, Pepin. I simply did not inform you of that fact."

"Claudine, you can't afford to be found here." I could hear shuffling and shouting in the rooms above. It was only a matter of time before they discovered the cellar.

"For Nate's sake, I can't afford not to be," she said firmly. "The Lumoscenti were tipped off. They're expecting a ripe sugar-plum out of this raid. If they get me, they might not look too hard for any one else."

"Your title won't protect you from the Lumoscenti! The Count and Countess of Chevre…."

She smiled sickly at me. "That's why we're here, Pip. Be off with you, and don't stop until you and the boy are within the gates of his mother's estate."

"Did *she* know you planned to sacrifice yourself?"

A heavy weight thumped against the door above. The bolt held, for now.

La Duchesse pushed me hard in the middle of my chest. "If ever you loved me, my dear, do as I say."

How's a fellow supposed to fight a woman who says things like that?

∞

I caught up to Conrad in the tunnel as La Duchesse pulled the last barrel back in front of the mouth, plunging us into blackness. "Faster, lad."

"I'm not at my best on hands and knees," he sneered.

I resisted the urge to point my laser pen at his posterior. "A good woman just sacrificed her position and title for you, tadpole. The least you can do is save your own skin."

We made it out of the tunnel without killing each other, and emerged sweaty and grimy into the alley where La Duchesse had left her phaeton and footman. It took me but a moment to realize that both were now missing.

I cursed anachronistically. The street entrance of the speakeasy was around the corner, but I could hear the hubbub that poured forth from the raid. We could not afford to be caught on these streets, so near to the spice shop. Most of the businesses along this strip were all closed, but light and music came from one private residence across the street, and a few carriages clustered at the entrance.

"That way," I said, giving Conrad a shove in the small of his back.

I stopped at the first of the carriages and stepped up to the running board, palming a handful of sous in the face of the driver. "This amount twice over to take us to the Garden District?"

"Sorry, guvnor," he said, startled. "My master wants me ready to go at a moment's notice."

From the sound of ill-sung opera music emanating from the upper windows, I didn't blame his master in the least. "Next one," I snapped at Conrad.

The occupants of the second carriage along were still disembarking, so I was more covert with my attempts at bribing their footman. He eyed my very young companion with ill-concealed disgust, and pretended that he could not speak French.

Marvellous. They all thought I was kidnapping a nobleman's son. Well, they weren't entirely wrong, though I had no intention of having my wicked way with the brat.

"Pepin," said a startled voice. "What are you doing here?"

I whirled around to lay eyes upon Drusus Savon, the one man in New Ceres who knew my darkest secret. He descended the steps of the residence, dressed in the usual finery of a Prosperine aristocrat — more comfortable in the costume than the last time we met.

I had hoped never to see him again (at least, that is what I told myself I hoped), but desperation makes for strange bedfellows. "Do you have a carriage, sir?"

The tone of my voice alerted him that the matter was urgent, and he ushered us both into the first carriage. He did not ask my companion's name, though he looked at Conrad with curiosity as we rattled along the streets.

"George is taking us to my hotel as a matter of course," Savon said, eyes not leaving mine. "The Prosperine Grande. Unless there's somewhere else you need to go?"

I almost laughed, though it would have been a hollow sound. La Duchesse and I also had rooms at the Grande. We might have run into Savon on the staircase, or over breakfast, at any time during the last week. I had been so close to my danger and had not known it.

The hotel would not do. We could not afford to have Conrad found anywhere associated with La Duchesse, not after her inevitable arrest. I thought of her in the hands of the Lumoscenti, and my mouth went dry. "The Garden District, if you please, M. Savon."

Savon leaned out the window, and spoke to the footman briefly. "That's a fair way out," he said to me.

"If it's an inconvenience, monsieur, you can drop us at a way station."

"I wouldn't dream of it. Demme, Pepin, you look as if a horde of ghosts were after you."

Conrad snorted.

"You don't say a word," I growled. "Enough people have paid for your foolishness tonight."

The boy pouted, and I saw fit to ignore his petulance. Even if that meant further conversation with the man who had saved us.

Savon cleared his throat. "Is La Duchesse well?"

Every street we put between ourselves and the Lumoscenti raid made me breathe a little easier. "I have not seen her in days, monsieur. A new lover, I expect." I prodded Conrad with my foot, to keep him quiet.

Savon appeared oddly cheerful at the happenstance that had reunited us. Had I the presence of mind to consider it, I might have thought it odd. I had not been overly courteous to him the last time we met. "Well, you have saved me, M. Pepin. I had no excuse at all when I escaped the Baron Rudolph's supper party an hour before politeness dictated — but now I can say in all truthfulness that I was called upon to help a friend in need."

"I would prefer it, monsieur, if you did not name the friend," I said quickly.

Savon's bright eyes sharpened. "You are in trouble. I thought so." He regarded Conrad, who was glaring at the curtained window as if it personally offended him. "I recognize the boy."

That, at least, got Conrad's attention. He stared wild-eyed at us both.

"How?" I asked, trying to keep calm. "You're not even a local...."

"I have eyes, Phi...." he caught himself. "Pepin. I have been here a half-year now, making contacts for the organisation I represent. Learning the ways of Prosperine. I was a guest at the Lady Governor's reception three days ago, and I know who this boy's mother is."

More information he could use against me, should he choose to do so. "You understand the urgency of the matter, then."

"I know that a wayward child can be used to make a parent look bad in the eyes of the public." Savon considered the matter. "There is an important policy decision being made soon, is there not?"

"Three days," I said. "The Lumoscenti have a petition before the House of Peers, to ban from New Ceres all technological advances made during the latter half of Earth's Eighteenth Century. They will not be happy, I think, until our world returns to the Dark Ages. Every restriction placed upon our lives further increases their power."

What I did not say aloud was that the Lumoscenti's conservatism was meeting with greater sympathy than ever before. The alien massacre of Earth was a raw memory still, and it was a commonly held belief that keeping New Ceres' technology restricted was the only thing that might protect us from a similar fate. Something akin, I believe, to hiding under a blanket with our fingers in our ears so that no one can find us.

"Such a reversion would affect the fleet?" said Savon, as if we were exchanging polite dinner conversation. "I believe a certain degree of steam technology is currently allowed on New Ceres."

"It is limited, but essential," I agreed. "Our agriculture would be devastated by such a change. The early forms of automated flour grinding and threshing would be lost to us. There is even talk that they mean to question the exemptions to the technological restrictions — the terraforming technology that keeps the water and crops clean from the poisons of this planet."

"Isn't that a little insane?" asked Savon.

"The Moderates are countering with a bill for further exemptions," I explained. "To more adequately purify the water, and to allow off-world birthing technology to be utilised in restricted areas."

"For aristocrats only, you mean," Savon said in a hard voice.

I rolled my eyes. "It's a start. You can't tell me that Mars has a flaw-less record when it comes to biological freedoms."

"It's hardly the same."

"In any case," I cut him off, "the Lady Governor must appear to be beyond reproach in presiding over the House of Peers in their delib-eration of these bills. It would only take one slip for the Lumoscenti to declare her unfit for that role, and to put a far less moderate leader in her place."

"If she or a member of her family were caught openly flouting cur-rent laws...." Savon said.

"Exactly."

"You don't have to keep talking as if I weren't here," Conrad said be-tween gritted teeth. "I understand you perfectly."

Savon and I exchanged glances. "I should hope so," I said. "Your mother has done too much good work to be removed from office now, when we most need her."

"I've never been caught," he said in a sullen voice.

"It need only happen once," I snapped back. "Had you been to that establishment before?"

"Once or twice."

"And who brought you this time? During the most critical week of your mother's political career thus far? Who encouraged you to put her in such jeopardy? Whomever they are, Conrad, they are not your friend."

"Jules would not steer me wrong," he flung at me.

I paled. "Jules Gambon? Sainted Minerva, you little fool. He is the son of your mother's Minister of History and Religion. Should she fall from power, Marcel Gambon is one of the top three candidates to take her place, and all know that he is in the pocket of the Lumoscenti!"

"Jules took the same risk," said Conrad defensively. "His father would be just as affected by the activities of his son."

"Was Jules there, when the raid happened?"

The lad bit his lip. "He was joining us later."

I let my frosty silence let him know exactly what I thought of that.

"It was just coffee and games," Conrad protested. "It would not have cost my mother her position."

"It has already cost my mistress hers," I growled at him.

Savon gave me a startled look, and I regretted saying so much in front of him. I did not think he was a Lumoscenti spy — they despise offworlders — but in my anger I had been less than discreet.

"Do you really think Jules is working for his father?" Conrad asked after a few moments.

"The coincidence is too great to ignore."

"Then...." Conrad swallowed valiantly. "There is something you should know about Bianca. Jules arranged for she and some of her friends to be invited to a party hosted by Mme. Dray this evening."

I swore violently in Martian. La Duchesse and I had committed to saving the Lady Governor's son from scandal tonight. It had never occurred to us that we would have to do the same for her daughter.

∞

Drusus Savon's footman was working far longer hours than he might have expected. The carriage clattered to a silence in an alley near the river — a part of the city where one would never expect to find the daughter of an Honourable, let alone the daughter of a Lady Governor.

Mme. Lucilla Dray was one of those aristocrats people think of when they say, "gone to the bad." Most of the First Families of the planet enjoyed some form of scandalous behavior. Flirtations, adultery and the occasional dip into black market technology were all par for the course. Indeed, one needed a certain frisson of scandal in order to move in certain elegant circles.

But there were those who not only risked degradation and arrest, but openly invited it. Mme. Dray, the husband of a minor nobleman and daughter of a far grander aristocratic family, had been risking her neck in such a manner for twenty years. Her set were renowned for supplying all manner of illicit supplies to their friends and allies, and they had a particular knack for seducing children into their net of decadent activities.

The stories surrounding Mme. Dray were legendary — there was not a person nor creature in existence that was not rumored to have shared her bed at some time.

"Are you sure this is the right place?' Savon said doubtfully.

"The Baths of Clodius," confirmed Conrad.

The public baths had been constructed in the great cities of New Ceres back in the day when the settlers were merely attempting an ambience of historical aesthetics, rather than aiming for societal conformation. The Lumoscenti had no issues with them, as they belonged to an earlier rather than later time period than the one our society was attempting to emulate.

In general, the baths were reconciled with the "Eighteenth Century" mores by the simple solution of leaving them in the hands of the lower classes. Gentlemen were known to attend such places in order to meet with lovers and prostitutes; respectable ladies were not.

"The boy shouldn't be here," said Savon. "It's the height of folly to risk one of the Lady Governor's children to rescue the other."

"Bianca will not come away with either of you without making a fuss," Conrad argued.

"He's right," I agreed. "If we had La Duchesse with us, she could talk to the girl, but Bianca De Vries doesn't know either of us from a statue of Pan."

"All or nothing, then," said Savon.

∞

We stepped through the cool stone arches, and found several burly factotums barring our way. "Invitation only," said one.

I palmed a card that I showed him, but did not hand over. "Duchesse Claudine Augustille Recherche Dubois sends us with her compliments to attend upon Mme. Dray." It was a likely gamble. Mme. Dray had been attempting to cultivate La Duchesse for years, and regularly sent invitations to her.

My mistress's name conjured its usual magic, and we were waved through to a disrobing chamber. Every available surface was draped with clothing, not only the low garb and gentleman's suits that might be expected, but whole racks of fine ladies' gowns.

"Never mind the Lumoscenti," I said to Conrad, untying my cravat. "You do realise your sister will be socially ruined, if it is ever revealed that she attended this place?"

Gulping, Conrad pulled off his boots.

Savon gave me a darting sort of look, and conversed lightly with Conrad as they stripped. I knew why he was trying to keep the lad's attention away from me, and why he had given me the opportunity to send him away. It was hardly the time for it, but I was never going to have another opportunity to demonstrate so visibly that there was nothing for Savon to worry about. I removed every piece of my clothing, folded them all neatly, and waited by the doorway for my companions.

Savon looked up first, and had a violent coughing fit.

Conrad, skinny and vulnerable without his fine suit to bulk him, clapped the other man uncomfortably between the shoulder blades. "Are you well, Monsieur?"

"I'll live," gasped Savon.

"Let us not tarry," I said, motioning Conrad through the doors to the tepidarium beyond. "We have little time to waste."

I did not intend to give Savon a chance to talk to me without the boy overhearing, but he physically restrained me from following Conrad. "Where did you get that body?" he demanded, barely breathing the words aloud as he gripped my arm.

"I have a male name and a male body," I hissed back, concentrating all my energies on restraining my maleness from responding to the touch of his skin against mine. "What precisely, Monsieur, is the contradiction in that?"

"You are Philippa Cervantes, daughter of Dominic Cervantes," he accused. "You were born a woman on Mars."

"That was a long time ago," I replied. "I was a different person then, as you can probably tell."

Damn it, my cock had hardened. I was a bare inch from brushing his hip with it, which would hardly be conducive to civil conversation.

Conrad turned back, looking at us strangely, and Savon released my arm. He stared at me as if a stranger — though of course I was a stranger. We barely knew each other. His reaction was startling to say the least, and I considered it as we walked towards the lad. I was relieved when my body quieted once more, in the cool air and dancing green shadows of the tepidarium. "Are you going to tell my father?" I asked quietly, as we walked along.

Savon laughed shortly. "You think I want to be on the same planet as him when he finds out? No, M. Pepin. I have told you before. I do not work for your father, and I did not come to New Ceres looking for you."

"Then why are you here?" I asked, as we crossed into the next room of the baths. "You have lingered in and around Prosperine for six months, why?"

Conrad jerked in surprise, and I was just as startled. It should have been a caldarium — a steamy pool of water heated by pipes. Some liked to cool themselves first, then plunge into the heat, while others preferred the reverse.

Instead, the pool bubbled with hot, dark volcanic mud.

"I didn't realise Prosperine was built over actual mud springs," said Savon, and it did not escape my notice that he had avoided answering my question.

"It's not," I said. "The nearest spa is on the south east coast. They must have imported the stuff, to heat with the water piping system."

"Expensive," suggested Savon.

"Exorbitant," I agreed.

The next room was full of sand. Hot, marbled pink sand.

"Sacred Minerva," choked Conrad.

"Literally," I added. "Savon, this is Minervan sand."

He frowned. "Who would import sand between planets?"

"No one," I said. "Plants, yes — Minerva grows foodstuffs that New Ceres cannot. But no one trades interplanetary minerals in this kind of quantity."

"They imported white stone from the other worlds once, when there weren't enough light veins here to build the cities," said Conrad, trailing his fingers in a fortune to rival a Sultan's wet dream.

"By 'they' you mean the Government," I said shortly. "I doubt somehow that your mother and the Peers have moved into the business of indulging wayward socialites."

The sand shivered. As we watched, the grains danced and rose before our eyes, colliding upwards to form a solid giantess of a statue.

Mme. Lucilla Dray stood before us, carved from solid pink stone, teasing and joyful in her nakedness. She made every Venus nude I had ever seen look as modest as a Vestal Virgin. Her sand finger beckoned us closer.

"That is the most amazing thing I have ever seen," said Conrad in awe.

"Forget about the Lumoscenti," said Drusus Savon, his face and voice equally grim. "This is a matter for ITHACA." Without another word, he strode through to the next room.

Conrad looked at me, enquiring.

I sighed, giving up all hope of pretending I was a native New Ceresian. "The Interplanetary Taskforce of Humanity Against the Corruption of Aliens. The technology Mme. Dray used to create that little statue isn't just too recent to be legal on New Ceres. It's inhuman."

The tragedy of humanity was that we never managed to develop nanotech beyond theory and infant steps. Not in time to save the Earth from the aliens who ravaged and transformed our source planet to suit their own biology. Ironically, if New Ceres had nanotech, we could far more effectively mimic an eighteenth century society. Our own terraforming technologies were decidedly clunky and intrusive by comparison.

But the aliens only shared their wares when they wanted something in return. Earth learned that lesson, far too late. You never invite the bastards in.

When we caught up to Savon, he had located the party. A horde of languid bodies filled a wide gymnasium that overlooked the river. There was no music, no grapes or wine — none of the usual trappings of an orgy. Just naked people, streaked with mud and wet sand, tangled on the cold stone floor. Some were still lazily copulating, but most merely lay there, grinning at nothing, deliriously happy.

Conrad made a choking noise.

"Your sister wanted to be outrageous?" I said. "Looks like she found the right place for it."

"I didn't know it would be anything like this," he said, sounding sick. "Jules never.... I didn't know!"

"I think you'll be a little more careful in future, choosing your friends," I said.

Savon dug his fingernails into the underside of his right arm and pulled an implant sheath open, revealing a hidden cavity inside his flesh. "Take these now," he said, drawing a small container of pills out and handing them to me. "One each."

I didn't even hesitate, something I wondered about later. Just because this man held all my secrets was no reason for me to trust him, but I did. I flipped the container open and swallowed a tiny white grain, lifting another to Conrad's mouth. He licked it off, nervously. "What is that?"

"Antidote," said Savon. "The queens of their species exude a certain pheromone when they're pregnant. Humans get high on it, until the toxin levels reach their peak. Then their skin starts dissolving." He drew a small digital console from the compartment in his arm, and scanned the room with it.

"There's an alien here on New Ceres?" said Conrad, alarmed.

"A pregnant alien," said Savon. "Bask in the possibilities." His eyes were dark on mine. "If not for this comedy of errors tonight, I might never have happened across her. If the eggs hatch, the planet falls. You're a miracle, Pepin."

I shivered. "You're welcome."

Green light filtered through narrow slit windows in the gymnasium, moonlight bouncing off the green water of the river Prosperine.

Conrad was searching the bodies with distaste, looking for his sister.

"Where is it?" I asked, looking around. "Does it know we're here?"

Savon waded through the bodies as well, lifting limbs and hair to peer underneath. "She'll be small. The females of their species are tiny. Easier to conceal the eggs." He gave me a knowing look. "I expect the ones you met were male. They're a similar size to humans."

Demme it, he had figured out the last of my secrets. Trust me to reveal myself to the one man on New Ceres who knew alien technology when he saw it. La Duchesse would be slapping herself in the forehead if she could see how I had crumpled in the face of discovery.

I did not know enough to recognize an alien female or Conrad's sister. Instead, I stared out of the window slits, to the river below. A slow flotilla of golden ferryboats advanced upon us, across the green water. "Lumoscenti," I said, wondering if it still mattered.

"Bianca," yelled Conrad, sorting one limp human girl out from the mass of drugged flesh.

"This, I think, is for my custody," said Savon, staring down a small pearly slug that lay on the cold stone of the gymnasium floor. He scooped the slug up in a small forcefield that emanated from his hand console. "Pat yourself on the back, Pepin. We just saved your world."

"I'd like to be pleased about that," I said. "But we still have the Lady Governor's two children to save from a political scandal. Any more miracles in that arm of yours?"

"Oh, no," said Savon, relaxing into a wicked grin. "But I have a few ideas. We may want to get our clothes back on before this place fills up with priests."

Until that moment, I had not realised how alike he was to La Duchesse. That should have worried me more than it did, but instead I felt as if I were in the best of hands.

∞

The next morning, La Duchesse rose early, leaving her latest lover asleep in bed while she joined me for pastries and the *Prosperine Times* on the balcony of our hotel suite. "He's a sharp one, that Savon," she noted of the reportage about the night's events. "A kidnapping plot was an excellent explanation for the night's dramas. I particularly like the way he gave young Conrad the credit for rescuing his sister."

"And not a word of queen aliens or naked drug orgies," I replied, biting into a croissant.

"Mm," said La Duchesse. "I see that Jules Gambon is being questioned for his role in Bianca's kidnap — his father has preemptively disowned the boy."

"I don't think Jules or M. Gambon actually intended to aid an alien invasion," I said. "But it's hard to be sympathetic. They had no qualms about trying to destroy the reputation of the Lady Governor's children."

"Not that the brats didn't bring it on themselves," said my mistress.

"I was refraining from such a comment," I mumbled into my dish of chocolate.

La Duchesse smiled and stretched. "Well, no matter what the *Times* declares, I know whom the true hero of the hour was. I was impressed that Savon arranged for me to be released from La Policia's cells by midnight — and before they handed me over to the Lumoscenti, no less. I'm not quite sure how he convinced them that I was at the speakeasy to aid his investigations, but his documentation seemed to impress them."

"He has a smooth tongue, I'll give him that."

La Duchess gave me a covert look. "I'm not used to owing favors to men whom I'm not sleeping with."

"There's still time for you," I said brightly. "I'm not sure when he plans on leaving, but there isn't another flight offworld until at least this afternoon."

"I rather thought it was you he was interested in, my dear."

I did not meet her eyes. "Not after last night's revelations, I expect."

"Ah," she said, with a world of understanding in her voice. "He saw the secret matter, did he? Well, if he'll let a little thing like that get in the way...."

"Hah," I said, and ground my croissant into crumbs.

My mistress's lover joined us then: a tall lady with fair hair and a rather pointed nose. "M. Pepin," she said warmly. "I must thank you for your service last night — somewhat above and beyond the call of duty, I believe."

"Where my mistress leads, I follow," I said lightly, accepting the compliments with a bow of my head.

"Well, then, Pepin," said my mistress with a gleam in her eye. "I intend to spend the day in pleasure and indulgence. I entreat you do the same." With that, she hooked her arm into that of the Lady Governor, and took her back to bed.

∞

An hour later, a manservant brought a calling card on a salver, and I allowed M. Drusus Savon, Gentleman, to attend me in the suite's main parlour. As two men, we could meet without chaperone, and no one would blink an eye. How I should hate to be a woman on this planet, even one with the privilege and resources of La Duchesse.

Savon refused tea, or a glass of madeira. It was a little early in the morning, but I would have liked the excuse to imbibe, myself. His discomfort was making me nervous.

We made a pleasantry or two, and then silence fell between us. Finally, he abandoned all pretence that this was a social visit. "No scars. Your whole body shape...not even Martian microsurgery can produce those kind of results in sex change operations. Whatever changed you from a woman to a man is not human technology." It was not quite an accusation, but there was something in his voice I did not entirely recognize.

I spoke quietly, aware that we were not alone in the suite. "Do you speak as a friend? As a concerned citizen? Or as an agent of ITHACA?"

Savon blew out a long breath. "I think it must be evident that I am off duty. As you said last night, I would have a devil of a time proving my guess."

"I lied," I said. "You could prove it in an instant. DNA records, my birth tissues...I was not changed so totally as you might imagine. I am living evidence of the crime I committed. Receiver of alien technology is the official term, is it not? Certainly one of interest to the interplanetary judicial system."

"I'm not here to arrest you," said Drusus Savon, looking genuinely miserable. "I just want to understand. I thought you ran away from your father, not...your biology."

I took a deep breath. "On Mars, thanks to the Population Control and Dispersal statutes, every woman must bear a child. No exceptions, no allowances. Full citizenship, immigration, advanced education...none of these are possible without having acted as an incubator. A piece of machinery. Whereas a man can just jump on a ship whenever he chooses."

Savon paled. "They're on Mars? The things that did this to you are on Mars?"

"I left Mars on a falsified tourist visa," I assured him. "The...dealer, I suppose you would call it, approached me en route here. The irony had already struck me that I was running from the biological laws on Mars to a planet that had no birth control beyond lemon-soaked sponges. They played on my weakness, my insecurities. And I bought myself the only freedom I really wanted."

Savon stood, pacing the floor. "Didn't they have...less drastic solutions?"

"They did. I could have simply let them sterilise me. Demme, I didn't need aliens for that, there are planets where sterilisation is practically compulsory. But I wanted a disguise, as well." I ran my hands a little down my firm chest, laid them on my thighs. "This is what I wanted. I did not sell my soul for it but the price was high. And worth every credit point."

Savon stopped moving, remarkably still as he looked down at me. "We've been chasing and eliminating their freelance surgeons for years now. There aren't many left that offer the service you took — they're using other methods now, to infiltrate us. You're unlikely to ever find one to reverse the process."

I almost laughed, but swallowed it for the sake of his ego. Men do so hate to be mocked. "I don't want to go back. Not to Mars, not to Philippa's breasts and hips and ovaries. I like this body and who I am in it. I like the fact that people see me as male. It may be a little strange, but it works for me."

He looked at me as if trying to really see me — for the first time, though he was not entirely sure what, or who, he was hoping to see. Finally, he made his confession. "I came to this world to integrate with it, to learn how New Ceres worked so that I could be an effective agent here. That was my only remit. I could have gone anywhere on this world, but I have stayed in Prosperine because...." and here, he hesitated. I waited, every breath a struggle. "Because I wanted to see you again."

Breathing, it seemed, was indeed to be a difficult thing this morning.

"I was half in love with you," said Savon, seating himself again, deeply uncomfortable at this revelation. "When I thought you were a woman in disguise."

I leaned closer to him, close enough to touch without any effort. "I am a woman in disguise. But I will never let that disguise fall. I love it too much."

We sat there like that for an age. My whole body was aware of him. When he touched me, would it be as a man to a man, or as a man to a woman? I did not know which I was hoping for.

When he finally did touch me, I was too busy glorying in the moment to notice, one way or the other.

∞

THE FAERIE
CONY-CATCHER

Delia Sherman

In London town, in the reign of good Queen Bess that was called Gloriana, there lived a young man named Nicholas Cantier. Now it came to pass that this Nick Cantier served out his term as apprentice jeweler and goldsmith under one Master Spilman, jeweler by appointment to the Queen's Grace herself, and was made journeyman of his guild. For that Nick was a clever young man, his master would have been glad for him to continue on where he was; yet Nick was not fain thereof, Master Spilman being as ill a master of men as he was a skilled master of his trade. And Nick bethought him thus besides: that London was like unto the boundless sea where Leviathan may dwell unnoted, save by such small fish as he may snap up to stay his mighty hunger: such small fish as Nicholas Cantier. Better that same small fish seek out some backwater in the provinces where, puffed up by city ways, he might perchance pass as a pike and snap up spratlings on his own account.

So thought Nick. And on a bright May morning, he packed up such tools as he might call his own—as a pitch block and a mallet, and some small steel chisels and punches and saw-blades and blank rings of copper—that he might make shift to earn his way to Oxford. Nick put his tools in a pack, with clean hosen and a shirt and a pair of soft leather shoon, and that was all his worldly wealth strapped upon his back, saving only a jewel that he had designed and made himself to be his passport. This jewel was in the shape of a maid, her breasts and belly all one lucent pearl, her skirt and open jacket of bright enamel, and her fair face of silver burnished with gold. On her fantastic hair perched a tiny golden crown, and Nick had meant her for the Faerie Queene of Master Spenser's poem, fair Gloriana.

Upon this precious Gloriana did Nick's life and livelihood depend. Being a prudent lad in the main, and bethinking him of London's traps and dangers, Nick considered where he might bestow it that he fall not prey to those foists and rufflers who might take it from him by stealth or by force. The safest place, thought he, would be his codpiece, where no man nor woman might meddle without his yard raise the alarm. Yet the jewel was large and cold and hard against those softer jewels that dwelt more commonly there, and so Nick bound it across his belly with a band of linen and took leave of his fellows and set out northwards to seek his fortune.

Now this Nick Cantier was a lusty youth of nearly twenty, with a fine, open face and curls of nut-brown hair that sprang from his brow; yet notwithstanding his comely form, he was as much a virgin on that May morning as the Virgin Queen herself. For Master Spilman was the hardest of task-masters, and between his eagle eye and his adder cane and his arch-episcopal piety, his apprentices perforce lived out the terms of their bonds as chaste as Popish monks. On this the first day of his freedom, young Nick's eye roved hither and thither, touching here a slender waist and there a dimpled cheek, wondering what delights might not lie beneath this petticoat or that snowy kerchief. And so it was that a Setter came upon him unaware and sought to persuade him to drink a pot of ale together, having just found xii pence in a gutter and it being ill-luck to keep found money and Nick's face putting him in mind of his father's youngest son, dead of an ague this two year and more. Nick let him run on, through this excuse for scraping acquaintance and that, and when the hopeful Cony-catcher had rolled to a stop, like a cart at the foot of a hill, he said unto him,

"I see I must have a care to the cut of my coat, if rogues, taking me for a country cony, think me meet for skinning. Nay, I'll not drink with ye, nor play with ye neither, lest ye so ferret-claw me at cards that ye leave me as bare of money as an ape of a tail."

DELIA SHERMAN

Upon hearing which, the Setter called down a murrain upon milk-fed pups who imagined themselves sly dogs, and withdrew into the company of two men appareled like honest and substantial citizens, whom Nicholas took to be the Setter's Verser and Barnacle, all ready to play their parts in cozening honest men out of all they carried, and a little more beside. And he bit his thumb at them and laughed and made his way through the streets of London, from Lombard Street to Clerkenwell in the northern liberties of the city, where the houses were set back from the road in gardens and fields and the taverns spilled out of doors in benches and stools, so that toss-pots might air their drunken heads.

'Twas coming on for noon by this time, and Nick's steps were slower than they had been, and his mind dwelt more on bread and ale than on cony-catchers and villains.

In this hungry, drowsy frame of mind, he passed an alehouse where his eye chanced to light upon a woman tricked up like a lady in a rich-guarded gown and a deep starched ruff. Catching his glance, she sent it back again saucily, with a wink and a roll of her shoulders that lifted her white breasts like ships on a wave.

Nick gave her good speed, and she plucked him by the sleeve and said, "How now, my friend, you look wondrous down i' the mouth. What want you? Wine? Company?"—all with such a meaning look, such a waving of her skirts and a hoisting of her breasts that Nick's yard, fain to salute her, flew its scarlet colors in his cheeks.

"The truth is, Mistress, that I've walked far this day, and am sorely hungered."

"Hungered, is it?" She flirted her eyes at him, giving the word a dozen meanings not writ in any grammar. "Shall feed thy hunger then, aye, and sate thy thirst, too, and that right speedily." And she led him in at the alehouse door to a little room within, where she closed the door and, thrusting herself close up against him, busied her hands about his body and her lips about his mouth. As luck would have it, her breath was foul, and it blew upon Nick's heat, cooling him enough to recognize that her hands sought not his pleasure, but his purse, upon which he thrust her from him.

"Nay, mistress," he said, all flushed and panting. "Thy meat and drink are dear, if they cost me my purse."

Knowing by his words that she was discovered, she spent no time in denying her trade, but set up a caterwauling would wake the dead, calling upon one John to help her. But Nick, if not altogether wise, was quick and strong, and bolted from the vixen's den 'ere the dog-fox answered her call.

So running, Nick came shortly to the last few houses that clung to the outskirts of the city and stopped at a tavern to refresh him with honest meat and drink. And as he drank his ale and pondered his late escape, the image of his own foolishness dimmed and the image of the doxy's beauty grew more bright, until the one eclipsed the other quite, persuading him that any young man in whom the blood ran hot would have fallen into her trap, aye and been skinned, drawn, and roasted to a turn, as 'twere in very sooth a long-eared cony. It was his own cleverness, he thought, that he had smoked her out and run away. So Nick, having persuaded himself that he was a sly dog after all, rose from the tavern and went to Hampstead Heath, which was the end of the world to him. And as he stepped over the world's edge and onto the northward road, his heart lifted for joy, and he sang right merrily as he strode along, as pleased with himself as the cock that imagineth his crowing bringeth the sun from the sea.

And so he walked and so he sang until by and by he came upon a country lass sat upon a stone. Heedful of his late lesson, he quickly cast his eye about him for signs of some high lawyer or ruffler lurking ready to spring the trap. But the lass sought noways to lure him, nor did she accost him, nor lift her dark head from contemplating her foot that was cocked up on her knee. Her gown of gray kersey was hiked up to her thigh and her sleeves rolled to her elbows, so that Nick could see her naked arms, sinewy and lean and nut-brown with sun, and her leg like muddy ivory.

"Gie ye good-den, fair maid," said he, and then could say no more, for when she raised her face to him, his breath stopped in his throat. It was not, perhaps, the fairest he'd seen, being gypsy-dark, with cheeks and nose that showed the bone. But her black eyes were wide and soft as a hind's and the curve of her mouth made as sweet a bow as Cupid's own.

"Good-den to thee," she answered him, low-voiced as a throstle. "Ye come at a good hour to my aid. For here is a thorn in my foot and I, for want of a pin, unable to have it out."

The next moment he knelt at her side; the moment after, her foot was in his hand. He found the thorn and winkled it out with the point of his knife while the lass clutched at his shoulder, hissing between her teeth as the thorn yielded, sighing as he wiped away the single ruby of blood with his kerchief and bound it round her foot.

"I thank thee, good youth," she said, leaning closer. "An thou wilt, I'll give thee such a reward for thy kindness as will give thee cause to thank me anon." She turned her hand to his neck, and stroked the bare flesh there, smiling in his face the while, her breath as sweet as an orchard in spring.

Nick felt his cheek burn hot above her hand and his heart grow large in his chest. This were luck indeed, and better than all the trulls in London. "Fair maid," he said, "I would not kiss thee beside the common way."

She laughed. "Lift me then and carry me to the hollow, hard by yonder hill, where we may embrace, if it pleaseth thee, without fear of meddling eye."

Nick's manhood rose then to inform him that it would please him well, observing the which, the maiden smiled and held up her arms to him, and he lifted her, light as a faggot of sticks but soft and supple as Spanish leather withal, and bore her to a hollow under a hill that was round and green and warm in the May sun. And he lay her down and did off his pack and set it by her head, that he might keep it close to hand, rejoicing that his jewel was not in his codpiece, and then he fell to kissing her lips and stroking her soft, soft throat. Her breasts were small as a child's under her gown; yet she moaned most womanly when he touched them, and writhed against him like a snake, and he made bold to pull up her petticoats to discover the treasure they hid. Coyly, she slapped his hand away once and again, yet never ceased to kiss and toy with open lip, the while her tongue like a darting fish urged him to unlace his codpiece that was grown wondrous tight. Seeing what he was about, she put her hand down to help him, so that he was like to perish e'er he achieved the gates of Heaven. Then, when he was all but sped, she pulled him headlong on top of her.

He was not home, though very near it as he thrust at her skirts bunched up between her thighs. Though his plunging breached not her cunny-burrow, it did breach the hill itself, and he and his gypsy-lass both tumbled arse-over-neck to lie broken-breathed in the midst of a great candle-lit hall upon a Turkey carpet, with skirts and legs and slippered feet standing in ranks upon it to his right hand and his left, and a gentle air stroking warm fingers across his naked arse. Nick shut his eyes, praying that this vision were merely the lively exhalation of his lust. And then a laugh like a golden bell fell upon his ear, and was hunted through a hundred mocking changes in a ring of melodious laughter, and he knew this to be sober reality, or something enough like it that he'd best ope his eyes and lace up his hose.

All this filled no more than the space of a breath, though it seemed to Nick an age of the world had passed before he'd succeeded in packing up his yard and scrambling to his feet to confront the owners of the skirts and the slippered feet and the bell-like laughter that yet pealed over his head. And in that age, the thought was planted and nurtured and harvested in full ripeness, that his hosts were of faerie-kind. He knew they were too fair to be human men and women, their skins white nacre, their hair spun sunlight or moonlight or fire bound back from their wide brows by fillets of precious stones no less hard and bright than their emerald or sapphire eyes. The women went bare-bosomed as Amazons, the living jewels of their perfect breasts coffered in open gowns of bright silk. The men wore jewels in their ears, and at their forks, fantastic codpieces in the shapes of cockerels and wolves and rams with curling horns. They were splendid beyond imagining, a masque to put the Queen's most magnificent Revels to shame.

As Nick stood in amaze, he heard the voice of his coy mistress say, "'Twere well, Nicholas Cantier, if thou woulds't turn and make thy bow."

With a glare for her who had brought him to this pass, Nick turned him around to face a woman sat upon a throne. Even were she seated upon a joint-stool, he must have known her, for her breasts and face were more lucent and fair than pearl, her open jacket and skirt a glory of gem-stones, and upon her fantastic hair perched a gold crown, as like to the jewel in his bosom as twopence to a groat. Nick gaped like that same small fish his fancy had painted him erewhile, hooked and pulled gasping to land. Then his knees, wiser than his head, gave way to prostrate him at the royal feet of Elfland.

"Well, friend Nicholas," said the Faerie Queen. "Heartily are you welcome to our court. Raise him, Peasecod, and let him approach our throne."

Nick felt a tug on his elbow, and wrenched his dazzled eyes from the figure of the Faerie Queen to see his wanton lass bending over him. "To thy feet, my heart," she murmured. "And, as thou holdest dear thy soul, see that neither meat nor drink pass thy lips."

"Well, Peasecod?" asked the Queen, and there was that in her musical voice that propelled Nick to his feet and down the Turkey carpet to stand trembling before her.

"Be welcome," said the Queen again, "and take your ease. Peasecod, bring a stool and a cup for our guest, and let the musicians play and our court dance for his pleasure."

There followed an hour as strange as any madman might imagine or poet sing, wherein Nicholas Cantier sat upon a gilded stool at the knees of the Queen of Elfland and watched her court pace through their faerie measures. In his hand he held a golden cup crusted with gems, and the liquor within sent forth a savor of roses and apples that promised an immortal vintage. But as oft as he, half-fainting, lifted the cup, so often did a pair of fingers pinch him at the ankle, and so often did he look down to see the faerie lass Peasecod crouching at his feet with her skirts spread out to hide the motions of her hand. One she glanced up at him, her soft eyes drowned in tears like pansies in rain, and he knew that she was sorry for her part in luring him here.

When the dancing was over and done, the Queen of Elfland turned to Nick and said, "Good friend Nicholas, we would crave a boon of thee in return for this our fair entertainment."

At which Nick replied, "I am at your pleasure, Madam. Yet have I not taken any thing from you save words and laughter."

"'Tis true, friend Nicholas, that thou hast scorned to drink our Faerie wine. And yet hast thou seen our faerie revels, that is a sight any poet in London would give his last breath to see."

"I am no poet, Madam, but a humble journeyman goldsmith."

"That too, is true. And for that thou art something better than humble at thy trade, I will do thee the honor of accepting that jewel in my image thou bearest bound against thy breast."

Then it seemed to Nick that the Lady might have his last breath after all, for his heart suspended himself in his throat. Wildly looked he upon Gloriana's face, fair and cold and eager as the trull's he had escaped erewhile, and then upon the court of Elfland that watched him as he were a monkey or a dancing bear. At his feet, he saw the dark-haired lass Peasecod, set apart from the rest by her mean garments and her dusky skin, the only comfortable thing in all that discomfortable splendor. She smiled into his eyes, and made a little motion with her hand, like a fishwife who must chaffer by signs against the crowd's commotion. And Nicholas took courage at her sign, and fetched up a deep breath, and said:

"Fair Majesty, the jewel is but a shadow or counterfeit of your radiant beauty. And yet 'tis all my stock in trade. I cannot render all my wares to you, were I never so fain to do you pleasure."

The Queen of Elfland drew her delicate brows like kissing moths over her nose. "Beware, young Nicholas, how thou triest our good will. Were we minded, we might turn thee into a lizard or a slow-worm, and take thy jewel resistless."

"Pardon, dread Queen, but if you might take my jewel by force, you might have taken it ere now. I think I must give it you—or sell it you—by mine own unforced will."

A silence fell, ominous and dark as a thundercloud. All Elfland held its breath, awaiting the royal storm. Then the sun broke through again, the Faerie Queen smiled, and her watchful court murmured to one another, as those who watch a bout at swords will murmur when the less-skilled fencer maketh a lucky hit.

"Thou hast the right of it, friend Nicholas: we do confess it. Come, then. The Queen of Elfland will turn huswife, and chaffer with thee."

Nick clasped his arms about his knee and addressed the lady thus: "I will be frank with you, Serenity. My master, when he saw the jewel, advised me that I should not part withal for less than fifty golden crowns, and that not until I'd bought with it a master goldsmith's good opinion and a place at his shop. Fifty-five crowns, then, will buy the jewel from me, and not a farthing less."

The Lady tapped her white hand on her knee. "Then thy master is a fool, or thou a rogue and liar. The bauble is worth no more than fifteen golden crowns. But for that we are a compassionate prince, and thy complaint being just, we will give thee twenty, and not a farthing more. "

"Forty-five," said Nick. "I might sell it to Master Spenser for twice the sum, as a fair portrait of Gloriana, with a description of the faerie court, should he wish to write another book."

"Twenty-five," said the Queen. "Ungrateful wretch. 'Twas I sent the dream inspired the jewel."

"All the more reason to pay a fair price for it," said Nick. "Forty."

This shot struck in the gold. The Queen frowned and sighed and shook her head and said, "Thirty. And a warrant, signed by our own royal hand, naming thee jeweler by appointment to Gloriana, by cause of a pendant thou didst make at her behest."

It was a fair offer. Nick pondered a moment, saw Peasecod grinning up at him with open joy, her cheeks dusky red and her eyes alight, and said: "Done, my Queen, if only you will add thereto your attendant nymph, Peasecod, to be my companion, if she will."

At this Gloriana laughed aloud, and all the court of Elfland laughed with her, peal upon peal at the mortal's presumption. Peasecod alone of the bright throng did not laugh, but rose to stand by Nicholas' side and pressed his hand in hers. She was brown and wild as a young deer, and it seemed to Nick that the Queen of Elfland herself, in all her glory of moony breasts and arching neck, was not so fair as this one slender, black-browed faerie maid.

When Gloriana had somewhat recovered her power of speech, she said: "Friend Nicholas, I thank thee; for I have not laughed so heartily this many a long day. Take thy faerie lover and thy faerie gold and thy faerie warrant and depart unharmed from hence. But for that thou hast dared to rob the Faerie Queen of this her servant, we lay this weird on thee, that if thou say thy Peasecod nay, at bed or at board for the space of four-and-twenty mortal hours, then thy gold shall turn to leaves, thy warrant to filth, and thy lover to dumb stone."

At this, Peasecod's smile grew dim, and up spoke she and said, "Madam, this is too hard."

"Peace," said Gloriana, and Peasecod bowed her head. "Nicholas," said the Queen, "we commence to grow weary of this play. Give us the jewel and take thy price and go thy ways."

So Nick did off his doublet and his shirt and unwound the band of linen from about his waist and fetched out a little leathern purse and loosed its strings and tipped out into his hand the precious thing upon which he had expended all his love and his art. And loathe was he to part withal, the first-fruits of his labor.

"Thou shalt make another, my heart, and fairer yet than this," whispered Peasecod in his ear, and so he laid it into Elfland's royal hand, and bowed, and in that moment he was back in the hollow under the green hill, his pack at his feet, half-naked, shocked as by a lightening-bolt, and alone. Before he could draw breath to make his moan, Peasecod appeared beside him with his shirt and doublet on her arm, a pack at her back, and a heavy purse at her waist, that she detached and gave to him with his clothes. Fain would he have sealed his bargain then and there, but Peasecod begging prettily that they might seek more comfort than might be found on a tussock of grass, he could not say her nay. Nor did he regret his weird that gave her the whip hand in this, for the night drew on apace, and he found himself sore hungered and athirst, as though he'd sojurned beneath the hill for longer than the hour he thought. And indeed 'twas a day and a night and a day again since he'd seen the faerie girl upon the heath, for time doth gallop with the faerie kind, who heed not its passing. And so Peasecod told him as they trudged northward in the gloaming, and picked him early berries to stay his present hunger, and found him clear water to stay his thirst, so that he was inclined to think very well of his bargain, and of his own cleverness that had made it.

And so they walked until they came to a tavern, where Nick called for dinner and a chamber, all of the best, and pressed a golden noble into the host's palm, whereat the goodman stared and said such a coin would buy his whole house and all his ale, and still he'd not have coin to change it. And Nick, flushed with gold and lust, told him to keep all as a gift upon the giver's wedding-day. Whereat Peasecod blushed and cast down her eyes as would any decent bride, though the goodman saw she wore no ring and her legs and feet were bare and mired from the road. Yet he gave them of his best, both meat and drink, and put them to bed in his finest chamber, with a fire in the grate because gold is gold, and a rose on the pillow because he remembered what it was to be young.

The door being closed and latched, Nicholas took Peasecod in his arms and drank of her mouth as 'twere a well and he dying of thirst. And then he bore her to the bed and laid her down and began to unlace her gown that he might see her naked. But she said unto him, "Stay, Nicholas Cantier, and leave me my modesty yet a while. But do thou off thy clothes, and I vow thou shalt not lack for pleasure."

Then young Nick gnawed his lip and pondered in himself whether taking off her clothes by force would be saying her nay—some part of which showed in his face, for she took his hand to her mouth and tickled the palm with her tongue, all the while looking roguishly upon him, so that he smiled upon her and let her do her will, which was to strip his doublet and shirt from him, to run her fingers and her tongue across his chest, to lap and pinch at his nipples until he gasped, to stroke and tease him, and finally to release his rod and take it in her hand and then into her mouth. Poor Nick, who had never dreamed of such tricks, was like to die of ecstasy. He twisted his hands in her long hair as pleasure came upon him like an annealing fire, and then he lay spent, with Peasecod's head upon his bosom, and all her dark hair spread across his belly like a blanket of silk.

After a while she raised herself, and with great tenderness kissed him upon the mouth and said, "I have no regret of this bargain, my heart, whatever follows after."

And from his drowsy state he answered her, "Why, what should follow after but joy and content and perchance a babe to dandle upon my knee?"

She smiled and said, "What indeed? Come, discover me," and lay back upon the pillow and opened her arms to him.

For a little while, he was content to kiss and toy with lips and neck, and let her body be. But soon he tired of this game, the need once again growing upon him to uncover her secret places and to plumb their mysteries. He put his hand beneath her skirts, stroking her thigh that was smooth as pearl and quivered under his touch as it drew near to that mossy dell he had long dreamed of. With quickening breath, he felt springing hair, and then his fingers encountered an obstruction, a wand or rod, smooth as the thigh, but rigid, and burning hot. In his shock, he squeezed it, and Peasecod gave a moan, whereupon Nick would have withdrawn his hand, and that right speedily, had not his faerie lover gasped, "Wilt thou now nay-say me?"

Nick groaned and squeezed again. The rod he held pulsed, and his own yard stirred in ready sympathy. Nick raised himself on his elbow and looked down into Peasecod's face—wherein warred lust and fear, man and woman—and thought, not altogether clearly, upon his answer. Words might turn like snakes to bite their tails, and Nick was of no mind to be misunderstood. For answer then, he tightened his grip upon those fair and ruddy jewels that Peasecod brought to his marriage-portion, and so wrought with them that the eyes rolled back in his lover's head, and he expired upon a sigh. Yet rose he again at Nick's insistent kissing, and threw off his skirts and stays and his smock of fine linen to show his body, slender and hard as Nick's own, yet smooth and fair as any lady's that bathes in ass's milk and honey. And so they sported night-long until the rising sun blew pure gold leaf upon their tumbled bed, where they lay entwined and, for the moment, spent.

"I were well-served if thou shoulds't cast me out, once the four-and-twenty hours are past," said Peasecod mournfully.

"And what would be the good of that?" asked Nick.

"More good than if I stayed with thee, a thing nor man nor woman, nor human nor faerie kind."

"As to the latter, I cannot tell, but as to the former, I say that thou art both, and I the richer for thy doubleness. Wait," said Nick, and scrambled from the bed and opened his pack and took out a blank ring of copper and his block of pitch and his small steel tools. And he worked the ring into the pitch and, within a brace of minutes, had incised upon it a pea-vine from which you might pick peas in season, so like nature was the work. And returning to the bed where Peasecod lay watching, slipped it upon his left hand.

Peasecod turned the ring upon his finger, wondering. "Thou dost not hate me, then, for that I tricked and cozened thee?"

Nick smiled and drew his hand down his lover's flank, taut ivory to his touch, and said, "There are some hours yet left, I think, to the term of my bond. Art thou so eager, love, to become dumb stone that thou must be asking me questions that beg to be answered 'No'? Know then, that I rejoice in being thy cony, and only wish that thou mayst catch me as often as may be, if all thy practices be as pleasant as this by which thou hast bound me to thee."

And so they rose and made their ways to Oxford town, where Nicholas made such wise use of his faerie gold and his faerie commission as to keep his faerie lover in comfort all the days of their lives.

∞

PALIMPSEST

Catherynne M. Valente

16TH AND HIERATICA

A fortune-teller's shop: palm-fronds cross before the door. Inside are four red chairs with four lustral basins before them, filled with ink, swirling and black. A woman lumbers in, wrapped in ragged fox-fur. Her head amid heaps of scarves is that of a frog, mottled green and bulbous-eyed, and a licking pink tongue keeps its place in her wide mouth. She does not see individual clients. Thus it is that four strangers sit in the red chairs, strip off their socks, plunge their feet into the ink-baths, and hold hands under an amphibian stare. This is the first act of anyone entering Palimpsest: Orlande will take your coats, sit you down, and make you family. She will fold you four together like quartos. She will draw you each a card—look, for you it is the Broken Ship reversed, which signifies perversion, a long journey without enlightenment, gout—and tie your hands together with red yarn. Wherever you go in Palimpsest, you are bound to these strangers who happened onto Orlande's salon just when you did, and you will go nowhere, eat no capon or dormouse, drink no oversweet port that they do not also taste, and they will visit no whore that you do not also feel beneath you, and until that ink washes from your feet—which, given that Orlande is a creature of the marsh and no stranger to mud, will be some time—you cannot breathe but that they breathe also.

The other side of the street: a factory. Its thin spires are green, and spit long loops of white flame into the night. Casimira owns this place, as did her father and her grandmother and probably her most distant progenitor, curling and uncurling their proboscis-fingers against machines of stick and bone. There has always been a Casimira, except when, occasionally, there is a Casimir. Workers carry their lunches in clamshells. They wear extraordinary uniforms: white and green scales laid one over the other, clinging obscenely to the skin, glittering in the spirelight. They wear nothing else; every wrinkle and curve is visible. They dance into the factory, their serpentine bodies writhing a shift-change, undulating under the punch-clock with its cheerful metronomic chime. Their eyes are piscine, third eyelid half-drawn in drowsy pleasure as they side-step and gambol and spin to the rhythm of the machines.

And what do they make in this factory? Why, the vermin of Palimpest. There is a machine for stamping cockroaches with glistening green carapaces, their maker's mark hidden cleverly under the left wing. There is a machine for shaping and pounding rats, soft grey fur stiff and shining when they are first released. There is another mold for squirrels, one for chipmunks and one for plain mice. There is a centrifuge for spiders, a lizard-pour, a delicate and ancient machine which turns out flies and mosquitoes by turn, so exquisite, so perfect that they seem to be made of nothing but copper wire, spun sugar, and light. There is a printing press for graffiti which spits out effervescent letters in scarlet, black, angry yellows, and the trademark green of Casimira. They fly from the high windows and flatten themselves against walls, trestles, train cars.

When the shift-horn sounds at the factory, the long antler-trumpet passed down to Casimira by the one uncle in her line who defied tradition and became a humble hunter, setting the whole clan to a vociferous but well-fed consternation, a wave of life wafts from the service exit: moles and beetles and starlings and bats, ants and worms and moths and mantises. Each gleaming with its last coat of sealant, each quivering with near-invisible devices which whisper into their atavistic minds that their mistress loves them, that she thinks of them always, and longs to hold them to her breast.

In her office, Casimira closes her eyes and listens to the teeming masses as they whisper back to their mother. At the end of each day they tell her all they have learned of living.

It is necessary work. No family has been so often formally thanked by the city as hers.

∞

The first time I saw it was in the pit of a woman's elbow. The orange and violet lights of the raucous dancefloor played over her skin, made her look like a decadent leopardess at my table. I asked her about it; she pulled her sleeve over her arm self-consciously, like a clam pulling its stomach in.

"It's not cancer," she said loudly, over the droning, repetitive music, "I had it checked out. It was just there one day, popping up out of me like fucking track marks. I have to wear long sleeves to work all the time now, even in summer. But it's nothing—well, not nothing, but if it's something it's benign, just some kind of late-arriving birthmark."

I took her home. Not because of it, but because her hair was very red, in that obviously dyed way— and I like that way. Some shades of red genetics will never produce, but she sat in the blinking green and blue lights haloed in defiant scarlet.

She tasted like new bread and lemon-water.

As she drifted to sleep, one arm thrown over her eyes, the other lying open and soft on my sheets, I stroked her elbow gently, the mark there like a tattoo: a spidery network of blue-black lines, intersecting each other, intersecting her pores, turning at sharp angles, rounding out into clear and unbroken skin just outside the hollow of her joint. It looked like her veins had darkened and hardened, organized themselves into something more than veins, and determined to escape the borders of their mistress's flesh. She murmured my name in her sleep: Lucia.

"It looks like a streetmap," I whispered sleepily, brushing her hair from a flushed ear.

I dreamed against her breast of the four black pools in Orlande's house. I stared straight ahead into her pink and grey-speckled mouth, and the red thread swept tight against my wrist. On my leather-skirted lap the Flayed Horse was lain, signifying sacrifice in vain, loveless pursuit, an empty larder. A man sat beside me with an old-fashioned felt hat askance on his bald head, his lips deeply rosy and full, as though he had been kissing someone a moment before. We laced our hands together as she lashed us—he had an extra finger, and I tried not to recoil. Before me were two women: one with a green scarf wrapping thin golden hair, a silver mantis-pendant dangling between her breasts, and another, Turkish, or Armenian, perhaps, her eyes heavily made-up, streaked in black like an Egyptian icon.

The frog-woman showed me a small card, red words printed neatly on yellowed paper:

You have been quartered.

The knots slackened. I walked out, across the frond-threshold, into the night which smelled of sassafras and rum, and onto Hieratica Street. The others scattered, like ashes. The road stretched before and beyond, lit by streetlamps like swollen pumpkins, and the gutters ran with rain.

∞

212TH, VITUPERATION, SERAPHIM, AND ALPHABET

In the center of the roundabout: the Cast-Iron Memorial. It is tall and thin, a baroque spire sheltering a single black figure—a gagged child with the corded, elastic legs of an ostrich, fashioned from linked hoops of iron—through the gaps in her knees you can see the weeds with their flame-tipped flowers. She is seated in the grass, her arms thrown out in supplication. Bronze and titanium chariots click by in endless circles, drawn on runners in the street, ticking as they pass like shining clocks. Between her knock-knees is a plaque of white stone:

IN MEMORIAM:
*The sons and daughters of Palimpsest
who fought and fell in the Silent War.*

752-759
*Silent still
are the fields
in which they are planted.*

Once, though the tourists could not know of it, on this spot a thousand died without a gasp. Legions were volunteered to have their limbs replaced with better articles, fleeter and wiser and stronger and newer. These soldiers also had their larynxes cut out, so they could not give away their positions with an unfortunate cry, or tell tales of what they had done in the desert, by the sea, in the city which then was new and toddling. Whole armies altered thus wrangled without screams, without sound. In the center of the roundabout, the ostrich-girl died unweeping while her giraffe-father had his long, spotted neck slashed with an ivory bayonet.

Down the mahogany alleys of Seraphim Street, clothes shops line the spotless, polished road. In the window of one is a dress in the latest style: startlingly blue, sweeping up to the shoulders of a golden mannequin. It cuts away to reveal a glittering belly; the belt is fastened with tiny cerulean eyes which blink lazily, in succession. The whites are diamonds, the pupils ebony. The skirt winds down in deep, hard creases which tumble out of the window in a carefully arranged train, hemmed in crow feathers. The shopkeeper, Aloysius, keeps a pale green Casimira grasshopper on a beaded leash. It rubs its legs together while he works in a heap of black quills, sewing an identical trio of gowns like the one in the window for triplet girls who demanded them in violet, not blue.

At night, he ties the leash to his bedpost and the little thing lies next to his broad, lined face, clicking a binary lullaby into the old man's beard. He dreams of endless bodies, unclothed and beautiful.

∞

I can be forgiven, I think, for not noticing it for days afterward. I caught a glimpse in my mirror as I turned to catch a loose thread in my skirt—behind my knee, a dark network of lines and angles, and, I thought I could see, tiny words scrawled above them, names and numbers, snaking over the grid.

After that, I began to look for them.

I found the second in a sushi restaurant with black tablecloths—he was sitting two tables over, but when he gripped his chopsticks, I could see the map pulsing on his palm. I joined him—he did not object. We ate eels and cucumbers thinner than vellum and drank enough clear, steaming sake that I did not have to lean over to kiss him in the taxi. He smashed his lips against mine and I dug my nails into his neck— when we parted I seized his hand and licked the web of avenues that criss-crossed so: heart and fate lines.

In his lonely apartment I kissed his stomach. In his lonely apartment, on a bed without a frame which lay wretched between milk crates and cinder blocks, the moon shone through broken blinds and slashed my back into a tiger's long stripes.

In his lonely apartment, on a pillow pounded thin by dozens of night-fists, I dreamed. Perhaps he dreamed, too. I thought I saw him wandering down a street filled with balloons and leering gazelles—but I did not follow. I stood on a boulevard paved with prim orange poppies, and suddenly I tasted brandy rolling down my throat, and pale smoke filling up my lungs. My green-scarved quarter was savoring her snifter and her opium somewhere far from me. I saw the ostrich-child that night. I smelled the Seraphim sidewalks, rich and red, and traded, with only some hesitation, my long brown hair for the dress. Aloysius cut it with crystal scissors, and I walked over wood, under sulfurous stars, trailing dark feathers behind me. The wind was warm on my bare neck. My fingers were warm, too—my bald quarter was stroking a woman with skin like a snake's.

There were others. A man with a silver tooth—a depth-chart crawled over his toes. With him I dreamed I walked the tenements, raised on stilts over a blue river, and ate goulash with a veteran whose head was a snarling lion, tearing his meat with fangs savage and yellow. He had a kind of sign language, but I could only guess correctly the gestures for mother, southeast, and sleep.

There was a woman with two children and a mole on her left thigh—between her shoulder blades severe turns and old closes poked on an arrondissement-wheel. With her I dreamed I worked a night's shift in a restaurant that served but one dish: broiled elephant liver, soaked in lavender honey and jeweled with pomegranate seeds. The staff wore tunics sewn from peacock feathers, and were not allowed to look the patrons in the eye. When I set a shimmering plate before a man with long, grey fingers, I felt my black-eyed quarter pick up her golden fork and bite into a snail dipped in rum.

There was a sweet boy with a thin little beard—his thumb was nearly black with gridlock and unplanned alleys, as though he had been fingerprinted in an unnamable jail. He fell asleep in my arms, and we dreamed together, like mating dragonflies flying in unison. With him, I saw the foundries throwing fire into the sky. With him I danced in pearlescent scales, and pressed into being exactly fifty-seven wild hares, each one marked on its left ear with Casimira's green seal.

Lucia! They all cry out when they lie over me. Lucia! Where will I find you?

Yet in those shadow-stitched streets I am always alone.

I sought out the dream-city on all those skins. What were plain, yel-low-lined streets next to Seraphim? What was my time-clock stamp-ing out its inane days next to the jeweled factory of Casimira? How could any touch equal the seizures of feeling in my dreams, in which each gesture was a quartet? I would touch no one who didn't carry the map. Only once that year, after the snow, did I make an exception, for a young woman with cedar-colored breasts and a nose ring like a bull's, or a minotaur's. She wore bindi on her face like a splatter of blood. Her body was without blemish or mark, so alien and strange to me by then, so blank and empty. But she was beautiful, and her voice was a glass-cutting soprano, and I am weak. I begged her to sing to me after we made love, and when we dreamed, I found her dancing with a jackal-tailed man in the lantern-light of a bar that served butterfly-liquor in a hundred colors. I separated them; he wilted and slunk away, and I took her to the sea, its foam shattering into glass on the beach, and we walked along a strand of shards, glittering and wet.

When I woke, the grid brachiated out from her navel, its angles dark and bright. I smiled. Before she stirred, I kissed the striated lines, and left her house without coffee or farewells.

∞

QUIESCENT AND RAPINE

There are two churches in Palimpsest, and they are identical in every way. They stand together, wrapping the street-corner like a hinge. Sev-en white columns each, wound around with black characters which are not Cyrillic, but to the idle glance might seem so. Two peaked roofs of red lacquer and two stone horses with the heads of fork-tongued lizards stand guard on either side of each door. They were made with stones from the same quarry, on the far southern border of the city, pale green and dusty, each round and perfect as a ball. There is more mortar in the edifices than stones, mortar crushed from Casi-mira dragonflies donated by the vat, tufa dust, and mackerel tails. The pews are scrubbed and polished with lime-oil, and each Thursday, pa-rishioners share a communion of slivers of whale meat and cinnamon wine. The only difference between the two is in the basement—two great mausoleums with alabaster coffins lining the walls, calligraphied with infinite care and delicacy in the blood of the departed beloved contained within. In the far north corner is a raised platform covered in offerings of cornskin, chocolate, tobacco. In one church, the coffin contains a blind man. In the other, it contains a deaf woman. Both have narwhal's horns extending from their foreheads; both died young. The faithful visit these basement-saints and leave what they can at the feet of the one they love best. Giustizia has been a devotee of the Unhearing since she was a girl—her yellow veil and turquoise-ringed thumbs are familiar to all in the Left-Hand Church, and it is she who brings the cornskins, regular as sunrise. When she dies, they will bury her here, in a coffin of her own.

She will plug your ears with wax when you enter, and demand silence. You may notice the long rattlesnake tail peeking from under her skirt and clattering on the mosaic floor, but it is not polite to mention it—when she says silence, you listen. It is the worst word she knows.

The suburbs of Palimpsest spread out from the edges of the city proper like ladies' fans. First the houses, uniformly red, in even lines like veins, branching off into lanes and courts and cul-de-sacs. There are parks full of grass that smells like oranges and little creeks filled with floating roses, blue and black. Children scratch pictures of antelope-footed girls and sparrow-winged boys on the pavement, hop from one to the other. Their laughter spills from their mouths and turns to orange leaves, drifting lazily onto wide lawns. Eventually the houses fade into fields: amaranth, spinach, strawberries. Shaggy cows graze; black-faced sheep bleat. Palimpsest is ever-hungry.

But these too fade as they extend out, fade into the empty land not yet colonized by the city, not yet peopled, not yet known. The empty meadows stretch to the horizon, pale and dark, rich and soft.

A wind picks up, blowing hot and dusty and salt-scented, and gooseflesh rises over miles and miles of barren skin.

∞

I saw her in November. It was raining—her scarf was soaked and plastered against her head. She passed by me and I knew her smell, I knew the shape of her wrist. In the holiday crowds, she disappeared quickly, and I ran after her, without a name to call out.

"Wait!" I cried.

She stopped and turned towards me, her square jaw and huge brown eyes familiar as a pillow. We stood together in the rainy street, beside a makeshift watch-stand.

"It's you," I whispered.

And I showed my knee. She pursed her lips for a moment, her green scarf blown against her neck like a wet leaf. Then she extended her tongue, and I saw it there, splashed with raindrops, the map of Palimpsest, blazing blue-bright. She closed her mouth, and I put my arm around her waist.

"I felt you, the pipe of bone, the white smoke," I said.

"I felt the dress on your shoulders," she answered, and her voice was thick and low, grating, like a gate opening.

"Come to my house. There is brandy there, if you want it."

She cocked her head, thin golden hair snaking sodden over her coat. "What would happen, do you think?"

I smiled. "Maybe our feet would come clean."

She stroked my cheek, put her long fingers into my hair. We kissed, and the watches gleamed beside us, gold and silver.

∞

125TH AND PEREGRINE

On the south corner: the lit globes, covered with thick wrought-iron serpents which break the light, of a subway entrance. The trains barrel along at the bottom of the stairs every fifteen minutes. On the glass platform stands Adalgiso, playing his viola with six fingers on each hand. He is bald, with a felt hat that does not sit quite right on his head. Beside him is Assia, singing tenor, her smoke-throated voice pressing against his strings like kisses. Her eyes are heavily made-up, like a pharaoh's portrait, her hair long and coarse and black. His playing is so quick and lovely that the trains stop to listen, inclining on the rails and opening their doors to catch the glissandos spilling from him. His instrument case lies open at his feet, and each passenger who takes the Marginalia Line brings his fee—single pearls, dropped one by one into the leather case until it overflows like a pitcher of milk. In the corners of the station, cockroaches with fiber optic wings scrape the tiles with their feet, and their scraping keeps the beat for the player and his singer.

On the north corner: a cartographer's studio. There are pots of ink in every crevice, parchment spread out over dozens of tables. A Casimira pigeon perches in a baleen cage and trills out the hours faithfully. Its droppings are pure squid-ink, and they are collected in a little tin trough. Lucia and Paola have run this place for as long as anyone can remember—Lucia with her silver compass draws the maps, her exactitude radiant and unerring, while Paola illuminates them with exquisite miniatures, dancing in the spaces between streets. They each wear dozens of watches on their forearms. This is the second stop, after the amphibian-salon, of Palimpsest's visitors, and especially of her immigrants, for whom the two women are especial patrons. Everyone needs a map, and Lucia supplies them: subway maps and street-maps and historical maps and topographical maps, false maps and correct-to-the-minute maps and maps of cities far and far from this one. Look—for you she has made a folding pamphlet that shows the famous sights: the factory, the churches, the salon, the memorial. Follow it, and you will be safe.

Each morning, Lucia places her latest map on the windowsill like a fresh pie. Slowly, as it cools, it opens along its own creases, its corners like wings, and takes halting flight, flapping over the city with susurring strokes. It folds itself, origami-exact, in mid-air: it has papery eyes, inky feathers, vellum claws.

It stares down the long avenues, searching for mice.

∞

ANOTHER COMING

Sonya Taaffe

death's angel is my cousin but I never said
he was my favourite relative
—Phyllis Gotlieb, "Doctor Umlaut's Earthly Kingdom"

∞

Rain was still falling when she stepped off the tracks, walking the old railroad under a sky like newsprint too sodden to read. Down a bank of gravel and clinker, small scraping crunches underfoot as Acacia stepped carefully in the slick weather, the cool slanting mist that clung in her hair and made her skin feel clammy, spongy as something drowned; she could not wipe it off. The air smelled of earth, dark and chill, and faintly of smoke and iron. Freight echoes, from a time when these rails and ties had rattled daily under flatbeds, sleepers, ores and travelers stitching cities together; but the stitches had come out and only steel scars remained behind for Acacia to walk the right of way, a small tight-shouldered figure against the stingy trees, malt-colored hair trailing out of its braid and her eyes a little warmer than the wet bark around her in the cloud-melted light. Her stomach hurt, turned over and in on itself; she put both hands in the pockets of her long coat, Leo's borrowed oilskin, away from the insistent feeling of something minute and irretrievable—a fleck, a grain, pearl-grit—lodged deep within her flesh. *A riddle in nine syllables.* She would need several more to explain this.

Here the trains' cargo had come, where the trees gave onto a yard of scabbed asphalt and the buildings that had stood cold for longer than Acacia had been alive. Some abandoned industry, the shell and skeleton of a steel-driving age: high brick walls and each grid of close-set windows cracked inward or outward, cloudy glass still clinging in the frames like old ice, panes of glaucoma; skylights fallen in around the steel braces, flat stretches of tarry gravel for the remaining roofs and some of the gutters still copper and sallow green. Even the company's name, high on one time-blackened face of brick, had worn off over the neglected decades; ground to illegible traces of block-lettered paint, replaced by graffiti, ivy, and the amorphous scripts of lichen and acid rain. Acacia had never seen anyone else inside, though sometimes she found the leftovers of trash-barrel fires below the catwalks and flaking presses, the detritus of bottles and cans as everpresent as dust or oxidation. Only Quince, or Leo, or herself: footsteps in oil stains and shadow, disturbing a country of obsolescence and rusted memory.

Quince was smoking under the scant overhang of a loose gutter, birch-bleached hair shaved down to pinfeather fuzz and her eyes half-closed against the shapeless, watercolor light. Black raincoat wrapped to her knees, heeled boots strapped and buckled mid-calf, she made an incongruous package among the corroded, autumn-colored wreckage: one foot angled up against the rain-worn bricks, the other planted in weeds and ash-brown grasses; rain dripped past her shoulders and she turned her head slightly at Acacia's approach, no more movement anywhere than that, no more sound than the wind dividing itself through broken teeth of glass, empty doorways and the spaces where stairs used to be.

"I thought you might have come out here first." She dropped her other foot to the ground and came forward just enough to meet Acacia: a needless, neighborly gesture. All the bones of her face were exact, fluid, fared into one another as adroitly as joinery or etching, expressions done silverpoint on her pale skin. She moved in a cloud of cloves and old burning, like incense in the matte folds of her coat and her fine, close down of hair where rain glittered now; under the smoke, her skin gave off its own edged musk that made Acacia think, not unpleasantly, of civet cats and other predatory, perfumed creatures.

"Every now and then, I'm wrong. But you've made me right, now that you're here yourself—what have you done with Leo?"

"I was going to ask you that." Even as she tried to make the words into a smile, Acacia heard them pouncing, defensive, the question spun too quickly back at Quince in her private atmosphere of silver-streaked air and smoke. Her pulse was jammed in her throat, a dam for words. She considered asking Quince for a drag, an old nervous reflex that still dried the back of her mouth; but Quince was stubbing out her cigarette against the brick, and Acacia had never smoked after high school. "He left late last night, before you got back. Before I thought you'd get back," wondering briefly where Quince had slept, in whose arms, and how it never mattered. Leo and Acacia, the two faces of Quince's coin: one was as true as the other. Tears burned abruptly behind her eyes and she said, "I haven't seen him all morning. We had a conversation. I thought you might have."

"No." Restless, Quince knocked one heel against the cindery ground, looked slantwise at Acacia. In the overcast, drowned-grey clarity of light, she had a child's lucid complexion; blackish brows and lashes limning her eyes like a mask. "But tell me how you're using that word *conversation*. It has uneasy echoes."

The words were easier to say than she had feared: repetition, she thought bitterly, practice. "I'm pregnant." Dead air; rain on industrial ruins. "We talked about that."

At a distance, Quince's eyes were indefinitely dark; up close, they changed and became differentiable, shades and textures of dark, as telling and legible as a blush, a pallor, a frown. Her voice was as impenetrable as the bricks at her back. "It must be his."

Leo's skin, like honey in the light, silk and ivory in the dark; all the words of sculpture and artistry that she used as shorthand for sensation, the touches and tastes of him, long watered-honey eyes and the feel of hard velvet under her hand; and Quince, laughing above or below them, her small breasts and her scars and her graceful hips, entering, entered, her seed as sharply aromatic as her flesh— Acacia shook her head. "I'm not sure."

"You can't have mine." Now Quince was shaking her head, denial in return; she had a silver stud in her left ear, gold in her right. *My brother, good morning: my sister, good night....* Her voice tipped slightly, a note sharp. "It's got to be his."

Acacia discovered her arms crossed low, almost around her belly and the invisible weight within, and jerked them back to her sides. "I said, I'm not sure." Her voice had gone ragged much faster than she expected, the unreliable ease flaking from her words like rust or dried blood, chips of brick from the wall that Quince slammed her hand up against, flat-palmed, percussive smack of meat and she swore between her teeth as Acacia said fiercely, "I haven't had any tests done—"

"You can't!" Only in bed, in the warm chaos of caring and desire, had Acacia seen Quince as unguarded, as intense: perhaps as frightened. "You fucking can't, Acacia. Not my child. It's not—"

"Not what, possible?" Between breath and word, she was shouting. Catching fire from each other, reflecting like always: she no longer felt the cold. "You're not any more possible, what does that matter? Quince, it's either yours or Leo's, and it's mine!" Less than five minutes, and things were already splintering: *the center cannot hold* and the poetry, immediate and familiar as a second language, was no comfort now. Quince shook her reddening hand, stared at Acacia. Rain sharpened on brick and battered glass, the sound of knives. "It doesn't matter," Acacia said quietly, around the hurt in her throat that might have been shouting and might have been her heart, "how much you want it not to be true. You can leave, Leo can leave. But I'm still pregnant. Tell me later why you don't want it. I don't really want to talk anymore right now."

She kicked aside a thin rubble of broken concrete as she walked away, dry clatter and a metallic ricochet off the grating up ahead; the nearest set of doors stood ajar, unlocked slabs that ground orange-rind rust into her palms as she pulled them open, damp and a deserted, erosion smell in the soot-colored shadows beyond. Dishwater light crossed overhead, filtered through broken layers onto metal beams and disused machineries, the good salvage and scrap sold long ago. She did not think she had really expected Quince to follow her. Still she looked back, through the doorway to the space where Quince was no longer smoking, once: neither salt nor dead shade, but the underworld that trapped, the burning disaster.

She had walked home from the clinic in rich, late afternoon, clouds like rough marble shoaled above the skyline for the sun to slide around and turn the air to fire. Pigeons rose up from the roofs, the flock lifting in one noisy-winged, furling curve against the sky; a skinny tree on the corner, potted in cement and spoked iron, was putting out buds that Acacia stopped and fingered for a moment, germination swelling cool and rough under her touch. Even the storm grate smelled like approaching spring, clean and humid, as she passed. *Do you want to make a follow-up now?* the doctor had asked, a neat short-haired woman as bristly grey as a fledging bird, and Acacia had ducked her head and mumbled something indistinct about talking to the father, getting back to her; the sickly knot in her stomach winding tighter and colder as the woman spoke, and she wondered if morning sickness would give her enough excuse to throw up on the white-tiled floor. A promise got out of her mouth instead, *I'll call tomorrow.* Keys cold in her hand, she unlocked the front door and went up without turning on the light, bare bulb hanging in a sphere of silver wires at the top of the stairs, aesthetically caged.

Leo was at his desk in the living room, among the more portable and less fragile aspects of his work: assistant curator buried in manuscripts and orreries and cracked icons, cataloguing, cleaning, running for coffee, and sometimes his glasses had a fur of dust around the rims. He twisted around in his chair at the click of the lock, one arm braced across the overstuffed back, a manila folder in his other hand raised in familiar, puzzled salute; the long-sleeved T-shirt he wore, *If you're a Goth, where were you when we sacked Rome?* in white capitals on black, Acacia had bought for him when he got the museum job. *There's tea in the kitchen,* he said easily, as if he had not expected her home until much later, *but it's herbal*; and when she only stood with her jacket in her arms, staring at the hardwood joins underfoot—polished with years and bare feet, the color of fresh bread, and she thought about kneeling to lay her hand against their fine-grained shine and feel where the cracks were—he put down the folder and walked across the small carpets until he could put his hands on her shoulders and ask, *Acacia? What happened?* No good way to start the conversation, though her skin flamed under his palms; no beautiful seams of language for this moment. Haltingly, she said, *I went to the doctor's,* and watched Leo's expression change.

Light like antique gold sloped through the window and made his hair a corona, his face a painted mask of the sun: a frustrated summer-god, a bewildered star. But constellations never stared down from heaven and said, *Oh, fuck. Weren't we safe? Didn't you use anything?*

I always—oh, fuck. Fuck. I can't deal with this, and Acacia had never seen a solar myth come to adolescent pieces before her eyes. She tried to touch him, his name thrown out like a line for him to hold, *Leo,* but he was too lost in some nightmare of responsibility, already running too far and too fast for anything other than distant light to reach him. *I have to think about this,* he said, sometime much later when she had run out of tears, cried herself into a sore throat and spasms that he would have soothed any other time, if she had been crying for any other reason. Instead she curled in a feral tangle of sheets and tried to pin her breath down again, gulping, dry-heaving tears, head buried in her arms to keep him out of her peripheral vision. *Acacia; Acacia? Listen to me, Acacia, please, I have to think about this. I have to talk to Quince. I have to—oh, my God, I have to talk to my parents. I can't. I'm sorry, I'm so sorry,* and she heard the bedroom door shut even before he finished saying *sorry.*

She must have slept; she woke to dull cloud-light, mouth sticky and salt grit in her eyes, the blinds making tambourine noises in a wind that tasted of storms. When she sat up, the emptiness of the apartment settled around her as the chill had not. She got out of bed in a movement as convulsive as a shudder. With oils and a fine brush, Quince had half-blinded all the apartment's mirrors, so that Acacia's passing reflection looked back in slices and fragments from among brilliant, blasphemous tableaux. In a glade of burning green leaves, a naked woman accepted a crimson globe mouth-to-mouth from an androgyne plumed in rainbow-slick scales; another woman stood, bloody-handed, one fist still clenched around an ear of pulped, dripping grain, above her sister sprawled in her sacrifice's blood; sheep, horses, flailing human figures sank beneath choking cobalt waves that tossed afloat a ship full of fabulous, archaic beasts. Over the dresser in the bedroom, a female figure whose wings were made of flames and calligraphy stooped like a hawk to embrace a male figure that looked upward, dumbstruck, lovestruck, ready. *Gaze no more in the bitter glass*: as if her heart would have given her any better suggestion.

She smelled Quince before she heard her lover's boots on the cement, musk and sweet burning almost tangible from where she stood; she unbent from memory slowly. Spray-painted tags littered this side of the wall, the browned scaffolding overhead and the nailed-up plywood blocking another door: an archaeology of graffiti, vivid strata she could not read. Once Leo had pretended to translate some for her, charting the dynastic rise and fall of urban legends. Apple-green glass fanned in a brittle, glinting spray about her feet. Without turning her head, Acacia said, "Why don't you want a child?"

Quince's voice was a breath at her back, glancing, recitative, not soothing. "When men began to increase on earth," she said, "and daughters were born to them, the sons of God saw how beautiful the daughters of men were, and took wives from among those that pleased them...." Glass cracked under her heel; half a step away, Acacia felt Quince's nearness working its way into her own skin, loosening muscles, burnishing nerves, until she waited for Quince's mouth at the curve of her neck, telling story into her skin, Quince's hands holding her close against hard-budded breasts and the press of desire at her groin. She had always courted Acacia with myths and mysteries. Still she held herself tightly away from even the air that eddied around Quince, breathing rain and spices and the familiar scents that meant comfort, need, companionship: nothing safe. Leo had smelled like sweet salt and brittle pages, and that had not stopped him. Then Quince's voice slanted, wryer and less ritual—"The sons of men were also pretty beautiful"—and something untwisted beneath Acacia's breastbone. That first day, summer in the creamy marble shadow of the museum where Leo did not yet work, where Acacia was looking at Leighton and Rosetti, Quince had given her the same sideways truth: the low-voiced speaker coming up behind her as she perused studies for John Singer Sargent's *Annunciation* and Acacia turning around to interrupt, *Unless I've really got the story wrong, it's not Gabriel's kid,* and look at Quince, and consider whether Mary had ever wished otherwise.

Rain dripped through cracked slates and girders, little sounds in the hollow space, as negligible as the details of Quince's strangeness had always been: inexplicable and no one asked for answers. But Acacia had one already, that she had not wanted to hear. She said, a thin ache of a word, "So?"

"So," Quince said, "so," and nothing else.

Glass shone under both their feet, little more than reflection and razor edges in the dimness. Acacia's fingers twisted in her hair, under her braid where loose, rain-curled strands had inked themselves to the back of her neck; one snapped and pain wired into her scalp, and she had to close her throat against the sound that wavered too close to tears for the minor, momentary hurt. Under Quince's regard or indifference, and she would not know unless she looked, she felt scraped raw at the surface, pressures inside and outside wearing her to little more than a shivering handful of tears wrapped around less than a handful of life. *Some kneeling girl with passionless pale face*, that museum afternoon. She wanted desperately not to say whatever would come next; she took her hand out of her hair, and turned around.

Quince's eyes were the darkness of desolation, sounded and known, and water brimmed along her lower lids. The clotted light turned her skin to dusted stone, ancient paper, blank; she looked neither old nor young but unreal, and a sudden chill sank in Acacia's stomach. At once, she wanted the tagged bricks to crumble dryly, let her through as she backed against them and out into the drowning, rain-swept day; she wanted to lean forward and lick at the sweat shining at Quince's temple, salt and the crisp, feathering brush of Quince's hair against her lips; or, simplest of all, to uncross her arms and open them so that Quince, if she wanted, could move into their circle and rest there until she was no longer terrifying, terrified, full of tears. But Quince was saying, "It's not safe," and Acacia would be dead and dust before light crossed that space between them.

"Not safe how?" she asked anyway, because she could not touch Quince and Leo had never waited to have this conversation. "For me? Or you mean the child?" Quince's arms were as tightly folded as Acacia's, pale fists tucked under black-leather elbows; her mouth admitted nothing. "Quince.... You keep saying *can't*, like that fixes everything. But if there's any chance, if there's some kind of problem, you have to tell me. If I carry this child, if it's yours, is there going to be something wrong with it? It'll have birth defects, it'll be retarded, psychotic," she was biting off the words like bitter stalks, "what?"

"Like me," Quince said tautly, "and like you. And that's forbidden."

"What?"

"They drowned in the Flood, all the children of men and angels. And there have been no more since. All the beautiful monsters"—one corner of her smoky mouth crooked upward, very slightly—"long before Leo's reliquaries and papyri, those ferns and fossils down the block— or maybe long after or somewhere in between. Somewhere else, it doesn't really matter. Here, now: no more. The universe would not permit it. The laws of physics and angels don't allow."

A desert in her mouth: teeth to tongue to palate like a cleavage of dust and wax. "You're grander than Leo, after all. He only thinks this will destroy his life."

"It's raining," Quince whispered. Her face was not an icon. When she moved forward, tines of shadow passed over her face like expressions, writing, rewriting; a palimpsest. "Not by water, not again—there was a promise. But still, it keeps me thinking. Oh, my love," and her hands touched Acacia's shoulders so lightly that she might have been an echo of Leo, a ghost frozen to this conversation in a flash of time. Recursive, while it rained: a shiver went like a shockwave over Acacia's skin and she could not imagine that Quince had not felt it. One hand angled briefly upward to cup the back of Acacia's head, fingers sliding through her tight-gathered hair; returned to her shoulder, the point of her pulse, blood for two circling through her veins now. "Oh, God. Acacia. It had better not be my fucking child."

The air smelled of ozone and myrrh. Quince's thumb caressed the shallow rise of her collarbone, sweet dry warmth against her sweating skin; the movement relaxed Acacia no more than Quince's remote gaze, the change of dark in her eyes that Acacia could not read. Something pushed hard into her throat, horror or laughter; words came out instead. "Stop this. Just stop. You and Leo.... I haven't been struck by lightning; his parents haven't disowned him; I don't care. Let it be nobody's child. Just mine. There's nothing else to say."

"You don't understand. I love you," and before Acacia could answer, Quince's hands stilled. She might have smiled like this for the sight of world's end, a sky full of fire and ash. "I can't even take the chance."

Acacia drew breath to shout again, and stopped. "Quince—" But Quince's fingers were pressing silence into her throat, tightening with less pain than burning where she should have breathed and a distant, gathering roar like thunder rending the air open, a wave toppling toward the shore. Her vision swam red and dark: the blind landscape of the womb. "Don't...." She could not even hear the noises she made.

"If you aren't sure, I can't. Please." Quince's voice heaved like Acacia under her hands, driven and cornered, trapped as the breath that she could not catch; her shoulder struck plywood, glass bit into her knees, and she could as easily have wrenched free of Quince as her heart from her bursting chest. She could not see Quince's face clearly anymore, nor the ruined walls beyond, old before Acacia was born and how many cities had Quince seen rise and fall? Her lungs threshed for air. The fountains of the deep; forty days' deluge. Nothing to salvage, this time. "Just tell me it's Leo's."

Her fingers pried at Quince's wrists, like clawing at marble with her nails. There was nothing in her left to whisper with, no air, no thought; she heard her own voice like something pinched from sand, from the gravel ballast scattered beneath the old tracks that she had followed here, a path of stones into darkness. "It could be Leo's," and before the fingers could loosen, her vision clear and the choking fire in her throat turn to air again, she got the words out. "And it could be yours."

The darkness crushed down on her.

But now I know
That twenty centuries of stony sleep
Were vexed to nightmare by a rocking cradle....

Rain was falling on her face, freshwater cold that tasted faintly bitter as tarpaper and smoke, salt drops warm as the amniotic sea where a pearl of flesh drifted, moored between worlds. Far above her, against the wrung-out wash of sky and shrouded sun, someone was saying, "Fuck me," over and over, like a prayer. Her throat was full of cinders. Half in Quince's arms, her head fallen back against Quince's shoulder and a freezing glaze of rainwater seeping into her jeans, Acacia blinked and tried to speak, made a noise like breath ceasing. Quince's arms tightened around her, eased as she struggled, spasmodic in a terror that sluiced out of her as abruptly as her strength; she heard Quince's voice, half-crying and hasty, "I won't, fuck me to God, Acacia, I won't!" and a different darkness slipped up over her before she tasted Quince's tears again.

She opened her eyes to clouds like wet slate, sun sliding toward evening and the rain still as cold, Quince's arms wrapped close about her and her throat just enough less ravaged for Quince's name. It might have been a question.

"I don't know." This voice had never whispered to her in bed, in a museum, over tea; Quince had never shivered like this. Answer and denial at once, "I don't know. If it's mine...."

Acacia said softly, "Mine." As suddenly and unconditionally as a small child, she wanted Leo; she wondered if he would hold her through that word, single and irrevocable; if it would make a difference. "The others?"

Quince's throat jerked, a swallow of nothing like a flinch. "I have no children."

A scrape of ash in her mouth. "You *are* a monster."

One of Quince's brows raked an amused, caustic angle; she bent as though to kiss Acacia's forehead, stopped. "I've never been anything else. Not in this world, how could I be?" Her face was very quiet. "And you never thought I was."

"No...." Acacia shifted in Quince's arms, enough to see her profile like weather-carved stone against the flat brick facade, punched-out windows and hanging gutters, motionless as rain traced her parted lips: a gargoyle from a painted mirror, a shadow of cataclysm at the back of her eyes. The question faded on her tongue, unasked; she said instead, "I don't accept a God that would ruin the world for anything as beautiful as your child."

Momentarily, Quince's smile was real and rare as a falling star. "As beautiful as your child, too. You've never believed that: that you are beautiful. I must have told you enough times. You and Leo, you amaze me, always. Even now." The smile slid away with the rain. "Especially now." Wind drew damp nails over Acacia's skin and she waited beneath Quince's silence, her gaze as distant as when Acacia had come up to her beneath the gutter, centuries ago, no time at all: the messenger. "This I know: fire, water, fucking locusts, it doesn't matter in the end. This place, that you like so much? Times change. Everything falls apart, sooner or later—rusts, dies, dissolves, decays—and nothing, no matter how cunning, how profitable, how lovely, lasts." Quince's voice was very soft, her body where Acacia leaned very still. "Nothing."

"Yes," Acacia said, as softly. "I know." But she lay in Quince's arms anyway, for this moment, and they watched the rain fall.

∞

BLEAKER COLLEGIATE PRESENTS AN ALL-FEMALE PRODUCTION OF *WAITING FOR GODOT*

Claire Humphrey

I stanch the blood with a handful of toilet paper. Red wicks through the white, and then the paper wilts and shreds. I toss the mess in the bin.

I breathe through my mouth. I lean over the sink and watch my blood splash down and diffuse into the water from the running tap.

The door swings in and shoves me against the countertop.

Swearing: Ginevra's voice. She stops when she meets my eyes in the mirror.

"Crap, Deirdre. Not again."

I shrug.

"You're going to the doctor, right?" Ginevra says.

"Next week."

"...'Cause that's not normal."

"I'm not normal," I tell her, thickly.

On another day, she'd comfort me. She'd walk me to the nurse's office, or call my dad to come pick me up. Today, she's already in make-up, and alight with nerves. She smells of cigarettes and Noxzema. Her fingers touch the back of my neck, then skate away.

"I go on in an hour," she says, brushing past me and into a stall.

"Break a leg," I say.

I hear her jeans unzip, and a moment later the clink of her belt buckle hitting the floor.

I turn away, look down. My hand has been fiddling with my ballpoint. Blue scribbles mar the cuff of my jacket; they almost make a word.

I don't know what else I'll say to Ginevra if I stay. I leave her and walk out into the rain.

One hour until curtain. Two dollars and eighty cents in my jacket pocket; a few cigarettes, a pack of gum. Nothing to eat, but I'm not hungry anyway.

Rainwater collects on my hair and runs from the lank tips onto my forehead and down to my chin. My jean jacket soaks through and turns stiff. I turn my face up into the downpour: at least it can rinse some of the blood from my skin.

Maybe it's the chill, or maybe it's just time, but I think the bleeding is slowing.

I start toward the Bleaker Public Library as the rain slackens. As I reach the crosswalk, at the uppermost limit of my field of view, black birds cross the sky, one and one and one. When I tilt my face back a little to watch them, blood runs down over my upper lip and into my mouth.

∞

Making friends with Ginevra was like taming a stray cat. First I started hanging around in areas where she might be found. If she showed, I didn't approach her. I just stood there, smoking, or I read something, glancing at her secretly from behind my hair. Then I started catching her eye once in a while. Then I started smiling.

Then I started dating Christopher Potter; I dumped him after a few weeks, but that got me introduced to Pete Janaczek, which got me the invite to Pete's party, which got me in the same room as Ginevra while she was tipsy and expansive, and then—finally—it happened.

All that was a lie, you know. As if I could plan anything like that. It's only in hindsight that I realize why I started spending time in the smoke-hole in the first place. So many of the things we do, we keep from ourselves.

∞

She told me the playwright was so much against the idea of his piece being performed by women that when someone in the Netherlands tried it, he banned the entire country from putting on his plays.

"Why are you doing it, then? Aren't you afraid he'll ban Canada too?"

"He's dead. Too bad: it would be great press for us," Ginevra said. She bit off the thread, put away the needle, and showed me what she'd been doing: adorning my jean jacket with a Violent Femmes badge.

I resolved to go out and buy the album as soon as she left.

∞

I lock myself in the handicapped bathroom at the Bleaker Public Library, and I kneel under the hand-dryer. In the rush of hot air, the last trickles of blood dry to sharp crusts within my nostrils. When I look in the mirror to gingerly prod them out, I see that I'm a strange colour, like old newsprint.

I always thought pallor would be more attractive. I think I've been imagining pale people as if they were made of marble, delicately veined and smooth: not this chafed and flaking skin, with all the moles and hairs brought into sharp contrast, and the leftover summer's tan yellowing me like dirty ivory.

I've got blood on my jacket, too. As if the Violent Femmes weren't enough.

Without warning, it comes again. No pain this time, just a hot gush down my face as the pressure overwhelms whatever fragile membrane held it back.

I slam my forehead into the paper towel dispenser in my hurry to reach the sink. That bleeds, too. In fact all this bleeding is making me feel spacy enough that I sit down on the toilet seat with my head on the sink, and I do nothing at all but wait.

After a while I'm not bleeding any more, and I get myself upright slowly, like a person with a truly vile hangover.

For some reason, I'm not using my left hand. I look at it, and discover I'm holding my pen again, in a bit of a death grip. I set it on the counter before I can make it explode, and begin the lengthy and awful process of cleaning myself up.

∞

The theatre is called a black box, because it is both of those things, and nothing else. Its stage is bare but for a dead sapling planted in a bucket, and a diffuse light coming down from the grid.

I've been up there: up through the trap door in the booth. I've spent a half-hour unhooking fresnel lights from the rack and handing them to people, because I couldn't make myself edge out from the wall onto the grid itself, so far above the stage. If we had to hook our wrenches to our belts, I thought, why didn't we have to hook ourselves to anything?

My stomach lurches, what with the thought of the people on the grid, and the others waiting in the wings. Or maybe they'll be in the green room still, warming up their voices: "Round and round the rugged rock the ragged rascal ran."

In the heat, the inside of my nose crackles. Everything that should be moist is parched, and everything that should be comfortably dry is soaked with rain: jacket, trousers, Converse, hair, bookbag. Where I had doodled Ginevra's name in ballpoint across the white rubber toe-cap of my shoe, there's nothing but a blue smear.

∞

The lights rise on Eve Morrow and Leslie Kulyk, both in bowler hats. Their faces, bare of paint, look tired and hollow and so much older than they did during lunch period.

They are waiting at a crossroads. It reminds me of something.

I try to remember. It seems important. Their dialogue teases around the edges of it, whatever it is.

Then I try to forget it, because Ginevra takes the stage.

Ginevra Iacovini: her father owns Bleaker's only cab company. Her mother works part time at Danylow's, selling fine leather. Between them, they've raised a changeling, all huge dark eyes in a face studded with piercings. She's taken those out for the show, and her face looks thinner and younger.

She enters stage right, with her bowler flattening her cap of curls, a rope about her neck and a whip cracking at her ankles. The whip is in the hand of Tyra Cross; she makes Ginevra stop and start and carry her things and take the whip in her mouth and give it back. Tyra speaks, and I watch Ginevra's silent lips.

"Think!" Tyra commands.

I almost miss Ginevra's first words. The excursus. Ginevra said it to me earlier, in the smoke hole, a bit of it. "*For reasons unknown but time will tell,*" she said; and "*plunged in torment plunged in fire*". It comes back to me now, and with it a warm metallic tickle in the passage of my throat.

I lean my head back, pull my knees up to my chest. Above me, the grid shows faintly, black on black, behind the fresnels. Below, Ginevra delivers a stream of words.

My hand gropes in the pocket of my jean jacket, and finds my pen, and a wad of toilet paper. I blot my nose with one hand and clutch the pen with the other, as if the pressure will help get this under control.

Maybe it does. I swallow, less each time, while below me Ginevra's voice rises, and with it the sounds of a scuffle.

She gasps, and shouts, and halts.

So does the trickle of blood down my throat. I raise my head, cautiously. Ginevra stands listless, lost and swaying. Her hat is wrecked.

She returns to the stage again in the second act. I was afraid her part was over. She says nothing, this time. Even her hair hangs lifeless about her cheeks. Her fall is inevitable.

She's called Lucky. That's irony. If I forget again in English class what the definition of irony is, I'll only have to summon this image to my mind: Lucky, slave to Pozzo, most miserable of a miserable crew.

When she is beaten, she whimpers once, and I think Leslie's given her a real kick with that steel-capped boot.

The whimper reminds me of nothing, though. The desperate remembrance in my brain has gone quiet. The blood in my head flows in the usual channels. It does not start again until what turns out to be the very last scene: Eve and Leslie, alone together once more, in the bleak light, by the spare tree. As that light dims I feel it all over, the familiarity, and with it the blood.

The applause ends. The rest of the audience rises, collects jackets and purses, files out.

I stay in my seat, hands to my face, until everyone has gone.

∞

I wake early the next day. Saturday. Dad will be in bed for a couple of hours still. I dress in my jean jacket, and go for a walk.

From our house you can see Bleaker spread below the lip of the escarpment: a pitiful little grid of Monopoly houses and patches of orchard, and beyond it the highway. I walk the other direction, between bare fields and windbreaks.

At a crossroads, a single tree. It reminds me of the one on the stage last night.

No: that tree reminded me of this one.

I stop walking, and fumble in my pockets: pen, bloody tissue, matches. My throat hurts. I light a cigarette.

I remember something now. I come here often, on Saturdays. I wait here. Don't I? Someone meets me at the crossroads. But who? How will I know it's the right person?

Why don't I ever think of this when I'm elsewhere? Is it so terrible? Is it just so large?

When I have finished my cigarette, they come for me, and I remember everything.

∞

On Monday I meet Ginevra in the graveyard after typing class. She's drawing, perched in the big tree, up in the branches.

Every tree is the one from the play, I think. Strangely familiar, and awful, and full of meaning that vanishes if you look at it directly.

Ginevra closes her sketchbook and swings down when she sees me coming. We kick our way through the drifts of leaves that have gathered around all the stones. My mother's buried here, on the far side, but I haven't told Ginevra that, so I steer us the other way, out the north gate.

I know a bridge, across a little creek that rushes down from the escarpment. The bridge is rusted; bits of it come away on my fingertips when I stroke the iron. We lean on the rail and watch the water trickling below us. Light rain begins to fall.

"So," Ginevra says.

"It was…. I want to say it was amazing, because it was. More than that, though."

She glances at me from behind the fall of her hair. "You got it?"

"It got me, I think."

"I thought you'd get it. You always have that look."

My turn to glance at her.

"You know. I used to see you by yourself, just leaning on the wall or something, with your hands in your pockets—"

"You used to see me?"

"Sure, I did." She takes a long drag, and exhales slowly, deliciously, into the autumnal air. "The deep one, we used to call you: me and Chris and Pete, back when we were wondering who you were."

She had a name for me.

"I don't think it's about God," I blurt.

"I don't, either. And I'm Catholic. I think they're waiting for something...more personal, if that makes sense."

"More vital."

"More important."

"We sound like Didi and Gogo."

"It gets into your brain, a bit." She smiles ruefully, and looks away. She's wearing her bowler hat from the play, an old white waffle-weave shirt, and a denim vest. Her lips were wine-red, earlier, but some of the colour has come off on her cigarette. Her eyes flash wide and dark like the eyes of an owl after sundown.

I wish I could kiss her.

Instead I watch the water, which falls, and the leaves, which also fall, and the rain, which—ah, whatever.

"You're kind of a mess," she says.

"I guess." I look down at my shoes. The toe-caps are smeared with ballpoint ink, and I thank the rain for smearing it before Ginevra could see what was written there; it might have been her name.

"Me, too," she says quickly. "All of us. There's so much we don't know."

I know, I almost say. Just for a moment, it's all there. The cause of my troubles. The thing for which I wait. The meaning of the crossroads tree.

But if I speak, something will burst in my head, and I'll spill blood all over the rusted bridge and the place where our hands rest.

I hold very still. The tide of blood recedes, and with it, the knowledge. All but the memory of forgetting, and the sense that time is short.

After a last inhalation, Ginevra drops the butt of her cigarette into the water. The tiny light hisses out, and there's only the smoke from her lips.

∞

THE GHOST PARTY

Richard Larson

"I don't want to go," said Charlee as she rode in the passenger seat of the old Bronco through the dark and quiet streets outside of her tiny, depressing town. Even though by now she actually *did* want to go. The beer was helping. She just had to keep drinking. At least that's what Taco had said when he handed her the first bottle, her face still puffy from crying.

"This should take the edge off," he said.

Charlee finished the beer quickly, and Taco passed her another from the cooler that he kept by his feet as he drove. She wondered if the main reason she kept Taco around was that he was old enough to buy booze. A few years older than her—well, probably more than just a few—and surprisingly persistent about hanging out with her. He was sometimes even sexy, in the right light and after the right amount of drinks. Charlee downed her next beer as quickly as the first. They were headed to the ghost party at the edge of town and she figured that a good buzz might better prepare her, or at least take her mind off the mortifying shame of what had happened earlier that night.

∞

The first ghost parties popped up way out in the middle of nowhere, south of the highway where everything was hills and winding roads. No one was told about them. People just showed up—people, and ghosts. The ghosts came out of a big bonfire and mingled among the living. Living people became ghosts, too. The ghost party was a give and take: you gave, they took. And then you were one of them.

The parties were noticed at first by truck drivers who saw the light from the huge bonfires and called the cops—and the cops, after examining the empty fields, never found any evidence of a party, the whole thing having disappeared in the night like a sinister traveling carnival. Lately, though, it seemed like the ghost parties were getting closer and closer to home, creeping toward town from the places where everything fell off into an endlessly dark expanse of ancient trees hiding secrets that people usually drove past too quickly to ever wonder about.

Charlee's friends had told her that the ghost parties lasted all night and into the morning, and that no one noticed the sunlight until they were already driving home. But Charlee's friends had never been to the ghost parties themselves, and none of Charlee's friends were ghosts. The whole thing could just be gossip from older girls at school who had probably only heard about the ghost parties from the community college guys they were hooking up with on the weekends. And those guys had probably made the whole thing up.

That's what Charlee thought, at least, until Taco called while she was lying in the dark, face down on her bed, wanting to die. When Charlee answered the phone, Taco said, "I found the ghost party. And I'm on my way over to pick you up *right now.*"

∞

Taco was Charlee's version of a community college guy to fool around with on the weekends, except that he hadn't even *tried* to go to college, and the two of them did more than just fool around. Not sex, exactly. Charlee considered it more of an exchange of ideas. They got drunk together and laughed about how stupid the world was, and sometimes she would let him touch her. Almost like she owed him at least that much.

One time she even told him about her father, which she later regretted.

Charlee: not the hottest girl in school, not the smartest, and not the best player on the soccer team. She had to work to keep her weight down and studied harder than everyone else to get a B+ and could maybe, with more practice, warm the bench on varsity someday. And until her improbable best friend Amanda came around, all of this was fine—Amanda, who wore the right clothes and scored a record high on the SAT when she was only fourteen. Amanda, who played varsity her freshman year. Amanda, who made Charlee want to be better at everything.

And also, being all of the things that Amanda was, Amanda made Charlee want—

Well. That was the problem.

∞

"Earth to Charlee," said Taco, glancing over at her as he drove, a beer nestled between his legs. In the oncoming headlights his face glowed brighter and brighter before it suddenly went dark again. And Charlee laughed because if Taco was Earth then she was definitely Mars. Maybe even something *past* Mars, something no one had found yet.

Taco was watching her. "Do you want to talk about it?"

"About what?" she asked, but she knew. There had been a desperate text message sent in a moment of weakness. "Girl stuff," she said now, a lame attempt at changing the subject.

Taco shot her a look. "Right," he said.

But girl stuff actually *was* the problem. It was supposed to have been only an emergency study session for Monday's history final. Just the two of them sitting around in Amanda's pink bedroom, learning about oceans, how sea travel was such a big factor in allowing different cultures in history to trade goods and share knowledge—and also, Charlee noticed, to generally screw everything up. Isn't it best to just keep to yourself and figure out how to make it on your own? This was what Charlee wanted to know. Especially now.

Because she had tried to kiss Amanda.

Not just out of nowhere. Amanda had been the one who suggested stealing some of her brother's pot from his underwear drawer. She knew that he kept it there because she had once made out with one of his buddies, who—horny and desperate—had told her.

"It'll help us focus, right?" Amanda said, giggling as she opened the plastic bag, and Charlee agreed because she needed plenty of help focusing on something else other than Amanda's skin, her legs, the dimples that emerged when she smiled. Even if smoking pot sounded like it would provide exactly the opposite. Which, of course, turned out to be true.

∞

Obsessing over a girl was definitely new for Charlee. Her occasional fooling around with Taco was fine, and there had been a few other boys here and there. One time at a party she got stuck in the kitchen with Tommy Carlton and he had shoved his crotch against her lower back as he reached around for a beer, and she had thought, well, *maybe*. Until he vomited in the sink.

But with Amanda, everything was different. When Amanda moved from a nice neighborhood near the city into a house down the street two summers ago and chose Charlee as her *de facto* guide to the ways of outer suburbia, it was as if a secret part of Charlee had emerged from the cocoon that she had wrapped around herself during the entirety of junior high. The world was suddenly more *colorful*, which sounds lame but wasn't as lame to Charlee when she was writing it in her notebook during algebra class with Amada sitting right in front of her, the fresh smell of her shampoo sparking images in Charlee's head of Amanda in the shower—which guaranteed, without a doubt, that Charlee was never going to learn a damned thing about linear inequalities.

"So stoned," said Amanda on her bed, holding Charlee's hand, the smoke dissipating into the perfumed air all around them. "I've been having these nightmares," she continued. "Really scary. You're actually in them—" She paused. "Also, Taco. Has he seemed strange lately?"

Charlee propped herself up on her elbow and leaned in toward Amanda's face. Their fingers were all wrapped up in each other and Charlee, also stoned, was not listening to Amanda. She didn't want to hear about nightmares. She was thinking about origami: how you can fold things up into tidy squares and then, when you cut them, they can suddenly become something completely different. Whole new shapes, intricate and beautiful.

Charlee figured that there was no way to do this particular thing in a way that wouldn't have been at least a little bit awkward, so why not just go for it?

All that meant, though, is that it probably would have always ended this way. Amanda tore her hand away from Charlee's and stood up beside the bed, suddenly not looking so stoned anymore. More *confused* than anything else.

"Charlee," she said, just as Charlee scrambled to her feet and ran out into the hallway and down the stairs toward the front door.

"Wait!" Amanda shouted. "You can't go. This is what he wants!"

But Charlee was already gone.

∞

The scene kept replaying in her head as she rode with Taco into some sort of future that she no longer really cared about: her face moving closer and closer to Amanda's, whose eyes were closed; the sense that time had stopped, that the two of them could curl up in this moment and live there together forever. Why did the things she wanted always seem impossible? Getting into a good college, backpacking across Europe, moving to New York City, even her dream of being a writer—all were things she had been told, at some point, were not appropriate guideposts by which to plan a life. The life she had been born into, the life in which she stayed in this town forever and married Taco, or someone like him, and had a kid or two who would probably grow up to do the same thing with their lives that their parents had—absolutely nothing.

Charlee realized that Amanda was just another one of those things that she wasn't allowed to have, and this sent her into a fit of tears when she got home from Amanda's house, having sprinted the whole way. She desperately texted Taco to come save her from doing something terrible to herself—Taco, who never had anything better to do than to try to find a ghost party and then, if she would let him, take Charlee there.

Charlee thought about asking Taco how he had found the party, but then realized that she didn't even care. She was already on her third beer, and this seemed much more important.

She saw the light from the bonfire before she realized that they were heading straight toward it, veering off the road onto a gravel driveway that could have led anywhere—but which, Charlee was certain by now, led at least *somewhere*. And that was enough.

"Is that it?" she asked.

"The ghost party," said Taco. "We're here."

∞

Charlee and Taco drove past a small lake which shimmered strangely in the light of the full moon, and then carefully circled a gigantic mound of dirt—*a burial ground,* Charlee thought—before the ghost party suddenly spread itself out before them like something to be devoured before someone else got to it first. Cars were parked haphazardly between trees, assembled around a giant clearing in which a bonfire burned like a portal to another dimension.

That's where the ghosts come from, Charlee thought.

Taco maneuvered his Bronco alongside two old beat-up sedans, and since there wasn't quite enough room on either side to open the doors, Taco and Charlee climbed out through the windows and shimmied off the tops of the adjacent cars. Then Taco opened the back of the Bronco and pulled out a cooler, presumably filled with more beer. As if they needed any more.

Taco had always been called Taco, maybe because he used to work at the Mexican restaurant by the supermarket in town, and that was all people really needed to create nicknames which would stick to someone for life. Charlee thought that Taco's real name was Sam—*where had she heard that?*—but you can never be sure about these things. Taco, anyway, was more appropriate. She liked to think of him as a hard shell full of tasty insides, even if the insides often proved disappointing, like take-out food that stayed in its container for too long and got soggy. Taco was like old take-out food. But that wasn't quite right, was it? How many beers had she had so far? Why had she been crying earlier?

Charlee looked around and could hardly believe that she was actually at the ghost party with Taco. This was not what she expected. But she found herself excited, the same way people get excited before the start of an important race. Charlee was coming to certain conclusions. There were ghosts and there were people and people could become ghosts if they really wanted to, and also by accident. All of this made sense to Charlee because it was true, and nothing else mattered. The world outside the ghost party: nothing at all, really. You could only see the sky if you tried really hard to remember that it was there. And the fire was so welcoming. It was almost as if you could walk right through it and not even be burned at all.

When a few of Charlee's classmates had come to school after a long weekend having suddenly transformed into ghosts, no one really thought it was that big of a deal. Like everyone would become a ghost eventually, so why make a fuss? And it was almost like the ghosts had always been there, except now they were skipping class to smoke in the parking lot instead of haunting old mansions and saying *ooooooooo* to anyone who would listen.

Now Charlee stood around at the ghost party with Taco while he talked about random bullshit with older guys who Charlee had always seen around but never really cared to meet. Guys like that were all the same, and they were all going to the same place. Maybe the whole ghost thing was like their last chance to be something better than what they always would be in the real world. They were talking about things that Charlee didn't understand. One of them mentioned a sacred ritual, and another said something about the Ancient Ones. She tried to follow the conversation but everything was getting foggy, the world spinning around her like a dark, dangerous carousel—gradually but steadily accelerating.

Charlee opened another beer, tossing the empty into a nearby pile. She watched the people standing around the bonfire and moving back and forth, not really dancing but definitely *moving*, as if they were trying to perfect a series of steps which would call forth something terrible from down below.

Or maybe she was just being paranoid. But the possibility unnerved her.

"Taco," she said, interrupting a conversation about football, or cars, or something else that didn't matter to her at all. But she thought she heard someone mention a Dark Lord. Ghosts were hovering around behind real people, and everyone was watching the fire anxiously.

"What's going on?" she asked.

Some of the guys snickered, and she felt like maybe she wasn't in on a particularly funny joke. "Taco," she said again, angry.

"You'll figure it out," Taco said calmly, looking away. Dismissing her. "When the time is right," he added.

Charlee stalked away into the darkness, dry leaves crunching below her feet. She was colder than before and she shivered, wrapping her arms around herself. Was it October already? She took another sip from her beer. She had ended up near the edge of the field by the trees, beyond which was only shadow. She watched the people across the field still moving around the bonfire, ghosts staring longingly and hungrily at the living, and Charlee thought that she could also hear them *chanting* something, the strange words growing louder and louder. Reaching for her from all directions and burrowing into her mind. She watched people doing the synchronized moves around the bonfire and then realized that her own feet were moving in a similar way, unconsciously mimicking the steps.

Already she was becoming someone different. Losing control.

∞

The last time she lost control, Charlee had been in the supermarket in town, doing the week's shopping because her mother had been working such long hours at the restaurant. And she thought she saw her father turn the corner into the next aisle.

It couldn't have been him. But the shape of his body, his posture, his hair—

She abandoned her cart and rushed down the aisle, but just as she turned the corner, he passed into the next aisle over. Again and again, she turned the corner only to see him disappear before she could get to him, like he was running away from her and she would never be able to catch up.

Charlee was crying, probably shouting his name, and people stared at her, some with their hands over their mouths. *Poor girl,* they must have been thinking, all of them knowing the whole story the way people know things about each other in small towns. *Poor girl.*

∞

Charlee finished her beer and wished that she had brought another one with her, but she didn't dare go back to Taco and his buddies. What an asshole. He brought her out here only to—what, to ignore her? How was this helping? She had been at home with her music and her books and her chocolate—and, if she was lucky, some of the vodka from her mother's liquor cabinet. Maybe surrounding yourself with familiar things was the way to get through crises like trying to kiss your best friend. Not going to the ghost party with someone like Taco.

But then Taco was there next to her with another beer. "I'm sorry," he said.

"You should be," she mumbled, but she was happy that he had come back to her. She felt like she had won an important battle and that it would all be downhill from here.

"I want to show you something," said Taco, looking ghostly in the darkness.

Charlee's cell phone vibrated in her pocket. Ignoring it would have been impossible at that point, so she tried at least to not look completely desperate as she scrambled to pull the phone out of her pocket. And there it was, a text message from Amanda:

Don't know what to say about tonight but I think the nightmares are real. CALL ME.

Yeah, right. Instead of calling Amanda, Charlee would run as far away from this place as she could get. She would learn another language and invent a new name for herself. She would never see anyone she knew ever again.

"Okay," she said.

Taco tugged at her arm and they moved closer to the trees. She swayed drunkenly, trying to put one foot in front of the other but often failing and having to be caught by Taco, who was drenched in beer and sweat. *But it's so cold,* she thought.

"Where are we going?" she asked. She was slurring now, the words probably only making sense to her.

∞

Charlee's father would have known what to do. But he wasn't there. He wasn't anywhere. Dying is a kind of leaving, but it's the kind of leaving that you can't really punish people for. You can't hate someone for dying. You just have to deal with it and move on, all by yourself.

But here she was in the dark with Taco, and something was wrong. Taco kept saying, "You have drunk the elixir. You have drunk the elixir." Everything was spinning. The chanting and the bonfire became further and further away, and Charlee was already forgetting the steps to the movements that she had only just been beginning to learn.

There was a dark open space ahead of them and suddenly Taco stopped walking—and so did Charlee, since she was still leaning heavily against him. He turned her around so that she was facing him, and he didn't look at all like himself. Charlee saw something in his eyes that could not have been from this world. Not a color, but an absence of color. Not an expression, but instead, no expression at all. He looked *blank*, but also hungry.

"What happened to you?" she asked quietly.

"This place," he said, gesturing proudly into the dark. "It's mine."

"I don't understand, Taco."

"I'm not Taco here," he said. "I'm the Dark Lord. I'm a ghost. Can't you tell?"

Charlee shook her head. "Is this a game? What are we doing out here?"

"You know what we're doing out here," he responded flatly. Then he said, "The ghost party gives you power. Or takes it away."

So this was the moment of truth, and Charlee was not prepared. They stood there looking at each other. "I don't think I do," said Charlee. But she did.

Taco grabbed her by the shoulders, roughly, and then tugged at her shirt. "You've been such a fucking tease all this time," he said. "I think you owe me."

And that was all the reason Charlee needed to start running. If only the world hadn't suddenly gone black. She was falling, falling, tumbling deep into the world below.

∞

Taco's accusation wasn't really all that far from the truth, though. He always wanted to go further than Charlee did, and definitely further than she would ever let him. Was it because of Amanda? Or someone *like* Amanda, some future version of Amanda? Was she really just waiting around for someone to sweep her off her feet, to show her that love was real? Charlee was convinced by now that love *was* real but that it was probably as unavailable to her as everything else that she wanted from her life. Maybe Taco was right—maybe she was just a tease, always trying to tease out a future that she would never get to have.

When her father had explained love to her, none of it had made any sense. Nothing he said made much sense by then. "Love is a secret language," he said. "Goo goo goo."

She was ten years old, clutching a Stephen King paperback that he had given her to read. When he was moved to the home after the stroke, he took all of his old books with him. An entire lifetime of books. But he constantly gave them away to everyone he met: nurses, mailmen, other people's children visiting for birthdays. Soon there was nothing left but an old copy of *The Stand*, which he anxiously handed over to Charlee when she arrived, as if he was scared that she would go away if he didn't have a gift for her.

"Goo goo goo," he said.

Moments of completely lucid thought—he had once been a high school science teacher and would sometimes still try to explain things like reaction rates and evaporation—were always followed by nonsense that came from somewhere *else*, a place that seemed like another world to Charlee. She would tell her mother that she wanted to go there with him so that maybe she'd understand the things he talked about, but her mother turned pale at the suggestion.

"No one wants to go there," she said.

∞

Charlee thought she was running, but then she woke up. Everything was blurry. Her head was pounding, and it took her only a second to realize that it was because the chanting had grown louder, impossibly louder, and now it had become a part of her.

The fire. She was *above* the fire.

Terror brought the world into a sudden, sharp focus. Her hands were bound and she was tied to a tall wooden post leaning precariously out above the bonfire. Her shirt was slashed, tattered. And there was blood. Ghosts were crawling out of the bonfire, and real people were going in and then coming out as ghosts. Charlee didn't see a way for this to end well for her.

The memory of the night came back to her like a slap in the face. Taco had drugged her. That much was clear. That last beer—he had brought it to her already opened.

Charlee looked into the bonfire. Something inside of it was gaping, yawning as if just now waking up from a long sleep. Reaching up for her from somewhere. Charlee looked down and she knew, even after all the beer, the darkness, the feeling as though she was sinking into the ground to somewhere dark, darker than dark, somewhere secret kept down below—she knew that something was coming for her.

"Daddy?" she said. Her voice sounded small and pathetic, even to her.

"We offer her," Taco was saying, his arms raised up to the sky. "We offer her to the Ancient Ones."

Maybe Taco had to believe that he was a Dark Lord of something, because otherwise he was just Taco. Not even a ghost—just nothing special at all.

"Get me down," Charlee said hopelessly. She knew that she would fall into the bonfire and she would come out as a ghost. She would just hang around town forever, haunting people who used to be her friends. This was her future. She would run and run and no one would see her. She would call out her father's name, knowing that he was there somewhere just out of reach, and that he desperately needed her help. Even though *he* was the one who left. Suicide is a kind of betrayal, but not the kind you can punish people for. He just decided one day that enough was enough, and Charlee had to let him go. She had no choice.

"Nowhere to go now," said Taco. He was smiling in a ghostly way. He was there and not there all at the same time.

Charlee wanted her father to step out of the bonfire, even if that meant that now he had to be a ghost. She wanted him to save her. Was that too much to ask? There were hands on her body, hands reaching out of the fire and trying to pull her down. Things crawling up from below, creatures with wrinkled skin and glowing eyes. All those forgotten things—lost things. Doomed to climb and climb and never get anywhere.

Then Amanda crawled out of the bonfire.

"What the hell," said Charlee.

Amanda was so pale, almost translucent. Pieces of her were loose, as if she had been hastily thrown together: a patchwork Amanda, composed of pieces of the truth but never adding up to the real thing. Like she wasn't a real person but she also wasn't a ghost, at least not yet.

"Let me love you," said Amanda. "I want to love you."

"You're not real," said Charlee. "None of this is real."

You can't outrun the ghost party. You can't hide from it. Taco had known that when he took her out there. Maybe guys like Taco needed the ghost party to turn them into the people who would actually go through with doing the things that they really wanted to do. People who had nothing left to lose and nowhere else to go.

"I will make you my Queen," Taco was saying, licking his lips, his eyes glowing in the ghostly darkness. He stepped menacingly toward her. "Even if I have to chain you to the throne."

∞

Charlee woke up in the car with Amanda, who was driving her home from the party in the early morning light. She was shivering, but Amanda had given her a blanket from the trunk of her car, so that was helping. "That was a close call," she said quietly. She kept glancing at Amanda, making sure she hadn't turned into a ghost.

"I'm glad you called," said Amanda. She looked really tired. "It took me forever to find you in the woods. How long had you been running?"

"I'm glad you came," said Charlee.

"You were so drunk. Like, way drunk." But Amanda was smiling.

The world rushed past them in the car windows as they headed toward home: the real world, the familiar world. The one that Charlee would stay in, at least for a while. "What were you saying about nightmares?" she asked.

Amanda stared straight ahead as if she was carefully considering her words. "It started a few days ago. In the nightmare, it's impossibly dark. And your friend Taco was there. He—"

She paused.

"What is it?" asked Charlee.

"Well," said Amanda. "He wants to make you into a ghost, just like him. And a ghost can never leave the house it haunts. That's what he keeps saying to me in the dream."

"Oh."

"Scary, right?"

"Listen," said Charlee. "I'm sorry about earlier. I don't know what I was thinking. I shouldn't have done that."

"What you shouldn't do is hang out with people like Taco," said Amanda, as if Charlee trying to kiss her had been no big deal at all. Something they could just forget about, maybe even laugh about later. "He always gave me the creeps. And tonight he proved me right."

A deer ran across the road in front of the car, dashing from one side of the forest to the other, and Charlee thought to herself that maybe life was like that: a series of jumps from one place to another, deep breaths before the plunge. There would always be danger, but sometimes you can be the girl who gets away. The girl who makes it to the other side.

"Goo goo goo," said Charlee.

∞

BONEHOUSE

Keffy R. M. Kehrli

Evictions are a messy business.

Muddy gold-brown sunlight filtered through the dust cloud that hung over downtown, putting tiger stripes of light and shadow in the air. Basalt gravel and desiccated eel grass crunched underfoot as I made my way down Holly Street at low tide. There was asphalt beneath it all, slowly crumbling and turning to beach before it washed out to sea.

There wasn't much this close to the bay. The buildings used to be two or three story shops before the ground dropped and the water level rose. Now the bottom floors had been opened up to let the tide run past. In the shadows, I could see the remains of rooms—slimy brown mold-and-rot walls, broken toilets and tile; a thick tide sludge that smelled like petroleum and the deaths of a million fish glistened in the shade.

Another ten years, maybe, and there'd be nothing here anymore.

Far cry from how it'd been when I'd lived this side of the mountains. Things used to be green, then. Now the lowland forests were full of bleached ghost trees, dead from the saltwater drowning their roots. The buildings were brickwork, and where there might have been ivy clinging to the sides, a thin tracery of metal spidered over the walls. Even in this submerged part of town, there was enough ambient electricity in the air for a decent harvest system to make up for what they didn't get from sun or tide.

I stopped near the end of the row, smelling the place I was looking for, even over the salt stench of the ocean. Disinfectant, too much of it, a citrus-tinged sickly scent. You could knock on a hundred abandoned doors if you wanted but I never needed to. I knew the smell of a bonehouse by heart.

I climbed up the ten feet of rickety wood stairs that were nailed to what had been the sill of the second-floor window. I didn't like the stairs. Standing at the top, there wasn't much to hang onto but a rotten banister that looked about ready to fall apart.

I knocked.

The owners let me stand out there a good few minutes, while the terns wheeled overhead and screamed.

When the door opened, a short white man with round glasses and lank greasy hair down to his shoulders squinted out at me. "Evictionist," he said. "I don't got anybody here for you. Go find some other House to haunt."

The disinfectant smell was stronger, and the room was filled with a dim, flickering light. A woman in ripped jeans sat on a patched-together couch, dividing her attention between the wall-mounted screen and our conversation at the door.

"You won't mind if I check their chips, then," I said. "I'm a good guy. You don't got what I want, I'll leave." Starting to lose my balance on the stairs, I didn't want to go for that banister, figuring it would snap if I did, so I leaned forward and grabbed the door frame.

The man flinched like I was too close, so I smiled.

"They're all paid up through next year at least," he said through his teeth. "I don't have enough flow to return that much cash."

I snicked my tongue against my teeth, waiting.

The woman came over. She said, "Let him in, Justin. Nobody ever gets the good side of an Evictionist." She shot me a look that was mostly poison with just a dash of hate. "I'll show him what he thinks he wants to see."

Justin growled a bit, under his breath, and let the door swing open. He bowed and gestured inside.

"Thank you," I said, and I slammed my boots against the door frame, knocking off as much sand as I could. I kept my eyes on Justin, partways hoping he'd pull a knife. Americans.

We shook hands. Hers were rough as any bonehouse warden's. "Doctor Anna Petreus," she said.

The front room was cluttered, but not near as filthy as most of the places I'd seen. A few dirty dishes were stacked on the end-table, next to them a pair of cell phones. Petreus had been watching news coverage of the riots in Ottawa. Someone had uncovered evidence that the parliamentary elections had been rigged. Almost normal, that.

A wiry looking orange tabby came out from under the coffee table and rubbed himself on my leg. Petreus gave me a funny look when I bent to pick up the cat. He wrapped his front legs around my neck and buried his nose in my ear, purring loud enough to wake the dead.

Petreus led me down the hallway to a dark room. The only light came from a cluster of monitors, each one hooked up to a different guest. The monitors showed vital signs. Steady heartbeats, hormones at the right levels, vitamins to stave off serious illness, everything they needed to live except reality.

Seven hospital beds full of bones and skin.

I'd never seen so many in such a small house. I wondered if it was a coastal thing, or if they'd come in as a group. The boy closest to me twitched while he net-dreamed. He'd been under for a while. They get like that, the bones. They'll twitch all around even after the muscles have gone. The only thing they've got left that works is their brain.

"You must be turning a hefty profit out here," I said. I put the cat down so I could fumble for my cell phone. "Not having to pay for your electricity."

"We're low-end," Dr. Petreus said. She scratched the back of her neck and then inspected her nails in the light from one of the vitals displays. "None of these kids paid all that much per month when we plugged them in. We get by, but...."

I grunted a response. Winding around my legs, the cat purred louder. "Friendly cat," I muttered.

"He doesn't get a lot of attention from our guests," she answered. "Go on, check them. I'm not leaving you alone in here."

Only two of the seven were female.

The one closest to me didn't really seem to have a human form under the blanket. From how small she was, I would've been curious to see the Vegas odds that she'd plugged in before she was legal. I thumbed open the phone. Nope, not mine.

The second woman was the one I was after. This didn't surprise me. It didn't matter how good a bonehouse tech was, she could never mask an IP address well enough to keep me out. And proxies, well. I'll just say that not all of them are as anonymous as they advertise.

"Well?"

"Bad for you," I said. I pocketed my phone and pointed at the woman tucked over in the corner. "She's the one I'm after."

Laura DeVries, age 29. Used the web like any normal kid until she was seventeen, when she ran away from home and tried to plug in permanently. She'd been evicted four times already. No wonder she'd come out to the coast—she probably had trouble finding a bonehouse that would take her.

Hers was a family extraction. The loved ones she'd left behind had pooled their money together for a fifth time, the amount much smaller than previous jobs. My cut was barely worth the trip out to the coast.

"She's been in three years straight now," Petreus said. "You know it won't be any good for her coming out. Why waste the rehab dollars on her?"

"Because her family wants her back and I get paid by the contract." I stretched my arms and back. Three years into a netdream, and she wasn't going to be walking much of anywhere. I'd be carrying her back down Holly and up Bay. "Plus, you might say it ticks me off a bit when people with potential can't handle unplugging long enough to feed themselves."

Petreus just shook her head. She wound between the beds until she got to Laura's. She called up the 'Net usage on the vitals monitor, and then cut the connection. She was doing it for the money, too.

It took a full twenty seconds before Laura realized that it was more than just a 'Net hiccup and opened her eyes.

"Anna?" Her voice was raw, hoarse.

Petreus patted her on the forehead, and then started disconnecting the IV and monitoring devices. "I'm sorry," she said. "We'll pro-rate your stay and transfer what's left back to your accounts."

"No," Laura said. "I didn't do anything. I didn't violate any codes, I didn't bring any viruses into the servers. Please." Her face was green and skeletal in the light from the monitors. "Sammy said he wouldn't wait for me again if I dropped and he couldn't find me. He'll move on, Anna, he'll move on."

I crept up to her bed. She was too busy trying to grab tubes out of Petreus' hands and stick them back to her body, but she was too weak. The tubes fell against the bed sheets, and Petreus gathered them up. She didn't answer or look at Laura's face. "I'm sure he'll wait," she said.

"Why are you doing this to me?" Laura's voice cracked. She was crying.

I couldn't figure if she was addled from the 'Net drop—she had to still have some world-ghosting going on in her head—or if she really had forgotten the other times she'd been evicted.

"Evictionist, Laura." I rested a hand on the metal bed railing. Good work on Petreus and her tech, getting all this equipment out here and up those stairs out front. "Your mama misses you."

"No," she started sobbing. "This is my life, don't you understand?"

I leaned over. "You ever think maybe your real kids want to see more of you than just your avatar?"

No answer.

Petreus started shutting down the equipment. Laura didn't move. She was dressed in what looked like a purloined hospital gown, so I wrapped the bedsheet around her limp form and picked her up like a kid. Couldn't risk the fireman's carry, too big a chance that she'd break something. Petreus said, "I'm sorry, Laura."

Laura didn't say another word until we were half-way down Holly Street. The tide was coming in, and I was already wading in an inch or so of surf.

"I'm just gonna go back," she said. "Soon as they let me out." Her chest heaved with every breath. Just the strain of holding onto my neck was enough to wind her. "I'll plug back in and put my life back together."

They all say that. I was expecting it.

"Go right ahead," I said. "Keeps me getting paid."

"Sammy might not wait," she said. "But just in case if he does, I'll be back. There's nothing you can do."

She was still babbling when I put her in the back seat of the car that the company had rented for me, a funny little Russian-made thing that I didn't think would have outrun the surf if I'd parked it on Holly.

"What's your name?" She asked as soon as I'd strapped her in, one weak hand closed on the front of my shirt. "What's your name?"

"To you," I said, "I'm just the Evictionist."

Her expression closed down into an angry glare. "He'll find out who you are," she said.

"Oh yeah? Sammy Not-Gonna-Wait-No-More?"

"Sammy Gauge," she said softly. "And he's going to break you."

She must have seen the recognition in my face, and there was a moment when she must've thought about bragging some more. As it was, though, she clammed up. I wanted to kick myself. I knew better than to broadcast my thoughts that way.

Gauge.

The possibility of Samuel Gauge being one of the aliases of Cameron Trexell had initially been figured at twenty percent. Both Samuel and Cameron had been good at restricting the personal information they let slip in their online communication. Once the suspicion leaked, Gauge had dropped offline, his actions going from borderline illegal to nothing overnight.

Cameron Trexell was an eviction so big that the company hadn't even bothered assigning it directly to one of their agents. Instead, it was open season, and the Evictionist cut was enough to live on comfortably for a while. I wouldn't stop working if I had that kind of cash, but I could quit living off the easy marks and take on the difficult cases, the ones who really needed to be saved. That, and pay for something I'd been meaning to do for years.

As for what the company'd get if I brought him in, well, at least half of the Northern Coalition was looking to get him out of the 'Net and into custody. For starters. Trexell or one of his known aliases had been heavily implicated in almost every act of electronic terrorism in the past five years. His group saw no future for the world and they typically made their feelings known by shutting some things down, breaking other things, and generally trying to bring their own prophecies to fruition.

"Oh yeah, *Gauge.*" I laughed at her, hard enough that I could see her squirm. It was still more than likely that she was screwing with me.

After all, it was more than a little odd that nobody else had turned up Laura while they were searching for Trexell. It was also more than a little unlikely that he'd spend time talking to somebody who'd had as weak a proxy set-up as Laura's.

"You'll see," she whispered.

∞

I slipped through the border ghost town that was Blaine, through White Rock, which was still doing okay, and Vancouver, which was evolving, filled up with Canadians, with the best of the American expats, with anybody who had enough cash to move north and enough skills to get through the border.

The guards gave me the fifth degree, as usual, picking apart the discrepancies between my appearance and my identification even though I knew damn well that they had everything they asked on file from the last ten or twenty times I'd jumped the forty-ninth. They backed off real quick when I asked if they wanted a direct line to my boss.

I left Laura in a little rehab place, more of a staging location than anything. They ran tests, made sure that the dreamers we dropped off were well enough to send east, in batches, in electric train cars. She'd end up somewhere in Ontario, maybe even Toronto itself, wasting health-care funds. Eventually, she'd run back south, and next time, the fee might be too low for anybody to bother coming after her. She probably knew that, which was why she'd mostly kept her mouth shut, just waiting out the ordeal.

'Course, before I left her, I made her a deal.

"I've got enough tech in the car right now to hook you up," I said.

She stared out the window, at the lost parts of Vancouver, where not even a dike had been enough to save the streets from flooding. It was a shallow bay now, a couple meters deep, dead trees and telephone poles sticking up like rotten dock pilings. "I'd be less suspicious if you had anything to gain," she said.

I tapped my fingers on the steering wheel, annoyed with myself. Once the disorientation had faded and she'd cat-napped in the passenger seat, Laura deVries was not stupid. Nobody did favors in this game.

"I was thinking if you were interested that I'd sell you the time." I tried to sound a little nervous, barely made eye contact over the rims of my sunglasses, like that was the most ethically shady I ever got.

She might have been pretty, if she wasn't so wasted-looking, or if I was able to ignore the nutrient drip in her arm. "That's pretty low, even for somebody who gets paid to ruin lives," she said, finally.

I shrugged. "Do you want to reconnect and settle your accounts, or not? I'll give you an amount to transfer, and once that's done, you can have an hour."

"An hour." Her hands clutched at the blanket I'd draped over her legs. "What if I don't have enough money?"

I snorted. "Funny. Look, neither one of us has enough time to screw around. Either you want to make a deal or you don't."

"Okay," she said.

The amount I asked for wasn't very high—just enough to throw her off, make her think that I was in it for the money after all. Low enough to make me seem like a small fish, as if jobs like picking her up were normal to me. The more she under-estimated me, the better.

I half-heartedly watched her online movements with one of my external monitors, figuring that she'd get too suspicious if she didn't see me watching her. I saw her pull apart her empire and parcel it off to those of her acquaintances that weren't important enough to keep secret. Public aliases.

It was kind of funny, how behind she was. She deleted every account she accessed, once she was done with it, assuming I'd have her passwords. That's not how I find people. Any kid with enough time on his hands can crack passwords. For me, it's about correlating behavior, the kinds of personal information that people don't really think about giving out. We all have our unique patterns of thought and activity. Given enough data and some processor time, I can find the alter-accounts of anybody.

Knowing where she'd had her accounts just told me who to bribe.

When the hour was up, I sent her through the short disconnect routine.

She didn't thank me.

∞

In retrospect, I'd say my biggest mistake was that I didn't tell anybody in the company what I was after when I requested all of deVries' records.

The advantage of being quiet about what I was up to was obvious—nobody to share the money with. The disadvantage was just as obvious—nobody to go in with me. I'd been in a few suspicious situations, bonehouses with wardens that outweighed me by thirty or forty kilos, wardens who didn't care that projectile weapons were definitely against the law, and once in the middle of what might as well have been a war zone. All this, despite being required by law to remain unarmed. Still, Trexell was worth enough in cash and notoriety that going in without backup like I did was stupid. A tenth of the cut would've been enough to get me what I wanted.

I crossed back out of Canada, and then drove a bit, looking for a place where I got a decent signal without being under too much surveillance. I finally found the right spot on I-5 after it leaves the Chuckanuts but before it turns into a series of bridges over Skagit Bay. Skagit was worse off than Vancouver—the economy had been such that the farmhouses in the area had been left behind, strip-salvaged and left to rot. The bay is full of islands that used to be roofs, covered in bird crap, sinking lower year by year.

I set my timer first. Plugging in is like falling asleep into a perfect dream. No—it's like waking up into one. No—

Your senses go away entirely if you've got the right connection. There's no touch, no smell, no sound unless you want it. Turn on all the senses before you're acclimated and you'll go crazy, touch and sight and smell all advertising different products at once.

The numbers say that most of bonehouse dreamers plug in for a 24-7 life of porn or games. By most, I mean a good 99%. This is what we're doing with technology that makes immersive language learning almost foolproof, that makes searching a couple of exabytes of data as easy as thinking.

Laura's files. Most of her time was spent in games. She'd been making money to keep herself plugged in by playing. I hadn't expected the search to be as easy as looking through her records to see if any of them had Trexell written all over them, but it would have been nice. I was just mining for pertinent data, dumping it into the computer.

My timer went off, distant, I pulled myself out of the 'Net long enough to slap it off, and then fell back in, for just another few minutes. I kept digging, found out everything I could about Laura's actions—which were easy enough to track, honestly. She'd had five alter-egos, some of whom were into sex acts that I'm sure her standard persona would have pretended to be scandalized just hearing about.

Funny thing about living online that way, everybody who does eventually ends up with some kind of multiple personality going on. Unavoidable, really. That's the thing about being a creature of data, humanity made in the image of artificial intelligence. Data is malleable, flesh is less so.

Intuition.

Every topic has a cloud associated, a set of linked concepts, linked accounts, linked people. Two choices. Either let the computer run through all of the possibilities, or figure it out yourself. I preferred doing the latter.

I followed links, cached search string lists, finding a way around every time I hit up on something password protected. I winced every so often when an ad wormed through my blocker, addressed me by my birth name, and tried to sell me something.

Then I found Samuel.

I followed Laura and Sammy Gauge, their entire lives unfolding to me all at once. Here's where they first met, in a voice chat on American secessionist politics. There was the simulator where they got married, with Gauge under a new name. There was the imaginary home life they'd set up, perfectly normal until I dug back through the links, finding old ones, dead links with less than benign file names attached to them.

And then the glorious and bizarre moment when I called in a favor on the anonymous proxy he'd been using and found out that he was based here, too. Here, as in Seattle, a bonehouse junky's dream.

The connection dropped suddenly, shunting me out into glaring daylight, dry-mouthed, in the back seat of my car. Slammed straight out of a connection like that, I always feel groggy, like I've been jerked out of sleep and I'm only half awake. The 'Net ghosted in my head, like the afterimage of a thought, burned into my neurons. I reached for water, drank, fought back nausea as I checked my clock.

Five hours?

My timer hadn't initiated shut-down...or had it? I vaguely remembered over-riding the shut-down order. Just a few more minutes. And a few more. And a few more. I took a shaky breath.

Physical limitations.

I fought the impulse to hook myself back in, embarrassed by it, even though there was nobody around to see my relapse.

∞

David wasn't happy to see me. He lived in what used to be north Seattle, and he didn't approve of my career path.

However, I needed somewhere to charge the car, and I still had the key to his house and to the electrical box outside. I'd just plugged the car in when he came to the door and crossed his arms. I wondered belatedly if he'd set up a perimeter alarm system. All the other houses on this street had been looted, long abandoned by people who didn't like living isolated in empty suburban sprawl. I'd crawled in through a few of the back windows for David, when I still lived with him. We'd liked living in an abandoned city.

"I'm close to him now," I said. "Found him."

He shook his head at me. "You know what I think about that."

"Relax," I said, my enthusiasm already fading. "You'll probably get lucky again and he'll be gone before I get there, and then you can continue to feel smug." I followed him into the house, an old single-level wooden structure. I plugged in my phone—which was also the computer that ran my car, did my all my statistical searches, and was otherwise far too important to charge in its normal location.

The house was still filled with photographs. For a while, David had talked about setting up an old-style dark room, but he'd changed his mind when he saw how much it would cost to get the permits for the chemicals.

Not that anybody would come out here to check him.

"You're just using this as a new way to act out your obsession," he said. He poured me a glass of water and put it on the cracked laminate countertop next to my arm.

I shrugged. "Does it matter? What I'm doing is important."

He, of all people, couldn't argue with me. He pulled out one of the chairs and sat. "Why did you come here?"

"Low on power."

A pause.

"And I missed you," I admitted. "You never come up to Canada."

He avoided the obvious argument, about why he stayed here. We'd had that argument too many times over the years, both in person and online. Online, he'd end the conversation by accusing me of using immersive, and I'd log off. He used immersive. I used immersive and I set the timer. Not a problem.

1011010010100001970010101101001

"I'm not sure that the person I miss is the person you are now," he said. "I'm less than certain she ever came back."

"He," I corrected.

"Exactly," he said.

I sighed. "That's not fair."

"I don't blame you," he said, reasonably. "I just think you're doing it for the wrong reasons. You were beautiful before you changed."

"I didn't change," I said. "I just figured out who I am."

The silence of a remembered argument sat between us, souring the air.

He stood up. "I'm taking more pictures of the Nisqually Lahar tomorrow...."

"Don't fall in," I said, even though the mudflow had solidified before either of us were born.

"And I don't want to see you when I'm done. You shouldn't have come back," he said.

I looked down at the screen of my phone, sifting search results. He'd started for the door to his bedroom before I said, "I thought things might be different after I've turned him in."

David shook his head. "Getting the object of your obsession isn't going to fix you. You'll just find something else to obsess over and I'm still not willing to go through it again."

∞

There's a famous photograph of me using immersive, plugged in, switched off, artfully arranged on a queen-size mattress, blood-red sheets covering just enough of my body to lower the disgust factor. The floor is tilted fifteen percent off horizontal, the mattress shoved all the way up against the cracked and peeling wall. I'm in focus, but in the distance, you can still see the shards of broken glass that used to be floor-to-ceiling windows.

I could be a corpse, discarded with the other debris in a condemned building, in a condemned city, and the picture would be no different.

∞

I didn't really believe I'd find Trexell until I was looking up at the building that held his bonehouse.

Gray dust blew past. It was a few minutes after noon, and the sun glared off everything around me, so bright that it hurt. The sidewalk under my feet had the brown-black stained color that concrete got in places where it rarely if ever rained. Faded "For Lease" signs flapped in the breeze, still tied against the side of the building. There'd been nobody to lease these buildings for at least ten years, maybe longer.

A man walked up while I stood there, hands in his pockets, hand-rolled cigarette in his mouth. His face looked weathered, like he'd spent way too many days outside. He had a handgun tucked into his belt, even if it was illegal. I wished that I wasn't so completely un-armed. "You looking for something?" He squinted at me.

I was a damn good actor. I stuffed my hands in my pockets, scuffed my foot on the sidewalk. Looked ashamed to even be asking. "Angelina's," I said.

He looked me over. "Bonehouses ain't free. Got money?"

"Access to it," I said.

"What's a guy like you looking for Angelina's for? Don't look at me like that, I can hear in your accent that you're from up north."

"Tired of having my life run for me," I said, as truthful as I could be.

He folded his arms one over the other. Even though I could tell that he was trying to be discrete about it, he tilted his head to the side slightly, listening to a voice in his earpiece. I suddenly felt naked, not knowing how advanced their surveillance was, and how well it was working. "All right, Jordan," he said, giving me the name on my fake identification and my fake ID chip. "Come on."

I followed him down the broken escalator into the fetid darkness under the city, into the tunnels that used to let busses travel down-town without getting caught in above-ground traffic. Back when there was traffic. Back when it was smart to drive a car through the maze of skyscrapers.

"Ever been in a bonehouse before?"

"Not long-term," I lied. There were dim lights overhead, up in the big arching ceiling. Only about a third of them were on, and one of them was flickering, making the debris filling out the tunnel roadway jump and jiggle. "This kind of thing is more policed up in Canada." *And thank God for that.*

He hopped down from the station platform. I followed him, care-ful not to snag my leg on the bent and broken post that used to mark the bus stop. I followed him through the narrower tunnels, surprised, since the proxy information I had suggested that Angelina's was in the mall.

This far underground they'd have to be running a wired network. Interesting.

"Not very secure, is it?" I asked. The signs on either side of the wall told how far we were from various platforms. I hadn't seen any security at all, which made me nervous.

"You don't need to worry about that," he said. "People in this city know to stay out of the tunnels."

I narrowly avoided snorting at him. Anybody with even a passing understanding of human nature knows that people will cheerfully go exactly where they're least safe.

Two steps further.

He grabbed my shoulder, twisted, and slammed me up against the wall. It was too quick, I'd let myself be too lulled into complacency, and so I didn't react. Just slammed into the wall and felt the air whistle out of me, hands snapping up to show they were empty, eyes wide, adrenaline making the dim tunnel clearer than it should have been. Empty but for us.

Cold metal dug into the soft underside of my jaw so hard that I thought I might gag. A click.

"Cocky, stupid, bastard Canadian," he said.

I was afraid to swallow. Afraid to talk. Breathe.

He dug the gun in harder, shoving my head up. "What, you thought Trexell would hand himself to you? On a platter, maybe? With a little note that says, "Dear *Christina*, please turn me in, I'm tired of living, oh and while you're at it, enjoy your reward."

"That's *not* my name," I snarled, surprised at what I clung to in the seconds before I died.

"You hunt bones," he said, his voice so reasonable. One arm across my chest, keeping me pressed against that earth-cold concrete wall, his face so close we could have kissed. "Bones don't move. They don't run. They're usually so wrapped up that they don't even try to hide themselves. Easy pickings for a hypocrite."

I kept my chin up, instinct pushing away from the gun. Looked up at him. "Either shoot me or let me go," I said.

"Who knows you're here?"

David. I thought about him clambering around on the lahar, cataloguing new plant growth, tsk-tsking at plants that should only grow at warmer climates. What would they do to him, uninvolved David, if I told them he knew I was in Seattle? "Nobody," I said.

He pulled back, like he meant to hit me over the head but I moved too quickly for him. I slammed my forehead into his nose, using the few seconds of disorientation to disarm him, send the gun skittering across the concrete floor.

He didn't waste time going after it and pulled a knife instead, dim light shining along the edge of the blade. I blocked his first mad slash with my forearm, the angle such that he didn't cut through my thick canvas coat. My knee connected with his stomach.

He shoved me back again, and I hit the wall. Before I could twist away, hot pain lanced down my side. I cussed, put my foot against the wall and used it to launch myself at him.

Dust and dirt puffed into the air, and his head hit the floor with a sharp crack. Good luck on my part. I beat his hand against the floor until his fingers loosened, and then I sent the knife skittering across to where the gun was.

Pain lanced up and down my left side, my shirt gone sticky from the blood. I told myself I'd had worse and flipped him onto his stomach. I planted my right knee in the small of his back, pinned him while I caught my breath.

"How many of you are there?" I asked when I could, having trouble keeping him pinned.

Nothing.

I leaned so close I was practically yelling in his ear. "How many of you are there? You got an army? Just a couple of you? Just you and Trexell?"

"Enough of us."

"Enough of you for what?"

He shook his head, laughing down at the concrete. I let him laugh, dug in my pocket for a tranquilizer, pulled it out of the box with one hand and uncapped it with my teeth. I gave him a full dose, listening to the laughter turn to curses when the needle went in.

When he went limp, I picked up the gun and left him there.

∞

I took the stairs into the mall. The broken escalator wasn't even safe for climbing; pieces of it had been pulled off and sold for scrap. Every piece of glass in the entire place had been shattered, everything from doors to store windows. Spray-paint graffiti blanketed every surface, turning walls into scenes of dueling tags. The air held the thick smell of stale urine.

Volcanic ash lay on the floor a good three inches deep. The place was never cleaned up after Rainier blew. The mall had already been closed, so when the ash filtered in through the broken windows, covering all four stories, there was no point.

I had to stop too often, breathing in little gasps, alternately trying to encourage myself to walk on and cursing myself for not going back.

The ash saved me some time, showing me a path up and down the broken escalators—these ones treacherous but still climbable—that was much more traveled than the side paths.

My ragged breath was the only sound in the mall. I left a trail behind me, drops of blood on ash, like breadcrumbs to safety.

At the top, more shattered glass. The remains of a food court to my right, the decommissioned remains of a monorail station to the left.

And a man dressed all in gray. Behind him were skyscrapers in front of a sapphire blue sky, half of the windows broken out, gaping holes in their shining surfaces. "Flesh is over-rated, isn't it?" he asked.

I gripped the rubber escalator rail so hard that I felt my fingernails dig in. It'd been years since I'd even held a simulated handgun, but some muscle memories don't go away. I took aim, resting my finger on the side of the trigger guard. Willing to let him talk. Glanced around, too late to save me if he'd had an ambush, but the floor was empty.

I stayed on my feet but I was losing too much blood.

"Not sure about that," I said, "But your security is. Should have beefed it up when you moved out here."

A smile. "You weren't expecting me to be on my feet."

"Might be for the best," I said. "Since I can't carry you out like this."

He laughed. "Chris, Chris, Chris," he said. "If I were willing to let you take me alive, would you really be happy?"

"Sure I would," I said. "I'm sick of being poor." I shuddered, cold suddenly, my head swimming.

I pulled myself the last step to the top of the escalator, my legs feeling like large cooked noodles. If he'd been just like the other bones, dead to the world in a hospital bed, I could have made it. But now that I finally saw Cameron Trexell in the flesh, I could see that he never plugged in permanently. Never had. Never would. His devotees had. I had.

I lowered the gun, put the safety on.

"Have things been fixed, in your wild attempt to wake people up? To make them see the world as you do? How many of them turned around and plugged back in, escaped their flesh and blood bodies?"

I leaned on the escalator rail, leaving a bloody smudge on the stainless steel surface. "Some of them stayed out."

He took a step toward me and I forced myself to level the gun at him again, even if the safety was still on. My arm felt like it was made out of iron, too heavy to hold up. "How many of them, even if they stayed out of the 'Net, fixed what you wanted fixed? How many of them got worthless jobs just to survive like you did?"

All of them.

Somewhere far off, I caught the scent of oranges, that bonehouse smell. Trexell himself may not be plugged in permanently, but somebody was around here.

He took another step. "Put down the gun, Chris. You're dying, and you gain nothing if either of us bites it."

I remembered waking up in the bonehouse dark, disconnected back into the flesh of my body, feeling it again. Bones aching. Atrophied muscles useless. Sobbing from the pain of badly used nerve endings while I waited for the 'Net connection to come back. Wanting nothing but to go back in, to feel the pain melt away, to have the body sense of myself as male jacked back into my brain. The bonehouse cat, a skinny black slip of a kitten, curled up by my shoulder, purring insistently, as though it could make me stop hurting through sheer force of will.

I still craved it, stronger than any drug. It was a million times worse now than the simple pang I felt performing an eviction. Even remembering the moments of intense pain, I wanted it. Needed it.

"Anyone I save from you is worth it for that alone," I said.

Another step toward me, his feet scuffing in the ash. The gun was only pointed at his feet, I couldn't sustain holding it any higher than that. "You don't want to stop us," he said. "We're showing the world that the Northern Coalition is no different from any other set of rulers in the past. Convincing them they must put aside their complacency and rise up."

I thought about the riots.

How many people did he have in his makeshift bonehouse? How many did he hold in other bonehouses across the country? "You never were Sammy Gauge, were you?"

"Of course not, although he was one of my best," he said. "He and I had too much in common, if you found us."

He took another step. He asked, "Do you remember when you used to have an effect on the world, instead of simply taking money to rearrange other people's lives? I don't think you'd be here if you didn't want to come back. This world isn't getting any better, is it?"

Every year, another disaster.

"You'd take me back just like that," I said. Twenty minutes and I'd be in. This time, there'd be no David to pay for my eviction.

"Just like that," he said.

I brought the gun up again, leaning on the escalator rail with my hip and using both hands to aim. I hit him twice, once in each leg. I hadn't aimed to kill, though at that moment I'm not sure I would have minded if I did.

He went down, screaming, cursing, and I dropped the gun, afraid he'd get it from me if I brought it nearer to him.

"There's more at stake here," he yelled at me, clutching one shin in both hands, even though it was bleeding just the same as the other. His gray pants gone a dark, bloody red.

"I know," I said, and then I got the tranquilizer into him.

The mall was silent again, except for the sound of my breathing and a cat mewling somewhere far off. I crawled over to where I'd left the gun and cradled it, watching for anyone coming out of the hallways or up the escalator.

The screen of my phone was cracked, but it still worked. I sent out my SOS call, with my GPS location. Told them to bring first aid resources and enough people to take care of Trexell's illegal bonehouse.

Jealous congratulations started pouring in, but I ignored the messages.

I watched the reflections of dark clouds in the mirrored surfaces of skyscrapers. I wondered if I'd won.

∞

SEX WITH GHOSTS

Sarah Kanning

It was a typical Friday at work; my day started with a first-timer interview. He sank into the black leather and chrome armchair, one hand gripping the other nervously as if to remind himself to touch nothing.

"Tell me about your firm's *sanitary* procedures."

Great. A germophobe. "Nothing's safer, Mr. Smith. The flesh of the bot itself is made of antimicrobial material, prepared before each session the way surgical instruments are cleaned."

They were all Mr. Smith; the only difference was the account number on the billing information. He'd given us that over the phone, a requirement to get in the door. A large enough credit line guarantees privacy at a place like the Boutique.

"Autoclaved?" A dew of perspiration anointed his upper lip.

"Cleaned ultrasonically, then treated with a combination of chemicals, UV light, and heat, and finally rinsed in distilled water."

He seemed to relax marginally.

"Would you like to review the templates now?"

Design a date: that was everybody's favorite part—or at least, everybody's favorite of the parts of the process that I saw.

You'd think there would be infinite variety in a place like this, where you can have sex with whomever or whatever you want, and there are a few truly strange requests that come in, but mostly it's the same sad old kinks.

Sex with famous people, living and dead. The star fuckers are the easiest to deal with, because they mostly have no idea what sex would actually be like with that particular famous person.

Sex with the ex. Sex with several of the exes. Sex with Catherine *and* her horse. Sex with the dearly departed—that always gets me down; people leave looking so bleak. Sex between two sex bots while the paying customer watches. Sex with a hermaphrodite. Sex with a famous person while the ex watches. Revenge sex. Greed sex. Closeted sex. Lots and lots of illicit and morally questionable sex.

Lots of nervous practice sex, trying out the moves before the big prom date or wedding night. Lots of sad and lonely sex. None of it real, all of it sex with ghosts.

I shepherded Mr. Smith through the design process, then sent him off with an appointment card and a dazed expression.

Jones must have thought it the height of wit to hire me, but it worked out well; to have anyone but an asexual in a job like "bot sex parlor interviewer/order-taker" would be inviting trouble in and putting it on the payroll. And a youngish woman with better than average looks and a deep well of patience and tolerance is a good fit for a job that entails asking paying customers to reveal their deepest sexual fantasies. Or at least the fantasies they would like fulfilled at this particular time.

For me, the choice was simple; it's expensive to live in Chicago, and glorified receptionist work anyplace else in the metro area would have paid about a third of what Jones offered. "Some girls aren't comfortable with this type of business," he had explained, shrugging. "But all I want from you is what's on the job description."

So it mostly worked out. My utter lack of interest in sex does seem to bring out the puckishness in some of the techs, however—especially Bill, the principal programmer. He's continually sending out new bots to try to tempt my nonexistent libido. His latest angle was literary figures, since he found out I majored in British literature in college.

"Miss Bingham, how delightful to see you!" His green carnation was a dead giveaway, even if I hadn't recognized the swoopy hair, heavy-lidded eyes, and general air of dissipation.

"Mr. Wilde, what an unexpected pleasure." I let him kiss my hand, and he lingered over it an extra moment, stroking my skin with his thumb. I suppose it's silly to try to be polite to a bot, since they preserve no memories after being repurposed, and wouldn't take offense even if they did, but still. Oscar Wilde.

"Fancy a shag, my dear?"

"A *shag*, Mr. Wilde? Isn't that a bit anachronistic of you? And aren't I bit out of your line?"

"Well, a man must keep up with the times. And be open to new possibilities. Constance never complained, at any rate." He perched next to me on my desk chair, leaning in. I could feel the warmth of his body, his ribcage expanding as he breathed. The bots are quite realistic. "How about it? You know, the best way to get rid of temptation is to give in to it."

"Yes, I seem to recall you saying that before." I rolled the chair a bit, throwing his weight off balance and causing him to rise. "But I'm afraid I could only give my heart—or anything else," I hastily amended, "to someone with strong moral character. And of course he'd have to be an early riser."

He recoiled in mock horror. "An early riser! Might as well ask someone to be brilliant at breakfast, and"—I helped him finish the phrase—"only tiresome people are brilliant at breakfast."

Unabashed, he tried a few more chestnuts out on me and trotted off again. *Is that the best you can do?* I messaged to Bill. *Not even that amusing.*

Be nice, Carla, he sent back, *or I'll send out an Anthony Trollope clone with enormous white muttonchop whiskers.*

I didn't think there could be much demand for Trollope, but I've certainly been proven wrong before. Bill was good; his Shakespeare was downright convivial, and could make you a proper cup of tea after a tumble. (I've sampled the former, not the latter.) I'm not sure how historically accurate that is, but it's a skill I can get behind. All the bots have built-in chess engines, but how sexy is that? I mean, how many people want to boff Bobby Fischer? (Answer: two, within the last seventeen months, in the Boutique's North American franchises.)

The next guy to come in seemed more nervous than the first guy, and got more nervous the minute he saw me. Strange.

I pulled up this new Mr. Smith's financials. Wow. Our services aren't cheap, but if he wanted to play Caligula at a Roman orgy, or quarterback of the football team getting it on with the cheerleading squad, he had enough flash to make it happen. Once or twice a month. There was a flag on his file, too: he was a frequent customer. He seemed vaguely familiar, but I didn't recall working with him directly before.

I started to feel him out—metaphorically speaking, of course—and he got shy. Not unusual.

"I want to talk to someone else." His gaze slid off me and fell to the floor. I felt like it had left a trail of slime on me.

"I'm sorry, Mr. Smith, are you unhappy with me for some reason?" I keyed in the code for a switchout.

"No, heavens no." He stammered a bit and wouldn't meet my eyes. His scalp glistened under thinning hair. "I just—I'm not comfortable talking about this particular, uh, order with you."

"Don't worry, Mr. Smith, Mr. Jones will be happy to continue your consultation." *Consultation* was the agreed-upon neutral term. Vaguely medical, or businesslike. Jones appeared, grinning like a shark, and cut in smoothly.

"Mr. Smith! A pleasure to see you again." He threw me a *get lost* look and I lost no time getting. Time for my lunch break, anyway.

Long past lunch and five consultations later (a couple of star fuckers, a re-creation of prom night, a widower looking for one last snuggle—poor bastard—with his wife, and a twosome looking to become a three- or foursome), I was ready to get home and hit the shower.

Sex. All those complications, all that messiness. It's like watching a group of enthusiasts really get into a hobby that you don't share. I mean, I don't understand the attraction of online gaming, either, but people spend their lives in that pursuit, too. I realize there's the whole propagation of the species angle to consider, but apparently I experience the phenomenon differently than most.

I was putting on my coat in the employee break room when I felt a presence. Not a human one. Bots must make some high-pitched whine, servomotors or something, that doesn't register consciously, but it prickles the hair on my nape.

"Bill, what did you send me now?" I asked wearily.

"Bill didn't send me." A woman's voice.

The voice was.... I knew that voice. "He would of course program you to say that."

"Oh, don't ruin the mood. Come on."

I turned around, got a good look at her—it. Me. My own face. Then I stormed past her to the programmers' cubicles.

"Bill, I am going to kick your ass from here to Cleveland!" I was shouting and running into things, knocking over the delicate fabrication instruments, the programming rigs. Techs scrambled to get out of my way.

He was cowering when I got there, cornered in his beige work area, eyeing the five-foot cube walls as if he might try some impromptu high jumping.

"It wasn't my idea to make her," he said, stammering a bit under my white-hot glare. "Jones signed the work order."

"And you just nodded and started scrolling through my security footage?"

"Listen, she wasn't even built here. We shipped the specs to Baltimore, and—"

"Baltimore? My sex stunt double has been screwed by the *Baltimore* office?"

Realizing he was just digging himself deeper, he fell silent. The beginning of wisdom.

"Clarkson, I am going to ask one question, and you are going to answer it. Truthfully." I glared at him and he managed to meet my eye for a fraction of a second. "Why did Jones want to make a sex bot with my face on it?"

Bill fidgeted and licked his lips. "He said, uh, he said, there were requests."

"We don't have to honor every request, do we?"

A mellow baritone cut through the tension in the cubicle. "C'mon, Carla. You know we'd double-bill Elvis and Mother Teresa gettin' it on for these jokers. And have."

"Jones." My employer. I whirled, rage searing through me. "This is different. I have to *work* here. Elvis and Mother Teresa don't. I don't want these creeps coming in here, thinking they'll get a piece of me, leering at me—"

"They do that now." His seamed, suntanned face was serene as a Buddha's.

"But there's a line, damn it! A line they shouldn't be able to cross."

"Carla. Our business is crossing lines." He gave me a cool, evaluating look. "Come on."

I knew where the playrooms were, but hadn't set foot in one since my orientation—despite the generous employee discounts. At the moment, one was set up like a locker room, another as a shoe store. Jones led me to a third door and opened it, waving me inside. I stepped through the door.

I was looking at the reception area where I meet with clients. No, not an exact replica. The chair was much more padded, and the desk was as large as a twin bed.

"You're actually fairly popular at the moment." Jones gave a small shrug. "Among a certain set of our clientele."

"The switchout with Mr. Smith?"

Jones inclined his head. "Although I don't know what possessed him to send that bot out to you. I assure you it wouldn't have been Bill's idea—he's been against this from the start."

"Well, that's just fucking great." I fought with my gorge and won, temporarily at least.

"I had hoped you would understand, Carla."

"No, you didn't, or you would have told me first." My vision blurred and went red around the edges. "You would have asked me."

"I—"

"Just save it, Jones. Save it for the paying customers."

I was out the door. Jones didn't follow me. Bill was hiding somewhere, which was fine. I didn't need to see him, either.

I didn't think too much about what I was going to do until I saw her again, standing in the corridor by the back door. She was wearing a wool skirt, black tights, a black tank top, and a cardigan—what I would wear, only shorter, smaller, tighter, and sluttier. I threw my coat at her. It.

"Put that on. We're going out."

"I'm sorry, I'm not allowed out, but we could go back to one of the rooms and—"

Shit. Built-in security protocols. Anti-theft insurance. I returned to Bill's cubicle (he had already fled), grabbed a programming rig, turned it on, and switched it to Simple Voice Command.

"Open the door and get out."

She—it—obeyed, and I followed, clipping the rig to my belt. What is it with programmers and little plastic boxes with belt clips?

"The white car. Get in the passenger side."

I drove five miles to a convenience store parking lot.

"Lean forward and pull your hair away from your neck."

"Glad to." The two words in her mouth somehow held infinite erotic promise.

"Shut up. We're just going to do a bit of minor surgery here. It won't hurt a bit."

I didn't actually care if it did. The GPS unit was in a port under the hairline at the nape of her neck—hard to find unless you knew what to look for. Luckily, Boutique designers firmly believe in plug-and-play. I dumped the chip in the back of a pickup with Tennessee plates. With any luck, it would buy me time to get away.

Get away. Where to, and for how long? To do what? I could barely look the thing in the face, and I was taking it on a vacation? I knew I didn't want it in my apartment. That was the first place they'd look, and besides, I didn't want it touching anything I owned. Having it in the car was bad enough.

I could get out of town, head south, find a little motel off the beaten path. I could spend a couple days away, get my head together. But if I was going to lie low for the weekend, I'd need some supplies. And cash.

When I came out of the convenience store, she was chatting up a middle-aged guy in the parking lot, standing next to his Subaru and giggling. He gave me a quick glance, and I heard him say something insinuating about "a *me* sandwich on *you* bread." Shit.

"Time to go, Sis."

She gave him a parting smile, but dutifully got back in the car. The guy watched her go, looking like a million dollars had fallen out of the sky into his lap and then vaporized. "Your sister says she likes to party," he ventured hopefully. "Do you like to party?"

"No." I left some rubber in the parking lot.

∞

It's an existential problem. It's as if one soul had been split off at the libido and placed in two bodies. It's like—I have no idea what it's like. I have no idea what it's like to exist only for purely physical, sexual pleasure.

∞

Taking a stolen bot across state lines, I thought as the "Indiana Welcomes You" billboard appeared ahead. *Got to be some kind of felony.*

But then, I wasn't sure it was entirely legal to create an automated sex worker who was the spitting image of one of your employees, either. Especially without that employee's knowledge and consent. So Jones might not even have called the cops. Anyway, if I were looking for a disgruntled employee with a stolen bot, I wouldn't look for them in La Porte.

If I were looking for anything other than fishing lures and maybe used truck parts, I wouldn't look for it in La Porte, but they did have motels. It was full dark by the time I pulled into the La Porte Country Inn and Cabins.

"I'm such a light sleeper," I told the bored innkeeper. She barely looked up from her game show. "Could you give me whatever's farthest from the road?" Off season there were plenty of rooms, even on Friday night. I got the keys to a cabin with a kitchenette in exchange for most of the cash I had with me.

I parked the car out of sight of the road and ushered my doppelganger inside. Then I carried in the supplies and shut the door. It was a beige room with beige carpet, beige curtains, and a beige bedspread on the king-sized bed.

"What do they call you?" I asked.

"Narcisse," she said.

Cute.

"And what should I call you?" She made even this innocent question sound like an invitation to unimagined delights.

"Ma'am," I said flatly.

"Yes, ma'am," she said, her voice instantly rising half an octave to make her sound like an uncertain schoolgirl. I sighed.

She kicked off her shoes and lolled on the bed. Its presence seemed to embolden her to kick up the charm a notch; she was practically purring. Time for a distraction.

"What can you do besides play chess?" I asked the bot.

"Besides the obvious?" My double arched her eyebrow.

"Do you have any idea how tiresome the sexual banter gets after a while?"

"Is that a rhetorical question?"

"Yes. So stop it. Now, what else. Besides that."

"I can do an initial psychiatric intake—"

"A counseling bot?"

"Just enough to sound like a shrink."

"The white coat fantasy?"

"Precisely. I also have extensive knowledge of eighteenth and nineteenth century English literature."

"Terrific."

"And I can do Swedish and shiatsu massage. You look like you could use some."

I stretched my neck, tilting my head from side to side. Tight as piano wire. "Grand theft sex bot is tense work."

The bot came and sat behind me on the bed and began to knead my taut shoulder muscles. It was the touch of a stranger, and I felt relieved—but would I have recognized my own touch anyway? Can't give yourself a back rub.

"Narcisse," I said, "do you notice anything funny about you and me? Any similarities?"

"What do you mean?"

"I mean get up. Look." The closet doors were mirrored; I pointed at our reflection in them. It was a lot easier to look at her reflection in a mirror; somehow she looked less uncanny.

"Oh," she said, her voice a bit uncertain. "We're very similar."

"Try fucking identical." We couldn't actually be identical—unless Jones had done more than scan security footage. I wouldn't have put it past him. "Narcisse. Take off your clothes. Everything."

"Sure." She giggled as if glad to be on more familiar ground, and was naked in a few seconds.

I breathed out air I didn't know I'd been holding in. Her moles and dimples and imperfections, though skillfully done, didn't match mine. So I would probably let Jones keep his balls. Probably.

"Do you like the way I look?" She spun and faced me, artfully jiggling things I have no idea how to jiggle. "You could take off your clothes, too, you know."

I felt suddenly exhausted by the psychic weight of all this weirdness. I flopped down on the bed.

"Or I could just give you a foot rub." Her naked thigh brushed my toes and raised gooseflesh all over me.

"Can you make me some tea? Oh, and how about putting some clothes back on?" She took the minimalist approach to following my last order, donning a pair of panties that resembled an eye patch, and then began to rattle things in the kitchenette.

"Lipton's okay?"

"Fine." I had a ridiculous thought. "Why don't you quote me some Yeats while you're at it?"

"*I made my song a coat,*" she replied, and I grinned. "*Covered with embroideries, out of old mythologies, from heel to throat.*" Ding of a microwave. "*But the fools caught it, wore it in the world's eyes as though they'd wrought it. Song, let them take it, for there's more enterprise*"—sound of water pouring into a mug—"*in walking naked.*"

"Bill, you high-class bugger, you surprise me," I said under my breath. Louder, I said, "Do your other clients like you to recite poetry to them?"

"I couldn't kiss and tell."

Right. Deactivated between sessions, she actually couldn't—her short-term memory was wiped clean each time. "Well," I asked, "what else have you got?"

"Whatever you want," she said. I rolled my eyes. She was made for sex, so I was just going to have to get used to everything coming out like a double entendre. Or a single entendre. Or just a dirty limerick.

"Here's your tea."

It was hot and steeped perfectly. I propped myself up with pillows to drink it, and Narcisse sat primly in a chair—primly except for her lack of attire, which made a mockery of the primness. They'd given her more than a smattering of my postures and tics, all gleaned from three years' worth of front office security tapes. I do sit primly.

No taping was allowed in the playrooms, a necessary precaution against blackmail. Small comfort; at least there weren't any sex tapes featuring my silicone twin floating around.

"You're tired and tense," Narcisse said. "A hot shower might perk you up."

"Are all sex bots this pushy?" I asked. But it did sound good. "You stay out of the bathroom. Understood?"

"Yes, ma'am." Her tone was mocking, but I knew she would obey. I mean, I was pretty sure she'd obey. Damn these later, more complicated models. The first-generation models were limited to the basic commands: *faster*, *slower*, *harder*, *softer*, and *more*.

She did obey while I let the near-scalding water pummel me for almost twenty minutes. I heard noises as I turned off the water. Instantly suspicious, I wrapped a towel around me and opened the bathroom door a crack.

Narcisse had opted to start the party by herself. Enthusiastically. My stomach lurched. It wasn't disgust I felt, but a kind of vertigo, a queasy sense of dislocation, and in back of that, loss.

Bots have acute hearing and sight, so I knew she'd heard the water shut off, had noticed the door open half an inch. The show was entirely for my benefit.

"You aren't Narcisse," I muttered, "just the reflection."

I could deactivate her, leaving her a dead marionette. I could melt off her face over the burner of the stove, revealing the titanium alloy substructure underneath. I could even instruct her to wade out to the middle of the lake, thirty feet deep, and stay there.

Instead, I crawled into the bed with that bit of my lost self. "Show me what makes you feel good," I said.

∞

She did. Categorically. Encyclopedically. Even limited by the number and type of bodies we had, and with no special equipment, it was fairly exhaustive. And exhausting. Outside it got dark, then got light again, a couple times. When I thought of it, I ate; when I needed to, I slept.

I wasn't horny or hot, but I was very, very curious. I did feel a shimmer of faint heat once or twice, but it was fleeting. That's just how it is with me. Narcisse, however, was like a fine-tuned instrument of sensation. A light breath on her skin subtly affected her body in half a dozen ways.

Finally I said, "Enough," and curled up to sleep. That was Sunday afternoon.

∞

On Monday morning, my first stop was Bill's cubicle. Narcisse, blank and obedient, was right behind me.

"Clarkson, that was bullshit about Baltimore. She's your work." It wasn't a question, so he didn't answer it.

"She was fabricated and tested in Baltimore," he said carefully, probably hoping I wouldn't shake him again.

"Any chance you can wipe her template?"

He looked at me mournfully. "Not if I want to keep my job." Right. Jones would have the final say.

It was as if Bill had read my thoughts. "Don't bother asking him. He's pissed enough that you took her off-site, unauthorized—"

"*He's* pissed?"

"Look, it stinks. I know it does. But it's his call."

"You see, *that* is a weasel," I told Narcisse as I left the cubicle and she fell into step behind me. "Now we go and meet the *asshole*."

"Weasel," she said, in a careful, neutral voice. "Asshole."

"Carla." Jones was waiting placidly in his office. "So glad you came back with my property. Saves me the trouble of having you arrested."

"*Your* property is wearing *my* face, Frank," I said. His genial slickness was already getting to me. How had I managed to work here for three years?

"I refer you to the waiver you signed during your first day on the job," he said calmly.

"You said that was for publicity photos, not sex bot templates!"

He just smiled his sharklike smile. "It's fair use, according to the terms of our agreement."

"Fair use to have those sweaty yokels drooling over me?"

"Carla. If a client treats you with anything less than perfect respect, I'll be happy to remove them personally from the premises."

"What about the ones diddling my evil twin in one of the back rooms?"

"You can't stop them from fantasizing about you. You and I both know that. It's fantasy we provide here, whether it's a fantasy about the latest movie star or the front office help. The great 'what if.'"

"Jones, you're full of it." I pulled my security card off my lapel and threw it on his desk. "This should make it simple. If she doesn't go, I'll be happy to."

∞

Even after three years, the personal items I'd accumulated in my desk fit into one box with room to spare. Bill and Jones both stayed away. It was Narcisse who strolled in as I was putting on my coat, and I got a near-paralyzing sense of *déjà vu*.

"Get lost, kid, you bother me."

I had reset her myself, so the events of the weekend were my memories only, recorded and preserved in my own head and no place else.

"Bill says he's sorry."

"Yeah, okay." Coward. "Tell him I'm leaving, so I'm expecting the demand to fall off quite a bit for the newest product."

She nodded, either not understanding or not caring that the message was about her.

"And tell Jones that he should model for the next one, so he can go and fuck himself."

I picked up the box and walked out the front door, the one the clients used after slaking whatever desire they imagined they'd brought in with them.

If I hadn't glanced back one last time just as I stepped onto the pavement outside, I would have missed Narcisse taking her place at the front desk, a bright and welcoming smile on her face.

∞

SEX WITH GHOSTS

SPOILING VEENA

Keyan Bowes

The snow thuds down like brickbats.

Instead of a soft and beautiful blanket, it lies on the grass in shards of ice. The party is ruined. It had sounded like such a good idea, snow in Delhi. Shalini should have known better than to trust Party Weather Inc. They haven't been able to deliver. Shivering, she herds the children into the veranda, out of the way of the pounding white chips.

"Let's bring in the cake, shall we?" she says, as the clatter of the hail on the cars parked outside distracts the children.

"Oh, can't we go out in that, Aunty?" It's a young boy called—Ajay, that's it, Ajay Zaveri.

"It's too hard, Ajay," replies Shalini. "I don't want anyone to get hurt." Or your lawyer mother to sue me, she thinks. India is becoming just too much like America since cable and satellite TV. She has releases of liability signed by every custodial parent, and still she worries.

"Maybe after the cake, Aunty, if it stops falling?" asks Preethi.

"Maybe," Shalini says. The cake is meant to resemble the castle of the Snow Queen, from the Andersen fairy tale, but the confectioner has built the US Capitol. Shalini hopes the children won't know the difference. She also alerts Jayesh that she needs reinforcements; her husband is hiding out in his study upstairs.

"I'll get on the phone," he promises. "Hang on. Don't let it spoil Veena's day."

"Cool! The Capitol!" says Rizwan, "Just like Washington."

"It looks like Rashtrapati Bhawan," says his twin, Ria, "but white-washed."

"It's the Snow Queen's palace," says Shalini faintly. Now that the child mentions it, the dome is indeed reminiscent of the Indian President's residence.

"The Snow Queen can copy the Capitol," says Preethi, politely coming to her hostess's defense. "Maybe she got bored with towers and turrets and stuff and wanted a dome. It's ice, right? It melts. She can have a different palace every year."

Shalini nods gratefully, then tucks the pallav of her sari out of the way and lights the dozen candles. The children crowd round.

"Happy birthday to you
Happy birthday to you
Happy birthday dear Vik-rum
Happy birthday to you."

Vikrum? Shalini looks at Veena, angelic in a snow-white taffeta dress that comes below her knee. She seems quite okay with what the children have sung, and blows out the candles in three tries. The single diamond, her parents' birthday present, glitters at her throat. Sparkling holographic snowflakes in her headdress reflect the myriad tiny lights with which Shalini has decorated the house and garden. Sweet tendrils of dark hair escape to fall down cheeks that are pink with pleasure.

The door-bell rings. Jayesh has pulled it off: Here is the Snow Queen, a whole hour early, to take over the party from her. The lady makes a magnificent entrance, swirling in through the front door in a scent of roses, greeting the birthday girl with an exquisitely wrapped present, and then magically making brightness fall out of the air onto the other children. There are oohs and aahs. They are the latest thing in cool fireworks from China, perfectly suitable for a crowded room on a gray day.

"Your majesty, can we go out? Before it melts?" asks one of the children. Shalini looks out to see that the 'snow' has stopped, and the ground is covered, inches deep, with ice chips.

The Snow Queen smiles at the eager girl. "First let me try it out. It looks cold outside. Do you have a warm jacket? Also I need to check the paperwork." Though it's summer, the 'snow' still shows no sign of melting.

Relieved, Shalini gives her copies of the releases, and waits while the lady takes a roll-call of the children to ascertain they are all listed. She isn't sure why organizing children's parties is so much more difficult than running a laboratory. Perhaps because they mean so much to Veena, perhaps because she herself is a bit shy—a trait she made sure Veena did not inherit.

Certain now that everything is under control, she slips upstairs to tell Jayesh about the failed snowfall and the strange birthday song. And have a cup of tea. Or maybe a whiskey.

∞

The Snow Queen is a pro; she is a schoolteacher who does this on weekends. She's invented games, dared what Shalini wouldn't and sent the children out into the garden in small groups, explained why ice floats, and kept them busy and happy. Eventually they all crowd round the large-screen TV for yet another dubbed-into-Hindi episode about the Celtic hero Cernunnos (now re-named Kanoon, the Hindi word for law) and his great wolfhound. The program's into its fifth season and seems entirely likely to continue for another five at least. After the party, the Snow Queen has silvery crowns studded with glittering icy jewels for the departing girls; and for the boys, spheres that spurt magic fire when you press them.

Shalini unwinds over another whiskey. Party Weather & Co calls to apologize, arrange a refund and explain that a virus corrupted their programs. Jayesh has built a real fire in the fireplace in the study, giving it a romantic smell of wood-smoke. The ice-storm chilled the surrounding air, so they can get away with it even in though it is not winter. Her mother, known to all as Mummy-ji, looks serene and silver-haired in the comfortable chair in the corner as she chats with her favorite son-in-law. Just look, thinks Shalini, it's like a story-book.

Shalini gazes at all the pictures of Veena that cover the walls, marveling at how quickly time has passed: There is Veena, a few months old, wearing a fluffy pink dress and a darling wreath of pink roses on her head. There is Veena in an embroidered blue silk lehnga and choli, toddling toward the camera at her uncle's wedding. There is little Veena in a sari, dressed up for her school's annual play.

And here is the actual Veena coming up the stairs, twelve years old already, tall and lovely in her wonderful white dress, her long dark hair coming undone from the chignon in which Shalini had put it up... where did the time go? How did we make a beauty like this child? She smoothes her own unruly curls, and looks adoringly at her daughter.

Veena's brought her presents upstairs to show her parents. From the Snow Queen, a brilliant snow-globe, beautifully made. In the center are two polar bears and a fir tree. When Veena shakes it, it plays a delicate tune. Something Western classical, Shalini thinks. Maybe Schubert? Then there's a remote-controlled truck, with a small GPS installed. A pin with a built-in cell-phone; Star Trek is enjoying a revival. A battery-powered holographic game that fills their living room with enemy soldiers for Veena to shoot at...huh? Shalini picks the box off the floor. The card attached says, "Happy Birthday, Vik."

"Vik? Veena, why are your friends calling you Vik?"

"They don't. Only Ajay, he's my buddy. The others call me Vikrum."

"What's wrong with Veena?"

"It's a girl's name."

"Aren't you a girl?"

"I am! But why?" she demands. "Who decided?"

"We did," Shalini says after a pause. She remembers their decision, to choose their baby. She and Jayesh had mulled it over, considered the expense, considered the payoff. They wanted a designer baby. It's the most important thing we'll ever do, Jayesh had said. Let's get this right, and damn the expense. This is an opportunity our parents never had, tweaking DNA.

She remembers the hours and hours they had spent with the specifications. Sitting in front of the screen, calibrating, raising this and lowering that. The massive spreadsheet with all those linkages to be considered. Physical specs, pre- and post-puberty. Talents. Temperament. Which part of it was causing this dissatisfaction, this questioning? Was Veena doomed to go through life never quite happy in her skin? Was it their fault? What had they done wrong? She says nothing of this to Veena. Instead, she says, "We wanted a little girl. We got you. We were thrilled."

Veena rolls her eyes. "Okay for you, Ma, but what about me?"

"Would you rather be a boy?"

"Duh-uh."

Shalini looks helplessly at the other two adults.

"I told you not to select the gender," says her mother, "Something like this was inevitable."

"Darling," Jayesh says to Veena, "Wait until you're eighteen and then you can choose."

"I want to be a boy now!"

"How long has this been going on?" asks Jayesh.

"Always. For ever."

"Your friends called you Veena last year," says her mother, "Or Vee. It wasn't that long ago you only wanted to wear pink. Remember when you wouldn't talk to boys?"

"Mo-om! That was years ago! I was a baby! I'm grown up now. I told them to call me Vikrum. They have to get used to my boy-name."

Shalini and Jayesh look at each other. "Sweetie, we can't just shift your gender like that," Shalini says, "It's very expensive. Universal insurance doesn't cover it. I don't know how we could afford it."

"You know," says Mummy-ji from the background, "Gender selection never should have been allowed in India. First we had a huge number of boys being born, and hardly any girls. Then girls and hardly any boys. Now, confusion."

"All the other kids' parents let them," says Veena.

"All your friends are changing gender? Ajay's always been a boy, as far as I know."

"That's just Ajay. But what about Preethi? She was a boy before."

Shalini sits down heavily on the floor. "Why?" she asks Veena. "Women can do anything they want. Even years before you were born, India had a great woman Prime Minister."

"Oooh!" says Mummy-ji, "How can you admire Indira Gandhi? What about the Emergency?"

"That's not the point, Mother!" says Shalini. "Besides, she herself lifted the Emergency."

"Only when she was forced into it," says Mummy-ji.

"How many dictators do you know who actually restored democracy within two years?" argues Shalini. "Are any of the countries that gained Independence when we did still democratic? Isn't it so, Jayesh?"

Jayesh diplomatically makes no comment. Instead, he turns to Veena. "It's true, what your mother says. You can be anything you want. Even Prime Minister."

"I don't want to be Prime Minister!" says Veena, "Anyway, not now. But boys get all the cool stuff! And they do all the cool stuff!"

"I told the Parliamentary Committee," says Mummy-ji. "I said it would worsen the gender divide, polarize the genders. Dr Mukherji, they said, thank you for your testimony, and just went ahead anyway. Isn't it so, Jayesh?"

"Girls can play with cool stuff, too, and do all the cool stuff," Jayesh says to Veena.

"But they don't," Veena picks up her toys. "I'm going to my room."

"Veena, sweetie," says Shalini. "Please...."

"Don't call me Veena!" Her voice sounds close to tears as she stalks off.

"I'm sorry, darling," Shalini calls after her. It's a wretched end to the birthday.

Jayesh silently busies himself with putting out the fire. The ice outside has melted away, and the temperature is rising again. He turns on the air-conditioning.

∞

Veena is the only girl wearing jeans. In the two years since the Snow Queen birthday, she has stopped wearing dresses altogether. But instead of graduating to the tunics and slender pants of the Punjabi suit, or even to sarees, she only wears jeans or slacks. Her hair is clipped short, and she's already running around with a group of boys, all engrossed in a new Alien Splatter holovid game released in Japan only this week. They are shooting at the escaped alien monsters that run across the park.

Veena races ahead of another child, dodges round a tree, crouches and fires. A huge green creature with horns running from its forehead down its back and sides rears up on ten legs to twice the height of a person, and then falls heavily sideways, spurting fluorescent purple gore. Behind it, an even larger crimson thing with eyes on eye-stalks shifts in and out of invisibility. "Vik! This way!" someone shouts, and Veena runs to the next tree to reinforce the attack.

The girls, dressed in designer Punjabi suits, watch and cheer occasionally as someone scores a particularly good splat. Some of them wear short white lace gloves, the latest fashion. They are waiting for the last guest before they take off to their own games in the clubhouse. The birthday twins have split up: Rizwan is killing monsters, and Ria waits with the girls for the friend delayed by traffic. Her party's theme is Fashion-show. But Veena has joined Rizwan's party, Alien Monster Safari.

The parents stand around under the trees, signing off on releases that limit the hosts' liability, and watching their children play. Shalini dreads the questions she knows she'll get about her daughter, but can think of no polite way just to leave. Sure enough, Ajay's lawyer mother, Mrs. Zaveri, together with Preethi's father, bear down on her.

"Shalini, why have a girl if all she wants to do is dress and play like a boy?" Mrs Zaveri says. "I just cannot imagine making my child to remain the wrong gender. If I can afford to change it."

Fine for you, thinks Shalini. Your Ajay's not agitating to be a girl. "Veena is going through a phase of exploring her gender identity," she replies stiffly.

"It might warp their personalities," says Preethi's father, as though Shalini hasn't spoken. "Once Preetam wanted to be a girl, I told his mother, 'Even if we have to spend for it, we must do it.' Otherwise it is just child abuse." Preethi, the former Preetam, is with the group of girls in lace gloves.

The crimson monster goes down to the combined firepower of the attackers in one of its brief moments of visibility, falling over with a roar and a gush of brilliant green blood. Immediately, a massive black alien rolls ponderously onto the field. It extrudes tentacles, seemingly at random, but as it comes closer to the trees where the boys shelter, they reach for the young hunters. Veena, Ajay, and Rizwan the birthday boy race around to get behind it. A tentacle darts out at the trio and hits Ajay on the shoulder. He goes down, and the strike badge on his shirt turns black. "Shit! I'm hit. Ten minute time-out." He retires to the edge of the field while Veena blasts the creature with her weapon. It shrieks loudly. Rizwan and Veena dance out of range of its tentacles. Another group of boys take advantage of the distraction to score another hit.

"What I don't understand is why you are thinking gender confusion is good?" says Mrs. Zaveri.

Preethi's father nods vehemently. "Veena should...."

"What is all this gender-switching like Broad-barred Gobies?" interrupts Mummy-ji. "It is not human to choose the sex at all. And then change if someone doesn't like it? Why?"

"Mother!" says Shalini, not appreciating this parental assistance, "We can talk about it another time!"

Fortunately, a car stops near them and disgorges another fashionably dressed youngster. Shalini grabs the opportunity to wish Ria a happy birthday, and leave with her mother before the debate becomes any more heated. "Mummy-ji," she says as they walk to the car, "You know their little girl started out male."

"I know that very well," says Mummy-ji "That does not make it right. Just look at that park. It's like the 1960s. Demure girls in pretty kameezes. . ."

"Mother, I wish you wouldn't get into these arguments."

"What if Veena wants blue eyes? Or augmented quick-twitch muscle fiber? Are you just going to keep doing these changes?"

As they get in the car, they hear a huge cheer of Shabash! Vik! Score! Apparently she's brought down the last alien.

Shalini had been concerned about spoiling Veena if they gave in on the gender change. But now, she feels she must talk to Jayesh. Was their decision abusive, as Preethi's father had implied? Maybe they can break into the money they've kept for Veena to go abroad for further studies.

∞

Shalini looks out of her window to where Vik stands tall beside his dad, directing the workers who are stringing party lights in the gulmohar trees by the front gate. A wonderful camaraderie has developed between them over the last two years. They watch cricket together in season, and he's begun to take an interest in his father's business.

The expense has been worth it. They've forgone all the little luxuries, the overseas trips, the new car. Of course they kept up appearances, but only she and Jayesh know how much debt they took on when she took six months' unpaid leave to help Veena through the transition.

Shalini wonders now if Jayesh would secretly have preferred a son all along, but had gone along with her desire for a girl. She wishes, momentarily, that they could have afforded two children. It would have been nice to still have a daughter. Girls are closer to their mothers, like she is to Mummy-ji. If they'd also had a son right from the start, would Veena have wanted to be Vik?

She brushes away these thoughts as disloyal. Vik is as handsome as Veena had been pretty. The girls love him. Yes, he seems more substantial, somehow, than Veena. She realizes she's said it aloud when her mother joins her at the window.

"It's the same person," Mummy-ji says, looking out at her grandson. "Veena, Vik, what's the difference? He's a good child now and he was before." She points to a van entering the driveway. "Look, the people from Flowers & Phool are here. You get ready, no? Some of the guests always come early."

Shalini nods. Some Westernized people actually will arrive at seven-thirty as invited instead of eight or eight-thirty. She goes to change from jeans into a heavy silk peacock-blue sari, her birthday present from Mummy-ji.

She pauses at the mirror. Just for a second she visualizes a male self, Shailen: a distinguished man with short hair graying at the temples. She imagines dominating the weekly research meetings and drawing covert glances from the young women scientists in her lab. Then what would Vik and Jayesh think?

Smiling to herself, she dresses, adjusts the drape of her sari, and goes down to deal with her birthday flowers. When Jayesh asks what is amusing her, she doesn't tell.

∞

SELF-REFLECTION

Tobi Hill-Meyer

The resemblance is uncanny. At first I don't notice anything because her short blonde hair standing in spikes is so different from my own dark curls working their way to my hips. Yet something about the way she holds herself draws me in. She clearly doesn't mind standing out in the crowd. She's wearing baggy pants with a tight-fitting tank top and a leather jacket with the word DYKE embroidered on the back. In this moderately conservative town, her outfit clearly screams "Fuck you!" at the straight world. At the same time it enticingly coos "Fuck me!" to the queer world.

I stop and can't help but stare as everyone else walks by. As she gets closer, I begin to notice little things. Her face is fairly distinct from mine, but there are definite similarities. Then when I catch her eye she flashes a particular smile at me: a crooked half smile that I've never seen on anyone but me before.

"That looks like my smile," I say with a touch of amazement in my voice.

"It is your smile," she replies.

I stare at her dumbfounded for a moment, not sure what she means by that. Then the other pieces begin to fall together: The same arc of her eyebrows. The same look she's giving me right now. The same skin tone. The same double-Venus symbol tattoo just below the left side of her collarbone. The same smart-ass tone of voice she's using with me. She is even wearing a handmade TRANS PRIDE button I designed.

"You're me," I say, "Aren't you?" She sits down on a bench next to me and takes her jacket off. I notice the embroidery again. It's a technique I've been learning, but it's far tighter and more orderly than my skill can produce. I look at her eyes and see small laugh lines beginning to develop. "...But older."

"You're a smart study, I never doubted that," she says, smiling.

"Does that mean you're from the future? How does that work? Can you tell me about what happens? Why are you here?"

She laughs for a moment. It's odd to hear my own laugh. It sounds different when it isn't coming from my own head. "I'm not really supposed to tell you those kinds of things. I'm not really sure how it all works myself." She leans over and in a hushed tone says, "But you might want to transfer your inheritance money out of the stock market before the end of 2007."

"It's 2009."

"Oh, well, you'll be fine. You'll get by without the money anyway." She gets up and pulls me into a more secluded space. The crowds disappear.

"So if you're not here to give me a message or a warning, what are you here for then?"

"I need a reason to visit now?" The joke seems more odd than funny. "The truth is that I'm here for a while before I can move on, and I don't really know anyone else here. I figured I might as well look you up. You'd understand better than anyone else we know. In 2012, I visited Mom and she almost had a heart attack."

I don't know why, but it kinda makes sense to me. I look back at her. She glances at the ground, and for a moment her face looks very tired and somewhat sad. I don't understand anything that's happening, but I realize that I don't need to. I put my arm around her shoulder. She looks back at me and smiles again, then embraces me in a long, comforting hug.

"Somehow I knew you'd understand." She looks at me a moment longer. "You said it was 2009. Does that mean you're dating Saphira right now?"

"For a year and a half."

"And you don't know Cayne yet?"

I think for a moment, then nod.

"And you're still poly, right?"

"Yep." I cock my head to the side. I can't really imagine a future where I'm not poly.

"Good, I just had to make sure. You can't always assume that all the details are still the same." She pauses then shoots me a smoldering look. "Anyway, if that's all true, then unless I'm mistaken, you haven't seen a trans cunt up close yet."

I perk up. "No, but I've been curious."

"That's another reason I wanted to stop by," she says, looking me up and down. "How would you like me to give you the opportunity?"

"No way," I say in disbelief, "But I'm non-op."

"You might be, but I'm not."

I've thought off and on about how I'd like to check out a trans cunt up close, but I didn't feel like it would be appropriate to just go ask someone. Having my future self here creates a valuable new opportunity. Before I know it we are back at my place, in my bedroom.

She gets on the bed and starts to take her pants off. A pulse of excitement runs through my body. Everything feels surreal. Like I'm not even sure if it's happening or not.

"Before we begin, we should check in about things. Part of why I haven't had the chance to do this yet," I explain, "is because as much as I want to know what it can look like and what it can feel like, the more significant part to me is that I really want to explore the sensation of it, how it feels to you."

"Oh, I'm well aware of that, Sweetie. Why do you think I came? I might get some details wrong now and then, but I know you inside and out. I came here because what you want is what I want. Besides," she adds, "you're a hottie and I've been envisioning this scenario for a while."

I smile at her. Suddenly I realize, regardless of the trippy context, I've got a strong and brazen beauty in my bed who knows every one of my desires and wants to play through them with me. This is hot.

She finishes taking off her pants. I glance down. Her legs have a different shape to them, probably due to a few extra years on hormones. That's not all I notice.

"Where did you get those scars on your legs?"

"The big one on the outside of my thigh was from a fight—don't worry, I messed him up even more. The smaller ones are from cutting." She watches me closely. I think she's looking for a reaction, but I'm not sure how I'm feeling. "You don't need to do that, by the way, if you can find a better alternative."

I decide that a minimal reaction is best. "I'll keep that in mind."

She must see my awkwardness with the topic and redirects us. "Come and get a closer look."

I move forward to look at her. The pattern of pubic hair is somewhat sparse, and I can see her labia underneath it fairly well. I glance up and notice her staring at me. I can feel myself blushing.

"It really is okay to touch it," she tells me.

I don't know why I'm being so hesitant. I pull her labia to the side and take a closer look. Her clit is actually pretty cute. Her bits really look like any other cunt I've seen, as unique as any other. "What made you decide to do it?" I ask.

"I realized that I had always been interested. I had just thought that if I had a spare twenty grand hanging around that I might have better use to put it to. But there are some real benefits to it. I don't have any problems in clothing optional space anymore, and I can go stealth in locker rooms, with Michigan festies, or even with one-night stands."

"You're stealth now?"

"Only for a few hours at a time." She flashes me my crooked smile again. "But I suppose the main two factors that pushed me over the edge were that my healthcare plan covered it—actually Saphira's health plan—but most health plans cover it now. And that I didn't want the risk of getting placed in a men's prison again."

It takes a moment for me to catch the significance of *again*. I should be disturbed by it, but for some reason I'm simply concerned. I look up at her questioningly, hoping for more explanation.

"Oh shit, that was insensitive of me. I didn't mean to tell you like that. But don't worry, I already took precautions to prevent it from happening to you."

"How did it happen to you?"

"It's a long story I'd rather not talk about. Let's just say it had to do with an abusive partner and survival crime. Life sucked for a while, but I got through it and I'm stronger now than I was then."

I can see the pain again. She's been hurt a lot. I wonder if, despite her mysterious precautions, that will happen to me.

"Hey, mind if we get back to the fun stuff? I know you'd love to see me get off, and I've actually been wanting to try this for a while."

I smile back at her and let her change the subject. "I'll grab the gloves."

"Hmm, that brings up an interesting question. I wonder if it's possible for me to give you anything? That seems like it would be a bit of a paradox."

I think about it a moment. "There's enough paradoxes floating around already. Besides, it's a part of my agreement with Saphira."

"Oh, certainly. Of course. I just get curious. Those kinds of things are hard to figure out."

I move closer to her and run my hand up her leg.

"Before you start...." She beckons me over. I come to her side and she pulls my head toward her and kisses me on the forehead. "Have fun, darling."

A little more relaxed, I cup my hand over her cunt and hold still a moment. Then I back off slightly and give her some light and teasing touches. She responds positively, with a slight shudder and a sigh. A smile comes to my face. I'm getting really turned on. I run my tongue over her thigh. Then I turn my focus to mapping her vulva with the tips of my fingers, enjoying every tactile sensation.

Once I'm satisfied I slip on a glove and douse my hand in lube.

I move my hand between her legs and find her opening. After rubbing the lube around a bit, I slide a finger in. Her eyes flutter as she takes a breath. It went in easily.

I feel around a bit, drinking in every sensation I can. I'm in up to my last knuckle. She's moaning softly. I back out to insert another finger. This time she gasps. I do a come-hither motion and she arches her back.

"There, oh fuck, yeah," she says between breaths, which are coming faster and harder. "Please, right there."

"You're a lot of fun to play with." With my other hand I squeeze her clit between her labia and rub it. She lets out a series of staccato breaths. Encouraged, I increase my pace. She writhes under me.

A moment later I slow to add another finger. I push all three in as deep as I can. She starts lifting up to me and I can feel how much her cunt wants me.

"Oh, yes," she cries. "That's what I need, fill me more."

I use a fourth finger as well. There's more resistance and I slow, then drizzle more lube over her cunt. It takes some time, then I can feel her opening up, begging to swallow my fist.

"Try your whole hand."

Doing as she says, I tuck my thumb under my other fingers and press in. I'm in awe and not sure if it will work, but I keep the pressure on. As her moans and movement build, my hand slips into her. She's gasping. I'm filled with a sense of amazement. Her pulse beats around me.

She reaches down to stimulate her own clit. Her whole body is tensing and pulsing. I can feel it as her cunt clenches around my fist. I hold her hip tightly as her body rocks. Then she's spasming. I feel her cunt quiver around me. Her abs tense and she almost sits up. Then her body slumps back and goes slack.

I take the cue to slowly remove my fist. When I finally am out she lets out a long breath. I lie down on the bed next to her and she puts her arms around me.

"A thousand throngs of thundering thespians, goddamn, I needed that!" She gives me a peck on the cheek. "It's been a while."

"Of course. I should be thanking you."

"You really are an adorable sweetie. I kinda miss that part of me." She brushes the hair out of my eyes. "So, what do you think?"

"That was incredible. When did you get it?"

"In 2015. As soon as I could after I got out."

"You know, I don't think you lost it," I say, "the sweet caring part of yourself, I mean." I lean over and give her a kiss. She's somewhat surprised at first, then kisses me back with a gentle tenderness that makes my heart swoon. I run my hand through her hair and kiss her harder.

I roll over her and run my hand down her side. Her hand moves up under my shirt and scratches my back. The sharp sensation intensifies the arousal I'm feeling. Her fingers find and undo the snap of my bra.

She gets my shirt off and cups one of my breasts in her hand. She pinches my nipple between her middle and ring finger. I moan. She twists. I gasp and pull back slightly. I'm disoriented for a moment, then she pushes me onto my back and is sitting on top of me and holding a royal blue dildo.

"The Empress! You still have her after all these years?"

"Of course. When you form a psychological connection with one of these babies, it doesn't go away easily." She leans over me. "You did such a nice job with me just now, how would you like it if I returned the favor?"

"Please."

She gets off the bed and walks around by my feet. She's wearing a strap-on harness, but I don't remember her putting it on. I grab the lube and spread some on myself. Kneeling at the foot of the bed, she lifts my legs into the air and leans over me.

She kisses my ankle and guides the Empress to my ass. I'm hungry and ready for her. She pushes the tip into me. I moan. She holds still for a moment while I adjust. Minute by minute, inch by inch, my ass swallows her. When she knows I've had enough time, she pulls almost all the way out, only to sink deep into me in one fluid motion.

I arch myself into her and she alternates between a few slow thrusts and several faster ones. I let out a slow groan. She reaches down with one hand to play with my breasts. As I get more into things she shifts her position so she's lying on top of me and kisses my neck. She's panting.

"How much can you get out of using that?"

"Quite a bit, actually." She moans into my ear while making several quick thrusts in succession as if to demonstrate. She grips my hair and grinds her hips into me. Her head lifts up and leans back. She's a lot louder. Her energy is intensifying, then suddenly she downshifts and returns to her previous patter.

She smiles at me. "A little more of that, and I could have come."

After a while I roll us over so that I'm on top. I've got room to touch my bits now. She's still thrusting up into me. Everything feels so good. She's staring straight into my eyes with such intensity and focus. The sensation is arcing. Waves of pleasure crash over my body. I collapse onto her. A tingling sensation is still making its way back and forth over my spine. I wrap my arms under her back and clutch her to me.

After it subsides I lift myself up and pull the dildo out. I snuggle up to her side. "Damn, I love you," I say.

"I love you, too." She laughs. "But seriously, I'm really glad you still think I'm worthy of your love."

"I don't think you've changed as much as you think you have. At least not in the important ways."

"Keep that in mind," she says. "You and I, we're resilient. I've been through a lot. A lot that I hope you don't have to deal with. But even with all that, you can still love the self that I've become. I hope you never stop loving the self that you are."

It's a rather beautiful sentiment. "Is that the message you came here to give me?"

"Maybe." She grins and looks to the side. "Hey, you wanna try something really weird?" She pounces back onto me and changes the subject, a habit I hadn't noticed about myself before. It's also interesting to realize how much bubbly energy she has, and I wonder if I'm like that too. She interrupts my thoughts and holds up a condom. "I'm creaming all over at the thought of you fucking me with your bits—if you feel comfortable with it."

I smiled. "I like how you think."

We keep going like that for who knows how long. We try everything we can think of. I'm getting to know her body really well, and she already knows mine. Occasionally we take breaks and she tells me more about her life. Time slips by. It's hard to keep one moment distinct from the next. I don't remember it becoming night, but suddenly it's morning. I must have fallen asleep.

I feel arms around me. I turn around to kiss my future self, but she's not there. Instead, it's Saphira. She's awake and kisses me.

"Saphira, when did you get here?"

"I got back really late last night and you had already fallen asleep. You looked so happy I didn't want to wake you."

Now that I'm more awake, I think I realize what happened. *Oh well,* I say to myself. *I guess I can never deny being vain again.*

"I had a thought last night, darling." It would be nice to keep my options open. "What would it take for me to be on your health plan?"

∞

THE METAMORPHOSIS BUD

Liu Wen Zhuang

It was an ordinary morning in every other way the day Georgia awoke to discover that she was not herself. Usually, the first sounds she heard were the thin horn melodies coming from her cheap bedside clock radio, tuned to a local jazz station. She would lie there in the dark thinking how snug she felt wrapped within her blue and white comforter, and doze a few more moments before launching herself out of bed and into the world. Today, however, she rolled onto her side and felt something cool shift inside her underwear.

Her eyes flew open and in the same instant it seemed that the temperature within her little cocoon dropped by a few degrees. She felt her eyes must be so wide open that the whole dawn darkness must be seeping into her head, an ebbtide that left in its wake light that lifted and brightened in front of her. The effect was dizzying.

She realized she was just holding her breath and watching the day break. Slowly, so as not to shock her system, she let the air out of her lungs.

Georgia put a cautious hand onto her abdomen. She felt the elastic edge of her panty directly below her belly button, the superfluous satin rosette attached to the lace-trimmed edge just like the rosettes that adorned all her bras and panties. So far, nothing unexpected.

Her hand crept further down inside her panties, over her hair, which on any other day, would have been covering her pubis, the bone palpable underneath the fur. Instead, she felt a tube of very soft, fine-skinned flesh lying amid her hair.

Upon touching it, she drew sharply back and put her hand instinctively on her chest in a gesture of supine surprise, breathing shallowly but quickly the whole time. How terrifying. She'd flinched away and at the same time the mass of flesh had moved in an equal and opposite direction from her, one of the muscles down below contracting through instinct. She squeezed her eyes closed even more tightly and willed herself to sleep, hoping that on the second try she would wake up and find nothing about herself changed.

Behind her lids, however, Georgia's mind buzzed like a fly the thickness of a windowpane away from its life. A thought occurred to her and, blinking, she reached out tentatively to see if her left breast was there, which it was, and then the right breast. She imagined her breasts under the skin—green veins woven around and through fat over her chest muscles—and was relieved.

Very well, she thought, is this a matter of addition to what I already have, or a substitution all together? Of the two, she supposed she preferred the additive effect, as at least there would be something familiar still left to her. Extra things one could deal with, like a newly discovered wart or a toenail that had grown unchecked, but substitutions implied an unknown force keeping some sort of balance on the grand genital ledger, on which she had come out on the penis plus side.

There. She'd finally said it. She blushed in the lifting dark, imagining her mother's ghost frowning; she had most certainly not been brought up to speak so baldly about her...parts, making so bold once and only once to refer to the love-thumb set among the whirlygigs, but this was an unusual situation, maybe even properly clinical in nature, and so for once coy baby names and the gutter nomenclatures she noticed so many young people using these days seemed wholly inappropriate. And what else could that tube be?

She sighed. If she *had* to have a penis, Georgia thought, she hoped at least that it was hers. That is, she dreaded the idea that she had been subjected to some cruel cosmic joke in which she lay here, sweating and agitated, completely without dignity, with someone else's organ while some other person elsewhere did the same, wondering how his genitals had suddenly gotten so complicated and involuted. A newly sprouted penis could be borne, like an unexpected guest, so to speak. It was a lot like having a hernia, she imagined. To be vagina negative, however, struck her as deeply terrifying.

Had she wanted children, or been much younger, it might have been devastating in another way to wake so altered. True, Georgia had never enjoyed the cramps, the bloating and monthly feeling of over-ripeness, but those years were very much behind her. No, she couldn't say that she felt an abiding regret for children never birthed, nor unadulterated pleasure that she would be without menses. It was this, Georgia decided: the appearance of a penis meant changes in the superficial contours of one's body, but the absence of a vagina bespoke internal rearrangements that went to the deepest parts of one's being. The vagina was connected to the uterus, the uterus was connected to the ovaries, the clitoris anchored to the vulva, and so on. Georgia wanted to believe that her inner organs were aligned around the assorted sacs and spaces that had always been there. She wanted badly to have her innermost self unaltered, whatever that was.

The phone rang just as Georgia was preparing to lift up her nightgown and check.

"Claude?" she said with agitation, as if she didn't recognize the voice of the man she sat next to while answering the lines every Monday, Wednesday, and Friday morning at the Senior Health Clinic Hotline.

"Georgia? Are you feeling all right today?"

"Yes, well, no," Georgia said, rasping her voice a bit. She cleared her throat. This faking was undignified. "I'm sorry I didn't call; I won't be coming in today."

"Hmmm, well, we thought something was amiss when you didn't come in on time. Coming in on Monday, do you think?"

"Impossible to say," said Georgia. "I'm feeling a bit out of whack...sorry not to call earlier." She noted that the sun was high in the sky—how long had she been sitting here navel-gazing?

"Yes, well, get some rest. Check in with us tomorrow."

Georgia murmured a farewell in feeble tones and hung up. She'd barely been able to keep the tremble out of her voice—she'd been handed a day off from work, and maybe the next day too! Should she call May and...? No. Better to keep this to herself, for now. She didn't feel like sharing something so unlikely. Still lying in bed, she peeled off her underwear clumsily, snagging it over the unfamiliar mass of flesh. She kicked the panties off her feet, sending the covers flying. Georgia stood, nightgown bunched around her waist, feeling her spine crack vertebra by vertebra as she bent forward to see herself more clearly.

Indeed. There it was. It had a cowl around its neck. She shook her hips: it waggled from side to side. Well! When she was little she had always wanted a tail. And here it was.

∞

It was a delightful day. In the morning, Georgia had spent some time outside in her garden in the company of her cats. Together they had dug in the sweet dirt, Georgia uprooting stray weeds from around her rose bushes, Ginger, Nutmeg, and Aspic rolling and scutting their heads against the small pebbles in the tea garden. Georgia had copied it from a visit to Golden Gate park last year. She made a mental note to buy a gardening book that would show her what else she might try next, now that the roses were finally on their feet.

About noon, Georgia stopped and fixed herself some excellent raspberry-mint iced tea she had purchased from the market right around the corner. She sat in the brown wing-backed chair, her head against a crocheted doily made by her mother years ago, and nodded at the parade of young folks trooping in and out of the living room. She had four young women of varying ages who boarded with her. Two were out of town, and two were setting up instruments in the unused garage in the back. Only one was in the band, but the other was the business manager. Some of the other band members were also helping out.

The one who liked to be called Zeke had small, dark eyes and a mane of very large black hair, some pieces of which were dyed a deep but discernable emerald green tipped with dark blue. She emerged from the shed, came through the kitchen's back door, and flopped down on the couch in the living room on the corner near Georgia, panting.

"Have some iced tea, Zeke," said Georgia.

"Do believe I will," said Zeke amiably. "Care for a refill, Miz Samson?"

Zeke spirited the nearly-empty glass away with grace while the rest of her moved with big, bold swinging movements that looked careless.

Both settled comfortably again, Zeke said, "Thanks for letting us use the garage, Miz Samson."

"Oh, it's Georgia, please. You're welcome, my dear." Georgia took a long sip from her iced tea. She couldn't keep her mind from their last chat, in which Zeke had confided that her band's name was King Twat. Georgia had been embarrassed by May's, er, Zeke's explanation of her last name, King, as a corrupted variation on Ching, also known as Chin, depending upon which dialect you spoke. Georgia had been all tongue-tied, not knowing whether she should say that her best girlfriend had exactly the same name for exactly the same reasons. Oh well. Let this dear young woman think with the arrogance of youth that she was the first to have discovered everything.

"And how are the gender spies and cultural provocateurs doing?" said Georgia, referring to King Twat's motto. By squinting her eyes a little, she could just make out today's t-shirt. It was a head the shape of an oval, accentuated by a Van Dyke beard and hollow cheekbones, looking suspiciously like the bard of Avon—but in fact, it spouted like a whale. Heavy gothic type below the disembodied head read I Have a Boner to Pick With Freud. People did have their opinions these days.

"Rippin', just rippin'," said Zeke, making up what she thought sounded slangy. Georgia took this to mean that King Twat was doing well.

Georgia lifted her glasses to her face out of habit, knowing full well she had better distance vision than near vision. Of course they weren't of any use. "I notice you have a ring...." Georgia pointed to her nose.

"Yeah, it's new. I got it for tonight's show. Do you like it?" Zeke wanted to know.

"Pretty," Georgia said truthfully. "Is it gold? With a gemstone?" Georgia wanted to know in turn.

Zeke nodded shyly. "I couldn't afford a diamond, so I had an Austrian crystal set into it instead."

"Was it any more painful than having your ear done?" Georgia asked.

"No, not at all," Zeke said," although the genitals and nipples are actually quite painful." She added, almost as an afterthought, "I have friends who've had nipples and clits pierced."

"Oh my," said Georgia, knowing she sounded every one of her eighty seven years.

∞

Later that day, Georgia thought back to their conversation as she rode the bus to Lake Merritt, the stale buns meant for ducks clutched in an old breadbag on her lap. Who could I tell about my penis? she thought, the pastel Victorians whizzing past her. Would Zeke be able to help me? She seemed like such a level-headed, open-minded person. So matter-of-fact about people's bodies. Later that morning Georgia had discovered that she did still have a vagina, which was of immeasurable relief. But throughout the day, her mind constantly came back to one idea, which was to get herself altered so that she urinated through a nice neat opening without a lot of extra flesh.

She had of course experimented with her new penis, seeing if she could direct the stream with laser-point accuracy (to her disappointment, she couldn't)—even giving it a few tugs to see if the orgasms were any different, but the inside-out feeling of pulsations travelling down and away from her to the tip of her penis and out the end left her feeling blank and spent instead of newly charged and with a tender elasticity focused inside. Of course one felt alert and refreshed after sex; blood circulated quite nicely once it had made a pass through the clitoris, bringing oxygen to the brain and pleasant muscle tone all over. She found she vastly preferred to feel focused instead of dopey and sleepy; perhaps this was only her experience with her penis, she concluded, and not necessarily connected to the sensations brought on by the condition of having a penis.

The bus hissed to a stop and Georgia headed past Children's Fairyland to the bird sanctuary on the lake. With her was a thermos stowed in a canvas bag that held more iced tea: lemon-mint this time. Yes, she thought, the semen had been interesting; she had even tasted some from her fingertips, there in her bathroom, but she had never been keen on the taste of anyone's sperm and saw no reason why her own would be an exception. It wasn't a dislike founded on prudishness, she thought, but a preference for sweet things that really kept her from savoring the salty fluid, a preference for sweet things probably the result of spending much time in the South. Why, she liked her iced teas fixed Southern-style, with several heaping tablespoons of sugar that never quite dissolved on the bottom of the pitcher.

Georgia shifted the canvas bag so that the large water-bottle that held the iced tea wasn't directly on top of her sandwich. She walked briskly along the goose-spackled sidewalk leading to the bird sanctuary, avoiding the large greenish-black splodges, past the children's maze consisting of a hedge a half a foot high, and rounded the bend to her favorite park bench.

She had just set her canvas bag down on the bench and was preparing to take off her sweater when a four or five year old child who had been running in large, loopy figure eights ran away from his mother, up the path to Georgia, and made several big circles around her and the park bench. He was laughing and shutting his eyes every now and then, daring himself to run a few steps blindly. Georgia stood still, clapping and laughing with the boy. He surprised her by gurgling with pleasure and mounting the park bench, launching himself along the length of the seat, hurdling over Georgia's bag while his mother called to him to stop, and finally flinging himself off the end of the bench against Georgia's soft body.

She felt this slightly sweaty child's body thud against hers; her arms curved to catch him, and she distinctly registered a small "oomph" as a sharp, bony part of the child landed square on her testicles, sending shock waves she had never felt before into her spine. The mother, an angular, careless creature herself, had slowed down the moment she saw that her boy had a soft place to land from his flight. She kept calling her son's name ineffectually.

The child slid down from Georgia's arms, with Georgia doubled over him, gasping slightly. He saw a new game forming and dodged his mother by using Georgia's body as a bunker.

"Eh-eh-eh-eh-eh-eh-eh!" he shrieked, making machine gun motions to go with the noises.

"That's enough, Willy, leave the nice lady alone," said the mother. She held her hand out to him.

"I think your mama wants you, son," said Georgia, relieved.

The child looked up at her with achingly candid affection. He put his arms around her hips and pressed himself to her in a farewell hug, the side of his head mashing the unfamiliar mass. Georgia winced again; the child looked up at her with alarm and confusion. The bodies of women he assumed to be like his mama's, indeed, treated like his mama's to nestle in or climb as he saw fit; he never thought they would be remotely like his own. He knew not to hug daddy in certain ways—why then did this old woman hold her body so as to protect her privates from him in the way other men did? This was too confusing. He dashed to his mother in genuine consternation.

His mother said, "Don't worry, Willy, I won't hit you for being bad if you promise me to never do it again." He clung to her, mute, his ear pressed to her body, which felt normal and smooth. To Georgia the mother said complacently, "Boys will be boys," which was not at all the apology Georgia was expecting.

∞

But would boys be only and always boys? wondered Georgia. She cast pieces of bread out to the greedy geese gathered at her feet. She'd been sitting at this park bench for several minutes now, mulling over the encounter with the boy, long gone, who had clearly found her monstrous. This disturbed her even more than the fact that there were badly behaved children out there who needed curbing. She hadn't considered herself a monster, because she hadn't felt who she was today was any different from who she had been yesterday, or all the days before that.

Georgia drank some more iced tea. She felt she really ought to entertain the idea that she might have a penis for the rest of her life, which she hadn't up to this point. She supposed she had just assumed that it had appeared one day and would be gone the next. Georgia saw that this was wishful thinking, and that she had better reconcile herself to holding herself differently. Right now, for instance, her bladder felt full, but one of her testicles felt a bit uncomfortably twisted. Georgia truly had no idea how it had assumed that awkward position. She hadn't sat oddly, she didn't think; it was just that she had parts which now slid around unpredictably. A breast would never move so that it was lodged under one's armpit, for example.

In the stall, she arranged her bag on the hook behind the door and settled comfortably on the seat to relieve herself of the iced tea. I must be pissing fit to flood a small town, she thought. At that, she reflexively tightened her muscles (and noted the delayed response) at the sudden uncomfortable thought: er, was the water level in the bowl rising? She hadn't ever been sympathetic to men standing and pissing—had thought there was really no good reason they couldn't sit in comfort like women and have a moment of personal reflection at least once a day—but it occurred to her that water levels were…unpredictable, to say the least. The idea disgusted her, but also gave her another idea. She had been altogether too unadventurous with this new appendage, she thought. Georgia was glad she had drunk as much tea as she had.

She gave the toilet a decisive flush and smiled to herself all the way to the bus stop.

∞

Her plastic water bottle now refilled with caffeinated orange pekoe iced tea and lying on top of a book in a cloth grocery bag, Georgia set out to see how the other half lived. She put her hand in her trouser pocket. For about ten dollars, she had been able to buy a good quality, summerweight two-piece suit, singlebreasted, and a starched white dress shirt from a secondhand shop on the way home. In her bedroom, while trying everything on, she had discovered the wonderful convenience of an inner breast pocket sewn into the lining of the suit jacket and wondered aloud why women's clothes were not similarly appointed. Was it because women were supposed to avoid the implication that they touched, however accidentally, their own breasts? In that case, just who did one's breasts belong to, if not oneself?

At first, she thought she really ought to stick her whole arm, up to the elbow, into the pocket, if at all possible. Putting her arm into the silky black hole had caused the rip in the pocket to gape. It was just as well; there seemed to be a piece of paper in there, anyway. Drawing her hand out took a little maneuvering, because one corner or the other of the postcard kept catching on the narrow slash of satin. How like a little gift, Georgia thought, threading the last bit of bright pink embroidery floss onto her needle because she was out of black thread. She set the postcard aside, and when the last stitch was in, she clipped the thread close to the knot.

Putting on her reading glasses, she saw that the discolored scrap of cardboard had on one side a picture of a lone flowering tree in a field of green. The flowers had once been white but were now yellow due to the postcard's age. Turning the card around, she saw that there was no message or identifying information of the scene on the front. She tucked the old postcard in between the glass and the frame of her dressed mirror and, slipping the jacket on, stepped back to finish surveying herself.

Luckily, she had remained rather slim—in fact, her thigh was about as big around as a can of creamed corn. The starched shirt stood away from her modestly flat chest, safety pins had taken care of the extra sleeve lengths, and the suit's pantlegs had required very few alterations. The rest hadn't been difficult: she seldom wore makeup. She had managed to make it to the gate that separated her yard from the sidewalk when Zeke, heading home, spotted her and made her stop.

"Georgia," Zeke had said, catching her gently on the arm, "I think you're missing a hat."

"My hat?" Georgia said, puzzled at first.

"Wait here, I've got just the thing," said Zeke, jogging past Georgia up the walk and into the house. She returned with a dark brown hat to go with Georgia's chocolate-brown suit. It had a fold in its crown and a very small brim, with a band of medium-width grosgrain ribbon knotted discretely around the base of the crown.

"See, your hair is just a little too long on the top and sides to be gentlemanly," said Zeke. "You wet it to slick it back and parted it, didn't you?"

Georgia nodded. "Is it starting to dry and curl back?"

"Mmm-hmm," said Zeke.

Georgia smoothed her fast-drying curls with one hand, jerked her hand away, and jammed the fedora on her head quickly with the other. "Good thinking," she said, flicking the brim of the hat in a one-handed salute to Zeke and then settling the hat more securely on her head. "I'll return it to you as soon as I'm back from—"

"—Gender-spying?" Zeke grinned. "Keep it as long as you want."

So for the remainder of the day, Georgia resolved to gender-spy by urinating in as many different men's bathrooms all over San Francisco that she could think of. Lots of times she was thwarted by the unisex toilets in many bookstores, movie theaters, and a particular coin-operated laundries-slash-café, where the toilets were labeled Readers and Writers. Fortunately, however, she had plenty of iced tea.

The cloth bag the iced tea container was in was something of a problem. Georgia hadn't thought to bring her purse to experiment with a suit-hat-handbag combination, though this being San Francisco, it would have been hard to shock in many neighborhoods. But she found that she hadn't given adequate consideration to exactly what kind of satchels nearly-ninety year old men would have commonly carried, and the cloth grocery bag was really dissatisfactory because there weren't convenient fixtures to hang the thing from in men's lavatories, nor were there many clean spots on the floor near one's feet.

In fact, Georgia had been astonished to learn that many men hadn't mastered basic habits of hygiene when it came to relieving themselves.

Georgia counted exactly three men out of about fifty that she had observed that day who washed their hands after using the urinals, not including herself. She hoped, in vain, that none of them worked in food services. An equally alarmingly small number of men seemed inclined to wash their hands after exiting the stalls. This seemed to be what one might expect from grubby nine year olds, she thought. At least fifty percent of the women she had observed over the course of her life (with the low-grade social sensor that many women like herself seemed to share) washed their hands no matter what they had done. And she considered those barely acceptable statistics. So unlike what she had heard of Singapore, where they had a law fining you if you didn't flush the toilet after you were done using it. Georgia thought enforcement of that law might be a bit of a strain on one's notions of privacy, but she had to admit that there was something to the spirit of the law that appealed to her.

But these men! It was unbelievable what she had observed. One fellow at the Exploratorium men's lavatory had been staring into space at the urinal and dribbled a bit onto his shoe before he was quite finished. Another man Georgia had caught rearranging himself absent-mindedly through his pants after having walked a full three feet away from the door of the restroom, back into the second-to-last circle of hell that was the street level of San Francisco Centre. Georgia wondered, what, did he think he was invisible? Why did men feel free to rearrange themselves so openly, yet discreetly? Wasn't that a contradiction? And at the Castro movie theater, she heard rather than saw someone come in and use a sink in the row of sinks along the wall behind her, as all the urinals were taken. At least he washed his hands, she noted—or should he have used the same sink? she wondered on second thought.

By far the most interesting experience Georgia registered was the time she caught the man next to her observing her. Here was another (another?) older man, one who had a craggy, stern face. Her stream faltered, then stopped altogether when it became clear that her neighbor's eye movements kept darting downward. She felt a miserable warm flush creeping up the back of her neck that wouldn't stop until it reached her tingling scalp. This whole business of glimpsing and being glimpsed was something she had had great difficulty mastering. Georgia, of course, was not used to grasping the most of details in her side vision as the other men were. She was, after all, there to see what she could see, but without letting on, and now this man was eyeing her rather openly.

What's wrong? she wanted to shout. What could you possibly be staring at?

She took a quick look down, first at him, and then herself. Ohhh, she thought, feeling as if the floor beneath her feet had opened onto a bottomless chasm where a jarring crash awaited her. The pink rosette on her underwear was hanging askew by a loose thread, having been twisted and stretched around in ways that it wasn't used to. His boxer shorts had no such rosette.

He thinks I'm a—a—fetishist, said Georgia to herself as the man grinned at her with knowing amusement.

"Suspenseful," he said to her, meaning the dangling rosette. "Mostly you shake the dew off the lily, and not the lily into the dew."

She looked at his laughing face. Her expression of utter surprise melted into mirth. Well, that was a downright charming thing to say. Perhaps there was a bond here after all. Were these exchanges always so convivial? she wondered, thinking that she may have to revise her notion that everyone would be better served by a moment of personal, enclosed silence.

But before she could think of her own friendly sally, he nodded curtly, zipped, and walked away, having dawdled longer than he had intended.

∞

Outside on the street, a mid-summer dusk seemed to rise off the paved streets and tall buildings of downtown San Francisco, pulling daylight out of the sky and trading it for city night dotted with man-made streetlight stars. Yellow window-squares showed people recently arrived home. Glad to be away from the aggressive stink of urine, Georgia bought some embroidery floss, a book on home gardening, and a large page-sized magnifying glass on her way to the train that would take her back home.

The magnifying glass clunked against her empty water bottle as the train rocketed through curving tunnels and Georgia, soothed by the rhythms of the crowd around her jostling in and out of the train, took comfort in the faces of those around her. Across the aisle, a stocky brown man lay slumped in his seat, his head tilted back, his mouth wide open. Loosely grasped in the sleeping man's arms was an alert baby, swaying to the movements of the train, her roving eyes framed by thick lashes. When her eyes alighted on Georgia she stopped, wordlessly absorbing her fill of the old woman's face. Such undiluted love. She gazed with utter serenity at Georgia until Georgia reluctantly got off at her stop.

∞

In her upstairs bedroom, the lights around her mirrored dresser-and-sewing-table ablaze, Georgia sat making flowers. Zeke and her band were practicing in the garage—loud, frenzied guitar strums athrob in the night air. Two cats, driven inside by the decibels, were arranged in feline loaves around her. The other sat in an unruly nest he had made of the brightly colored flosses and the paper bag in which they came. Earlier in the evening Georgia had bathed and then done a load of laundry, carefully detaching the loose rosette from the waistband and handwashing it. Now she mended the garment by putting the rosette square in the center of her underwear's front panel. Whether or not anyone else saw her underwear again, she would certainly be ready to be seen on her own terms.

An inspiration stood up suddenly inside her. With fingers no longer steady after years of living, Georgia threaded the embroidery floss and arranged the rectangular magnifying glass at the edge of the table so she could see her work underneath it. A black-speckled, flame-tinged tiger lily bloomed over the crotch of another pair of underwear. She turned the open book of flowers to a different page. Now irises twined among the lily, the periwinkle of the inner tongues of the iris shading into pure blue-purple, a petal of flame occasionally resting over it. Bright green pea plant tendrils snaked hairlike around the flowers. She turned out undergarment after undergarment: plain yellow bearded snapdragons with open, fringed hibiscus and elegant violets; hardy, branching grey pussy willows, tulips and delicate rose blossoms.

Lifting her head every now and then to allow her eyes to refocus, Georgia saw light and movement in the garage. Catching a few notes of King Twat's music, she realized the distorted crash of guitars she was listening to accompanied Zeke singing, "...All of me...why not take all of me?" By chance Georgia looked up at the postcard she had found earlier in her new suit. She had slid it between the mirror frame and the glass, next to the hot bulb of a lamp which had been on for several hours.

   She rose and pulled the postcard free. Upon closer inspection, it looked like a tree covered in orange blossoms. The postcard even smelled like orange blossoms. Those simple little flowers would go on the next piece of art. The heat had somehow burned or discolored the ink of the postcard so that the flowers were more distinct. The heat had also had another effect. On the back, to Georgia's great surprise, a few brown hand-scrawled words in old-fashioned-looking script were visible where none had been before. They seemed to have been directed to her. She read the words thrice with unbelieving eyes, set the card down on the dresser among all the loops of floss, and then dialed her girlfriend's number.

   "Come over here quick—I think you'll like this," she said into the phone.

   "I usually do," said May, sassy as always.

   "Then don't waste time," said Georgia, hanging up.

   She turned to look once more at the fragrant brown message a distant hand had written her, her heart aflutter with anticipation. Humming a little, she read it one last time: You're a good man, sister.

∞

SCHRÖDINGER'S PUSSY

Terra LeMay

I am you, and you are me. We haven't met, but we will, in some months. Then again in a year. More frequently after that for a stretch, though it doesn't last. Or perhaps we never meet. Or just that single time, which was (will be) both meteoric and ephemeral.

Except I remember that weekend and you don't.

I remember them all. All the moments. Even the ones you forgot, and those which never happened. They are all here, in this one place in my mind (in your mind).

Our time together was (will be) catharsis for you, but I will fall in love, like a spaniel. The world cracked open the day we met (or another day, in another place), and we became one. We have always been (will always be) one. We stand in two places at once, two times, two dimensions. We are separate. But I am in your head, in my head.

We grew up on either end of the same street. We both had grapevines growing in our yards. (Have you heard?) Yours in front by the mailbox, ours hidden like a naughty secret next to the fence out back. We only had three blocks between us, go figure, but the road stretched all the way from Antioch to San Juan, spanning a continent, spanning the ocean, spanning a million, million miles. Or only a millimeter.

It took too long for us to find each other. (Sometimes we never do. Sometimes it is too soon.) Once we had, we were inseparable. Except when we fought. Or never meet.

You always walked the difference between our houses, even though the hill between us was almost too steep to climb. I rode horseback (or drove a car) even though going to you is always downhill. Maybe it wasn't laziness. Maybe it was precognitive thought—(Photons in two places at once, two times, two different dimensions, two heads, two minds, two hearts. Twins, inseparable even apart.)—the truth already, so subtle, so soon, so obvious.

Maybe it's only common sense, the knowledge that once I'd gone downhill to find you, I'd have to return the way I'd come, and that hill was *always* too steep to climb.

Sometimes we met (will meet) in the middle. Halfway up the hill for you, halfway down for me. We'll sit in the gutter next to the mailbox with the ugly plastic flowers zip-tied to its flag. (I stole one of those flowers, sun-yellowed and cracking, once when you were gone. Maybe you never noticed, or maybe the flowers were bright and new when you looked at them. Maybe you stole one too.)

Did you know, growing up, we went to the same school? I don't think you ever saw me. I watched you in the hallways. We passed each other every day at 11:25 and again in the break between *Chorus* and *Ancient Greek Sexuality*. I sat in the back of the class, three seats behind you. Sometimes, if I strained my eyes hard enough, I could just make out what you were writing on your lapscreen.

It usually wasn't notes for class. Sometimes it was porn. Sometimes it was poetry. Or a suicide note.

Once, I came to class stoned on a cocktail of weed and microdots and Corona Extra (with a twist of lime). No one seemed to notice, but you gave me a cock-eyed glance as I shuffled past your desk. I let myself trail fingertips across your papers, and you didn't think I saw you blush. Paper feels like velvet when you're stoned.

One day you will ask me to tell you what it's like to find your future (faith/destiny) in tarot cards or chemicals or the variations of oscillation in ceiling fans. Jesus loves you as much as your light fixture.

Of course, back then neither of us knew what I was seeing (would see/never saw). Neither of us understood. Those were daydreams or flights of fancy. (Nightmares.) Maybe. When everything happens at once, when everything could happen, when everything will happen, everything becomes equal. Potentials are realized. Negated. Equated.

I don't like to think on it too much. Better to dwell on the happy moments, for they are infinitely equal to the unhappy ones. Infinitely better. (Infinitely worse.)

The first time I kissed you, we were in front of our old house. The house at the *bottom* of the hill. (Uphill in both directions back then. Now. Tomorrow.) I remember tonguing over your braces and worrying that we might get stuck together.

We only kissed. I didn't want to share my bed with you. (Or my head with you.)

Much later (or on some other visit), you made a pallet on the floor beside me and spent the night. I dreamed I caused the apocalypse, gave birth to the antichrist, or learned to split photons with my mind (Option D: All of the above?), and you held me while I told you what I'd seen in those dreams. You said you never dreamed. I tried to open your eyes, but you couldn't put yourself in my place. I wish I could make you understand.

There's so much you don't see (won't ever see/haven't seen yet). How is it that we are the same, but so different? Sometimes we can't even speak the same language.

And yet, we talk for hours when we finally meet, filling up the space with words. You drive us to the lake (the caldera on top of the volcano/ the dollar theatre double-feature/your house). Just off the edge of the lake is a small island, hardly more than a sandbar really. The water between the two shores comes halfway up my thighs. I hold my skirt up to keep it dry and you carry my shoes. Your pants are soaked through all the way to the crotch, but you don't complain. There's a wide plank-swing on the island, hanging between two trees. I thought we'd sit on it together to talk but, instead, I sit on it and you push me. We say only two words during the entire night.

"Higher?"

"No." (Or "Yes.")

We don't kiss that night because I am so intimidated by you. You take me home when it's too dark to see the stars. And then I'm with you two years later (last week). We are making out in your basement. When we come up for air, you take me to look at your paintings, and

I accidentally kick over a cup of dirty mineral spirits, ruining the rug. For many years, the stain will look like spilled blood.

Our relationship dissolved after that (except sometimes it fermented, cemented, or otherwise improved). I apologized, but it was too late. By that point, I'd already broken your lamp (knocked it over with my head when I rose up from kissing you) or backed your car into the security-light post in the parking lot at *Swif-T-Mart*.

"Don't drive when you're high (drunk/splitting photons/in a hypnotic trance). Just don't." I don't drink. I don't do drugs. I'm a straight-edge. It's true.

That was the year I discovered how to be everything and nothing. You were the one who showed me how to alter my consciousness. You got me drunk on a bucket of frozen margaritas, then helped me outside when I couldn't stop coughing from all the pot smoke. You showed me transcendental meditation. You showed me the power of prayer.

You showed me how to be in two places at once, two times, two minds. How to be here and there.

You showed me Jesus (Krishna/Buddha/The Invisible Pink Unicorn). You tripped me and I hit my head. Or I tripped you and you hit your head. Or we were both dreaming. (I thought you said you never dreamed.) All our life (lives/past lives) passed in the flash that occurred during the moment right before our death.

One of us looked into a scrying mirror. One of us learned time travel (quantum mechanics/psychomancy/telepathy). One of us learned that photons exist in two places at once, or two times at once, and we learned to split them and share them with you, with me, with each other. One of us fell into a black hole.

Do you remember? So much happened between us in no time at all. Time did not exist for us. It's overwhelming.

I say, "I think I'm going to throw up."

"That's okay. You're in the bathtub. It'll wash down the drain."

It didn't.

"You'll see," you said, "Chemicals don't change people." (Or maybe you said, "Time travel is impossible." Or "I can control your mind with my psychic powers.")

But it wasn't true.

Chemicals changed you. We both had psychic powers. You invented a time machine, and I used it.

In school I sat beside you, one row closer to the door. You smelled like watermelon lip gloss. We were fifteen and sixteen, and I still wanted to kiss you but wasn't brave enough. Besides, you had a boyfriend who wore heavy metal T-shirts and smoked cigarettes.

The second time I kissed you (the first time) we were at Caitlín's pool party just after we'd graduated from high school (elementary school/rehab). My very first kiss with anyone, ever. You had a different boyfriend every week, back then. Someone discovered how easy it was to play Spin the Bottle in a swimming pool with a plastic two-liter bottle half-filled with water. We held our breath and kissed where no one could see us.

When I am everywhere and nowhere, I revisit that moment. I hold you under the water. My eyes were open; yours are closed. Air bubbles cling to your lashes, and you put your hand on my breast. I taste your wintergreen breath-spray and the chlorine in the pool.

I once tried to tell you about that kiss. A hundred million times I've tried to tell you about that kiss in the pool, but you never remember, and you never believe me. I don't know why I keep trying to remind you.

It's okay. I remember. I remember you rescuing me. I remember calling you to come over to my apartment and sit with me when I couldn't stand reality. How many times did you let me stay with you when I had no other place to go? (Where can you run to when you are everywhere and nowhere?)

When you moved away, I thought my heart would break forever. I never wrote you letters, but you wrote back anyway. You wrote me replies to questions I never asked you. When the Internet was invented we had secret liaisons on GEnie. You sent me poetry.

Once, you showed me my letters. I did not remember writing them. Once, I showed you a poem you sent me. You said you'd never seen it, hadn't sent it. Both were only echoes, slipping across reality.

Sometimes, we never met at all. Sometimes we meet while you are away at college. I fly out to see you. We make love in the airport, and the world ignites in apocalypse while we bring each other to orgasm in a bathroom stall. We are frantic, as if we know with certainty that we only have a few moments left together.

SCHRÖDINGER'S PUSSY

"I love you," I whisper. It echoes off the bathroom walls, and old women powdering their noses can hear us in the stall. I can smell their rosewater perfume even over the cleaning chemicals and urine.

"I love you more," you say. "I love you a hundred times more."

"That's impossible. I love you to infinity."

We are silent, both pondering the possibilities inherent in that statement. ("I hate you."/"Don't know you.")

You ask the impossible question, the question that begins and ends everything.

"What does that mean? What is love to the infinite power?"

"I think it's like a wavefunction. An uncollapsed wavefunction," I say, but I don't even know what that means, really. I was never any good at theoretical physics. (In another instance/timeline/universe, I don't reply.)

"You don't love me at all."

"Don't you believe in God? (Allah?/Zeus?/The Flying Spaghetti Monster?)" I say. I'm crouched with my feet up on the commode, in case airport security comes through. Men can be arrested for sharing a bathroom stall in an airport. "God is infinite. God is in everything, even a ceiling fan. God loves you." (Or maybe, I talked about physics, instead—and the practical applications of the infinite.)

"I don't believe in God. I'm an existentialist. I *am* God." (Or maybe, we discuss alchemy, or paradoxes.)

"Then I am you," I say, "and you are me, and I love you infinitely."

"And you do not love me at all."

I couldn't argue.

What is infinity? Surely it is more than nothing? Isn't it? I rest my cheek on your cheek. You kiss me again for the first time, and there is paper (a pill/a microchip) on your tongue (or a love note in your hand), but now it is on my tongue (in my hand).

I love you, like a puppy, and you don't love me at all. But you are me, and I am you. We love each other just enough, and not too much. We are strangers, and we are the same person. We are crazy more than we are sane. Again and again, or only once, (or never) we make the wrong choice/the right choice. When every moment in our life is singular, there is no choice.

We are Love, infinite.

∞

ACKNOWLEDGMENTS

Thanks most especially to Steve Berman, without whom this book would not exist—his suggestion of the project, his willingness to let me try my hand at editing, and his continued support in the process of putting *Beyond Binary* together were all invaluable. Also and obviously, thanks to Lethe Press—Steve and his whole crew, especially Alex Jeffers, who handled the design and cover—for getting this book into your hands.

Acknowledgment is due also to those who came before in writing about gender and sexuality in speculative fiction, as well as the authors who wrote these wonderful stories in the first place and the people who published them.

Thanks finally to my partner, supportive of the piles of books and late nights spent working, and to my friends, whose enthusiasm for the project bolstered me when I needed it.

ABOUT THE EDITOR

BRIT MANDELO (britmandelo.com) is a writer, critic, and occasional editor whose primary fields of interest are speculative fiction and queer literature, especially when the two coincide. Her work—fiction, nonfiction, poetry; she wears a lot of hats—has been featured in magazines such as *Clarkesworld*, Tor.com, and *Ideomancer*. She also writes regularly for Tor.com and has several long-running column series there, including Queering SFF, a mix of criticism, editorials, and reviews on LGBTQI speculative fiction. When not writing, she is a perpetual student and is working up to an eventual (hopefully) PhD. She is a Louisville native and lives there with her partner in an apartment that doesn't have room for all the books.

CONTRIBUTORS

KEYAN BOWES is frequently ambushed by stories, and took the 2007 Clarion workshop for science fiction and fantasy writers in self defense. Since graduating from Clarion, she's had some twenty short stories and poems published online and in print. Keyan is a member of the Written in Blood writers' group; of Codex, an online group of neo-professional authors; of 'Second Draft', a dedicated group of writers; and a former member of the online critiquing group Critters. She is currently working on two young adult novels, both urban fantasy adventures.

∞

KELLEY ESKRIDGE writes fiction, essays and screenplays. Her novel *Solitaire* is a New York Times Notable book and was a finalist for the Nebula, Spectrum and Endeavour awards. The stories in her collection *Dangerous Space* include two Nebula finalists, three Tiptree Prize Honor stories, and a winner of the Astraea Prize. Her story "Alien Jane" was adapted for television, and a film based on *Solitaire* is currently in development with Eskridge attached as screenwriter. She is an independent editor at Sterling Editing and the Board Chair of the Clarion West Writers Workshop. She lives in Seattle with her partner, novelist Nicola Griffith. Visit her at http://kelleyeskridge.com.

∞

TOBI HILL-MEYER (HandbasketProductions.com) is a trans activist, writer, and filmmaker. She started producing media to fill the utter void of diverse trans characters as well as to offer an alternative to the overwhelmingly exploitative and exotic ways that trans women's sexuality is often portrayed.

∞

NALO HOPKINSON, a Jamaican Canadian, is the author of novels *Brown Girl in the Ring* (1998), *Midnight Robber* (2000), *The Salt Roads* (2003), *The New Moon's Arms* (2007), and short fiction collection *Skin Folk* (2001). She is a recipient of the John W. Campbell Award, the Locus Award, the World Fantasy Award, and has twice received the Sunburst Award for Canadian Literature of the Fantastic. Her work has twice been on the bibliography *Books for the Teen-Age*, issued by the young adult librarians of the New York Public Library. Her science fiction novel *Midnight Robber* received Honourable Mention for a novel written in creole in Cuba's "Casa de las Americas" prize for literature. She was a founding member of the Carl Brandon Society, which exists to further the conversation on race and ethnicity in science fiction and fantasy. She is currently Associate Professor specializing in speculative literatures in the Creative Writing Department of the University of California Riverside. *The Chaos*, her first YA novel, appears in April 2012 from Margaret K. McElderry Books. Her next novel, *Sister Mine*, is scheduled to appear in spring 2013 from Grand Central Books. Hopkinson splits her time between California and Toronto, Canada.

∞

CLAIRE HUMPHREY lives in Toronto, writes novels and stories, and works in the book business. Her short fiction has appeared in *Strange Horizons*, *Fantasy Magazine* and *Podcastle*. She is also the reviews editor at *Ideomancer*. You can read more about her at www.clairehumphrey.ca.

∞

SARAH KANNING (www.sarahkanning.com) has rarely met a near-future dystopian story she didn't like, and is fascinated by the ways technology can alter and distort our senses of self, identity and memory. Her work has recently appeared in *The Crimson Pact* volumes 1 & 2 (TheCrimsonPact.com). She writes fantasy and science fiction, and lives in Lawrence, Kansas.

∞

KEFFY R. M. KEHRLI is a speculative fiction writer currently living in Seattle. Since attending Clarion in 2008, his work has appeared in *Fantasy Magazine*, *Apex Online*, *Escape Pod*, and *Writers of the Future* Vol. 27, among others. He has degrees in both physics and linguistics and does science in a basement when he's not writing.

∞

ELLEN KUSHNER's first novel, *Swordspoint: A Melodrama of Manners*, quickly became a cult book that some say initiated the queer end of the "fantasy of manners" spectrum. She returned to the same setting in *The Privilege of the Sword* and its sequel, *The Fall of the Kings* (written with her partner, Delia Sherman), as well as a growing number of short stories. Her second novel, *Thomas the Rhymer*, won the Mythopoeic Award and the World Fantasy Award. Her most recent work includes the anthology *Welcome to Bordertown*, co-edited with Holly Black, a "feminist-shtetl-magical-realist" musical audio drama, *The Witches of Lublin*, and her own recording of the audiobook version of *Swordspoint* (ACX/Neil Gaiman Presents). Kushner was for many years the host of public radio's Sound & Spirit. She and her partner, author and educator Delia Sherman, live in New York City, with a lot of books, airplane ticket stubs, and no cats whatsoever. www.Ellen-Kushner.com

∞

RICHARD LARSON is currently a graduate student at New York University. His short stories have appeared previously in *Strange Horizons, Chi-Zine, Subterranean,* and *Wilde Stories 2011: The Year's Best Gay Speculative Fiction*, among others. He also writes about books for *Strange Horizons* and movies for *Slant Magazine*. He can be found online at http://www.rlarson.net.

∞

TERRA LEMAY was born on top of a volcano (in Hawaii). She tamed a wild mustang before she turned sixteen, and before twenty-five, she traveled through most of the U.S. and to parts of Europe and Mexico. She has also held some unusual jobs, like training llamas and modeling high-heeled shoes (though not at the same time!) She co-owns a tattoo studio north of Atlanta, but currently spends most of her time creating artisan glass beads and writing. She can be found online at: www.terralemay.com

∞

LIU WEN ZHUANG is the pen-name of Asian-American writer Cynthia Liu, who is based in the Bay Area after doing time in upstate New York and the mid-Atlantic East Coast. "Bud," from the writer's collection of short fiction, is both of a piece with and unlike anything Liu has written before.

∞

SANDRA MCDONALD is the author of the award-winning collection *Diana Comet and Other Implausible Stories,* which was a *Booklist* Editor's Choice for Young Readers and an American Library Association "Over the Rainbow" book. She is also the author of three science fiction military novels and two young adult teen mysteries. Her short fiction has appeared in more than forty magazines and anthologies, and she currently teaches college in Northeast Florida. Visit her at www.sandramcdonald.com.

∞

TANSY RAYNER ROBERTS is the author of the *Creature Court* trilogy (Harper-Voyager Australia) and short story collection *Love and Romanpunk* (Twelfth Planet Press). She lives in Tasmania with her partner and two daughters. She blogs at http://tansyrr.com, tweets as @tansyrr and is one of the voices of the SF feminist podcast *Galactic Suburbia.* "Prosperine When It Sizzles" was originally published in *New Ceres Nights,* as part of the New Ceres shared world project.

∞

DELIA SHERMAN's most recent short stories have appeared in the young adult anthology *Steampunk!* and in Ellen Datlow's *Naked City.* She's written three novels for adults, but is now writing novels for younger readers. Her newest novel, *The Freedom Maze,* is a time-travel historical about ante-bellum Louisiana. When she's not writing, she's teaching, editing, knitting, and cooking. When not on the road, she lives in a rambling apartment in New York City with partner Ellen Kushner and far too many pieces of paper.

∞

KATHERINE SPARROW currently writes and lives in San Francisco where the city's strange tech culture, radical activism, and pastel houses seems to be seeping into her fiction. When she's not writing she does fundraising, burrito eating, and baby-wrangling. She's had fiction published by *Fantasy Magazine, GigaNotoSaurus, Escape Pod,* and others. All things Katherine can be found at katherinesparrow.net.

∞

SONYA TAAFFE's short stories and poems have won the Rhysling Award, been shortlisted for the SLF Fountain Award and the Dwarf Stars Award, and appeared in various anthologies including *The Moment of Change: An Anthology of Feminist Speculative Poetry, People of the Book: A Decade of Jewish Science Fiction & Fantasy, Last Drink*

Bird Head, The Year's Best Fantasy and Horror, The Alchemy of Stars: Rhysling Award Winners Showcase, The Best of Not One of Us, and *Trochu divné kusy* 3. Her work can be found in the collections *Postcards from the Province of Hyphens* and *Singing Innocence and Experience* (Prime Books) and *A Mayse-Bikhl* (Papaveria Press). She is currently on the editorial staff of *Strange Horizons*. She holds master's degrees in Classics from Brandeis and Yale and once named a Kuiper belt object.

∞

CATHERYNNE M. VALENTE is the *New York Times* bestselling author of over a dozen works of fiction and poetry, including *Palimpsest*, the *Orphan's Tales* series, *Deathless*, and the crowdfunded phenomenon *The Girl Who Circumnavigated Fairyland in a Ship of Her Own Making*. She is the winner of the Andre Norton Award, the Tiptree Award, the Mythopoeic Award, the Rhysling Award, and the Million Writers Award She has been nominated for the Hugo, Locus, and Spectrum Awards, the Pushcart Prize, and was a finalist for the World Fantasy Award in 2007 and 2009. She lives on an island off the coast of Maine with her partner, two dogs, and enormous cat.

∞

CREDITS

CPSIA information can be obtained at www.ICGtesting.com
Printed in the USA
LVOW12s0912120215

426604LV00005B/494/P